Y0-BSW-115

# SPELLBOUND

"Hush now, *cara*," he soothed. "Nothing is so bad as that."

He moved to take a seat beside her, putting one arm about her trembling shoulders as silent sobs shook her. She rested her head on his shoulder, and suddenly the flame of desire leapt to life within him.

*She is forbidden to you,* warned the voice of reason.

But this might be his only chance. . . .

He leaned toward her. Their mouths were a heartbeat apart, their breaths mingling on a sigh.

When his lips touched hers, Giulietta forgot everything in the wake of the strange and exciting feelings that rippled through her. Surely, he was a Gypsy sorcerer, and she was caught in his erotic web. But she didn't care. She wanted more—she wanted what had been withheld from her for too long.

"Love me," she whispered. . . .

# TODAY'S HOTTEST READS
# ARE TOMORROW'S SUPERSTARS

**VICTORY'S WOMAN** (4484, $4.50)
by Gretchen Genet
Andrew—the carefree soldier who sought glory on the battlefield, and returned a shattered man . . . Niall—the legendary frontiersman and a former Shawnee captive, tormented by his past . . . Roger—the troubled youth, who would rise up to claim a shocking legacy . . . and Clarice—the passionate beauty bound by one man, and hopelessly in love with another. Set against the backdrop of the American revolution, three men fight for their heritage—and one woman is destined to change all their lives forever!

**FORBIDDEN** (4488, $4.99)
by Jo Beverley
While fleeing from her brothers, who are attempting to sell her into a loveless marriage, Serena Riverton accepts a carriage ride from a stranger—who is the handsomest man she has ever seen. Lord Middlethorpe, himself, is actually contemplating marriage to a dull daughter of the aristocracy, when he encounters the breathtaking Serena. She arouses him as no woman ever has. And after a night of thrilling intimacy—a forbidden liaison—Serena must choose between a lady's place and a woman's passion!

**WINDS OF DESTINY** (4489, $4.99)
by Victoria Thompson
Becky Tate is a half-breed outcast—branded by her Comanche heritage. Then she meets a rugged stranger who awakens her heart to the magic and mystery of passion. Hiding a desperate past, Texas Ranger Clint Masterson has ridden into cattle country to bring peace to a divided land. But a greater battle rages inside him when he dares to desire the beautiful Becky!

**WILDEST HEART** (4456, $4.99)
by Virginia Brown
Maggie Malone had come to cattle country to forge her future as a healer. Now she was faced by Devon Conrad, an outlaw wounded body and soul by his shadowy past . . . whose eyes blazed with fury even as his burning caress sent her spiraling with desire. They came together in a Texas town about to explode in sin and scandal. Danger was their destiny—and there was nothing they wouldn't dare for love!

*Available wherever paperbacks are sold, or order direct from the Publisher. Send cover price plus 50¢ per copy for mailing and handling to Penguin USA, P.O. Box 999, c/o Dept. 17109, Bergenfield, NJ 07621. Residents of New York and Tennessee must include sales tax. DO NOT SEND CASH.*

# Tender Rogue

## Linda Lang Bartell

**ZEBRA BOOKS**
**KENSINGTON PUBLISHING CORP.**

ZEBRA BOOKS are published by

Kensington Publishing Corp.
850 Third Avenue
New York, NY 10022

Copyright © 1994 by Linda Lang Bartell

All rights reserved. No part of this book may be reproduced in any form or by any means without the prior written consent of the Publisher, excepting brief quotes used in reviews.

If you purchased this book without a cover, you should be aware that this book is stolen property. It was reported as "unsold and destroyed" to the Publisher and neither the Author nor the Publisher has received any payment for this "stripped book."

Zebra and the Z logo Reg. U.S. Pat. & TM Off.

First Printing: October, 1994

Printed in the United States of America

"She stepped into my heart so vividly,
A thing of light and warmth!—as, all unknown,
A princess, having wandered from her throne,
Might crowd a peasant's hut with courtesy."
                                        —Petrarch (1304–74)

# Prologue

*8 June, 1478--Monteverdi, Italy*

"*Save* him, Maddalena!"

The words were softly uttered, yet weighted with urgency in the hush of the night as the Prince of Monteverdi's eyes locked with those of the ageless Gypsy woman.

"I'll grant you anything within my means!"

Lightning flashed, its blinding silver tracery turning the dark into daylight for a suspended moment, and seeming to lend divine support to the prince's promise.

And then it was gone, leaving only the muted growl of distant thunder, and the glow from the campfire . . . the latter revealing four people within its immediate circle.

The balmy breeze picked up suddenly. Firelight flared across the Gypsy woman's features, casting them in rose-gold; shadows danced in the recesses of her still-handsome face, making her odd, brilliant blue eyes glitter like twin sapphires.

Durante de' Alessandro lowered his gaze to the wounded servant lying on a blanket upon the ground between them. "You *must* save him!" he repeated with quiet desperation as his eyes sought hers again.

"*Sì, principe,* and then I will burn for witchcraft." Her vernacular was heavily accented by her native Romany.

"Pah!" he said, his handsome features twisting with derision. "Surely you must know that I am not superstitious." He inclined his head toward a fourth figure nearby. "Neither is my brother Vittorio." He paused. "No one need know how you do it—you have my word as an Alessandro, and you will be under my protection should anyone ever question aught."

The wounded man, who was lying upon his side, moaned softly, his dark lashes fluttering briefly before they stilled. He sighed then, his eyes remaining closed.

Dante felt the chill of fear waft over his heart, for surely Aristo was breathing his last. The physicians of Florence had done nothing but shake their heads in defeat, in spite of even Lorenzo de' Medici's exhortations.

But Aristo himself had given his master new hope. "Mad-da-lena . . ." he'd whispered. "Zin-gara . . ."

Of course. Maddalena was one of Aristo's own—a *Zingara*. A Gypsy. And so, here he was with his half brother, literally begging the aid of the woman called Maddalena.

"Why would you want to save this man? This lackey to the maleficent Bishop of Florence? The man who would have killed you and your wife this day?"

"Aristo *saved* my life, woman. Don't you understand—with all your wisdom, your Sight? He saved *la principessa* from the bishop. Then he killed him—his own master—to save me. He is a good and courageous man, of utmost importance to my family. He cannot die!"

She stared at him for long moments, as if she would see into his heart—his very soul. The smell of wood smoke and her strange perfume came to him, the wind caressed his warm face.

"Anything within your power to give, you said?"

Dante looked down at Aristo, suppressing the impulse to leap across the fire and strangle the woman. Surely the dwarf couldn't last much longer. *"Sì!"*

Maddalena straightened and came around to where Aristo lay. She leaned over him, examined the two dagger wounds to his back. "Then leave us and I will do what I can. I will send for you if and when he is out of danger."

Dante opened his mouth to speak, then decided against it. There was no mistaking her tone of dismissal. He straightened slowly, looked down at Aristo once more, then swung away and strode toward his waiting brother.

*Castello Monteverdi—September, 1478*

"The time has come, Excellence."

The Prince of Monteverdi put down his writing quill and looked up at the small man standing across the desk from him. In spite of the servant's uncanny way of appearing and disappearing with little more than a whisper of sound, Dante had grown accustomed to Aristo's shadowlike movements. He showed no surprise as their eyes met.

"Maddalena?"

*"Sì,"* came the answer in the servant's raspy voice.

The faint scent of rose water came to Dante then, distracting him briefly. He suppressed a smile. *Dio mio,* he thought, biting his lower lip. But it was better by far than the repulsive asafetida that in the past Aristo had religiously smeared over his body to ward off evil. . . .

"What does she ask of me in return for having saved your life, *maestro?*"

Before Aristo could answer, Dante stood to his impressive height and moved around the desk. The sunlight from one of the small windows above him touched his golden hair, limned his extraordinary profile. As he came to stand before Aristo, the contrast in their height and appearance was startling. While Dante de' Alessandro was tall and gifted with Adonis-like features, his servant was a dwarf of a man with a pronounced hunch in his back, and a face that was almost simian in its ugliness.

But the warmth that shone in his dark eyes told anyone who cared to look beyond the physical that Aristo was a good man. A man who had gone through hell and come out alive. A man who was the better for it.

Aristo shook his head slowly. "Mayhap you should have let me die, *principe*," he said quietly.

Dante's eyes narrowed, his look turning somber. "Come now, *maestro*. Naught could ever make me regret the promise to Maddalena—and least of all the privilege of having you live with the Alessandros at Castello Monteverdi."

Color stained the dwarf's cheeks. His eyelashes lowered for a moment as if he sought to gain his composure. *"Grazi,* Excellence."

Dante put one hand on Aristo's shoulder. "Tell me now. What did Maddalena say?"

The dwarf's eyes met Dante's. "She asks that you take an oath of secrecy before she reveals what she has to tell you . . . and her subsequent request."

Dante's brows raised. He was quiet a moment. "Do you know what this is about?"

*"Sì.* But first I, too, was sworn to silence."

*"Ebbene* . . . very well. I swear upon the Alessandro name that I will not reveal what either of you tell me if that is what Maddalena wishes."

Aristo nodded. "I am afraid you are in for a shock, *principe*." He paused, seeming to cast about in his mind for the right words. "But there is no easy way to tell you except the plain and simple truth. At least the truth according to Maddalena."

Dante nodded.

"It seems that five years before Giuliano de' Medici's death, he sired a son by Maddalena's daughter, Ginevra. She died in childbirth, after making Maddalena promise never to reveal the identity of the child's father."

The color had leached from Dante's face. "Giuliano's child?" he whispered, stunned.

"So she swears."

Dante leaned his hip against the desk, trying to absorb this. "Why has she said nothing about this until now?"

Aristo shrugged. "It seems she had no opportunity until recently. Who could she trust enough to keep such a secret but an honorable man sworn to repay a debt?"

Dante frowned. "Surely Giuliano would have known if—"

"No one knew except Maddalena, Ginevra, and the couple who took the child in as their own."

With a slightly trembling hand, Dante poured a half glass of wine from a decanter sitting near one corner of the heavy walnut desk, his agitation clearly visible. He offered some to Aristo who declined, before he downed it. "I cannot believe this!"

"So Maddalena anticipated. She asks that you come to the camp at your convenience."

Dante's bright, blue-green gaze cut suddenly to the dwarf. "Have you seen the boy?"

*"Sì, principe."*

"And?"

Aristo said only, "You must see for yourself."


Once again Dante stared across firelight at the Gypsy woman known as Maddalena. This time the glow was from a small, ornate brazier that lit the interior of the decorated wooden caravan with the play of light and darkness among the various furnishings within.

It had already been dark outside when Dante had arrived, as per Maddalena's request. As he'd approached the camp on his white stallion, he'd observed other small campfires here and there. The faint murmur of voices and activity came to him, although no one approached him as he strode toward one particular caravan. The bark of a dog, the wail of a child, the *whirr* of a bat streaking among the trees overhead . . . all faded into the background as Durante de' Alessandro, Prince of Monteverdi, knocked upon the open door at the back of the wagon, then stepped up and inside at Maddalena's bidding.

He had come alone, in good faith, for not only did he need to see the boy himself, but he also did not want to arouse suspicions around Monteverdi regarding either the Gypsy woman or the child.

Someone began to sing a haunting love song on the other side of the camp. The muted strains of the lover's lament drifted to them through the open door. Others joined in.

In spite of the music, Dante could feel the sense of expectancy building within him. He waited in silence, however.

Finally Maddalena spoke. "You have come to see the boy, *principe?*"

Dante nodded, feeling as if he were reliving a similar scene of only three months ago as he watched the firelight flicker over her features, casting shadows over her face and reflecting the burning blue of her eyes. Strange eyes, Dante thought, for a *Zingara*. Most were dark-haired and dark-eyed. Yet, in Dante's experience, every race of people had its aberrations, either through some freak of nature or from mixing occasionally with other peoples. . . .

"My blue-eyed father was not Rom, but one of your own," she said unexpectedly, as if reading his very thoughts. She leaned forward slightly then. "You have agreed to keep the secret, *sì?* If so, then there will be only four who know."

"Five. I keep nothing from Caressa, Maddalena. She can be trusted."

She nodded with what looked like reluctance.

"I find it hard to believe that you wouldn't have told me but for what happened with Aristo."

" 'Twas written in the stars . . . that you would find out one way or another. I was merely awaiting the right sign, *principe*."

Dante wasn't so sure about that, but he kept his thoughts to himself. "What of the boy?"

"He need not know. What good will it do him to yearn for that which he cannot have? Cannot be?"

"A man shapes his own destiny if he but has the drive, and can make of himself that which he wishes."

"Maybe. But the boy will never know. You've already sworn as much, Il Leone." For emphasis she used his old sobriquet, a reminder, obviously, of his reputation.

She turned her head aside and, in a low voice, said something in Romany.

For a long moment there was only the spit and snap of the fire and the faint song in the background. Then, a small boy materialized from the shadows behind Maddalena. He looked to be about five, as Aristo had said, and as the child moved to stand beside Maddalena, Dante's breath caught in his throat.

It was like looking at Giuliano de' Medici at five or six years of age.

An eerie feeling passed over Dante, and the flesh prickled along his neck and scalp. Yet he also felt the press of emotion behind his eyes, for the boy's beauty was very like that of Giuliano . . . yet even greater.

"Rodrigo, bid good evening to *il principe*," his grandmother said softly.

The boy's gaze had been on the glowing brazier, the shadow of his lashes spiking the delicate skin beneath his eyes. Now, he slowly raised his gaze to Dante. Even in the play of light and darkness Dante could see that his eyes were as blue as semiprecious lapis, just like Maddalena's. Beneath his unruly mane of sable hair, his features bore the distinct beauty of childhood that promised even more with maturation.

*His mother must have been stunning,* Dante thought. No wonder the carefree and fun-loving Giuliano had loved her, whether for a night or longer. . . .

*"Buona sera, principe,"* the boy murmured shyly, one bare toe tracing a line in the colorful rug at his feet. But his eyes remained on Dante's face with frank curiosity.

*"Buona sera a te,"* Dante answered, coming to his senses and allowing a slow smile to curve his mouth. He held out his hand. "Come closer *nino,* so we can become better acquainted . . . *si?"*

# One

*"Skewer him!"*

Rodrigo da Valenti watched from the shelter of several saplings, fearing to try and slip away unobserved and, at the same time, fascinated by what was happening in the glade before him.

Two boys, both a little older than he, one with light brown hair, the other blond, were engaged in swordplay, the very skill that so intrigued Rodrigo. The very skill in which *il principe* drilled him for hours on end outside of the camp. But here . . . here were two youths engaged in the sport, completely unaware of his presence, and both very good in movements and strategy. Sons of nobility, obviously. And because of that fact, among the best without a doubt.

Two younger children—a boy of about thirteen, and a girl a few years younger—watched and cheered on the combatants.

"Run him through, Mario!" the young boy urged again.

Automatically, Rodrigo's gaze went to the girl beside him in expectation of her response.

But he never heard exactly what she said—only the sound of her sweet, melodic voice, like that of what he imagined an angel would sound. He forgot to breathe for moments—forgot the contest—as he studied the young girl with her long, gently curling, fire gold hair and her face like a miniature

Madonna. She jumped with childish exuberance and clapped her hands once, her eyes, of indeterminate color, wide and sparkling with excitement. A smile of delight curved her rosy mouth, revealing saucy dimples, as the youth for whom she was cheering managed to knock the sword from his fair-haired opponent's hand.

*"Bravo!"* she cried, then clapped her hands over her mouth and looked at the boy beside her.

*"Hush,* Giulietta!" he muttered fiercely. "Else you are discovered here instead of at your studies and Papa puts you in a convent!"

She sobered instantly, and Rodrigo watched as the joy faded from her face, her expression taking on a budding if reluctant maturity—controlled, ladylike. He was reminded of a cloud passing over the sun as the light in her eyes dimmed, and he wanted to tell her brother to let her be. But he'd caught her name. Giulietta. The prince's daughter. The boy must be her brother then, Niccolò. . . .

The sandy-haired youth was turning away from his weapon-less opponent, sheathing his sword and saying, "You'll have to work on that one, Mario, for it seems I took you completely by—"

"Nardo!" Giulietta's soft cry pierced the air as Mario snatched his sword from where it lay and launched himself at the young man who had just bested him.

*Bernardo.* It registered immediately in Rodrigo's mind. Bernardo de' Alessandro. The prince's nephew. . . .

Without thinking, Rodrigo sprang from the bushes to come to Bernardo's aid. It was the supreme act of cowardice to attack a man when his back was turned, so Durante de' Alessandro had told him long ago. And Rodrigo never doubted the prince's wisdom. He never doubted anything the Prince of Monteverdi said or did . . .

. . . or that Mario was anything but serious.

Giulietta de' Alessandro's expression turned shocked as Rodrigo materialized from the trees at the edge of the glade and attacked Mario di Corsini—to whom she was betrothed.

Her brother Niccolò tried to intervene, but Bernardo de' Alessandro swung back to face them at the sudden sound of activity behind him, and quickly grabbed his younger cousin around the waist. "No!" he said softly into Nicco's ear.

Meanwhile Mario, older and more experienced than the newcomer, had managed to pin him to the ground. Rodrigo spat in his face. *"Coward!"* he snarled, blood trickling from his nose. "You attacked a man after he'd turned his back!"

Before the outraged Mario could answer, Bernardo stepped in. "And you did exactly the same thing," he told Rodrigo evenly, reaching out a hand to bring Mario to his feet. "And made a mistake, as well. Mario is no coward . . . rather he likes to play a trick now and then." He shook his head, a tolerant smile lighting his hazel eyes as he reached to help Rodrigo up, as well.

Rodrigo, however, was suddenly appalled at having made such a mistake before these noble youths. And especially the beautiful woman-child who, after throwing an openly adoring look at Mario, narrowed her gaze at Rodrigo as if he were a snake.

Pointedly refusing Bernardo's outstretched hand, Rodrigo scrambled to his feet, suddenly conscious of how he must look. And smell. He'd been working with several horses his adoptive father, Andrea, had obtained in trade for work he'd done, and then planned to improve their health and appearance, and train them before selling them for a profit.

Rodrigo loved horses, and had a way with them. After many hours of hard work he had been on his way to a stream near the eastern periphery of Monteverdi lands to bathe. Today was his eighteenth birthday, and the prince had hinted of a surprise.

Except that his innate curiosity had unexpectedly landed him in the midst of a most embarrassing situation.

He opened his mouth, intending to apologize, much as it went against the grain to exhibit any regret before this haughty Mario; but the latter didn't give him a chance.

"You've the look—and *smell*—of a *Zingaro*," Mario stated, making a face of contempt and wrinkling his nose as if at something offensive. "Are you from yon camp? The camp His Excellence the prince so generously permits your kind to use?"

Rodrigo sucked in a breath, and Bernardo looked at his friend in startlement. Giulietta, however, continued to stare at Rodrigo with a frown between her eyes, her mouth tightened in a distinct moue of disapproval.

With a swift, smooth movement Rodrigo bent and snatched Mario's fallen sword, then turned on him. "At least my *kind* have enough grace to avoid insulting a man for making an honest mistake," he returned.

"A *man?*" Mario jeered. "I see naught of a man holding my sword, but rather a stinking Gypsy boy who would aspire to manhood."

"Mario," Bernardo warned in a low voice. "Enough of—"

Mario waved one hand at his friend in dismissal. "Now, boy . . . you will return my sword!" He held out one hand confidently.

"Why don't you borrow your friend Bernardo's," Rodrigo challenged against all common sense, fighting to rein in his suddenly seething temper, "and see if a man must smell of roses to skillfully wield a weapon!"

Mario di Corsini represented everything Rodrigo had learned to resent, in spite of the influence of Durante de' Alessandro. Wealth, position, haughty good looks . . . and inborn arrogance. His anger began to consume him beneath his humiliation, and grew so quickly that he felt sweat break out under his arms, upon his brow. It slicked his palms. He suddenly felt his hair

cling to his damp face, like a filthy, set-upon urchin after steal-
ing from a vendor in the *mercato* in Florence and fleeing for
his life.

But he had a sword of the nobility in his hand, and it felt
comfortable—as if it were a natural extension of his arm,
thanks to Dante de' Alessandro's tutelage. He had *that*. at least,
before this sneering son of the aristocracy.

"Just who *are* you?" asked Nicco. "Mayhap the *Zingaro*
Papa has taken under his wing? The boy known as Rodrigo?"

Rodrigo's attention was momentarily snagged by the query.
He wasn't aware that anyone outside of the camp knew of his
relationship with the prince.

*"Sì,"* added Giulietta unexpectedly. "Maddalena's grandson—the Gypsy who saved Aristo's life!"

As Rodrigo's attention shifted to Giulietta and her brother,
Mario added snidely, "A relative of that skewed dwarf Aristo,
mayhap?" He drew up one shoulder, hunched his back, and
went lurching around Bernardo and Niccolò, imitating the
dwarf's clumsy gait.

Rodrigo missed the darkening of Giulietta's expression at the
obvious insult to the Alessandro servant, for in that instant,
Mario capered close enough to Bernardo to rip the latter's sword
from its sheath before he realized Mario's intent. "Now, *Zingaro*
thief," Mario challenged, "let's see you defend yourself!"

A soft cry escaped Giulietta, and Bernardo stepped toward
Rodrigo in an obvious attempt to intervene. A most unwise
move. . . .

Rodrigo, reflexes primed, flicked the tip of his borrowed
sword in Bernardo's direction in reaction, slashing the silken
sleeve of the older youth's arm and drawing a ribbon of blood
across the white material.

"Why you . . ." Mario lunged, his sword pointed directly
at Rodrigo's middle. Rodrigo spun aside, blood blossoming on
his own shirt. He didn't even feel the nip of the blade, however,

as Mario took advantage of his successful move and quickly
went for him again.

Rodrigo spun away again, and felt the air stir with the passage of the blade a heartbeat away.

Nicco's laughter dimly reached him. "See how he spins
round and round . . . like a top!" the boy cried. "He has no
chance against Mario's skill!"

It was true, Rodrigo thought angrily as he ducked and
swiped once, twice, ineffectively at his adversary. Not so much
that he had no chance, but rather, he was being outmaneuvered
by an older and more experienced opponent. For every lesson
in swordplay given him by the prince, Mario di Corsini probably had received three or four.

It seemed, Rodrigo acknowledged, that he'd bitten off more
than he could chew, and all in the name of pride. . . .

*"Maledizione!"* swore Bernardo, clutching his bleeding
arm. "That's enough!"

But Mario was lunging once again directly at Rodrigo's
belly—a blow meant to impale.

Using a last-ditch trick Dante had taught him, Rodrigo
clutched the hilt with both hands and slashed sideways at
Mario's blade with all his might, knocking it out of the latter's
hands. Rodrigo dropped his own weapon and lunged for
Mario's throat, sending him staggering backward. Mario's heel
caught on a fallen branch, and arms windmilling wildly, he
pitched toward the bole of an oak tree.

Rodrigo pulled back and froze as he watched Mario come
up solidly against it. His blond head cracked against the solid
trunk with the impact, then jerked sideways before stilling. His
limp body folded and slumped to the earth, his head settling
into an unnatural cant.

For a moment the silence was so complete it was deafening.
Then the disbelieving words of yet a sixth person sounded in
the shocked stillness: *"Madre di Dio!"*

The sound of the voice snagged Rodrigo's attention, and before anyone could say or do anything else, he looked over his shoulder toward the speaker . . .

And saw the Prince of Monteverdi astride his huge white stallion, his handsome face a mask of fury.

"His name is Morello. He is my birthday gift to you," Dante told Rodrigo gravely. "And now he will take you away to France . . . and safety."

Rodrigo's hand stilled upon the ebony horse's velvet neck. He threw an angry look at Dante. "You will send me away?" he asked. "To France?"

"It's best."

He whirled to face the prince, his youthful features taut with anger. He was clean and presentable now, but he felt every bit as soiled as he had earlier. "Best? To flee and hide like a criminal?" His fingers fisted at his sides. " 'Twas an accident! You saw it!"

"Try and explain that to the Corsinis, Rigo." Dante's voice was low, taut. Concern creased his brow.

They were near the Gypsy camp. It was late afternoon, and pots and cauldrons on the cooking fires gave off mouth-watering aromas; but the luring smells were lost on the two men.

Rodrigo had never been angry with Durante de' Alessandro, for he loved him like a father . . . worshipped him. He'd never had the slightest reason to be angry. But he was angry now.

"You mean try and explain an accident with a *Zingaro* involved," he corrected bitterly. "You couldn't convince any like the Corsinis that it wasn't outright murder."

Dante ran the fingers of one hand through his golden hair, obviously searching for the right words. Rodrigo wanted to tell him that there *were* no right words to cover up the truth, in all its ugliness.

"Come," the prince said finally, and turned to mount his stallion.

Rodrigo mounted Morello, failing in his agitation to notice the beautifully detailed leather saddle. Failing to fully appreciate the magnificent animal beneath him while his emotions played havoc with his reason.

They left the camp and rode more deeply into Monteverdi lands. As the disk of the sun began to sink into the molten horizon, Dante pulled up at the edge of a meadow. Unexpectedly, the sun gilding his fair hair reminded Rodrigo of Mario di Corsini. Outrage assailed him again, for he knew exactly what would happen now. And why.

They sat in silence for a few moments before Dante said, "A man must learn when to allow insults to roll harmlessly off his back. A mere word cannot harm you unless you let it."

"You are a prince, my lord. A noble. 'Tis easy enough for you to say such a thing—"

Dante's gaze cut sharply to his. "Don't *ever* use that as an excuse, Rigo. It reeks of self-pity. A man is not born noble, but rather becomes noble. His name at birth means nothing, nor do his antecedents."

"He would have killed me! If you believe your nephew capable of honesty, then ask him. He saw it all."

"I'm not accusing you of aught but allowing Mario to draw you into a duel."

"Have you ever been called 'stinking' or 'thief'?"

Dante dismounted and moved to stand before Morello, stroking the latter's nose. He looked up at Rodrigo. "There was a time, my son, when I was called worse."

Suddenly every other consideration faded before the words "my son." How many men could claim to be considered a son by a prince? To be told that a man was born with the capacity to acquire true nobility, not born into it? Emotion tightened

Rodrigo's throat, and he felt the press of those feelings behind his eyes.

"Then I—will leave, *principe*." Rodrigo said huskily, fighting to hold back the tears. "If that is what you wish."

" 'Tis *not* what I wish, but we have no choice. If you remain in Tuscany, the Corsinis could easily declare a feud against my family for protecting you."

Dismay filtered through Rodrigo. A vendetta? Because of him?

"I'm not afraid to fight—even to die. But innocents will die, too, and that I cannot allow. Why fuel hatred and shed blood unnecessarily if it can be avoided? That's common sense, Rigo, not cowardice, and don't ever let any man tell you differently."

Rodrigo nodded, hoping his acute misery didn't show. "For how long?"

"A few years . . . just until things settle down. Until I can soothe ruffled feathers."

Rodrigo felt his entire world crumbling before him. Years?

"What if I travel with my grandmother's people? They wander throughout the provinces of Italy . . ."

Dante shook his head, then placed one hand over Rodrigo's. "You must go far away—to a foreign land. I will send you to people I know in France. You can train as a professional soldier in King Charles's army. You will be so busy learning that you won't have time to pine for Tuscany, eh? And when you return you will be a true *condottiere*."

Rodrigo nodded. But something else suddenly came to mind, as well. Something that unexpectedly seemed of utmost importance, even in the face of his leaving all that he knew and loved.

"Giulietta . . ." he began, feeling outrageously bold at even mentioning her name to her father. He swallowed and cleared his throat, feeling the heat rise in his cheeks.

"*Sì* . . . most unfortunate she had to witness Mario's death.

She should be safely in a convent, but her mother won't have it."

"Will you explain to her—and Niccolò—that 'twas an accident? They are young, and . . ." He trailed off, words escaping him.

"I will talk to them. Nardo knows it was unintentional; he is old enough and has a level head on his shoulders. But, *sì*, the younger ones . . ." He shook his head, then searched Rodrigo's eyes. "Mario di Corsini lost his life—that can never be restored—but I will find my Gietta another husband, if that is what concerns you."

Rodrigo's chest tightened inexplicably at the thought, but he ignored the strange feeling. He reached to run his fingers through Morello's mane in an effort to redirect his thoughts. "He is beautiful, *principe. Grazi tante.*"

Dante nodded and remounted Sirocco. "He is the son of one of the Medici's finest horses, after whom he was named."

"The horse you rode in the palio in Giuliano de' Medici's name? And won?"

*"Sì,* Giuliano . . ." Dante murmured, a distinct catch in his voice. Then, as if remembering himself, his expression hardened. "How did you know about that? You were only a child."

"Everyone knows about that, my lord prince. The story will be retold long after we are gone."

Rodrigo knew only a smattering about Giuliano de' Medici: He had been like a brother to Dante and considered the most skilled horseman in all of Tuscany. And he'd been loved by his fellow Florentines for his good-naturedness, then cut down at twenty-four by assassins in the cathedral of Santa Maria del Fiore during High Mass. The Prince of Monteverdi had been present, and had helped Lorenzo de' Medici to safety. But he couldn't save the younger Giuliano.

Rodrigo had the feeling, however, that for some reason his

bringing up the subject did not sit well with his mentor, and he couldn't fathom why.

He changed the subject. "When do you want me to leave for France?"

Dante's expression cleared. "I don't *want* you to leave for France, Rigo. Not now, not ever. But you must." He leaned over to adjust a stirrup, then straightened and said, "Come. Let's take Morello for a run, then you must collect your belongings. You should be gone from Monteverdi by dawn."


Caressa de' Alessandro held her sobbing daughter in her arms and let the girl's grief and anger run their course. She pressed her cheek against Giulietta's bright head, her own raven hair a vivid contrast to the strawberry-gold curls.

"There, there, *mia piccola Gietta,*" she soothed. "My little Gietta . . . all will one day be well again, you'll see." She kissed Giulietta's warm, flushed cheek, then returned her own to its resting place.

"I sh-shall go to the c-convent," Giulietta declared in a broken voice. "If I cannot have M-Mario, I want no one."

"That is up to Papa, *cara.* You know that."

"Papa will understand. There is no one like Mario . . . he was f-fair as Papa and almost as tall. He was handsome and—"

"Giulietta!" Caressa said, holding her daughter suddenly at arm's length. She took in the misery in the girl's eyes and almost kept her silence. But Giulietta was old enough to understand. She was only a few years younger than many married women. "You know that marriages are arranged for political reasons. Your father is Prince of Monteverdi, and must think of the good of his principality and its people. He cannot be selfish, and neither can you."

They sat upon a stone bench in the central courtyard of Monteverdi. The scent of potted lemon trees and jasmine perfumed the air. The sun-heated cobblestones were warm beneath their feet. And the singing fountain, with its trident-wielding Poseidon in the center and four water-spewing dolphins around its perimeter, masked their conversation.

It had always been Caressa's favorite place in the great bastion of the Alessandros.

Giulietta appeared to consider her mother's words. She nibbled her lower lip thoughtfully, and her tears slowed to a trickle.

"Don't even get your hopes up, daughter," Caressa said. "You will marry when and whom your papa chooses. 'Tis natural. And, although you—all of us—mourn Mario, you will find contentment with another one day."

Giulietta's amber eyes met her mother's. "I'll speak to Papa," she insisted, reminding Caressa for the hundredth time just how outrageously her father spoiled her. The auburn cast to her blond hair, inherited from Caressa's maternal side of the family, also brought to mind just how prone Giulietta was to spurts of temper. And in those instances, Dante was most effective at wheedling or cajoling her free of them.

"Papa isn't here right now. And even if he were, *nina,* he—"

"Where is he?" Giulietta interrupted her. "With the Corsinis?" Her eyes darkened with pain.

Caressa hesitated, then decided to tell the truth. "I think your uncle is with the Corsini family."

*"Zio* Vittorio?"

*"Sì,* Papa . . . is at the *Zingaro* camp."

Giulietta's eyes narrowed. "Protecting that . . . that son of iniquity?"

"Giulietta!" Caressa exclaimed, shocked. "Where did you ever hear such a thing?"

"Nardo."

"Bernardo? He used that expression in front of you? And Nicco, I suppose, as well?"

Giulietta shook her head, her cheeks coloring, and stood. She moved toward the fountain. Caressa followed, determined to hear the answer.

"I—I overheard him and Mario one day when—"

"You're not supposed to be trailing after the young men! Were you eavesdropping?"

Giulietta avoided her mother's eyes and ran one finger over the smooth Carrara marble of the fountain's rim. She finally nodded.

"That is an *awful* thing to say of someone, child. And Rodrigo da Valenti is no such thing."

Giulietta raised her gaze to meet Caressa's. "Why did Papa ever decide to have anything to do with such a boy?" she asked, looking genuinely perplexed. "He's a dark and dirty *Zingaro* who has no worth—"

Caressa took hold of Giulietta's chin and held it firmly as she searched her daughter's eyes. "Your father would be furious if he heard you say such a thing! He would say that you shame the Alessandro name."

"Mario told me the *Zingari* were worthless beggars and thieves. Lazy and stupid and—"

"And Mario, God rest his soul, was small-minded to ever say such a thing. Every man has his worth, and who are you, Giulietta Maria, to judge *anyone?* Especially the Valenti boy, whom you've only seen once?"

In the wake of her mother's rare anger, Giulietta remained silent.

"And what of Aristo?" Caressa asked with slightly narrowed eyes as she released her daughter's chin. "He is pure *Zingaro.* He is dark and ugly. He is malformed—"

"Aristo is *not* ugly!" Giulietta said indignantly.

"Ahh . . . I see. Most people, *nina,* would not agree with you. But you know Aristo is beautiful inside—and that is the important thing, no matter what he looks like."

Giulietta's features took on a stubborn set. "Aristo is good and kind and would never *kill* someone."

"Your father said 'twas an accident—even Bernardo concurred. Yet you blame the Gypsy boy?" She shook her head. "I hope 'tis only your agitation that makes you sit in judgment of a man—and his people—whom you know nothing about. And remember, too, that 'twas Rodrigo's grandmother who saved our Aristo . . .

"And now, I think you'd better go to the chapel and pray for Mario's soul." She took a step back. "And for the ability to put into practice the love and tolerance for others that your father and I have tried to teach you."

She watched as Giulietta moved across the courtyard, her steps dragging with obvious reluctance. In spite of the girl's bowed head, her semisubdued demeanor, Caressa knew she was struggling with a natural obstinacy . . . a flare of temper that ran through her blood, a legacy from both her grandfathers.

Caressa de' Alessandro was glad, in spite of the amount of emotional pain Dante believed it would cause Rodrigo, that the boy was leaving Italy. Not only for Rodrigo's safety, but also for the time his absence would allow Giulietta's pain to heal, her anger to dissipate.

For Caressa knew that whether Giulietta liked it or not, sooner or later Rodrigo da Valenti would reenter her life through Dante and his promise to Maddalena. And perhaps, too, for a reason much closer to her husband's heart now that Mario di Corsini was dead.

# Two

*Soon, Giulietta mia. Soon you'll have a husband . . .*

The words reverberated through Giulietta de' Alessandro's mind, scoring her heart like a sharp dagger-point, and serving only to reinforce the fact that she was already seventeen years old—well past marriageable age—and still a maid. In fact, she was nearing the age when some might consider her matronly.

*Mamma didn't wed until her seventeenth birthday the first time.*

Aye. But Mamma was a serene person, more accepting of what life threw her way . . . and what others told her to do.

*Mamma never fled to a convent, either.*

"I am not Mamma!" she declared softly.

What was her father *doing* to her? Giulietta thought in utter frustration. Was he deliberately humiliating her? Punishing her for some sin she'd unwittingly committed?

It was dark. The sun had set, and thousands of stars dotted the Stygian tapestry of the night above her. The moon shone full and bright, like a newly minted florin waiting to be spent in the *mercato*.

Giulietta allowed her eyes to adjust to the darkness, then glanced about her from where she stood flattened, in the deeper shadows, against the outer castle wall. She hadn't sneaked away for months, having outgrown the need to do such a thing.

It wasn't really dangerous, she told herself, and she had every right as an adult to come and go as she pleased.

*No you don't,* whispered a voice. *You are unwed and under your father's jurisdiction.*

"And see where it has gotten me," she muttered bitterly. "I am like an overripe olive . . . bursting to be picked before I drop to the ground and shrivel."

Frustration and anger threatened to swamp her. In a bid to hold those emotions at arm's length, she directed her concentration on her escape. She glanced about her, narrowing her eyes against the umber night with its layers of shadows. No one was about. At least on this side of the castle. The woods beckoned to her, the scented breeze sighing through the leaves on the trees. An owl hooted.

Wishing belatedly that she'd worn darker clothing, Giulietta moved swiftly away from the sanctuary of the east wall and began to run toward the trees directly opposite. She would go to the convent of Santa Lucia and speak to the sisters there. At the same time, she'd gain a few hours of freedom, and escape the sound of her father's empty promise repeating over and over again in her mind. . . .


The sound of singing voices and clapping hands lured her toward the eastern edge of the lands adjoining the castle. The faint scent of wood smoke came to her. It had been a long time since she'd clandestinely traipsed off in Nicco or Bernardo's wake. Bernardo was wed now, and Nicco too wily for Giulietta to fool anymore.

Besides, the need to do so had faded somewhat with maturity, although by no means altogether.

The convent was at the edge of the town of Verdi, east of the castle. And when the Gypsies were in that part of Tuscany, they camped nearby—between the eastern edge of the castle

lands and the portion of the principality of Monteverdi that
included the town. The smell of campfires told her that they
were there now.

Unbidden, the image of the Valenti boy rose before her
mind's eye. She could only conjure up unruly dark hair and
strange eyes for a *Zingaro*. . . . Why she got the impression
of strange, she couldn't remember.

She hadn't seen or heard of him since that tragic day six
years before. He'd just disappeared, and her father had never
mentioned him again.

Sudden, unexpected curiosity propelled her toward the
sounds of the camp, her own problems temporarily pushed
aside. She had never been among the *Zingari* before. Never
seen how they lived or any of *them* for that matter except
for Aristo and the Valenti boy. Of course she'd heard of Maddalena and her magic; but Dante had told her that Maddalena
had no more special powers than he had, and the rumors were
only circulated out of ignorance and fear. There was no such
thing as a witch, he'd told her. . . .

She slowed her steps, trying to catch her breath and avoid
the briars and low-hanging branches that caught at her gown,
that clawed at her hair and pulled it loose. If she moved slowly
enough, she could see her way by the scraps of moonlight that
penetrated the leafy branches overhead.

Suddenly the trees thinned and gave way to a clearing ahead.
Giulietta stayed within the shelter of a huge, double-trunked
oak, wishing once again that she'd worn something dark . . .
and light or dark, a pair of Nicco's trunk hose and a tunic
would have served her much better in the woods.

A few people moved about, but most of the Gypsies sat
around several fires, talking and gesturing animatedly. Some
of the women were clearing away remains of the evening meal,
and two boys in brightly colored tunics and baggy breeches

teased a mongrel dog as they tossed a ball back and forth over its head.

She wondered which of the women was Maddalena . . . until her attention was unexpectedly snared by one man in particular.

He was a young man in his mid-twenties, seated cross-legged upon the grass at the periphery of the circle of light from the campfire nearest Giulietta's hiding place. His dark head was bent over a full-bodied lute, his fingers working experimentally over the instrument's strings. As he grew more confident in his strumming, the activity around him ceased; other sounds faded. The attention of those immediately nearby shifted to him, and he began to sing, the lute a soft and sweet accompaniment to his melody.

For some inexplicable reason, Giulietta found her gaze riveted to him, caught securely by his voice and his music . . . and some indefinable aspect about the man himself.

His voice was deep and mellow, his words in perfect tune with the lute he played so beautifully. The words were not Italian, or Romany, Giulietta realized, but rather, French, of which she knew a smattering, and the tune was unfamiliar. Yet there was no mistaking the beauty of it . . . and the spell the man's performance seemed to cast over his audience.

Giulietta watched with fascination his long fingers play over the lute strings, his hold on the wooden instrument as loving as if it were a cherished thing. When, after a time, he looked up, she felt her throat tighten, her mouth grow dry, at the splendid profile unknowingly offered to her.

He gazed into the night as he sang, and the sight of that unfamiliar yet provocative profile, the strong, clean lines of his throat and jaw, stirred strange yet profound yearnings deep inside Giulietta. She remained concealed, utterly mesmerized by the man and his music.

He wore his hair short, just covering his ears; his dress was more subdued in cut and color than that worn by the other Gypsies among whom he sat—a simple, pale-colored tunic and dark trunk hose. Yet he appeared perfectly at ease, as if he belonged among them.

His song ended, and something within Giulietta mourned it. Applause followed, and shouts of praise. She thought she detected the rise of color in his high cheekbones, but couldn't be certain it wasn't a trick of firelight and shadow. A young woman approached the lute player . . . a lovely woman with long, straight hair as dark as the night. Dainty bare feet and ankles peeked from beneath her full skirt. She bent and said something into his ear as he looked up at her. He flashed her a smile and nodded, and she knelt beside him as he appeared to commence an impromptu lesson on his lute.

Giulietta's fingers unconsciously curled at her sides. . . .

With the greatest of efforts, she dragged her attention from the couple, wondering what strange spell had come over her for a time, and made to turn away and continue on toward Santa Lucia. A shout went up just then, and in response, a middle-aged man sitting on the opposite side of the campfire stood and moved into the shadows beside what evidently was his family's caravan. From the light of the fires and torches, Giulietta could make out the compact wooden wagon's ornateness—designs of every conceivable color decorated its outer walls. What made it look even odder to her were the wheels that held it above the ground. What a strange home, she thought, and tiny compared to her own.

The man emerged from behind the caravan then, and all thought of the handsome lute player fled. *Dio mio!* she thought . . . was she seeing things?

A large, furry creature lumbered along on all fours behind the Gypsy until it came into the circle of light from the fire. Its owner gave it a command in a language utterly foreign to Giulietta, and the animal stood on its hind legs and pawed the air.

She gasped softly, then felt her heartbeat steady when she saw the leash in the Gypsy's hand. It was attached at the other end to a leather muzzle over the creature's snout.

She watched in fascination as the animal began to perform tricks at its master's command. It danced clumsily about in a circle several times, then performed a slow bow. Amidst the sound of scattered applause, the creature sat, accepted a tidbit from the Gypsy, then heaved itself to its feet again.

Without warning, it turned its head in Giulietta's direction . . .

. . . and she realized what it was. She'd seen such an animal in the menagerie in Florence. *Orso,* her mother's voice came to her from the past as Caressa de' Alessandro had identified the different animals to a young Nicco and an awestruck Giulietta.

A bear.

Had it caught her scent? she wondered as it continued to look her way for a long moment before its owner regained its attention. She took one step backward, then another, trying not to make any more sound than she had to. She had a mission at Santa Lucia, and had no business spying on the *Zingari.* A sharp stone split the thin leather of one of her slippers and penetrated the delicate arch of her foot. She winced, but continued to carefully step backward . . .

Until she came up against something solid. She bit back a cry of surprise, the image of the bear still in her mind.

*Don't be a fool,* said her sensible side. *There are no bears in—*

She whirled, putting her back to the camp, attempting to dodge whatever or whoever was directly behind her. But the abruptness of her move and the tenderness in her bruised foot as it took her weight caused her to twist her ankle.

To her dismay, her knee buckled. . . .

\* \* \*

Firm hands were suddenly on her shoulders, lifting and steadying her. She looked up and into the face of a man, a stranger, whose features she couldn't make out. The back of one hand came up to her mouth to stifle a scream, yet even as the urge to dodge her way past him once more came to Giulietta, his hands tightened on her shoulders as if he could read her mind.

"Let me go!" she said in a low, strained voice. "Who do you think you are to . . ."

She trailed off as she caught the flash of even white teeth against his shadowed visage. "Rather, *cara mia,* who are *you?*"

His voice was rich and smooth, carrying a trace of an accent She wasn't so much afraid of him, however, as embarrassed at being discovered alone in the middle of the shadow-shrouded forest, eavesdropping on these people, whom she really knew nothing about.

Reluctant to reveal her identity to a stranger—he could easily have been a brigand or worse—she hedged, "I asked you first, signore. *You* accosted *me."*

"I did no such thing," he said, dry humor lacing his voice. "I was merely taking a walk. As I returned to camp, there you were . . ."

He knew exactly who she was . . . he'd dreamed of her a thousand nights—not as the half-grown child he remembered, but as a young woman. He would have had to be a mindless *idiota* to have mistaken her identity, even now, after six long years and beneath the semiconcealing canopy of the trees, so close to the present campsite of his people.

Aye, here she was, having appeared as if conjured up by his grandmother, and having all but fallen into his arms.

She smelled sweet—of jasmine and woman.

Giulietta de' Alessandro . . . Forbidden.

That thought, and the feel of her in his arms, was like a powerful aphrodisiac to his already heightened senses beneath the full Tuscan moon and in the caress of the sultry, late summer breeze.

*"Per piacere,"* she was saying softly, a quaver to her voice. "Please, let me go. I—I shouldn't be here . . . with *you.*"

She hadn't meant to say it aloud, but he'd admitted to being one of those from the camp. Heaven knew what he might do to her, she thought as her mind suddenly echoed with every unsavory rumor she'd ever heard regarding the strange *Zingari.* Any people who kept *bears* among them—

"You weren't frightened by Lily, were you? Piero's bear?"

"I *must* leave," she insisted, missing the teasing note in his voice. She pulled away, fighting panic, and felt his hands unexpectedly fall away from her.

"As you wish, *madonna,* but at least allow me to escort you—"

"No!"

She lunged around him in her eagerness to escape and began to run in the direction (she hoped) of the castle.

Giulietta hadn't gone twenty paces when she came to a small, moon-dappled clearing. The extra light, however, didn't prevent her from treading on a small broken branch in her frantic flight and sinking to her knees. The pain in her foot shot up her ankle as a piece of the offending wood invaded the torn leather of her shoe . . . and the abused flesh of the cut she'd suffered only moments ago.

He materialized behind her, his tall, imposing form backlit by moon glow.

*Dio!* she thought in frustration. She was virtually helpless before him. But pride prevented her from showing her fear. "If you'll stop trying to frighten me, I can return to . . . Santa Lucia," she said in her loftiest tones.

The convent? he thought. Not likely, from her clothing and the fact that she was out alone in the woods.

"I agree you should be . . . er, home," he told her, "but at least allow me to carry you—"

"No!" She pushed to her knees. To allow a perfect stranger to *carry* her? To hold her in his arms and. . . .

"Or you can allow me to tend your foot, and then perhaps you can walk home yourself."

This alternative was infinitely preferable to Giulietta, and her immediate reaction was to nod in agreement.

He bent, touched one knee to the ground, and lifted her into his arms with seemingly minimal effort. But as he stood with her in his firm embrace, Giulietta knew instantly she'd made a mistake.

His hold was steady but gentle, and his chest against the side of her breast felt like the touch of fire. She tried to ignore the latter as he turned to the right and took her away from the camp—and also the direction of the castle—with long, lithe strides.

She began to struggle against his hold. "*Signore,* you cannot just hie me off into the forest and—"

"I promise to return you home, *madonna,* and if naught else I am a man of my word."

He looked down at her in the darkness—she could just make out the blur of his profile, feel his warm breath feather across her cheek.

"Who *are* you?" she asked, fighting her rising alarm at the ease with which she'd submitted to his suggestion . . . surrendered herself to his care.

She felt him shrug. "A man. No more . . . no less."

A finely stated answer she thought with irony. It told her absolutely nothing. "A *Zingaro.*"

The word hung in the air between them for a moment.

"So they say." The smooth register of his voice roughened here. The words were terse.

Recognition dawned suddenly. The lute player.

Giulietta opened her mouth to speak again, but she abruptly perceived that they were near water—a creek or stream, from the tinkling sound of it as it gurgled along its course. The trees thinned; moonlight silvered the clearer area of the bank.

He set her down on a fallen log that spanned the glittering ribbon of water. Her dangling feet sank ankle-deep into its welcome coolness. Then she remembered her shoes.

"My shoes—" she began.

". . . are already ruined," he said, a trace of humor in his voice again as he bent to remove them. He placed them both on the log to one side, then lifted her injured foot, noting that she wore no stockings, and gently probed the area around the laceration.

Giulietta had never felt a man's hands on her bare legs. One held her ankle while the other explored carefully. Heat seeped into her cheeks. She reflexively jerked her foot, but succeeded only in almost unseating herself.

He slanted her a look through his lashes, his eye color still indiscernible to her. "Let the water cleanse the cut for a few moments," he said, and lowered her foot back into the water.

"I—I'll be missed," she blurted.

"Your husband, *naturalmente.*"

He was probing deliberately, and cursed himself inwardly for a romantic fool. Of course she was married. It was all but inconceivable, considering her age, her fairness, her lineage, that she should not be.

Instead of exhibiting affront, however, Giulietta averted her face as renewed misery swept through her. Her loose hair shielded her face from the faint celestial light, but there was no mistaking her attitude of despair.

*"Perdonami,"* he said. "Forgive me. I didn't mean to pry." He lifted her foot from the water and looked at the cut again, narrowing his eyes against the dimness.

His dark hair formed an enhancing frame for his strong,

even features, Giulietta decided as she pulled herself from her misery long enough to venture another look at him. In the bright light of day, she thought—or even the muted glow of firelight, as she'd already observed, he would be an extraordinarily handsome man, although as dark as her father was fair.

"I meant I'll be missed at the convent," she said in an attempt to change the direction of her thoughts. "Santa Lucia. I wish to dedicate my life to God, for my father evidently does not think me fit to be wed."

He looked at her averted face, inexplicable hope surging through him at her unexpected confession, despite the bitterness that curdled her words. It couldn't be. Nothing, he'd discovered in his four and twenty years, was ever that simple. . . .

*Of course not,* jeered a voice. *She is out of your reach. She always has been, always will be, whether she's married to another or not.*

He watched in silence as she succumbed to acute misery once again, his thumb massaging the silken flesh of her ankle as if he could smooth away her anguish.

She began to shiver, although he couldn't quite discern why. Was she weeping? he wondered. "Hush now, *cara,*" he soothed. "Nothing is so bad as that."

He moved to take a seat beside her, putting one arm about her trembling shoulders as silent sobs shook her. She leaned her head onto his shoulder, and suddenly the flame of desire leapt to life within him. He pressed his lips to her hair, taking in its light, clean fragrance. Heady stuff, indeed, one rational part of his mind registered . . . jasmine. But jasmine enhanced by her own unique scent.

*She is forbidden to you,* warned the voice of reason.

But this might be his only chance. . . .

*The world is full of innocent young maidens,* reason insisted, *just waiting to be comforted.*

He ignored it as Giulietta raised her tear-tracked face to his in the moonlight. "You—you are very kind, but I have shamed myself with such a display before you." A troubled frown formed between her eyes.

"No one need know," he said softly. "Your secrets are safe with me."

He couldn't seem to prevent himself from leaning toward her. Their mouths were a heartbeat away, their breaths mingling on a sigh.

When his lips touched hers, Giulietta forgot her emotional pain in the wake of the strange and exciting feeling that rippled through her midsection, a renewal of the earlier sensations she'd felt as she'd watched him perform. The few stolen kisses she'd experienced—which she could have counted on the fingers of one hand—had been nothing like this.

Tentative, hesitant at first, his touch was infinitely tender as his mouth played over hers. His tongue teased the smooth surfaces of her lips, the sweet line where they met, still closed in heart-rending innocence.

He threaded the fingers of his free hand through the tumbled mass of her hair, gently gripping her head and holding her face to his, his reason swiftly dispersing into the mists of mind-less passion.

Giulietta felt her mouth relax, and his gently questing tongue took instant advantage. It touched hers, then retreated briefly, touched it again, stoking the tiny flame of desire in her belly to a roaring fire. It flicked along the pearly edges of her teeth, then filled her mouth with an almost unbearable sweetness.

A groan of purest pleasure escaped her, and the hand that had been holding her head moved to stroke the silken lines of her neck and throat. His lips followed, his tongue teasing her warm, sweet-scented flesh, and searing her wherever it touched.

He nestled his mouth in the hollow where her neck met her shoulder, nipping lightly before resting his face in that sweetest of havens while he reined in his runaway passion. He tried to retain his grip on his sanity as jasmine teased his nostrils, invaded his very brain; tried to conjure up the fury of Il Leone when he heard of his daughter's seduction at the hands of a man who, many would say, had no right to touch the hem of her gown.

Giulietta held him to her, savoring the new and wonderful feelings wending their way through her body. *Dio mio,* but she never dreamed of such sensations, making her tingle from the top of her head to the tips of her toes. A warm wetness bathed the area between her thighs as his hand caressed one breast through the silk of her gown. With a groan of primal need she arched against his fingers, needing suddenly to feel his flesh pressed to hers.

Surely, she thought in a flash of lucidity, he was a Gypsy sorcerer, and she was caught inexorably in his erotic web. But she didn't care. She wanted more—she wanted what she felt had been withheld from her for too long.

She felt his hot breath through the cloth over one nipple, and felt it tighten in response. He took the bud, damp fabric and all, between his teeth, and Giulietta felt tears of frustration form behind her eyes.

*"Cara . . . cara mia,"* he murmured, dragging his mouth back to hers, tasting its delectable corners, slipping his tongue between her teeth once again.

"Love me," she whispered as his kisses traveled over her eyes, her cheeks, the slope of her jaw. Her hands explored his shoulders, then the broad expanse of his upper back as her arms twined about him. She marveled at the latent strength beneath his shirt, the sheer size of his masculine form.

Suddenly he was slipping one arm beneath her knees, then lifting her from their perch above the water. He carried her to the bank and stood her up against him, their bodies fused.

Her fingers threaded through his hair, and she savored the

clean, crisp feel of it, the strength beneath her hands as they moved down the corded column of his neck, then back to his shoulders. By all rights, she should have been mortified at her brazenness—and with a stranger—yet not only was Giulietta intoxicated by him, but also inundated by her own long-denied yearnings and needs.

Here was a man to dream about, she thought with a sudden stab of bitterness, in her chaste cell at Santa Lucia. And if she were to spend the rest of her life wed to Christ, then she would finally discover in this stranger's arms what her father had seen fit to deny her.

Except, she wasn't quite certain what to do to aid the process. . . .

Then inspiration struck. She moaned softly.

"What is it?" he asked, the concern in his voice unmistakable. "Your foot?"

*"Sì,"* she lied with sudden, naughty ease, and allowed her knees to buckle, throwing her body even more securely against his.

He helped her to sit upon the grass beneath them and moved to examine her injury again. Giulietta shamelessly leaned back on her elbows, having decided that whatever it was she wanted from this man would be more easily accomplished in a supine position.

He looked over at her in the moonlight, perceived her lovely mouth parted and ready for more of his kisses, her eyelids heavy with obvious desire, and slowly brought her instep toward his lips, thinking she was truly her father's daughter in more ways than one. Not only was she a temptress, with the Alessandro sensuality, but a creative actress, as well—a role that had once perfectly suited her father while he secretly served as an informer to Lorenzo de' Medici. . . .

As his lips touched her foot, he watched her eyes fly open,

her mouth form a rounded *O*. He smiled slightly. "Is that better, *cara?*"

She nodded, her words trapped in her throat as his lips skirted the injury and sent waves of pleasure shooting up her leg. His mouth moved insidiously to her ankle, causing her entire foot to hum with sensations that had little to do with pain. The ache centered deep within her increased in direct relation to the movement of his mouth upon her calf, then her knee and the sensitive depression behind it, then upward even farther. . . .

She reached for the thick, soft cap of his hair, gripping with the exquisite tension born of anticipation of fulfillment. He obliged, pushing back the rich material of her gown and undergarments to gain access to the satiny stretch of her thigh, driving Giulietta to distraction. . . .

She moaned softly, her head thrashing back and forth, erratic tremors spurting through her and shaking her to the core. When his mouth suddenly stopped just short of the area between her legs, Giulietta made a sound of frustration.

Immediately his lips silenced her protest, and one hand moved down to take the place of his mouth. "I would not leave you so," he said softly, in that velvet voice of his. He gently penetrated and stroked the silken folds of her, trying to ignore his own arousal in order to give her pleasure.

Yet what did it matter, he thought, if this young woman was the Prince of Monteverdi's daughter? Hadn't Dante de' Alessandro sent him away from all that he had known and loved six long years ago?

*'Twas for your own good,* a voice reminded him.

No!

*Aye! And 'twasn't the prince's fault that you chose to defy him and remain in France for two more years after you were summoned back to Monteverdi.*

A battle raged within him . . . until his finger encountered the fragile barrier that proclaimed her a maiden. Even as he felt the woman beneath him begin to shudder with her release, he knew he couldn't betray his former mentor in this manner. There would be hell to pay as it was, with him having shared such intimacies with Giulietta de' Alessandro, but he was willing to bear any punishment, for she had all but spoiled him for any other that day he'd first glimpsed her . . . and was well worth any retribution.

She clung to him, and his lips found hers as he held her close, feeling the tension ebb and leave her body in exchange for the utter relaxation of sexual surcease.

He buried his head in the luxuriant spill of her hair lying across her shoulder, savoring what he knew in his heart he would never evince again. Reveling in the feel of her in his arms, soft and compliant and fulfilled.

And, because of an accident of birth, silently acknowledging it would never—*could* never—happen again.

# Three

"That ungrateful whelp! I could just wring his neck!"

In the veil of twilight gently descending over the Tuscan countryside, Aristo could see the heat in his master's cheeks. And as the dying sun touched Durante de' Alessandro's golden hair, Aristo could also make out the subtly blended streaks of silver here and there, the only indication aside from a few more lines about the prince's eyes and mouth that he was only a few years away from his fiftieth birthday. The vigor that had always been a part of Dante de' Alessandro was still just as evident as the day Aristo had first met him almost twenty years earlier.

"Valenti?" he asked, knowing the answer.

Dante turned angry eyes on his servant. "Who else? If it weren't for him, I wouldn't be traipsing all over Tuscany searching for a husband for my daughter! And especially to Antonio Sarzano . . ." He looked ahead, his fair brows lowering as his frown deepened. "I had such plans for him! *Dio*, 'tis enough to shrivel a man's soul."

Aristo smiled to himself, despite the discomfort of riding a horse with his crooked spine. He would have walked over burning coals however, for the man he served, and gave no outward sign of his pain. "There are other eligible young men besides Sarzano's son, Excellence," he offered, clinging to the saddle as a slight but treacherous depression in the earth caused his docile mare to break her even gait then right herself.

Of a certainty, Aristo thought, he must look like a great beetle perched upon the horse's back, his short legs sticking out to either side like spindles from beneath his dark robe, his badly hunched back flattening him now, in middle age, until he felt almost parallel with the mare's back.

Dante, ever perceptive, threw him a probing look. "Are you comfortable?"

It was an old game they played. *"Sì."*

Dante's lips twisted. *"Sì,* indeed," he echoed. "You'd suffer the tortures of hell before you'd admit it." He returned his gaze to the road ahead. "And there are other eligible bachelors to be sure, *maestro,* but not nearly as pretty of face as Leon Sarzano. And to a young woman Giulietta's age, 'tis important."

Aristo merely grunted, keeping his thoughts to himself. Giulietta de' Alessandro was shamelessly spoiled by her father. It was not for her to be concerned about the looks of her prospective husband but, rather, how advantageous a match for the Alessandros it would prove to be. And she should have been, as custom dictated, in a convent until she was wed, although Dante was certainly not the first father to raise his daughter at home.

And who could blame *il principe?* the dwarf thought, for Giulietta was vivacious and high-spirited, and more than a little devilish even when on her best behavior. She would either have driven the good sisters of some convent to drink, or would herself have pined away for the freedom she obviously loved so well. But she was also immature in many ways. . . .

"I know what you're thinking," Dante said, breaking into Aristo's thoughts. "That she is nothing like her mother was at her age."

" 'Tis not my place to compare," came the reply. Yet Aristo silently acknowledged that Giulietta's mother had put little value on looks, even at Giulietta's age. Caressa de' Alessandro had been the first person to look past Aristo's deformity, his unattractive features, and accept him on a level with every other human being within her circle.

Madonna Caressa had given him a chance to find the goodness within himself, and for that and much more, he would always love her.

"The tarot cards say he will return soon."

Dante slanted him a wry look. "You've been saying that for the last year."

Aristo shook his head. "I feel it in my bones—he is either on his way home or . . ."

"Or?" The wry look turned to a frown.

"Or he is already here."

Dante swiped at a fly hovering near his face, then raised a golden eyebrow at Aristo. "Are you certain 'tisn't rather the creak of old age in your bones? Mayhap 'tis time to visit Maddalena and see which it is . . . although I don't know which would be worse—his deliberately remaining in France or his having returned secretly."

"I will go first thing in the morn, Excellence. You will know then whether to seek a husband for Mona Giulietta in earnest."

*Or if your troubles are just beginning.*


Utterly replete, Giulietta savored the euphoria that enveloped her, and the haven of his arms as he carried her through the woods. She never even gave their destination a thought . . . until he set her on her feet at the periphery of the trees just across from the east wall of Castello Monteverdi.

Reality deluged her. She was suddenly back home, the very place she had fled earlier that evening, and not Santa Lucia.

More importantly, she'd allowed this absolute stranger extraordinary liberties with her. Surely, she thought as shame swept through her, she'd ruined herself for marriage—wantonly thrown away her virtue in a moment of undreamed-of ecstasy.

*What does it matter,* an imp taunted. *You were on your way to the convent, remember? God won't mind a soiled bride.*

As if sensing her hesitation, he said, "Shall I carry you to your doorstep?"

In the midst of her shame, his words sounded mocking, as if to deliberately remind her that his carrying her in his arms to the very gates of Monteverdi would shred her reputation to ribbons. And in the dead of night, no less, for she had no idea how much time had passed while she'd lain in his arms like some *puttana.*

The rebellious side of her nature wanted to dismiss it as of no real importance. She would more than likely take her vows.

Her conscience, however, was another matter. . . .

"No!" she blurted in a low but emphatic voice. Did she sound as suddenly uncertain and guilty as she felt inside?

Before she could even contemplate an answer, he bent his head and touched his lips to hers, a softly uttered *addio* caught and swept away in the night breeze. The kiss was light, yet reassuring. It also conveyed something more to Giulietta that was disappointingly elusive . . . a mixture of whimsy and reverence, perhaps? she thought. Then dismissed reverence as impossible. Why would any man ever respect a woman who'd thrown herself at him without even knowing his name? Or he hers?

"Here," he murmured, placing one arm about her shoulders. He bent to catch her behind the knees. "Let me—"

"No!" she repeated and pulled away from him. She'd already spent an indecent amount of time in his embrace, and in those moments wanted nothing more than to discourage him from taking her directly to the keep. All hell would break loose if someone saw them.

Essaying to ignore the stabbing pain in her foot, Giulietta spun about, emerged from the trees and headed incautiously toward the castle, praying he wouldn't follow. That concern outweighed any others in those moments.

As she limped along, she chanced a look over her shoulder once to see if he was behind her. She could only discern what looked like the silhouette of his tall form, standing in the same place she'd left him, and watching her. Or it could have been merely another pocket of shadow.

Halfway to the castle wall, Giulietta suddenly remembered the possibility of guards—certainly two at the castle entrance—and maybe more in the four towers.

She slowed her steps and glanced up at the tower at either end of the east wall, straining to see, but in vain. It was too dark, and it was also too late to turn back. Surely, she reasoned, if the two towers on this side of the keep had been unguarded earlier, they would still be so now.

She picked up her pace, toward the small door through which she'd exited Castello Monteverdi . . . and was brought up short at the sight of a man standing directly in her path. He'd materialized from nowhere, or so it seemed to Giulietta. She heard the soft grinding sound of a sword sliding free of its sheath.

"Who goes there?"

Giulietta recognized Paolo's voice. Paolo—the captain of the guard.

She instantly answered him in her sweetest tones, allowing distress to infuse her words. " 'Tis I . . . Gietta," she said, also using her childhood nickname, and hoping to further win his sympathy instead of his censure.

"Mona Giulietta?" he said, obviously surprised. He stepped toward her and peered into the dimness.

"*Sì.* And I'm injured . . . I hurt my foot and almost drowned in the stream when I tried to cleanse it."

He slid his sword back into its place and took her by the arm. "Are you all right now?" he asked, concern in his voice.

"Aside from my foot, *sì*. Can you help me back into the keep?"

He visibly hesitated a moment, his duty obviously overcoming his concern now. *"Sì*, but what do you here? Alone outside the castle . . . at night?"

She managed a sniffle, hoping she sounded close to tears. "I—I was angry with Father, Paolo," she confided in a small voice. "He still hasn't found me a husband—surely I'm the oldest maiden in Tuscany!—and we argued earlier."

She thought he nodded, and was glad he wouldn't question her about such personal matters. "Come," he said, and began to guide her to the door. "You shouldn't try to run away, *madonna*," he chided. " 'Twill solve nothing."

"I know, Paolo," she said with contrition, and feeling guilty at the same time for her outrageous exaggeration. But she was desperate. "I didn't really run away—I just needed to be alone and—"

"You could have found any number of places to be alone within *il castello*." The uncharacteristic eloquence of the man in itself (for Paolo was normally a man of few words) revealed to Giulietta just how serious a transgression she'd committed in his eyes.

They reached the small wood-paneled door. "I know," she said with a sigh. "But I wanted to be outdoors and . . . away from Monteverdi." She turned to him, trying to read his expression in the deeper blackness of the stone wall. "You'll not tell Papa, will you?"

Caressa had once told her daughter of wheedling the taciturn Paolo into allowing her to disobey Dante's orders in the prince's absence. Paolo had suffered severe punishment, for Caressa had unwittingly put her life—and those of several men—in jeopardy. Caressa had explained this to Giulietta to make a point: If one knowingly disobeyed or did wrong, one only compounded that wrong by dragging others into the deceit necessary to cover it up. And, equally important, one did not force a servant, or anyone else for that matter, to choose between loyalties.

Giulietta's conscience squirmed even as she thought of her mother's story, for Paolo had received a disciplinary whipping, and Caressa had felt such remorse that she'd begged her husband to allow her to apologize to Paolo and then tend his wounds.

"Paolo?" she whispered in the wake of his silence. *"Per favore?"*

There followed a brief silence. Then, "Your father is not here, *madonna* . . . so I cannot tell him now, can I?" He opened the door carefully. "I wondered why this door was unbarred," he said under his breath.

"And later?" she pressed, feeling monstrous.

She could just discern one corner of his mouth lift beneath the shadow of his steel helm, in what looked like a half-smile of resignation. "I am getting old, *nina*. I cannot always remember things like I used to. But only this once," he added, his tone hardening. "And if someone else sees you, you must explain yourself." He propelled her gently inside. "Bar the door, *sì?* And see to your foot," he said, then closed the panel quietly but firmly behind her.

Rodrigo stood long after Giulietta disappeared, and stared at the castle of Monteverdi. A host of emotions ran through him as he stood within the trees, hidden like a thief in the night, he thought with a bitter twist of his lips. Although Rodrigo the man could understand and forgive Durante de' Alessandro's actions of six years past, the simmering sense of betrayal he still felt, just beneath the surface, would not disappear. His love for the prince fought through layers of old anger and resentment, half-faded now with time and wisdom.

But the sense of disloyalty remained. Had Rodrigo been a nobleman born, Dante would never have sent him away. And although he knew the circumstances of his birth were a whim of fate and not the prince's fault, he still smarted deep within.

And could remember the day of his humiliation before Giulietta, Bernardo and Niccolò de' Alessandro as if it were only yesterday. Mario di Corsini's death had been an unfortunate accident, nothing more.

*. . . my father evidently does not think me fit to be wed.*

He felt a sliver of guilt for having robbed Giulietta of her betrothed, for the anguish in her voice as she had said those words had been obvious. Yet for some strange reason the prince had not found another husband for his daughter. Why? he wondered. She had to be seventeen or eighteen years old by now . . . an unseemly age for an unwed young woman, and especially a noblewoman.

After some time, Rodrigo turned and retreated into the trees, toward the camp. If Giulietta said nothing of her sojourn into the night, no harm would really be done. He'd left her maidenhead intact, he thought wryly as he acknowledged the slowly fading pressure in his loins. If he'd done things to her that only a husband was entitled to do . . . well, it was too late now. There certainly could be no taking it back.

Her biggest problem, as he saw it, would be explaining the cut on her foot. And the loss of—

He headed toward the stream. He'd forgotten her shoes in the heat of passion. She, obviously, had also forgotten about them.

They were sitting on the log beneath the moonlight, just as he'd left them. He retrieved them and examined the split leather of the one sole. Even in the dimness he could see the bloodstain. She had to be in pain, he thought, wishing suddenly that he could wipe away that pain by distracting her the night long.

His fingers unconsciously tightened on the fine kid leather

before he reached beneath his tunic and tucked them both into the waist of his trunk hose. After one last, lingering look around, Rodrigo swung away and left.

Avoiding the campfires and the few remaining Gypsies still sitting around them, Rodrigo paused before the back entrance to Maddalena's caravan. He dipped his cupped hands in the pail of water for washing on the side of the top step and splashed his face with it. A swim in the stream would have served him better, he acknowledged with rue, for more than his face still felt overheated.

As he picked up the towel to dry his hands, his grandmother's face appeared in the open doorway. "Alessandro will nail your beating heart to the battlements for this," she warned him softly. "You deal with the Prince of Monteverdi now . . . not merely the Corsini family."

He met her gaze levelly, hiding his surprise at her words. "I did no more than she was willing to do . . . and none will be the wiser."

"And if she accuses you of ravishment, then what will you do, my fine *condottiere*? Go back to France?"

"No." He should have known. It was difficult to hide anything from Maddalena. She'd not earned the reputation as a witch for nothing. She possessed the Sight, as well as the ability to read the cards and chart the stars with uncanny accuracy.

He dropped the towel and ascended the few steps to the threshold. Maddalena moved back into the lantern light of the caravan, her blue eyes studying her grandson, a dark frown between them. "No one will ever send me away again," he told her.

Maddalena shook a finger at him. "No one will *send* you anywhere, for you'll be forced to flee for your life if you aren't careful. Not only did you ignore Il Leone's summons to return, but you are deliberately staying away from Monteverdi. And now you dare to trifle with his only daughter?" She swung away, toward a small table with an array of tarot cards spread over it. "You push the boundaries of his love for you."

"And you taught me that love has no boundaries. Is the affection of a prince different then?"

*"Sì!* I also taught you that blood runs thicker than water, and you are not of his blood."

Rodrigo felt the first spurt of anger. "I need no reminding."

"Then you will go to him?"

Rodrigo didn't answer.

"You'll pay the consequences," she said over her shoulder, her fingers lightly moving over the cards before her. "And not only that, grandson. She'll break your tender Gypsy heart."

"I did nothing to Giulietta de' Alessandro," he insisted, ignoring her last words. "She was on her way to Santa Lucia—so she said. I ran into her after Piero began to show us Lily's tricks. She'd cut her foot—I tended it and returned her to Castello Monteverdi."

"Your face still bears the tint of a flush, my grandson. Your entire body emanates the tension of unfulfilled desire . . . you think me ignorant of such things?"

No, he certainly didn't think her ignorant of such things. Quite the contrary. "Naught happened."

She turned back to him, the silver streaks in her long, unbound hair catching the lantern light. She seemed to deliberately hold her position between Rodrigo and the tarot cards, as if she did not want him to see them.

Surely she knew, he thought, that he didn't put store in such nonsense. He could more easily accept her clairvoyance than any accuracy of tarot cards, for he'd occasionally evinced the power himself, although on a much smaller scale.

"So, she was fleeing to the convent," Maddalena mused aloud. "She wants for a man—small wonder she was like warm clay in your hands."

Rodrigo ran his fingers through his hair in visible agitation. "You talk as if I make a habit of seducing innocents." His eyes met hers, his voice suddenly strained with emotion. "Does that mean you also think I murdered the Corsini boy, Maddalena? If you are truly a seer, you would know unequivocally 'twas an accident." Without waiting for her to reply, he added, "In truth, I spent every spare moment while I was away learning my trade—honing my skills with sword and lance."

Maddalena raised an eyebrow. "Which lance do you speak of, grandson?" she said softly, slanting him a meaningful look.

His ink blue eyes locked with hers. "The one I employed when I entered every tournament possible in France . . . and used those developed skills to my gain. I thought about many things in the past years . . . and not least of all the carelessness of noblemen when it comes to pleasuring themselves on women of lesser station. I've no intention of siring bastards all over the countryside, I can assure you of that."

One corner of his mouth lifted suddenly. "I have enough gold in Parisian banks to convincingly prove to any doubters exactly how I spent my time in France. Shall I build you a villa, Grandmother? Or will you wander about the countryside until you breathe your last in this cramped wagon?"

Maddalena lowered herself to the wooden bed that was suspended from several chains bolted in the caravan wall. It also served as seat and sometimes table. *"Zingari* blood runs stronger in me than you, Rigo. I could never settle down in one place." She cocked her head as she studied him. "But you are more *gorgio* than I, aren't you? Not only through your great-grandsire, but your sire, as well." She nodded. "You'll build yourself a home—a grand villa, mayhap, like you said . . . *if* you make your peace with the prince." Her frown returned with the last words. "And *if* naught comes of your encounter with Giulietta de' Alessandro."

She was probably right, he thought. It was time he went to

see Dante, and it would be better—to say nothing of proper—for him to go to Dante instead of forcing the prince to come to him.

"Very well, then," he said softly, wondering if Giulietta de' Alessandro was asleep yet. "I will send him a message on the morrow."

Giulietta lay abed, wide-eyed. Her entire foot throbbed . . . no doubt from walking on it after *he* had set her down, and then scurrying through the keep to her room without being discovered.

She sat up. Aristo. He was a master of alchemy. She would ask him for something to dull the pain and help her sleep.

The soft snores coming from the direction of her small pallet near the antechamber told her that Lisa, her young handmaiden, was sound asleep. Good . . . she didn't need Lisa to insist on performing the errand for her. An odd restlessness filled her, and Giulietta felt a need to *do* something, although she wasn't sure what it was.

She reached over to the foot of the bed, retrieved her shift, and pulled it over her head. As she stood to let it settle over her hips and thighs, however, her injured foot protested. Gritting her teeth with determination, Giulietta limped toward the door. The cool terrazzo floor felt good against the heated flesh of her swollen, injured arch. . . .

Her father would be back by now, and the dwarf with him, for Aristo was rarely far from Dante de' Alessandro's side. She thought she'd heard returning horses shortly after she'd gone to bed, and from the amount of time she estimated she'd spent tossing fitfully in her bed, it had to be the middle of the night—well past the time for normal comings and goings.

The corridor was cool and dimly lit, and as Giulietta moved along one wall toward the northeast tower, she wondered what story she could tell the dwarf concerning her injury that wouldn't give away her earlier flight. He was very canny, and missed little that went on at Castello Monteverdi.

She neared the tower, then paused to peer around the corner into the adjoining passageway, a thoughtful frown furrowing her forehead. The servants' quarters were on the east side of the keep, near the chapel. No one was about. . . .

She rounded the corner, hugging the wall, her shadow flitting over the stone walls every time she neared one of the regularly spaced flambeaux. The hemline of her shift rippled with her movements and the drafts that endlessly played about the corridor. The acrid smell of burning oil stung her nostrils.

She glanced at the open door of the chapel as she passed it . . . and hesitated. The chapel contained several windows on the outside wall. The east wall.

Giulietta turned into the chapel automatically, her thoughts suddenly diverted from her foot. And from Aristo and the excuse she must give him. Her body responded to the memory of the man who had given her such pleasure. The sight of his profile in her mind's eye, his burning touch upon her flesh, sent a curling heat through her midsection. It spiraled downward, downward, stoking the half-banked embers of desire. . . .

Giulietta looked around in the candle-lit dimness with a kind of desperation. She *had* to see him again, or at least view the spot where he'd stood watching her. It was like a spell he'd cast over her, pulling her toward him, even through the thick walls of Monteverdi, with his sweetly potent lure.

If her foot hadn't been hurting so, if she could have easily left the shelter of the castle in those moments, she would have eagerly gone a-running through the night to see him again, even if only from her hideaway in the forest.

She espied a stool near the side of the chapel door through which she'd entered. She glanced back at the two windows above her, mentally calculating the distance between them and the floor. The stool, she decided with a wrenching disappointment, wouldn't raise her high enough to see outside.

*And the windows are stained glass, anyway, foolish girl,* reminded a scalding voice. Then it turned beguiling: *But mayhap you can see from the tower . . .*

She leaned one warm cheek against the rough, whitewashed wall. It felt cool, refreshing. The disappointment began to dissipate. Of course. Even in the presence of a guard, she could plead insomnia and say she needed to feel the caress of the night wind.

Giulietta pushed away after a few moments, forgetting her original intentions, even when her foot rebelled against the weight she unwittingly put on it in her haste. She hobbled across the chapel, ignoring the scent of incense and candle wax, the serene silence of the room and the comforting image of the altar with its glowing tapers, as if pulled by some powerful yet unseen force.

*What's wrong with me?* she thought with one tiny part of her mind as she gained the door. The rush of cool air bathed her face as she turned the corner . . .

And collided with someone. . . .

The scent of rose water came to her; someone's hands steadied her.

"Mona Giulietta? Is that you?" Aristo squinted up at her in the gloom, his head irreversibly canted from his handicap.

*"Sì,"* she said with resignation in her voice. She'd been foiled.

"What do you here, *madonna?* "

"Why, I was looking for you, *maestro,* " she managed to lie with some glibness.

The dwarf's obsidian eyes narrowed fractionally. "For me? In the chapel?"

Everyone knew Aristo was not a religious man. Spiritual, her father had once told her, but not religious in the ordinary sense. He'd been too badly abused at the hands of the late Bishop of Florence, whom he'd finally killed almost a score of years before.

He never entered the chapel of his own volition.

Ignoring the deeper question beneath his simple words, Giulietta added, "I was on my way to your quarters, for I hurt my foot. And I . . . thought I smelled roses."

"I see." He nodded, as if the excuse were perfectly legitimate, which it could have been under more ordinary circumstances. "Can you walk on it?"

She nodded. "I can move well enough, but I cut it on a sharp stone. It hurts so badly that I cannot sleep." She managed to conjure up a tear then and lowered her lashes. It shimmied down the lush length of them, hovered, then fell like a single drop of rain.

Aristo, she knew too well, was totally vulnerable to tears; specifically, Caressa's tears, and her own.

He looked down at her bare feet, then back up at her face. He sighed. *"Ebbene*—well then, come along. I'll tend it . . ." His mouth tightened almost imperceptibly, but Giulietta missed it. "And you can tell me what mischief you were up to while *il principe* was gone, eh?"

In spite of her confidence in the effect of her tears, Giulietta felt as if the subtle springs of a cleverly laid and inescapable trap had closed around her as he took one of her hands in his twisted fingers and placed it upon his bent shoulder.

*"Viene,"* he repeated softly, and led her down the passageway and toward his chamber.

# Four

"I cannot believe my eyes," Dante said with heavy irony. "The prodigal son has returned . . . albeit it in his own good time." But he was secretly pleased with the young man before him as they stood in the library.

The morning promised a bright and beautiful day, Dante mused, in more respects than weather. It seemed that Rodrigo da Valenti had decided, for whatever reason, to appear on his doorstep before Aristo could even fetch him. And if Dante was any judge, in spite of the years of separation, the initial hard feelings, the anger that had prompted Rodrigo to ignore Dante's earlier summons, Giuliano de' Medici's son was glad to be back.

"I find it difficult to believe you consider me a son—unless you mean it figuratively, of course, Excellence." A faint edge of bitterness tinged his words.

There it was, Dante thought. The crux of the problem, the existence of which he'd suspected ever since Rodrigo had ignored his instructions to return to Tuscany.

"You will always be a son to me, no matter what you wish to consider yourself . . . or the degree of your anger. You know very well that I did what I had to for your own protection."

"And if my name had been Alessandro?"

"No matter what my affection for you, in the eyes of most others—the Corsinis specifically—you were *Zingaro*. You would have been dead by an assassin's dagger within days of the accident." He studied Rodrigo through narrowed eyes. "The other alternative would have been a vendetta against the Alessandros, and you know what I once went through to end the old feud between the Alessandros and Caressa's family."

Rodrigo nodded. "I would never want to be the cause of such a thing. If there are any accusations still being hurled, let the Corsinis deal with Valenti the man, not the stripling."

Dante wanted to embrace him in the worst way. To welcome him, in spite of the years and misunderstanding. But he wasn't sure if any physical display would be welcome now, and he didn't want this young man, whom he loved as much as Niccolò, to feel obliged to reciprocate purely out of respect for Dante's title and station. Instead, he held his joy within and maintained a composure worthy of a prince.

He walked to a portrait of his father on the wall, the late Rodrigo de' Alessandro, and studied it thoughtfully. "Did I ever tell you my father's name was Rodrigo, as well?"

"No."

"'Tis a noble name—a name of stature." He swung back to Rodrigo. "It suits you well as a man.

"As for the Corsinis, the father is dead, and most of the family perished of the plague a few years back. Mario's mother, Gabriella, returned to her family in Rome after she lost her remaining children." He shook his head, his look turning somber. "An unfortunate end to them but I sometimes wonder if you would have ever been able to return had the immediate family survived."

"I had witnesses, *principe,* including you. I am innocent of murder."

Dante nodded. "And so you are, we know that. But some men are unreasonable when faced with the loss of a son, no matter the nature of the child. To tell you the truth, I had second thoughts about the betrothal within a year of having signed the contract, for Salvatore di Corsini was a tyrant . . .

and fathered half the bastards in Tuscany. Caressa had reservations about the union from the first, and she was right."

"How is she?" Rodrigo asked. "And Niccolò and Giulietta?"

"Well. They are all well, although my Gietta is extremely unhappy with me for not having found her a husband."

Rodrigo looked across the room at the unshuttered window, seemingly unable to meet Dante's gaze. "'Tis nothing short of miraculous that a woman like her is yet unwed."

Dante frowned slightly, puzzled.

"I remember her well as a child. If she is half as lovely now, she is a prize well worth winning, even were she poor as a peasant girl."

Dante continued to watch him carefully, extremely interested in the younger man's every reaction to the mention of his daughter.

At last, Rodrigo seemed to recover enough to meet the prince's eyes.

Dante grunted in answer, a thoughtful look still on his face. Then he changed the subject. "Despite everything, Rigo, you cannot know how happy I am to see you again—safe and sound and a man grown."

*"Grazi.* And I you."

What did he really feel? Dante wondered, but decided it was wiser to let some time pass and heal the hurt.

*"Ebbene,* did Leroux and Fauchet teach you all they know? Can you best me with a sword now, *figlio mio?"* He smiled, in spite of himself.

For the first time, Rodrigo allowed his mouth to curve slightly, and Dante felt as if he were seeing Giuliano de' Medici again, only a slightly more serious version of him, and one also more classic of feature. "We will have to see, won't we?"

"Come, have a glass of Trebbiano with me, eh?" Dante clapped his hands, and a servant slipped through the door into the room. "Surely 'twill be good to taste Tuscan wine again . . . although the French make excellent wine, too." He laughed aloud with pure pleasure. "Then we can take advantage of the day and ride about Monteverdi. We have much to catch up on, *sì?* And, of course, you'll dine with us this eve . . . we have so much to celebrate!"

*Where* is *he?* Giulietta thought in a near panic.

Her mother had just left with Lisa to see that a tray was brought up to Giulietta for the noon meal, and would no doubt remain to make certain Giulietta ate a token amount. How long could she remain abed on so beautiful a day? she thought in frustration, her gaze going wistfully to the unshuttered arched window on the north wall. How long could she pretend she wasn't feeling well enough to get out of bed . . . something completely out of character for her?

Aristo's tending had soothed the pain in her foot during the wee hours of the morning, and then enabled her to fall asleep. But when she'd awakened this morning, the foot had swelled again, making it impossible to don even her loosest slippers. Her sharp-eyed father—or nosy Nicco—would surely notice her limp . . . to say nothing of Caressa, who was always concerned about the slightest indisposition of either of her children.

Giulietta leaned back against the pillows Caressa had plumped and propped behind her. *Dio!* but she hadn't even the slightest fever from her injury to support her claim of illness, so well had *he* cleansed it in the stream.

As she watched chubby-cheeked clouds cavorting across the patch of blue sky visible through the confines of the window, her thoughts returned to *him.* Who was he? she wondered for the hundredth time since the night before, and felt her resentment toward him and the liberties he'd taken increase as the

morning wore on. Gone was the darkness, the spell of the
moon, the sounds of the forest that were magically transformed
into something almost mystical by the shadowed serenity of
the night.

And gone the ineffable yearning that would have driven her
to the nearest tower had Aristo not appeared.

In the bright light of day, Giulietta was confronted by a
smarting conscience—and the knowledge that she'd thrown
away what might have been her best chance to seek a haven
at Santa Lucia. All for the brief pleasure of lying in a man's
arms and doing things reserved for husband and wife.

She felt fire creep into her cheeks . . . and a flutter of desire
deep within her at the memory.

*Lust!* she amended angrily. *And for a stranger who could
have been a thief or—worse!—a murderer.* As it was, she
thought darkly, he was a seducer of unsuspecting women.

*What did you expect from a Zingaro? He's undoubtedly very
much like his fellow wanderer, Rodrigo da Valenti, who killed
the man you were to marry and then conveniently disappeared.*

Her thoughts were unfair and unkind, and she knew it. But
in those moments Giulietta was grasping at anything that
would shift the blame for not only her own behavior the night
before, but also for her untenable position as an unwed sev-
enteen-year-old. Indeed, if Mario di Corsini hadn't lost his life,
she would have been married with children already, like her
cousin Lucia, Bernardo's sister, and most normal young
women of her age and station.

So she sat and directed her guilt and anger and frustration
at Rodrigo the Gypsy boy. And the lute player who'd brazenly
toyed with her virtue. . . .


Caressa returned with Lisa right behind her, the young girl
bearing a tray of enticing edibles. She placed it across Giulietta's

knees and moved away. Caressa seated herself on the edge of
the great baldachin, or canopied, bed.

Afraid to meet her mother's concerned gaze, Giulietta pretended great interest in the food before her, then remembered
that a sick person usually had little appetite.

Caressa's palm on her forehead startled her, and her eyes
met her mother's. "You have no fever that I can tell, *nina,* yet
your cheeks are flushed."

A muffled cough came from the tall, ornately carved wardrobe where Lisa appeared to be searching among Giulietta's
gowns.

Hoping that with Caressa in the same room the young servant wasn't looking for the soiled gown she'd hidden the night
before, Giulietta quickly said, "I have an unusual taste for
sweets, Mamma," and reached for a small bowl of sugared
almonds.

Caressa smiled, her clear gray eyes lighting. "What is unusual, Gietta, isn't the taste for sweets. Rather 'tis *any* type of
appetite for one who isn't feeling well enough to rise from
bed."

Giulietta popped an almond into her mouth, then belatedly
offered one to her mother.

Caressa declined. "I have some news for you that might
cheer you," she said, and immediately caught Giulietta's interest. "Your father is near a decision concerning a husband for
you."

Giulietta's hand paused in midair as she reached for another
sweetened almond. Aristo's words came back to her: *His Excellence paid a visit to Antonio Sarzano this night . . .* Yet she
didn't dare question her mother and reveal what she'd whee-
dled from Aristo. And then, too, why would she have been
talking to Aristo so late last night? When everyone else was
asleep?

"I didn't realize he was actually searching," she said, sarcasm weighting her words. She instantly regretted them, for she knew her mother was her staunchest ally in all things.

*"Perdonami,"* she said with a sigh as she lowered her lashes, her mind suddenly racing behind her carefully neutral expression. Leon Sarzano was the only unwed Sarzano son. He was fair-haired, tall, and handsome, like Mario di Corsini had been . . . and her father whom she adored (although no man could ever compare to him in her eyes). The Sarzano family was wealthy and Giulietta often wondered why her father hadn't arranged for a match with Leon. He was their firstborn, and a widower for over a year now. His first wife had died in childbirth, leaving him with a son. He was only about seven and twenty years old—still young enough to appeal to a young woman. Although it was rumored that he continued to pine for the wife he had come to love . . . currently a most unfashionable emotion in matrimony.

"Gietta? Are you listening?"

Giulietta retrieved her thoughts from Leon Sarzano and focused them on her mother, hoping Caressa would think her distracted because of her illness, and not because she was building a plausible scenario in her mind concerning Leon Sarzano.

*"Sì, Mamina,* but who is it?" Her eyes took on a glow that was anything but sickly.

A slight frown creased Caressa's alabaster brow. "I cannot tell you until the arrangements are made final, *nina."*

Giulietta couldn't help but purse her lips with disappointment, then remembered she was supposed to be ill. Yet, she thought, who could it be but Leon Sarzano?

"Does the news please you, Gietta?"

Giulietta looked at her mother, her mouth tightening briefly. "How could it not? My present situation is humiliating at my age."

Caressa placed one hand over her daughter's. "Your father

loves you dearly, child. He couldn't bring himself to separate you from the family by sending you to a convent, nor could he bring himself to wed you to just anyone, politics or no. Surely you can appreciate that?" Her dark, winged brows raised. "Or is that why you are abed? Because you are angry with Dante?"

Giulietta felt a telltale heat stain her face as guilt kicked up its heels once again. Her silence added to her mutely proclaimed guilt.

Caressa sighed and looked at the very window Giulietta had been contemplating only moments before, then down at the gimmal ring on her left hand that Dante had placed there nearly twenty years ago. "I didn't wed Silvio Ruggerio until I was your age."

Giulietta instantly regretted her words at the pain in her mother's quiet voice. As much as Caressa loved her husband, she obviously still felt the dull ache of an old wound at the memory of her murdered husband and lost child.

"Forgive me, Mamma, for being so thoughtless," Giulietta said with genuine contrition. She laced her fingers through Caressa's, still resting across her hand, and squeezed gently. "'Tis just that my situation is different, is it not? I'm the daughter of the Prince of Monteverdi. 'Tis even more unseemly for me to be yet a maiden, I believe."

Their eyes met. "And so it may be, at least in your mind, for you are proud as a lioness, my Giulietta. A Leo like your sire. But you must learn humility, as Dante had to do, outwardly at least."

"But he had a valid reason! He played a role, and thus helped guard the interests of his principality." She tossed her head in an unconscious gesture of defiance. "I play no part; have no ulterior goal."

Caressa smiled as Giulietta pouted prettily. "And so you don't. But your father will do well by you, don't ever doubt it. Within the year, you will be wed, *nina,* and God willing, you will find the contentment you seek." She released Giulietta's hand and stood. "'Tis all I can say for now."

Giulietta felt hope fill her. Her eyes lit with enthusiasm as she momentarily forgot that she wasn't supposed to be feeling well.

"And now—" Caressa leaned over and pressed her lips to her daughter's forehead—"I have somethings to see to. We are to have company for dinner this eve, and I would hope you feel well enough to join us."

She arched her brows questioningly, thus hinting she had serious doubts about Giulietta's indisposition.

"Eat what you can," she added before she swung away. "And take a nap. Mayhap you'll awake feeling well enough to join us later, *si?*" She moved toward the door, throwing a curious glance at Lisa, who was still rummaging in the wardrobe.

When she'd closed the door behind her, Giulietta hissed, *"Lisa!* What are you *doing?"*

The girl pulled her head from the wardrobe, her face flushed, her dark hair escaping its knot at the back of her head. She looked at her mistress. "I was going to clean the gown you wore last night, but then I remembered 'twas a secret. Your lady mother was here and I couldn't—"

"Never mind," Giulietta cut her off, trying to rein in her impatience. Lisa wasn't the brightest girl at Monteverdi; but her mother, also one of their servants, was devoted to the family, and Lisa (who'd been born out of wedlock) was single-mindedly faithful as well. She served Giulietta with slavelike devotion, and Caressa would never have considered giving her a more menial position.

Lisa stood and held up the bedraggled dress in triumph. "And the shoes at the bottom of the wardrobe are neatly arranged now, Mona Giulietta," she announced as if she'd accomplished the most difficult task at Monteverdi.

Giulietta eyed the sodden hem and dirt splotches on the skirt and bodice. "Can it be saved?" she asked with a dubious look as Lisa turned it around for her to see the back.

"*Sì.* I think so. At least let me try."

"*Ebbene,* do it. But don't tell anyone . . . and do it right here instead of the laundry. Fetch hot water and we will see, but can you remember to seek out Aristo first?"

"For your foot?"

"Yes, but don't tell anyone, do you hear?"

Lisa bobbed her head with vigor, then put the dress aside and quit the room. When Giulietta was alone, she tackled the food before her with a vengeance.

She wondered what had happened to the dwarf . . . and who was to dine with them that evening.

By the time Aristo returned to Castello Monteverdi, Giulietta was in high dudgeon. Her temper simmered, for as evening grew nigh, her foot was little improved and she hadn't a clue as to Aristo's whereabouts. She certainly couldn't just ask Caressa, for her mother would want to know why she needed the dwarf. And it was very difficult for Giulietta to lie to her mother. Her father, as well, but more so Caressa. And she had already told Caressa one lie.

At last, as the afternoon grew late, she hobbled across the chamber to her wardrobe, and stood staring at her assortment of gowns with a deep frown pulling her nutmeg-hued brows together. Even if she had to hop down the corridors to the dining hall, she would dress in her best and make an appearance at dinner. Or Aristo could carry her, she thought darkly, for failing to come to her aid.

Leon Sarzano was reputed to be a handsome man, even if

a little melancholy since his young wife's death upon the birth of their son. This was probably her best—and mayhap her last—chance to end her hated and humiliating unwed status. Why, Sarzano's late wife hadn't even been as old as Giulietta when she'd delivered her babe!

"How is your foot," Lisa said as she entered the room.

Giulietta shook her head and stuck out her swollen foot from beneath her shift. "I could *die* from the wound for all Aristo cares!" she said darkly. "Not only does it hurt to put weight on it, but I cannot even wear a shoe. What good to have all the gowns in Italy if I cannot dress properly and walk to the hall?"

"Madonna Giulietta?" Aristo asked from the doorway, startling both young women.

"Where have you *been?*" Giulietta exclaimed in a low, distraught voice. "Look at my foot! And Leon Sarzano will be here for dinner . . . I think Papa is arranging for our betrothal and I'm in a fine fix!"

The dwarf ambled into the room, and Giulietta noticed there were bits of leaves and other specks of debris in his dark hair, stuck to his robe. He seemed even more hunched over than usual as he held up a small packet and said, "Forgive me, Mona Giulietta. I had to search the woods for a particular ingredient for this powder, and then prepare it, of course."

"All this time you were searching the forest?" she asked in disbelief.

"*Sì,*" he answered quietly. "As far as the Gypsy camp even."

Gypsy camp? she thought.

A host of feelings collided within her as she thought of the lute player, and what they had shared last night. A languid warmth coiled through her belly, and she felt her face grow warm. Would she ever wonder about him when she was wed? Would she wonder what having him for a husband would be like?

You probably won't ever even see him again, her realistic side bluntly told her whimsical side.

"Would you bring me a bowl of warm water, Mona Lisa?" As she never failed to do, Lisa blushed at the formality of the way he addressed her, and hurried to do his bidding.

When she was out of earshot, he said, "I'm sorry, *madonna,* but I cannot move quickly . . . and the bending and searching took its toll. I dared not ask for assistance, either, without furthering the lie."

Giulietta instantly forgave him. "I thank you maestro. And I'm sorry you are hurting." She bit her lower lip, feeling responsible for his aches and pains. He resembled, in his middle age, a dark spider curled up in a permanent attitude of defense.

But she couldn't ignore the question uppermost in her mind now. "Will I be able to attend dinner this eve?"

He nodded, placed the packet beside her and bent to examine her foot. "This will ease the swelling and numb the pain. 'Tis stronger than the other I used."

"I slept like a babe after you tended me," she reassured him, "but this morn it swelled once more." Her brows drew together again. "Oh, how will I wear a shoe, Aristo?" Her distress was genuine—she didn't have to feign it as with Paolo the night before.

"We can always slit the leather," he said, turning to receive the bowl of water Lisa brought just then. "'Twill be hidden beneath your gown, *sì?*"

Her expression brightened, her topaz eyes sparkling with hope. "Ah, yes! You are so clever! I never even thought of it."

Already the evening loomed brighter for her, and she wondered just when the betrothal ceremony for her and Leon Sarzano would take place. . . .

* * *

"Do you think 'twas wise, Dante? To invite Rodrigo da Valenti the same night as Leon Sarzano?"

Caressa de' Alessandro frowned, for she wasn't certain her husband—who usually exercised great judgment—was doing so now.

Dante winked at her and gathered her to him. He was barechested, clad only in his trunk hose. "Let me wipe that frown from your lovely brow, *dolce* . . ." He lowered his mouth to join it with hers.

As always, when her husband kissed her in such a way, Caressa tended to forget everything else. Still . . . even after nineteen years of marriage.

When he finally released her, he looked into her eyes. "Trust me, *cara*. You always have . . . why doubt me now?"

She watched him don a silk shirt, the exact color of his blue-green eyes. It slipped down his torso with a sigh. "Because your daughter is involved here—the apple of your eye. And a decision made in haste is not always the best."

"True," he admitted. "Yet I would see her reaction to both men."

"But why, Dante?" she said with a shadow of her former frown. "You've already decided . . . or have you changed your mind?"

"Sandro will be here, as well. And Vittorio and Gianna. 'Tis only a typical family affair, with the added presence of a few friends, as far as I am concerned."

Caressa's eyes narrowed at him. "And I am the Pope!"

Dante laughed aloud. "You'll never know how glad I am you're not. His Holiness can't compare to you in any way."

"Leon Sarzano is not a family friend. And Rodrigo da Valenti has never graced the board at Castello Monteverdi. It could be a very uncomfortable evening." With a sigh, she seated herself to allow Marina, her maidservant, to coif her glossy black hair.

"I have my reservations about this whole affair," she mused aloud.

Dante stood before her, his knuckled fists on his hips. His short yellow doublet was in place, the turquoise silk of his shirt visible through the slashes in his doublet sleeves, and at his neck. His long legs were encased in parti-colored trunk-hose—one leg yellow, the other aquamarine. His short, golden hair was neatly in place, catching the lamplight when he moved a certain way.

It never ceased to amaze Caressa how well he carried off any fashion, no matter how absurd it might have looked on another. Sometimes, she thought, he did it for the sheer pleasure of watching others' reactions.

His eyes glowed as he looked down at her. With love and admiration—something she still treasured. Yet tonight, they were lit with the anticipation of a challenge.

"I invited Sarzano before I knew Rodrigo was back. 'Twould have been rude to cancel. And as for Rodrigo . . . well, the sooner the rest of the family meets him, the better. He's no *Zingaro* child anymore, Caressa. Wait until you see him!" He grinned and rubbed his hands together. "By God, he does his father proud! He's ambitious and intelligent—and more mature than Giuliano was at his age." His smile faded, obviously at the thought of his friend's violent death at the age of five and twenty.

Marina signaled her work was done with a brief, assessing look at her mistress's head. She handed Caressa a small flask of her favorite perfume, jasmine, and wordlessly withdrew.

Caressa applied the cologne, restoppered the flask and replaced it on the table that held her paints and powders, other fragrances, and brush and comb. She moved toward him and linked her arm through his, the soft rose-colored silk of her gown whispering with the movement. "I never doubted your judgment as far as a husband for Giulietta," she told him, " 'tis just that . . . well, I'm apprehensive about the mix of guests. And the shock of Rodrigo's unexpected presence after all this time."

They paused before the door, and Dante smiled down into her silvery eyes. "Have faith, *amore mio*. You were never one to back away from a challenge . . . and neither am I. We'll deal with any problems as they arise."

# Five

"The peach, *madonna*," Lisa said. "It brings out the gold in your eyes—the creaminess of your skin." She sighed with obvious approval as Giulietta nodded and reached for the peach-hued gown Lisa was holding.

"And how is your foot now?" Lisa asked.

Giulietta lay the gown carefully across the bed and looked down at her bare foot. She held it out for Lisa's inspection as the latter bent for a better look.

"The swelling has gone down," Giulietta said, "and I feel only a twinge when I walk on it. *That* I can manage!" She threw Lisa a conspiratorial look. "If we must, we can cut the leather of my right shoe, as Aristo said, but it may not even be necessary."

Lisa nodded and helped Giulietta slide the satin underskirt over her head, then returned to the wardrobe for the sleeveless overgown. It was of apricot silk, with delicate lacings down either side, revealing the paler garment beneath; it was also cut into a deep vee at the neck and down the bodice, but the undergown formed a straight, demure line across her breasts. Both garments tapered at the waist, with the added advantage of more laces at the back of the overgown, before flaring outward, hinting at the perfection of the feminine form beneath. The advantage of such a gown was that on a less shapely woman, the tapering would have been less, the laces arranged loosely, thus concealing any figure flaws.

"We'll save the shoes for last," Giulietta said as Lisa began brushing her hair. "And I want to wear it down," she added, studying her image in the polished metal mirror before her. "We can hold back the sides with my pearl combs, *sì?*"

Her tone was mildly cajoling, for she knew very well that only a more daring maiden would wear her hair in so flamboyant a style. Yet Giulietta was proud of her gently curling, fire gold hair and wanted to show it off to Leon Sarzano. Maybe he wouldn't notice her limp if he was busy admiring her hair.

Lisa did as she was bid, and then, as the finishing touch, wove several strands of seed pearl-studded apricot ribbons through her mistress's coppery tresses, placed seed pearl cluster earrings on her prettily shaped ears, and a single strand of the same pearls about her throat.

"Ahhhh!" Lisa exclaimed, and clapped her hands. *"Che bella!"*

Giulietta smiled at her compliment, then picked up a soft, sable brush and feathered a sprinkling of rouge over each cheek. She also touched a bit of lip color to her mouth, then stood. She gingerly tested her foot before moving with little discomfort toward the chest at the foot of the bed, where she kept the extra slippers that wouldn't fit in the wardrobe.

Shoes in hand, she sat on the bed and put on the left first. Then the right. The latter was slightly more snug, but not uncomfortably so. Lisa handed her a feathered fan, and Giulietta stood. She walked slowly toward the door, hoping she wouldn't have to slit one of her prettiest leather shoes, yet prepared to do exactly that if she had to.

Lisa opened the door. " 'Tis hardly noticeable," she said with a bright look.

Giulietta nodded. "If I walk slowly, and keep more of my weight on my left foot, I think 'twill work."

"Gietta!" exclaimed Niccolò from the antechamber doorway. "You look beautiful!"

Giulietta greeted her brother with a warm smile. *"Grazi,* Nicco. And you, too."

She waited for his reaction, but he was getting too old to fall for her deliberate but good-natured teasing. "I agree, sorella mia. In their own way, men can look as beautiful as women."

He moved forward, reminding Giulietta—as he often did now that he was a man grown—of her uncle Vittorio, her father's half brother. His gray eyes were alight with admiration . . . and a barely hidden mischief.

"Are you feeling better this eve?" he asked, his smile fading. "Mother said you were abed most of the day." He slanted a look down at her. "Or were you displaying your pique with Father?"

"I'm better now," she said absently, her thoughts already concentrated on Leon Sarzano.

Suddenly, as they turned a corner, the sounds of a lute came to them from the dining room. The music reminded her poignantly of another lute player, and her steps faltered.

"Father must be playing his lute already," she said.

Nicco shook his head. "Father doesn't play that well, *nina."* His look turned thoughtful. "So who could it be? I don't recall any among our guests who are so accomplished . . . unless 'tis Leon Sarzano."

But as the haunting, mellifluous notes floated down the passageway, they seemed to reach out and coil about Giulietta's heart. Just as the sweet strains of another lute had recently done. . . .

It was considered an intimate gathering, and therefore held in the dining room instead of the great hall. The dining room also had the advantage of being directly above the kitchen.

Giulietta and Niccolò entered, both with smiles of greeting lighting their faces, for not only were they accustomed to being cordial to any guests at Castello Monteverdi, but among those milling about the room was a close friend of their father's, Sandro Botticelli, a favorite of everyone. Uncle Vittorio and Aunt Gianna, who also lived at Monteverdi during the summer months, were present, as well.

Caressa came forward and gave Giulietta a quick hug. "I'm so glad you're feeling better, *nina.*" She held her at arm's length and looked her over from head to toe. "You look lovely," she added with an indulgent smile.

"And so do you, *Mamina.*" Giulietta reciprocated, marveling as always at her mother's dark-haired beauty and utter serenity. Caressa de' Alessandro was the calmest person Giulietta knew, and she often wished she'd inherited more of her mother's disposition.

Dante came to meet them with Leon Sarzano at his side. Giulietta felt her heart skitter unnaturally as she looked at the man her father had chosen for her. However, beside the scintillating presence and awesome form of the Prince of Monteverdi, Sarzano looked absolutely lackluster.

*He's barely out of mourning, what did you expect?*

Giulietta managed to keep her smile in place as Dante kissed her forehead and introduced her to Leon. The latter bent his wheat-colored head over her hand, then straightened to meet her curious gaze with his hazel eyes.

"I am enchanted to meet you, Mona Giulietta," he said solemnly, and Giulietta felt as if a cloud were suddenly passing over her hopes and dreams.

It must have shown in her expression somehow, for as if he realized how sober he appeared upon meeting the Prince of Monteverdi's daughter—and possibly his bride-to-be—he smiled. It was a nice smile, Giulietta decided, and it lit his otherwise melancholy eyes. For some reason, however, the notes from the lute were distracting her . . . yes, that was it. How could she ever concentrate on Leon Sarzano when her eyes wanted to seek out the source of those incredibly seductive notes?

"How is your son, Leon?" Dante asked, breaking into her thoughts as he obviously attempted to fill in the brief silence that ensued.

Sarzano's entire face brightened. "Fine, *principe.* Daniello never ceases to amaze me. Why, just yesterday . . ."

Giulietta allowed her attention to wander briefly around the room while Leon expounded upon the childish exploits of his year-old son. Nicco was talking animatedly to Sandro Botticelli, the brilliant artist. The latter was gesturing toward the other side of the room, where a tall, dark-haired man stood near the only window, staring out at the deepening dusk while he strummed a lute, unwittingly giving Giulietta his unnervingly familiar profile.

She went absolutely still.

". . . like to introduce you to our other new guest," Dante was saying to her, "for it appears that Nicco is about to make his own introduction, and the others here have already been presented." He took her by the arm. "You will excuse us for a moment?" he asked Sarzano in his naturally disarming manner.

Leon nodded, and Caressa moved closer to him, renewing the discussion of his little son.

Dante led Giulietta forward, her hand on his arm, his hand over hers. She forgot her sore foot. She forgot protocol and allowed shock to register on her features. She forgot everyone else in the room except the man who ceased his lute playing to speak to Nicco and Sandro.

She moved toward him on her father's arm, a thousand thoughts flashing through her mind, all of them disjointed: *He* was the lute player . . . here in her own home. Her surreptitious lover from the night before. The man who'd intercepted

her, lured her from her course to the convent and then proceeded to teach her things that most assuredly had driven others to Santa Lucia to atone for their carnal sins before her.

Suddenly, like magnet to metal, his gaze shifted beyond
Sandro and Nicco, to Giulietta. . . .

Giulietta was vaguely aware of Sandro and her brother parting for her and Dante as the prince said, "Rodrigo, my daughter Giulietta Maria . . ."

"Mona Giulietta," the lute player murmured, his startlingly
blue eyes delving into hers. Then, with the full-bellied lute
tucked beneath his left arm, Rodrigo took her automatically
extended hand in his other and brought it to his lips. His lashes
lowered briefly, and Giulietta could only think how absurdly
long and thick they were . . . until his mouth touched the delicate flesh of the back of her hand.

His lips singed her skin and caused her to flinch ever so
slightly. . . . Heat shot up her arm and shoulder, then crawled
into her cheeks in unwilling acknowledgement of the intimacies they'd shared the night before.

But the worst was yet to come.

"And, Giulietta, allow me to formally introduce Signor Rodrigo da Valenti."

Rodrigo da Valenti straightened, her hand still in his, his
gaze meeting hers again as the name registered in Giulietta's
beleaguered brain. Valenti? she thought, stunned. The *Zingaro*
youth who'd killed Mario di Corsini? The youth who'd simply
vanished into thin air?

"Valenti?" she heard Nicco echo from somewhere nearby.

*Of course,* sneered a voice. *Didn't he all but admit he was
one of* them?

Her entire body stiffened in reaction, and she pulled her

hand away as if he'd bitten it. *"Buona sera,"* she managed through stiff lips.

She felt her father's eyes on her, and the blue of Valenti's gaze darkened with some emotion she didn't care to define. His chiseled features tightened almost imperceptibly, and Giulietta knew instinctively he'd guessed the bent of her thoughts—and remembered that tragic day as vividly as she did.

". . . should like to paint you, signore," Sandro Botticelli— ever on the lookout for subjects for his paintings—was saying to Valenti. "You remind me so much of Il Superbo. And yet . . ." He trailed off, but Giulietta caught his meaning. And was appalled.

Il Superbo. The murdered Giuliano de' Medici. Her father's dear friend. Surely, Giulietta thought with disdain, a black-a-vised Gypsy couldn't compare in any way with a man like Giuliano de' Medici.

Some distant part of her mind registered how very unkind and unfair to judge a man—any man—without knowing him. She remorselessly allowed its echoes to sink into the quagmire of her roiling emotions.

". . . you are the antithesis of Dante," Sandro concluded. "Similarly beautiful of feature, but dark as he is fair."

Giulietta watched color climb Rodrigo da Valenti's bronzed face. He dismissed the compliment with a shrug of his well-set shoulders and smiled at the artist. *"Grazi,* Maestro Botticelli. Coming from someone of your renown, 'tis truly a compliment."

"I don't know if I like the idea of someone equaling my looks in Sandro's eyes," Dante said lightly. "But if you think him striking of feature, wait until you see him handle a sword. *Dio mio,* and ride a charger! He's a *condottiere* now, newly returned from training in France."

Giulietta tore her eyes from Rodrigo da Valenti's countenance and looked at her father. Why, he was actually *proud* of this . . . this grown-up waif!

*But your sin is even greater,* reminded a voice. *You allowed this man you supposedly detest—Mario di Corsini's killer— every liberty with you.*

"Then I'll have to challenge you," Nicco said, obviously taking his father's cue. "Mayhap you've learned some tricks from the French that my father didn't teach me, eh?"

*The traitor!* Giulietta thought fiercely, her gaze going back and forth from Dante to Niccolò . . . *anywhere* but to Rodrigo da Valenti.

"Can you play something else for us, Rodrigo?" Caressa asked from behind Giulietta.

But for once the calm voice and soothing presence of Caressa de' Alessandro had no effect on her high-spirited daughter; Giulietta felt as if one more of her family had betrayed her. The shock of having the man responsible for Mario's death within their midst was bad enough—but she could have dealt with that. Her father had emphasized to both Nicco and herself that the incident was entirely accidental. He, himself, had witnessed Mario's untimely death, and anyone present when the tragedy had occurred who thought differently was either blind or a monumental fool. Their cousin Bernardo had stood firmly behind his uncle in his declaration.

But to discover that the same man—guilty or not—had *duped* her . . . Had taken wicked advantage of her when she was alone in the forest and injured . . . It was reprehensible. Totally, she thought nastily, in character with the actions of the hot-headed Gypsy youth of six years ago.

She found herself watching Rodrigo gift his hostess with a brilliant smile, the flash of his even, white teeth a vivid contrast to his swarthy skin. "Of course, *principessa*. Have you something in mind?"

Caressa considered a moment, and Giulietta tore her gaze

away and backed up to give her mother her place. "Something French, perhaps?" Caressa said.

Giulietta didn't hear the answer as she turned away abruptly, refusing to give *him* an audience. Her uncle Vittorio and aunt Gianna, who had been speaking to Leon Sarzano, moved toward the others standing around Valenti. Giulietta, however, went straight for Leon and put a hand on his arm.

Her seeming urgency obviously surprised him, for his eyes met hers questioningly. "I would know more about your . . . about little Daniello, and the rest of your family, *sì?* I've not much interest in listening to another lute player," she lied, for she loved music and admired a skilled musician, "when Papa plays at all hours of the day!"

*Albeit not nearly so well,* a pesky imp pointed out.

"But won't we be considered rude?" he said uncertainly, obviously flattered at Giulietta's sudden attentions.

She tossed her head in an unconscious gesture of defiance . . . and quite accidentally met Dante's stern gaze. The profound displeasure in that beloved and normally good-natured countenance brought her up short.

Even Giulietta knew when she'd gone too far.

*"Ebbene,"* she said with a distinct sigh of resignation, "we can stand behind the others." But she whispered incessantly into Leon's ear while they stood as far back as Giulietta dared, until it was apparent to anyone who cared to notice that she was much more interested in Leon Sarzano than Rodrigo da Valenti and his lute.

She absolutely refused to succumb to the magic of his music. Enough damage had already been done, she acknowledged with the distressingly substantial part of her mind that couldn't focus on Leon. And his voice. . . .

No. It was far safer to direct her attention toward Leon Sarzano—and certainly less humiliating to her pride. Yet even Leon seemed enthralled by Valenti's performance, which made it more and more difficult for Giulietta to keep his full attention.

When the song ended at last, it was rewarded with enthusiastic applause. Rodrigo da Valenti bowed briefly, then allowed Nicco to engage him in animated conversation. If Giulietta hadn't been so caught up in her own emotional turmoil, she would have found it amusing. Her brother was a devoted student of fencing, and was considered a superb swordsman. The last notes hadn't even died away—the applause still ringing in the air—when Nicco attached himself like a leech to Valenti.

"Don't you find it unusual that a bloodthirsty *condottiere* would have any interest in playing the lute?" Giulietta asked Leon as the group around Valenti began to break up and move toward the table at Caressa's direction.

"If it weren't for those 'bloodthirsty *condottieri*,' daughter, many of us would not be safe in our homes," answered the prince from beside them. "Mayhap you need to know about the slaughter at the river Taro by the French army."

They both looked over at Dante, who was frowning at Giulietta.

To her surprise, Leon stepped in with unforseen grace and diffused the moment. "How true, *principe*. And a professional soldier can have artistic pursuits outside of his livelihood. Signor Valenti plays well, and has a voice to match his singing lute strings."

Giulietta glanced up at Sarzano and noticed that his chin wasn't quite as weak as she'd first thought; his hazel eyes were alight with interest now. But if she had hastily and mistakenly judged him as introverted and boring, so much the better that perhaps she had been wrong. She would sooner flee to Santa Lucia than wed a weak man.

It was with relief that she found herself seated in the high-backed chair beside Leon Sarzano. Her relief was quickly replaced by dismay however, as, at her mother's direction, Rodrigo da Valenti took the seat on her other side. She dimly felt Caressa's hand touch her shoulder as her mother moved to take her place at the left end of the board. Nicco sat to Valenti's left, and Sandro Botticelli, Gianna and Vittorio de' Alessandro sat across the table.

It was going to be an endless and uncomfortable meal, she thought as her silk-clad arm briefly brushed against Valenti's. Tingles rushed up her arm from the contact, and setting her teeth, Giulietta shifted to the right side of her chair as unobtrusively as possible.

Rodrigo da Valenti may have gulled her once, but it wouldn't happen again. She reached for her wineglass. . . .


The animosity that emanated from Giulietta de' Alessandro would have made a lesser man quail. Rodrigo saw the anger in Dante's eyes as well, and went out of his way to engage Giulietta in light conversation. Which only made things worse.

Especially when he asked, sotto voce, "How is your foot?"

He physically felt her stiffen, felt the outrage suffuse her, in spite of the fact that he was genuinely concerned and meant no harm. Yet how would she know? he thought with rue. She really didn't know him . . . didn't know how he felt about anything.

When her tawny eyes met his, he *felt* her offense like a physical thing as she bit out in a low, choked voice, "Better, *grazi*." Her lips curved upward, but those leonine eyes . . . oh, yes, they told him what she really wanted to say to him. They held no hint of the good humor her smile was obviously meant to convey.

His gaze fell to the snowy tablecloth, for surely she had every right to be angry with him—at the liberties he'd taken with her. Yet he'd left her virginity intact . . . and she had no reason to fear he would ever give their meeting away. He would have cut out his heart first; but, then, she had no way of knowing that either.

And he certainly wasn't about to apologize for the fleeting taste of heaven she'd afforded him.

Fortunately—or unfortunately—Niccolò de' Alessandro plied him with a fusillade of questions about France and the French methods of swordplay. Caressa was graciously attentive, as well, as if to make up for her daughter's lack. And Dante's half brother, Vittorio, who sat across from Rodrigo, was curious about Charles of France and his army . . . especially since that very army had marched through Italy only three years past when the French king had decided to reassert the Angevin claim to the Kingdom of Naples. Had Rodrigo been in the ranks when they'd entered Florence?

Rodrigo noted Giulietta's sudden attention as her uncle awaited his answer. "No, my lord," he replied, glad of one less supposed 'sin' to fuel Giulietta de' Alessandro's animosity. "I was not."

" 'Twas the night when Piero de' Medici and his family were forced to flee Florence," Leon informed Rodrigo around Giulietta. "Did you hear of that in France?"

"*Sì*. 'Twas a sad day for the Republic."

The Medici fall from grace was a touchy subject at Monteverdi, for Dante had been very close to the Medici family— even closer to the late Lorenzo than his brother Giuliano. Lorenzo's son Piero had been as poor a ruler as Lorenzo had been good.

"And Florence hasn't been the same," Dante declared sourly. "That hook-nosed monk fancies himself above even the Pope. Now let him stew in his own heretical juices!"

"*Sì!*" Nicco added, obviously for Rodrigo's benefit. "Savonarola was excommunicated by His Holiness in June," he told Rodrigo. "He's been quiet ever since."

Several glanced at Botticelli, who was dressed in dark, flowing *lucco* instead of his usual gay splash of colors. Dante had told Rodrigo that Sandro had been "reformed" by Girolamo Savonarola—had even allowed some of his more "licentious" paintings to be burned atop a pyre of priceless art objects and other items considered "vanities" and the "devil's invitations to vice."

*"Firenzi* needed reform," the normally mild-natured Sandro insisted, "in the wake of its excesses!"

Dante drained his wine goblet and looked at the artist. "I do not like to debate before dinner is finished," he said affably enough before his tone hardened, "but I do not consider illuminated books and chalices, candlesticks and crucifixes in convents and monasteries sinful."

"He's gone so far as to urge death to all those who advocate the restoration of the Medici," Vittorio said with a twist of his lips. "Since when does a true man of God campaign for death?"

Rodrigo answered, "When he is afraid . . . or a blind fanatic." His gaze briefly touched Botticelli.

The latter held up his hand. "You are entitled to your own opinion, *signore,*" he said to Rodrigo. "And you have been gone for a number of years. Much has happened of late."

"And I believe things will get worse before they get better," Leon added. "Past experience has shown us the Dominican won't just go away. Even though His Holiness attempted to bring the independent Tuscan Dominicans under Roman control so that he could then send Savonarola far away from Florence, the friar refused to acknowledge Pope Alexander's jurisdiction in the matter."

Giulietta looked at Leon Sarzano through new eyes in the wake of his words. He was quickly revealing more interesting aspects of his nature while engaged in conversation at her father's table. Even though it was typical of men to enjoy talk of war above all else—and therefore bring even the most reticent to animation—Giulietta was heartened a bit by this facet of the man her father had chosen for her.

Mayhap she could concentrate on Sarzano to the exclusion of the man sitting to her left and actually begin to enjoy herself somewhat in spite of the awkward situation. . . .

"Tell us about the French army," Nicco said eagerly, as the first dishes were served. "I remember them marching through Florence with Charles at the head."

"A man easily underestimated if one acts on first appearances alone," Rodrigo said. He accepted a dish of fancily dressed quail in aspic from Giulietta, and deliberately met her eyes. Her lashes lowered in seeming demureness, but he'd caught the flash of ire within their claret depths. Her perfume—jasmine—teased his nostrils, and he caught the fine curve of her cheek as she turned her head away. "He's a small man," he added, "with a twitching affliction in his head and hands. His very gait is unappealing to many—he walks with a crouch and a limp."

"Aristo's gait is ungainly, yet he is a beautiful man," Giulietta interrupted without warning, her eyes clashing with Rodrigo's.

He nodded in agreement, secretly exulting in what she'd just revealed about her natural compassion and tolerance . . . except, he mused wryly, when it concerned *him*. "Exactly. I wouldn't say the French king is beautiful inside"— one corner of his mouth lifted, and a dark, up-slashed eyebrow raised, reminding Giulietta of a demon with those burning blue eyes beneath—"but he is certainly capable of maintaining a first-rate army." He sobered. "Woe to the man who judges Charles VIII too hastily."

The meaning-laden message seemed somehow particularly aimed at Giulietta. She felt her face warm, in spite of her best efforts to remain unaffected by anything he said.

"One only has to remember the slaughter at the Taro in '95," Dante said in reply. "Even though they were greatly outnumbered, the French artillery and cavalry were our undoing." His eyes rested on Giulietta for a brief but intense moment before they moved on to Rodrigo and Vittorio, then back to Leon. "After a short and ferocious battle, Italian losses were enormous. A pitiful showing for all our supposed virtues and talents, wealth, past glory and experience . . . for all our purported skill as military engineers. We could not withstand the advance of the French army." He shook his head. "Thank God Florence played no part in that horrendous farce—'twas more than likely the best thing Savonarola ever did for the Republic, wittingly or nay, this fawning over Charles . . . proclaiming him as sent by God and therefore Florence's liberator. No doubt we would have lost the flower of Florentine youth had we engaged Charles then."

There gathered a brief silence. Then Giulietta spoke. "I don't see what a Frenchman has that one of our own does not! What is lacking in any soldier from our city-states that he cannot defend against a foreign army like the barbarian French?"

Her disdain was meant for the man on her left and what she considered his cowardly flight to France; not only to escape retribution, but to learn from a foreign army that couldn't possibly—in her mind at least—compare to one comprised of her own countrymen. She didn't think, however, that anyone would notice her veiled insult except her father. And, of course, Rodrigo da Valenti.

"Would you be so kind, Rigo," Dante asked, a steely tone underlying his even words, "as to apprise my daughter of exactly what you observed firsthand concerning the differences between the Italian soldier and the French?"

Rodrigo braced himself inwardly for what he must reveal. More than likely most at the table—at least the men—knew exactly what he was about to say. The women—and especially young Giulietta, he was guessing—would not know. And, he thought with irony, would not take kindly to what he had to say.

"No one doubts that the Italian soldier can fight bravely when he has to fight," he said. "But most of the time his commanders make certain he is busy plundering rather than fighting . . . driving cattle with his lance rather than shooting the enemy with his crossbow. Most of us know the typical Italian infantry troops march along to fife and drum looking more like strolling players in their parti-colored tights and smart jerkins than men of war—"

"But aren't the commanders to blame for this?" Leon interrupted.

"Indeed," Rodrigo agreed. "We must begin with them, for like the French commanders, they must teach their men to be professional through actual experience; they must train them to kill rather than posture and plunder."

Here Nicco jumped in. "And Father says they have cannon that fire iron balls instead of stone . . . larger and heavier."

Rodrigo nodded, his gaze on Giulietta's fingers tightening around the stem of her empty goblet. He reached to refill it and glanced at her pure profile, offered to him rather than a direct look. She nodded her thanks, obviously unable to even speak to him at this point.

"And their cannon are also hauled on carriages drawn by horses and not the slower oxen, Nicco," he added, turning his attention to the younger man. "Thus they reach the walls and set in position there with incredible speed." He looked over to catch Leon's eye as the latter hovered close to Giulietta in an obvious effort to hear every word Rodrigo had to say. His gaze was snagged, however, by Giulietta's narrowed eyes. "And they use this most effective weapon right in the field as well as for besieging cities," he finished, wondering if he would ever again look into those very fine eyes and see them liquid with desire. . . .

"So we've work to do," Vittorio said, his eyes moving to every man at the table before coming to rest on his brother.

Dante nodded. "And above all the Republic of Florence, for that meddling monk has persuaded many to look to him for guidance—as if he were God himself!—to the exclusion of every other sensible course."

This time, no one threw any apologetic looks at Sandro Botticelli, and the mild-mannered artist, evidently seeing he was outnumbered among those who did not support Savonarola, held his silence.

Silver dishes of red fried fish were served in a spicy sauce, followed by plates of silver galantine—boned and stuffed fish that was poached and served cold. Silver vegetable cakes and fresh almonds came around as well, before a new round of perch and another dish of fowl prepared in a tongue-tingling sauce.

The conversation slowed for a while as the diners ate. Then, as fresh fruit was served to soothe the palate before the lemon candy and light and airy marzipan dessert, Leon Sarzano asked Rodrigo: "I've been thinking . . . the name Valenti is familiar. Wasn't that the name of the lad who tangled with Mario di Corsini a few years ago?"

# Six

An awkward pause gathered about them like an impending storm, swiftly altering the atmosphere of congeniality. Suddenly the air pulsed with tension.

Several gazes cut to Rodrigo—notably Leon's as he waited for an answer to his question . . . and Giulietta's.

Before Dante could step in to defend him, Rodrigo answered Leon Sarzano in quiet tones, "It was . . . and I am." He couldn't help but meet Giulietta's eyes, for she was staring at him from only an arm's length away. As he spoke to Leon, his words were really for her. "I assure you, Leon, that I did not kill Mario di Corsini. 'Twas an accident—and there are three witnesses here at the board who can attest to that."

*Including you,* his look told Giulietta before it returned to Leon.

"If Rodrigo was guilty of anything," Dante interjected, "it was coming to what he thought was the defense of my nephew, Bernardo, who had turned his back to Mario after a bit of swordplay. Mario went after Bernardo—in play, we assume. But Rigo here, who was watching from the trees, assumed no such thing."

*Nardo!* Giulietta's soft cry of alarm came back to Rodrigo suddenly, for the fear in that sweet voice had been every bit as compelling as Corsini's rear attack upon Bernardo de' Alessandro.

"Then he should have taken his cue from us," Giulietta said with as much asperity as she thought she could get away with.

Nicco opened his mouth to speak as he leaned forward, but it was Rodrigo who answered her. "I'll always remember your cry of concern for your cousin, Mona Giulietta," he said quietly.

"*Sì,*" Nicco added. "I remember it now. Don't you, Gietta? You cried *'Nardo!'* as if he were about to be slain." His mouth curved in a superior grin. "Of course, you were so *young* then, and impetuous, *sorella* . . . and shouldn't have even been with us."

A delicate blush swept across Giulietta's cheekbones for she *shouldn't* have been with the young men; and, of course, even she had to admit to herself that it was hypocritical to accuse Rodrigo da Valenti of overreacting when she, too, had been momentarily uncertain of Mario's intention.

"My son said Corsini lost his balance and came up against a tree. It was an awkward fall and, unfortunately, cost Corsini his life," Vittorio de' Alessandro told Leon. "Bernardo never said it was aught but the most tragic of accidents. Dante concurred." He looked at Giulietta one eyebrow raised, then reached for a ewer of wine nearby to refill his goblet.

A servant spoke into Caressa's ear, and she nodded. A small, raised platform had been put into place at one end of the dining room before the diners had arrived. Now she clapped her hands softly for attention and pointed toward the stagelike structure. "We have something special for you tonight, my friends. Enjoy our Marco's culinary skills with desserts, at your leisure, while Piero shows us what his Lily can do."

While the others turned their attention expectantly to the platform, Giulietta had to resist the urge to slide downward in her seat. *Madre di Dio,* wasn't it enough that she had to sit beside Rodrigo da Valenti? Now she had to be subjected to this barbarian form of entertainment by another *Zingaro?*

*Or is it that you don't wish to be reminded any more than necessary of what happened last night?*

All eyes were trained on the small stage except for Giulietta. She chanced a look through her lashes at Rodrigo da Valenti . . . and he was watching her with what looked very much like amusement lighting his eyes. She raised her lashes, revealing the full extent of her anger, then narrowed her eyes at him in outrage.

How *dare* he laugh at her? The Gypsy rogue!

As if reading her very thoughts, Rodrigo leaned over and murmured (much too close for her liking) into her ear, "I'm not laughing at you, *cara*. I was merely thinking how you would enjoy Lily's performance if your first fascination with her was any indication." His smile widened, deepening the creases splayed about his eyes, and accenting the whiteness of his straight teeth against his skin. "Don't you like animals?"

In a daring move—considering the surrounding company and her father's suddenly omniscient presence—Giulietta lowered her voice to a soft rasp as she said into his face, *"Briccone!* You knave! How could you—"

The gasps of surprise and wonderment from the diners cut across her words, and Rodrigo straightened, his gaze going to the stage and leaving her to sputter at the empty air.

". . . was a gift from Rodrigo," Piero was saying as he stood before them with Lily on her leash. "She was given to him by a French nobleman, whose pet had outgrown his children. As I understand it, the distraught man was considering having his huntsman dispatch her, but feared the reaction of his family if they ever learned of Lily's true fate. Rodrigo quite accidentally learned of the doomed animal and requested her as a 'surprise' for his family back in Italy." Piero grinned at Rodrigo. "Lily bears him a special affection, and becomes entranced whenever he plays his lute . . . as so many whom I've observed." His voice rang with pride.

*Why, the man is as self-inflated as Valenti!* Giulietta thought. *It must run in their blood.*

The dark and burly Piero spoke to the bear in Romany, and the sow sat on her powerful haunches, paws dangling before her like some great dog. Her small eyes roamed the room. "She begs for some morsel from your bountiful board, *principe,*" Piero said to Dante, who'd turned his chair toward the dais beside him. "Please forgive her—she has manners like her former French owners."

Laughter broke out at this.

"She obeys commands even more quickly in French," Piero added with a sly wink, one eyebrow waggling. "But she's picking up Romany quickly enough."

"A bilingual bear!" Nicco exclaimed, and the laughter was renewed.

"Wait until she learns Italian," Botticelli added, still laughing. "She'll be the talk of Tuscany!"

"And I couldn't think of a better teacher, Sandro," Dante said. He looked at Piero. "Maestro Botticelli here is very good at whatever he does, Piero, and works cheaply."

Sitting amidst the laughter and good-natured banter, Giulietta decided she had no choice but to join in, for surely she would appear churlish if she sat through the remainder of the evening with her features set in grim lines. Even she knew when to ease up in her father's presence. As his only daughter, she might have him totally captivated with her, but Giulietta knew when she'd gone far enough. Her father was kind and loving, but he'd not earned the sobriquet Il Leone for nothing . . . which was why she'd gone to such pains to keep him from learning of her flight from the castle the night before.

Besides, she thought darkly, her pride pricked, if Rodrigo da Valenti could dismiss their interlude last eve with such apparent ease—if he could act as if it were of no significance and naught was amiss—then so could she.

Piero gave Lily a tambourine, and she proceeded to shake it with exuberance. At another command, she began to lumber about the platform at the end of her leash, and Giulietta thought how mammoth the sow's frame compared to Piero; yet the animal appeared to be under his control.

The audience clapped at Lily's antics, and Piero grinned with pride. "But you should see her with Rigo," he said behind his hand to those closest to him.

In spite of herself, Giulietta was fascinated by the bear. She hardly heard Piero's words, she was so absorbed in Lily's clumsy dance.

"That animal stinks," Leon whispered to her with a fastidious wrinkling of his nose. Giulietta nodded, although she was not in agreement. How absurd. Bears didn't bathe to keep from offending human sensibilities.

"Perhaps we could sprinkle him with Aristo's rose water," she said, casting him an impish look. He grunted, seeming to miss her humor.

Rodrigo pushed his chair back, catching Giulietta's attention. She watched him collect his lute and move to stand beside the dais. In spite of everything, she found herself staring at his long legs encased in sapphire trunk hose, his trim flanks beneath the short sapphire and scarlet doublet. No wonder his eyes looked so blue, she mused, then wrenched her thoughts away from him and back to Lily.

A ripple of applause greeted Rodrigo's first soft chords on the lute which instantly snared Lily's attention. The animal swung toward the sound and, with obvious interest, moved toward Rodrigo. He grinned, and Piero quipped, "She is literally transformed by his lute, you see. Or mayhap 'tis Rodrigo himself who mesmerizes her."

Light laughter skittered around the board.

*No doubt,* Giulietta thought sourly, feeling her improved

mood dissipating. *No doubt he could charm any creature on God's earth.*

*Including you* . . . Soft echoes of laughter tripped through her mind.

Then it happened, and with frightening speed.

Tambourine discarded, Lily swiftly drew back one huge paw just as Rodrigo glanced down at his lute.

"Rigo!" Dante warned, alarm infusing the word.

Too late . . . the lifting of Rodrigo's head coincided perfectly with the bear's forward swing, and two of her claws scraped across his cheek before he could jerk his head clear.

Instantly two streaks of crimson appeared on his flesh. Shock flashed through Giulietta, and hard on its heels a real fear that the bear would attack him.

Piero gave a mighty tug on the leash with both hands, his oath shattering the stunned silence, and Lily let out a growl of irritation. Rodrigo shook his head in obvious warning to the other man and continued to strum the lute as if nothing were amiss; but now he put words to the music. French words, which seemed to calm the animal. Lily stood towering before him on the dais, her small eyes pinned to his face. Her great body began to sway slightly from side to side as the man before her crooned soothingly in French. Giulietta could discern sighs of relief around her.

Her own gaze remained glued to the slashes across Rodrigo da Valenti's cheek, queasy fear roiling through her.

It would hurt him to flash that bright and beautiful smile now, came the thought, unbidden . . . and the world would be a duller place for the duration.

*You're under his spell as much as the sow . . . and you know better!*

*Or do you?*

Dante was standing, his body rigid, as he watched the bear through narrowed eyes. Vittorio was on his feet as well, and

Caressa, her forehead creased with concern, had already dipped a clean napkin in a nearby ewer of water and was obviously awaiting a signal from her husband. One of the serving girls stood at her side.

Soon the song ended, with Lily settled calmly on her haunches, her eyes still on Rodrigo. As the last notes died away, he turned back toward the others. "Please don't be concerned," he said lightly. "She meant me no harm, but rather was showing her, ah . . . appreciation of the music, and also the language of the children who raised her from the time she was a cub."

Piero led Lily, who appeared totally docile now, toward the back of the dais to polite applause, and followed a servant, with Lily in tow, out a side exit.

Both Dante and Caressa approached their guest as he set his lute against the dais. "What happened to her?" Dante asked as he watched his wife touch the wet napkin gently to Rodrigo's cheek.

He smiled and took the cloth from his hostess. "Such distasteful work for so beautiful a lady, *principessa*. And the scratches are nothing."

"That animal is dangerous," Leon Sarzano declared with a frown.

Dante escorted first Caressa, then Rodrigo to their seats. "Not really," Rodrigo said as he resumed his place beside Giulietta. "Piero wanted to have her declawed, but 'twould only diminish Lily as a means of making a living for Piero. Next he would want her fangs removed, despite the fact that she wears a leather muzzle . . . and who would pay to see a clawless, toothless bear?"

He felt Giulietta's gaze on his face as he answered Leon and looked directly at her. For a fleeting fragment of time he saw concern darkening her lovely eyes, and he wondered what it would be like to be loved by such a woman.

Concern—and something more subtle—took over as Giulietta removed the dampened napkin from his hand and touched it to his cheek in imitation of her mother. Their eyes locked; a light flush brightened her face becomingly.

Like one in a trance, she was suddenly powerless to pull her gaze from his, and only belatedly noticed a droplet of ruby-bright blood thread its way downward and toward his white shirt above the neckline of his doublet. By the time she recovered enough to swipe at it, it had already stained the pristine garment.

Just then Aristo entered the room with a small chest. He looked at Dante, who inclined his head toward Rodrigo, and the dwarf moved toward him. His arrival interrupted the short but intense moment between them, and Giulietta set the cloth back down and dropped her hand to her lap.

"Is this really necessary?" Rodrigo asked ruefully. He looked into the dwarf's face.

"You're bleeding, signore," Aristo replied simply.

"Then I should leave the board," Rodrigo answered, throwing an apologetic look at Dante, then Caressa.

"That won't be necessary," Dante said. "Aristo can touch a bit of alum to the gashes and you'll be good as new."

Rodrigo concentrated on Giulietta's bright auburn hair as Aristo did exactly that, for it stung. In fact, so sharp was the sting that it made his eyes water, and as the seed pearls woven through her hair began to waver he dropped his gaze to her lap where her fingers were tensely entwined. Then Aristo was blocking his view of her. . . .

Giulietta was vaguely aware of scraps of conversation around her as her parents tried to smooth over the situation, but for some reason couldn't attune her mind to what was being said. Not with Aristo tending Rodrigo da Valenti's injury to her immediate left.

"There." Aristo deposited the cloth and small jar of styptic in his small chest, tucked it under his arm, and backed away.

Rodrigo nodded. "Thank you, *maestro*," he said to the dwarf. To the other guests, he said, *"Per favore,* forgive the disruption."

"Think nothing of it," Dante said, and grinned. "I've been wondering since you returned from France if you had any battle scars. Now Lily has given you several."

Nicco and Leon laughed, and the somber mood was broken.

"Do you *have* any battle scars?" Nicco asked.

Rodrigo laughed, one side of his face already stiffening. "You'll have to observe me bathing if you wish to know, for I don't make a habit of . . . displaying them."

"And Nicco shouldn't make a habit of asking about such things . . . especially in mixed company," Caressa chided.

Nicco sighed and sat back, properly chastened, but his sister didn't notice. At the thought of Rodrigo da Valenti's nude form, blood pounded through Giulietta's head, banishing her earlier concern and compassion for the headier feeling of forbidden desire. And sharp images of remembered passion on the bank of a stream beneath the moonlight. . . .

She abruptly turned her attention to Leon Sarzano.


"If there had been any doubt in my mind during the last years, it's been banished completely," Dante said.

Caressa paused in the act of brushing her long, dark hair and looked at her husband in the polished metal mirror before her.

"As to who will marry our Giulietta," he explained.

She replaced the brush slowly on the small table of rouge pots and perfumes and turned to him. Her lips were parted slightly, happiness sparkled in her clear gray eyes.

"I take it you approve, *cara*," he said. He arched one brow, his expression wry. "Or did you have someone else in mind . . . like Sarzano?"

Caressa's mouth curved in a warm smile; her heart warmed, too, at his words, for Dante had always consulted her behind closed doors, acknowledging her intelligence and demonstrating his respect for her opinions. "The man I would choose for her is not the man she thinks she wants—but that normally isn't an issue in an arranged marriage."

Dante strode toward her, still fully clad, and kissed the top of her head. His fingers began to knead the muscles in her shoulders with soothing movements.

"And?" he pressed.

"She would come to detest Leon Sarzano in no time," she said. "Mayhap even entertain thoughts of fleeing to Santa Lucia to escape what she would consider a dull existence."

"Giulietta Maria would not be so irresponsible," he said. "I hope we've taught her better than that." He paused, then added with a twist of his lips, "Although 'tis no secret that she is spoiled."

"And Leon's family is not so rich or influential as to add anything to the security or prosperity of Monteverdi," Caressa continued, pleased that Dante had acknowledged that his daughter was accustomed to having her way.

"But their lands adjoin ours," Dante reminded her.

"Only a small portion on one border."

"But times are uncertain. Every ally counts."

"Whenever are times certain? And the Sarzanos are too much in awe of you to ever turn against you. I could more easily picture them hiding behind Monteverdi's walls than attacking them."

"Ah, *cara mia,*" he sighed, caressing the slender stretch of her throat. "You are so wise."

"And it would be better for all to have a man like Rodrigo da Valenti in the family—a professional *condottiere* with absolute allegiance to you, in spite of lingering hard feelings. Monteverdi and its people will benefit greatly from his love for you . . . and he's a man with Medici blood running through his veins. When I think of his late uncle's administrative abilities—his many talents . . . and Rodrigo's natural father's ability to draw men to him in absolute loyalty, it gives me chills."

"Even now that the Medicis have been banished from the Republic?"

She nodded. "It wouldn't make sense to wed Giulietta to anyone else." Her eyes met his in the mirror. "And then, of course, 'tis obvious Rodrigo is already half in love with her, in spite of her abominable behavior toward him this evening. I don't think you could have made a better choice, husband."

Dante's fingers paused in their magic, and she watched a frown transform his expression as he obviously remembered his daughter's actions during dinner. "And I couldn't have said it better if I'd tried," he told her then. His frown returned. "I only hope he accepts—especially after the way she treated him. I wouldn't blame him if he beat her before they were even wed!"

At the sudden distress that darkened Caressa's eyes, he quickly added, "But such is not Rigo's way. He is good-natured to a fault if he is anything like his sire. He is normally slow to anger—a strength in a man, I've always thought."

"He has changed over the last six years?"

He nodded, his fingers drifting from her shoulders to her unbound hair. "He seems to have accepted certain things he didn't understand as a youth. I think, *amore mio,* he will make her an excellent husband."


Morning dawned bright and beautiful, promising an extraordinary day. Voices from outside drifted to Giulietta's window, teasing the periphery of a light sleep. She burrowed deeper under the light covers, unconsciously seeking silence and un-interrupted slumber, thanks to Aristo's ministrations before she'd gone to bed the night before.

But it was not to be.

An insistent rap on the antechamber door woke her fully. She sat up, held the sheet to her chest with one hand and rubbed her eyes with the thumb and forefinger of the other as Lisa hastened to answer the knock. Who was inconsiderate enough to interrupt her sleep after a late—

"Gietta? Wake up, *piccola sorella!*" Nicco strode into the room and headed straight for his sister without hesitation. They were close, even at this age, and neither had ever denied the other access to their bedchamber at any time, or for any reason.

He wore a steel-plated brigandine over his shirt, a sword belt and sword, and carried a buckler.

Giulietta, however, was irritated at her brother's exuberant entrance this morning, no matter what his reason. It had taken her a long time to fall asleep, but not because of her foot. Thoughts of Rodrigo da Valenti had kept her awake, much to her annoyance.

The thought of him brought an unconscious frown to her delicate features. "What? You're not overjoyed to see your favorite brother?" he asked.

"My *only* brother." The frown disappeared with her arch reply, and a saucy smile replaced it.

He sat on the edge of the bed and rested his buckler across his knees. It bore the Alessandro shield, a black rampant horse on a gold background. "No matter how many brothers you may have had, I would have been your favorite, *nina.* And when I am wed to Gina and set up my own household one day, you'll miss me terribly."

Giulietta hugged her knees to her chest and planted her chin there. That was certainly true, she thought as she regarded him with sleepy eyes. But she didn't want to think of him wedding and one day becoming Prince of Monteverdi just yet. "And Castello Monteverdi isn't good enough for you and your future family?"

"Of course. Rather, *you* will be the one to leave Monteverdi when you wed."

*I pray God 'twill be so,* she thought, meaning entering a state of marriage as opposed to leaving her home. Then, "Indeed, Nicco, I will miss you . . . although it appears that you have brought your accoutrements of war to convince me of it."

He laughed. "Sometimes I think Father ought to use such means to keep you in line, Gietta, but I have no such thing in mind." Excitement shone in his gray eyes as he changed the subject. "We are engaging in a few contests of war on the morrow at the quintain field. At first light Father sent a message to Nardo and Angelo, inviting them to participate. But today we practice."

She brightened immediately, all thought of sleep banished. "Lucia will come then with her Angelo . . . and Elisabetta with Bernardo!"

"And Leon Sarzano and his father," he added. "Father told them to bring several of their best condottieri—and Paolo was given the task of choosing a few to represent Castello Monteverdi from our men." He slapped her leg lightly beneath the sheet and sprang to his feet, ready to take on the world with all the exuberance of healthy and optimistic youth. "There's much Rodrigo can teach all of us, Father says, if we are to hold our own against those like the French."

He saluted her and swung toward the door.

Rodrigo? she thought in bewilderment.

But why not? Hadn't the men hung on his every word concerning war and weapons and methods?

Before she could think further about the unwelcome news,

Lisa's voice came to them from the antechamber. *"Viene qui! Viene qui!"*

Brother and sister looked at the door in unison just as a fluffy fur-ball bounded through it on long legs.

"He found you!" Nicco said, laughing, and bent to scoop up the dog with one hand.

"Where did he come from?" Giulietta asked, thinking how beautiful its snow-white coloring, and warming to it instantly.

"An admirer," Nicco answered as he stroked its downy head.

"Leon?" Giulietta asked as she took the small sealed note Lisa handed her, after shaking her head at the pup now nestled in the crook of Nicco's arm.

"No . . ."

Giulietta broke the wax, and the words of the message jumped out at her with a kind of calligraphic arrogance: *Meet Beau—a faithful friend to guard you at night against wolves and brigands. . . .*

"Rather," Nicco was saying, and scattered her thoughts, "Signore da Valenti." He placed the puppy beside Giulietta. "He said 'twas from France . . . some kind of mountain dog used by shepherds for centuries in the Pyrenees, I believe. They grow to be very big . . . look at his paws." Giulietta examined one of the animal's paws. The pup, indeed, had much potential for growth, she thought. At first, the inclination to give it back to the man who'd given it vied sharply with the urge to keep it. The dog couldn't choose its owner . . . or on whom the owner chose to bestow it.

But if Rodrigo da Valenti thought to make up for his outrageous, libertine treatment of her the other night. . . .

As Nicco strode from the room, Giulietta took the irresistible ball of fluff into her lap, and stroked its thick fur. It raised its head and looked at her with its deep brown eyes that seemed to combine mischief and understanding . . . trust and adoration.

Giulietta was taken, completely, in those brief moments.

"Beau . . ." she murmured, savoring the sound of the French name—the name given the animal by Rodrigo da Valenti. "Handsome," she translated softly and put her nose to the pup's. His pink tongue tickled her with a canine kiss.

As she thought of the man whose very name was anathema to her, she wondered briefly what excuse (if she dared to even attempt one) she could offer to remain abed on the morrow.

# Seven

"Mayhap your potion is different enough to be effective," Aristo said to Maddalena. "I've become immune to my own, it seems, and my joints pain me almost constantly now."

*Especially from my recent exertions on my hands and knees,* he thought with a mental grimace.

Over the years, Aristo had formed a bond with Maddalena—not only because she was *Zingaro* like himself, but because she'd saved his life. They also shared an interest in alchemy and the stars, although Aristo had always believed Maddalena had a special gift of clairvoyance that he felt made the accuracy of his own predictions child's play in comparison.

After Rodrigo da Valenti had come to Castello Monteverdi, Aristo decided to visit Maddalena for his own reasons.

Maddalena nodded. "I have plenty and would be glad to share it." She gestured for him to sit. "San Gimignano?"

His dark eyes lit up. *"Sì . . . grazi.* But just one cup."

" 'Tis wise, especially if you take a dose of the medicine before you leave here."

He looked down at his skewed fingers resting in his lap, thinking, wondering if he should take the risk. Yet he would feel better about his small (and utterly uncharacteristic) deception, if he had more information . . . mayhap even reassurances that Giulietta de' Alessandro's virtue was still intact. "Would you also have something to numb the pain in a delicate area? Say . . . the arch of the foot?"

He watched Maddalena stiffen. She slowly looked up from the ewer of San Gimignano in her hands. "One of Monteverdi's peasants?" she asked.

He stared at her for a long moment before he spoke. "No."

She handed him a cup of the wine, and his gaze slid away from hers. "Clever man . . . you have told me what you will without breaking your patient's confidence, haven't you?"

He nodded and raised the cup to his lips. "Do you know aught about it?" he asked after he drank.

"Only that Rodrigo took her back to Monteverdi," she replied. "But that is between you and me. Your prince need not know, for Rodrigo assured me that nothing untoward happened."

Aristo shook his dark head. "I don't like this at all. Too many secrets! I serve Il Leone, not just anyone who feels at liberty to confide in me!"

"Madonna Giulietta is not just *anyone*. Nor am I. If nothing happened, then what harm will be done by saying naught of her . . . outing? On the other hand," she added, "your prince should know that his daughter is very unhappy. She was fleeing to Santa Lucia, so she said."

Aristo stood and set his cup down. "All that will be changed soon. *Il principe* has found a husband for her. As soon as arrangements can be made, he will tell her." *Provided the groom-to-be is in agreement,* he added silently and immediately swung away to avoid her penetrating blue gaze.

He looked up at her shelves of potions and elixirs, salves and powders. Having extra for his own stores would save him another painful sojourn on hands and knees should he run out. . . .

" 'Tis the blue bottle, middle shelf—you may have it. Take a *small* swallow thrice a day as needed," she specified with an arch of one eyebrow, then moved away with the empty cups and ewer.

As Aristo reached for the bottle indicated, a flash of yellow nearby caught his eye. Tucked behind a closed bed plank on the closest wall, was the top portion of a shoe—sole facing outward. Aristo blinked to clear his vision, and looked harder, for it looked out of place in the humble Gypsy wagon. A dark stain surrounded what looked like a tear in the leather of the sole. The tip of its mate was unblemished.

The color and richness of the slippers proclaimed them the shoes of a noblewoman . . . possibly Madonna Caressa's. More likely Giulietta's. Had Maddalena found them? Or had Rodrigo kept them?

The dwarf absently reached for the blue bottle on the middle shelf, his attention still on the slippers. Then he pulled his gaze away and removed the stopper. With an inward sigh of relief—for he would have done anything to numb the discomfort that had been sorely exacerbated by his foray into the forest—he took a modest swallow. Then another for good measure, in spite of Maddalena's instructions. He restoppered it and placed it in the purse hanging at the waist of his dark robe.

By then Maddalena was rummaging in a small chest toward the front of the caravan. She straightened and turned back to him, holding out a packet of powder. "Dissolve a pinch of this in warm water and soak the foot in it morning and night."

"*Grazi*," he repeated as he took the package and made to swing away.

"Can you not remain? We haven't spoken for a while . . ."

Aristo stared into her handsome face, tempted. She was *Zingara* . . . and very appealing to him. And not only had they many interests in common, but she treated him as an equal, too. He sighed heavily. "I shouldn't stray far from Castello Monteverdi, for Giulietta de' Alessandro is attempting to hide her tryst and the resulting injury from *il principe*. I am caught in the middle and that could mean—"

He shook his misshapen head in obvious foreboding and lurched to the door and down the steps with more than his normal awkwardness, upsetting the washbasin on the top step in the process.

*Dio,* he thought as his feet touched the ground and the basin bounced past him, splattering the hem of his robe with water. He paused to get his bearings, for he suddenly felt strange.

"Aristo?" Maddalena queried from behind him. "What is it?"

He ran his hand over his face and slowly shook his head. "Naught, I think . . ." He bent to retrieve the basin, now lying upside down and felt the world begin to spin. A dark-haired Gypsy child skipped into his line of vision and quickly retrieved the basin. "Here, Maddalena," the little boy said with a grin. "Your basin tried to run away!"

*"Grazi,"* Aristo mumbled to the child, and continued on away from the wagon. Maddalena's voice faded behind him.

"Aristo!" greeted a man who appeared from seemingly out of nowhere. "Come look—"

The dwarf squinted at him. Piero?

Suddenly a huge furry creature loomed before the dwarf. But instead of being frightened, Aristo could only stare in wonder at its thick brown fur and think how beautiful it was.

". . . Lily," the man was dimly explaining.

A female, Aristo mused as he stared up at the bear. "Ah, *sì* . . . Lily from last night!" His lips curved into a stupid smile, the ache in his bones suddenly gone. *"Che bella!"* he murmured, staring into the animal's small brown eyes.

A hand on his arm swung him around without warning, and Maddalena was before him . . . *towering* over him. She had never looked so appealing, with her bright blue eyes and long, silvered hair . . . Why hadn't he noticed before?

"Aristo? What ails you?"

He reached for her hand. "Naught ails me, beautiful Maddalena, for the very sight of you is balm to my heart." His lips touched the soft backs of her fingers, and he breathed deeply of her faint perfume—was it lilacs?

He missed the look she exchanged with Piero before the latter led Lily away.

"And a tonic for my loins as well," he added in his most alluring tones, his grin widening. "Come for a walk with me, *sì, bella* Maddalena? Grace the woods with your beauty . . ."

"Tonic?" she interrupted with a puzzled frown.

He sighed, his hold on her fingers tightening, and stared up into her eyes.

She bent to reach into the folds of his robe for his pouch.

He giggled. "Ah, *bella strega,* you feel it, too! You cannot wait, can you?"

"Don't be absurd—" she began. She pulled out the bottle he'd taken from her medicine stores.

Rodrigo's adoptive mother, Luciana, came up to them. "What is it, Maddalena?" she asked.

"He's taken the wrong medicine," Maddalena said wryly, trying to stifle a smile.

"Medicine?" Aristo repeated. *"Sì.* Never have I taken such a wonderful potion." He flashed a grin at Luciana, but had eyes only for Maddalena. "You aren't taking my medicine away, *dolce,* are you?" He reached with his free hand for the bottle.

"Ah, ah, ah," she cautioned, holding it up out of his reach. "You may have it later . . . first you must come back to the wagon. You forgot the rest of the potion."

"Rest? Wagon?" he said.

*"Sì."*

He brought her hand up to his lips again. "We'll be alone then, won't we?"

She nodded, intending to give him something to sleep until the love philter he'd taken by mistake wore off.

"Shall I ask Andrea or Carlo to help you? Or one of the other men?" Luciana asked in a low voice obviously meant for Maddalena alone, for the dwarf was extremely strong for his size and it was obvious that the situation could easily turn disastrous if his anger were aroused. But just then Piero reappeared.

Maddalena shook her head. "I think not . . . yet." If she kept him happy, hopefully he would do as she suggested until he fell asleep.

"Come along then, *maestro*," she said, and swung back toward her wagon.

"I'm coming, *bella mia*," he said with a sly grin, and followed her with the rolling, awkward gait that had once reminded Dante de' Alessandro of a broken-winged bat.


"I'm forming my own company of *condottieri*."

Dante gave Rodrigo a thoughtful look in light of the revelation as they rode the paths of Monteverdi lands, near Verdi. He shook his head. " 'Tis too dangerous, Rigo."

In spite of ambivalent feelings, Rodrigo laughed goodnaturedly, finding that he couldn't remain resentful of Dante de' Alessandro for long when in his presence . . . and especially after last night. Being hundreds of miles distant and in a foreign country, away from friend and family, was one thing; being back at Monteverdi and beneath the prince's benign aegis was completely another.

"I've already recruited Carlo, and several others who seek a more exciting—and lucrative—way of life. My brother is most enthusiastic and would never forgive me if I discarded the project." He glanced sideways at Dante as they rode toward the *Zingari* camp, his expression sobering. "Besides, there is little else for me to do—unless I want to farm, which I do not. Or wander about Italy with the band, eking out a living from sharpening weapons, or as a smithy, or entertaining the masses with a trained bear or my lute."

Dante shook his head. "After last night, I wonder about your luck with trained bears . . . But seriously, I think you're wrong. You're too intelligent to throw your life away like that. You've noble blood running through your veins, whether you acknowledge it or nay."

Rodrigo frowned. "My fellow *Zingari* do not consider their way of life a waste. Yet it isn't for me. And as for my mysterious sire, I wouldn't be surprised to one day discover he was a *contadino*—a wayward peasant who somehow charmed my mother into lying with him." He couldn't keep the taint of bitterness from his voice.

Dante reined in his mount and watched Rodrigo follow his lead. "Do I hear self-pity in your voice?" His mouth tightened in obvious and uncharacteristic irritation. "If so, you are unworthy of your father. Surely no peasant's son could have accomplished what you have."

"And most self-respecting peasants wouldn't have sown their seed so carelessly as my supposedly well-born father. An honest *contadino* is too busy laboring to feed and clothe his family to engage in such irresponsible behavior as siring unwanted children all over the Republic!" His dark brows drew together in anger. "There is much to be said about an honest man of humble origins—mayhap more than many nobles."

Dante held his silence, his eyes locked with Rodrigo's.

"And you were the very one who told me that a man isn't born noble, but rather becomes noble." Surely, Rodrigo thought, the prince could not deny the reprehensible carelessness of the nobility when it came to matters of the flesh. Although Dante was a prince, with the option of any man (as custom allowed) to engage in extramarital dalliances, Rodrigo didn't believe for a moment that Dante had ever been unfaithful to his beloved Caressa. And while the prince might not participate in such behavior like many of his fellow aristocrats, neither had he ever outwardly condemned it . . . at least to Rodrigo.

Dante touched the sides of his horse and moved forward. "I need a dependable man to keep abreast of the activities of the Prior of San Marco . . ."

"Savonarola?"

*"Sì.* He was excommunicated by the Pope in June—had you heard?—and is uncharacteristically quiet for the moment—no doubt planning his next move. I would know what he's up to, for even though it appears that his supporters are losing ground, I believe he still has enough influence to bring Florence to its knees—to make the Republic even more vulnerable to its enemies now that the Medicis have been banished by the *Signoria."* He looked at Rodrigo. "Are you interested in such an undertaking?"

Rodrigo ducked a low-hanging bough on the path before he answered. "It sounds intriguing, to say the least. I could approach it several ways, couldn't I?"

Dante nodded, then grinned. "You could become a most devoted follower of the Prior of San Marco, eh? Or you could join the ranks of the *Compagnacci*—those noble young men bent upon causing such mayhem as to humiliate him enough to drive him from Florence."

Rodrigo nodded.

"And then I would hire you and your company to work for me, if you insist on being a mercenary."

"But what of Tristano Bossi and his men?"

The corners of Dante's mouth turned down. "Bossi died two years past. Many of his men are getting old, losing some of their vigor. Monteverdi's soldiers need an infusion of young blood."

But being near Giulietta de' Alessandro day in and day out would be pure torture, he knew already from their brief but sweet interlude, and then last night. He was—had been for years—infatuated with her.

". . . can think about it," Dante was saying. "I don't need an answer now." They were nearing the campsite and Dante nodded his head in its direction. "I'd like to see your grandmother again. Shall we?"

"*Sì*." But Rodrigo's mind wasn't on Maddalena at that moment. How could he refuse the prince's offer? he was thinking. Yet wasn't this a big part of the reason he'd stayed away from Castello Monteverdi since his return to the prince's domain? Anger had been a part of his reluctance to show himself at Castello Monteverdi, yes. But so was his reluctance to see Giulietta—knowing that he could never have her. . . .

"What's all the commotion?" Dante asked as they broke through the trees bordering the camp.

Rodrigo was immediately struck by the number of people around his grandmother's caravan—which was rocking precariously on its wheels.

"Maddalena!" he exclaimed softly, and slid from Morello's back. Tossing the reins unthinkingly to Dante, he turned and strode across the remaining distance to the wagon, then began shouldering his way through the small crowd.

"What's going on?" he asked Maria, the pretty Gypsy girl to whom he'd given a lesson or two on his lute.

"The dwarf," she replied as he moved past, putting her hands to her cheeks in chagrin. "He's after Maddalena . . ."

Marco, a somber, sullen young man who was like Maria's shadow, snorted with derision, but Rodrigo didn't hear the rest as he reached the rear of the wagon and vaulted to the threshold in two springing steps.

Piero and another man were fighting to hold Aristo down on the floor. The dwarf resisted, his short, bowed legs working in a tangle of brown wool and pale flesh as he cried out, "What are you *doing* to me? Unhand me!" He thrashed against their hold like a miniature bull. "Maddalena? Where are you? Come back to me! Ahh . . . !" His face contorted with pain and frustration and the two men on either side of him were hard-pressed to keep him down. Though he was diminutive, his strength was equal to that of several strong, normal-sized men, even though he was more than two score years of age.

Pity moved through Rodrigo, for Aristo had suffered terrible abuse before he'd ever met Durante de' Alessandro. He'd done a complete about-face nineteen years ago when he'd turned against the master who'd caused him such mental and physical anguish, all in the name of a twisted form of nurturing from infancy on. Now the dwarf was a devoted servant to the prince and his family and here he was . . . pinned on his malformed back by two burly *Zingari* brothers and in obvious distress.

"What is it?" Rodrigo said as he moved into the shifting wagon and bent so that Aristo could see him. He could almost feel the smaller man's pain.

Piero, sweat pouring from his brow, said through set teeth, "Ask Maddalena . . . surely the dwarf's gone mad!" The other man, Rino, grunted in agreement as he struggled to control the dwarf beneath them.

"He took the wrong potion from among my medicinals," Maddalena said from beside Rodrigo. He looked into her eyes as she crouched shoulder to shoulder with him, and saw her concern.

"Will he—?"

She shook her head. " 'Twas a love potion, not poison. If I can get him to take this—" she held up a small flask of milky liquid—"he'll sleep until the potion wears off."

Rodrigo said to Rino, "Let me take your place," and the other man relinquished his viselike hold on Aristo's shoulder. "Turn him to his side, Piero, you're hurting him."

*"Per favore,* . . . . please, Rodrigo," Aristo begged, "let me go. I've done nothing. I just want to see . . ."

"I'm here," Maddalena said to him. She reached and pushed the dark hair from his brow, and he instantly quieted. "They'll turn you loose after you take this elixir to calm you down. You're frightening my people, Aristo, with your carrying on. If you would take that walk in the woods with me, you must cooperate, *sì?*" Her lips curved upward in a smile worthy of a young temptress.

"Do you hurt still?" Rodrigo asked.

"Only my heart," Aristo sighed, his eyes on Maddalena as she poured some of the elixir onto a small wooden spoon.

A figure appeared in the doorway, blocking the daylight for a moment. Rodrigo glanced up, and was not surprised to see the prince, the bright afternoon sunlight forming a nimbus about his fair head.

No one said a word as Rodrigo shifted his attention to Aristo and cradled his shoulders to hold up his head. Piero retreated then, and the dwarf obediently took the proffered liquid. "If 'twill please you, *bella mia,*" he said to Maddalena, "I will do what you ask."

Dante came farther into the room. Those outside had quieted by now, and a hush descended within the caravan as the prince approached his faithful servant.

"What is happening here? Is he hurt?" Dante asked in a low voice. His blond brows were flattened with concern.

Aristo glanced at his master, and a slow flush crept up his neck and face. "Excellence," he muttered, appearing suddenly drowsy. "I came for medicine for my aching bones . . ." He trailed off, his dark lashes lowering.

Dante took Maddalena's place as she knelt beside his servant. "You owe me no explanations, my Aristo," he said softly, then looked at Rodrigo questioningly.

"He did no harm," Maddalena said. "He merely took the wrong philter—a love potion, no less—and had to choose between Lily and me." Her mouth curved with good humor.

"Beautiful . . . beautiful Lily from last night," the dwarf murmured. "But Maddalena is . . . *la bellissima . . ."*

"I'll take him home," Dante said, shaking his head. "He'll awake in his own bed and mayhap we can cajole him out of what surely will be his humiliation."

Rodrigo nodded. "I'll help you—"

"No," insisted Maddalena softly as she reached down to cover Aristo's exposed calves and ankles. "Let him remain here so I can watch him. One never knows with a love po- tion—especially if, as I suspect, he took more than a mouth- ful." She looked at Dante. "Will that be acceptable, *principe?"*

Rodrigo caught the confidence in her voice as she properly requested Dante's permission. He knew, as well as any of those in the camp, that she was her own woman. No one told Mad- dalena what to do—not even a prince.

But did the Prince of Monteverdi know that? Rodrigo won- dered. And would he yield to her wishes?

"He will be mortified."

Maddalena shook her head. "I will see that he is not. When all is set to rights again, I will send him home to you."

Dante looked as if he would disagree, then nodded. He stood, and the others silently filed out. Rodrigo suddenly re- membered the brightly colored slippers directly across from where Aristo lay. If Dante saw them . . .

But the prince thanked Maddalena for her kindness toward Aristo. "Caressa will be concerned about him, for he normally stays close to the keep." He bowed briefly to her. "If I may, I'll take my leave." He looked at Rodrigo. "I'll see you in the morn," he told him, and exited the wagon.

# Eight

"She's here," said Carlo as he handed Rodrigo his lance. "There is no mistaking that hair."

"The perfect frame for her vivid features," Rodrigo answered, the uninjured side of his mouth curving ruefully. "I can't imagine why she isn't wed yet." He shifted his weight more securely in the saddle and looked down at the ground for a moment.

"And you don't know if you can work for the prince and be near her within the walls of the keep, yet aware of how out of your reach she'll always be."

With undisguised surprise, Rodrigo looked up into the face of the man he called brother. Was he that easy to read?

"Better she were wed already and spoken for, eh?" Carlo continued in a low, empathetic voice.

"Nay . . . better, I think—" his voice lowered huskily here as he confided bluntly—"that I had remained in France."

"You are infatuated with a phantom, brother," Carlo told him. "The memory of a lovely child from six years past. 'Tis no secret that Giulietta de' Alessandro is outrageously spoiled . . . everyone knows it, although 'twould never discourage a man from marrying her. She's beautiful and desirable . . . and her father is the Prince of Monteverdi."

Rodrigo said nothing.

"But you'll not always be here," Carlo added. "You said His Excellence has other duties for you aside from heading

Monteverdi's mercenaries." He grinned knowingly. "We'll find you another woman to heal your heart . . . and warm your bed at night, *sì?*"

Rodrigo slowly, thoughtfully, swung Morello's head in the direction of the quintain. He looked over his shoulder at Carlo. "I appreciate your concern, but I don't think you have any idea how great a task you've undertaken on my behalf." His words were weighted with rue.

"So you gave her the pup to protect her, eh? From whom?" Carlo laughed with soft irony. "You, mayhap?"

"Believe me, brother," he said, absently threading his fingers through Morello's mane, "when I say that if I had the remotest chance of winning her for my own—if I had the least *right* to do so—'twould take more than a three-month-old pup—even a Great Pyrenees—to stop me."

"Beau would never harm you. He loves you . . . and you are attached to him as well."

Rodrigo's fingers stilled. "He's young enough to transfer his love and loyalty to Giulietta de' Alessandro. I wouldn't want to cross him in a year or so."

Carlo shook his head, throwing up his hands in resignation. Then, "Maria is here to watch you, brother," he said with a sudden, sly grin. "Surely she's more woman than any pale-skinned *gorgio.*"

"And the jealous Marco is here to watch *her,*" Rodrigo added wryly. "Besides, I have no designs on her."

"There are some who think otherwise."

Rodrigo laughed softly, and instantly felt his injured cheek muscles protest. It would be impossible for him not to smile or laugh—it was as natural to him as breathing. "I don't love Maria," he insisted softly and, ignoring the bothersome burning in his cheek, touched his rowels lightly to the stallion's sides. The animal surged forward in response.

*How I wish that for once you were right in underestimating a woman, Carlo.*

In this case, however, he knew better.

The rectangular tilting field, which was being used this morn as a practice area, was marked by ropes hung with colorful pennants. They rippled and flapped in the breeze like bright-winged birds. Tiered benches flanked the two longer sides of the field with simple awnings stretched over them to protect the spectators from sun or drizzle. A large tent called a "refuge" stood across from one end of the field, where participants could don or remove their armor, have their injuries attended to, or just rest.

No particular preparations had been made, there hadn't been time. And since it wasn't to be a formal, full-sized tournament, the number of spectators, as well as participants, would be small.

Giulietta stalled as long as she dared before making an appearance. To her delight, Bernardo's sister Lucia arrived with her husband, and the two young women made their way to the viewing stands after catching up on gossip and news. Bernardo was there, as well, although he explained to Giulietta that Elisabetta was too near her time with their third child to travel to Monteverdi.

In spite of Lucia's chatter about events in Florence, Giulietta found herself watching the man dressed in simple black and white as he took his turn at the quintain, a pole with a sandbag attached at one end that pivoted on a board when a lance hit the small wooden target on the opposite end. If the contestant hit the target squarely, he passed safely under the sandbag. If his aim was off in the least, the sandbag swung around and knocked him from his horse.

There were fifteen or sixteen participants in all, including

Niccolò, Bernardo, Vittorio, Dante and Rodrigo. Leon and a few of the Sarzano retainers were participating also, as well as Paolo and several of Monteverdi's best mercenaries.

It was a hot, sultry August day, with only an intermittent puff of wind to stir the air which was redolent with the rich scents of late summer. An occasional cloud dotted the cerulean vault of the Tuscan sky.

The contestants wore little armor—mostly plated or scaled brigandines to protect their chests. To a man they evidently chose to eschew helms, for not only were the weapons to be blunt, but also, Giulietta suspected, because it was just too warm. Had it been a true battle—or even a formal tourney—more armor would have been worn. As it was, the impromptu contests did not warrant much heavy, protective gear for men or steeds.

First, to lend at least a touch of the pageantry that normally accompanied a tourney, each man who so chose rode up to the stands to receive a favor from his lady. Giulietta noted with satisfaction that Rodrigo da Valenti remained to the side, calmly watching as wives bestowed ribbons or bright scraps of cloth upon their husbands, or unwed ladies upon the men of their choice. When Leon rode his horse to stand before Giulietta, she made a deliberate show of tying a strip of cloth of silver to his lance.

A few applauded her gesture, for cloth of silver was very expensive—a most extravagant way of showing favor. When Giulietta cast a furtive glance through the spray of her long lashes at the very man she sought to ignore, she saw a dark-haired, barefoot Gypsy girl—was she the one she'd seen learning to play Valenti's lute?—walk shyly, hesitantly, toward him a scarlet ribbon streaming from one hand. Even from where she sat, Giulietta could make out Valenti's warm smile of obvious encouragement. He leaned over in the saddle and accepted her token with a flourish, saluted her smartly, and wheeled his ebony stallion away and toward the others gathering at one end of the field.

Unforeseen irritation uncoiled within Giulietta at the Gypsy girl's audacity. And it was then that she noticed a small group of *Zingari* standing to the side to observe the proceedings, including a tall, handsome older woman with streaks of white in her long, dark hair. She stood with all the bearing of a queen.

Maddalena, Giulietta guessed, Rodrigo da Valenti's grandmother.

That thought made her deliberately turn her attention to the quintain . . . but that activity provided only partial escape from her hectic thoughts and feelings. Every time Rodrigo da Valenti took his turn, although she pretended great interest in what the effervescent Lucia had to say about any subject Giulietta could think to introduce, of their own volition her traitorous eyes would peek through her lashes at the sound of the solid thwack of lance against wood. Her traitorous ears registered the resounding cheers that inevitably followed. And her traitorous memories conjured up vivid images of his lean, powerful form pressed against the length of her own. . . .

Of all the participants, only Dante and Rodrigo had not missed the crest on the target. Leon (a surprise to Giulietta) had only just been sandbagged on the turn before. Then, to Lucia's obvious horror, her father was sandbagged unexpectedly. He tumbled from his horse.

"He's too old for such things," Lucia exclaimed, concern mirrored in her soft brown eyes. "He's nearly fifty! Angelo and Nardo are in their prime—and Nicco is even younger—so 'tis natural. But why do our fathers feel the need to prove their prowess at their age?"

Giulietta smiled. " 'Twill be so as long as they both can sit a horse," she said. "Although Paolo appears to have more sense. See how the head of the castle guard watches from the sidelines!" Yet it was Paolo who rushed to Vittorio de' Alessandro's side after his tumble and helped him to his feet.

"Your father is tougher than you think, Lucia," Gianna told her daughter, appearing unruffled. "Look . . . your brother knows he's not so fragile as marzipan. He doesn't seem concerned."

"I must be getting overly protective," Lucia sighed, glancing over to where her two children were playing outside the fenced-in area under Lisa's watchful eye. She looked at Giulietta. "Having little ones can do that to a woman, I suppose." A sudden, sheepish grin softened her mouth.

Even from the distance, Giulietta could see the flush of obvious embarrassment in her uncle's cheeks. He waved a hand toward Gianna in obvious dismissal of his fall before he spun away to remount his horse.

Dante rode up to him and said something that made Vittorio laugh, and the brothers left the tilting field to watch the younger men who hadn't yet had enough. Giulietta watched as again and again, Rodrigo da Valenti hit the mark unerringly, untiringly.

"See how he struts and attempts to outshine the others like a *pavone,*" she said in a low voice to Lucia. "Peacock!"

Lucia, her eyes on Rodrigo, answered with a lift of her eyebrows, "In such subdued colors?" She shook her head. "Angelo said Valenti trained in France. We all know of the efficiency of King Charles's army. It forced the Italian states to their knees, so Angelo said. No wonder Valenti is so skilled." She narrowed her eyes as she continued to watch Rodrigo. "He is a handsome one, *si?* Like a dark angel . . ."

Giulietta shrugged, feeling the sweat trickle down her back beneath her lightweight gown, in spite of the protective awning above them. But they couldn't escape the humidity of the day, she thought, as a sharp twinge in her foot served as a sudden and unwelcome reminder of the reason she disliked Rodrigo da Valenti in the extreme. "If you like *Zingari*, I suppose," she answered her cousin. *And murderers*, she added silently, shrewishly, knowing full well that she was the only one who persisted in blaming him for Mario di Corsini's death.

With uncharacteristic singlemindedness she refused to examine her motives for continuing to do so.

She missed Lucia's questioning glance in her direction, so busy was she trying to find fault with Valenti. Neither did she feel Caressa's gaze upon her.

Perversely, every time Rodrigo da Valenti hit the target, her disapproval of him grew. Then Dante and Vittorio joined them. "Infantry is more important now," Dante said to the women, accepting a kerchief from Caressa and dabbing at his dripping brow. "Knights on horseback have seen their day, I'm afraid. Now they must dismount and face any adversaries on foot—'tis acknowledged by better tacticians."

Dante looked at Giulietta. "Sarzano is reputed to be quite skilled with a sword." There was a mute message in his bright eyes that Giulietta couldn't quite decipher. "But so are the Alessandros known for their exemplary swordplay. Your grandfather taught your uncle Vito and me and I taught Nardo and then Nicco . . . and had some influence on Rodrigo when he was younger." He paused, one blond eyebrow lifting. "Were you not impressed by his skill at the quintain, daughter?" Without waiting for her answer he added, "Nicco already worships him, and can learn even more from—"

" 'Tis Leon's skills that have made a favorable impression on me, Father. I don't see why my brother admires a—" She thought better of offering any insult to Rodrigo da Valenti when her father obviously was as taken with the man as Nicco was. "Er . . . admires Signor Valenti when Leon holds his own so impressively. His antecedents are excellent—a true nobleman born—and he handles himself as well as any I've seen."

"Ah. I see. And, in your long life you've seen so very much,

Giulietta *mia,* haven't you?" Amusement lit his eyes, but he didn't wait for an answer. To no one in particular, he said as he watched the men on the field, "I think when they are done, we'll retire to the keep for the hottest part of the day. We can resume in late afternoon then."

Giulietta watched as one by one each man was eliminated from the competition as the morning wore on. Each time Valenti hit the mark, Giulietta felt a contrary spurt of anger, until one of the servants brought Beau to her on a leash.

"He was whimpering, *madonna,*" the young page said in explanation. "Marina told me to take him to you." He handed her the leash, and the frisky pup flung its front paws onto her knees, his tail swishing furiously as his small, black nose investigated her lap.

She couldn't help but laugh, her irritation momentarily forgotten.

"He's beautiful," Lucia said. At the sound of her voice, the pup alertly lifted his head and glanced at her, then returned his attention to his new mistress. "Where ever did you get him? And what kind of dog is he?"

*"Le Grand Chien de Montagne,"* a male voice from just behind them answered. "A Pyrenees Mountain dog."

Valenti. Giulietta would know that voice and the fluent French *anywhere.* Lucia turned toward him as he stood respectfully beside Giulietta, obviously awaiting her permission to join them.

"Ah . . . you must be Signor da Valenti, *si?* "

Giulietta made the introduction through stiff lips, her gaze skimming over Rodrigo, as if he were of no consequence, when she pronounced his name. Suddenly it seemed as if the seats around them were emptying with dismaying speed. Giulietta glanced at the field as Beau transferred his exuberant attention to his former owner. The men were examining pieces of what appeared to be a suit of armor in a small cart to one side of the tilting field. Included in that group was Leon Sarzano.

Her earlier annoyance returned, much of it now directed at Leon, as well. Suddenly, it was of utmost importance that Lucia remain at Giulietta's side, for she had no wish to be alone with Rodrigo da Valenti . . . even with so many others in the vicinity.

"I am honored to make your acquaintance," he said politely, accepting Lucia's hand and briefly pressing his lips to it. Giulietta could think of no way to avoid asking him to join them without being rude.

"Please join us," she heard herself say, her eyes tracing the angry red lines across his right cheek. For some inexplicable reason, as he seated himself on the other side of Lucia, the sight of his injuries caused a queer little lurch deep within her . . .

"The dog is from France, then?" Lucia asked.

"Yes, given me by a priest who raised such dogs. He's indispensable to shepherds against wolves and bears, and also a valued sentry for chateaux—castles—in the area."

Beau made his way across Giulietta's lap, to Lucia's— briefly suffered her attentions—then enthusiastically clambered onto Rodrigo's black-clad knees in obvious recognition.

" 'Tis obvious he's attached to you," Lucia observed. She glanced at Giulietta, then back at Rodrigo and the pup. What she didn't say hovered in the air even more pronouncedly than her spoken words. *Why would anyone ever give up such a dog?*

Recalling her manners, before he could reply, Giulietta said, *"Grazi,* signore. Thank you for Beau."

The words hung in the air for a moment as their eyes met and held across Lucia.

" 'Twas my pleasure."

"I . . . understand we'll be seeing you regularly when we visit Castello Monteverdi," Lucia said.

Giulietta gave her a strange look.

Word certainly traveled fast, he thought, but answered simply, "If I accept His Excellence's offer. Your brother is excellent at the quintain," he added deliberately, changing the subject. "I met him some years ago and observed firsthand his ability with a sword, as well."

Giulietta stiffened at the reminder, searching suddenly for an excuse to escape his presence.

"Thank you," Lucia said with a smile. "Speaking of Bernardo . . ." She glanced over at the men standing around the cart across the field. "He's gesturing to me." She stood suddenly, and Rodrigo courteously did the same, crooking one arm about the wriggling Beau as she added, " 'Twas a pleasure making your acquaintance, Signor da Valenti. Giulietta, I'll see you inside later, *sì?*"

Then she was gone.

Giulietta stood, too. His hand on her arm startled her . . . and stopped her cold.

"Forgive my boldness," he said in a low voice, "but, I thought you might be interested in some of the history of the breed."

She looked at his bronzed fingers resting on the silk of her sleeve, then up into his deep blue eyes. "I would rather know, *signore,* just what kind of . . . *offer* you spoke of to Lucia. Why ever would you be seen regularly about Castello Monteverdi?"

He removed his hand, although not, Giulietta suspected, because she wished it, but rather because he chose to. "I regret that you aren't pleased at the prospect." He set down Beau, maintaining his hold on the leash

Her eyes narrowed at him. "Pleased? *Pleased?*" she said through set teeth, her voice low. "After you took deliberate advantage of me the other night? When you *knew* who I was, yet you dared seduce me like some common—"

His voice was calm, quiet, yet utterly firm. "There is nothing common about you, Mona Giulietta, nor was there anything in the least bit common about what we . . . about our meeting."

Her mouth tightened. Surely he thought her an *idiota* to be taken in by such unadulterated flattery.

He watched the changing expressions play across her face, knowing that perhaps an older, more experienced woman—one who knew him better—would have taken his words as they were meant.

But not Giulietta de' Alessandro. He was a fool a hundred times over, but he couldn't seem to help himself. It was as if he were compelled to leap out from the foliage again in the name of the Alessandro family, as he had six years past, in spite of the risk of appearing the fool.

Yet the last thing he wanted was to cause her distress. "And should anyone ever ask, it never happened."

*"I'll* know it happened! If your cheek weren't already cut . . . if we were alone, I would slap your face, signore!"

She ignored the voice that whispered, *What of your behavior after you returned to the keep in the chapel . . . ?* and watched the left corner of his mouth as it curved slightly. "You would be perfectly justified, *madonna,* although it's a little late. With all due respect, however, I don't think your response would be so violent."

Giulietta cast a quick, clandestine look around them, fearing someone would overhear their exchange. But it was as if everyone else had forgotten their existence. She felt perspiration gather beneath her arms, trickle down her ribs. Renewed warmth bathed her face. "If you possessed one bit of gentility, you would never imply that I *enjoyed* our . . . interlude. That

my response to you in any similar situation would be aught
but outrage!"

He turned his head and stared unseeingly across the tilting
field, his lean jaw suddenly looking as rigid as carved granite.
"What claim of gentility would a *Zingaro* ever have before a
prince's daughter?"

His answer gave her pause; not only the very words, but
the brittleness of them. Here, she thought, with a sudden, unexpected sense of triumph, was a chink in the armor of his
irritating confidence . . . and his unwelcome humor (his
mouth certainly wasn't curving now!). Rodrigo da Valenti
wasn't quite as even-natured—quite as imperturbable—as he
would evidently have the world believe.

And the evidence of that very susceptibility where his pride
was concerned was soothing salve to Giulietta's own; for *he*
seemed able to dismiss what they'd shared on a recent moonlit
night—what had been a major occurrence in her life—as
merely one more trophy among the scores of others he'd no
doubt collected in his dealings with women. Oh, how he must
have savored her fall! she thought. Yet here he was, obviously
upset by her reference to his failure to act the gentlemen.

That was because, as he'd said, he was not genteel . . . but
a Gypsy born. She'd evidently struck at the heart of his vulnerability.

*All men are equal, Giulietta. Don't ever forget that. Any
man may rise above his circumstances, for no one is born
noble, but rather becomes noble.*

Her darker side made her ignore her father's words, for they
didn't apply in Rodrigo da Valenti's case. He was a knave, a
scoundrel, a rogue . . . and had taken unfair and wicked advantage of her and her ignorance in matters of love, without
the slightest bit of remorse. And all the while knowing who
she was and the havoc he'd created in her life before he'd
blithely hied himself off to France.

"And your self-pity adds further proof of . . . other flaws, as well, signore." Some small part of her—a part that was still able to stand back and condemn her unkind observation—regretted the words the instant they were out of her mouth. But it was too late. There was no way she would ever apologize for anything to the man who'd committed such an outrage against her.

He slowly turned his head and looked at her, the blinders beginning to slip from his eyes. Could it really be, he thought in growing dismay, that the Giulietta de' Alessandro he'd held in his heart was truly a fantasy of his own making? A fantasy without substance, as Carlo had implied, that he'd nurtured over the years? Could any daughter of Durante de' Alessandro, his mentor and hero, be so unfeeling toward others? So unfairly judgmental?

Beneath her haughty gaze, he felt the urge to step away; but he resisted. Momentarily Rodrigo da Valenti felt as dirty and unworthy as he had some six years ago after he'd unnecessarily come to Bernardo de' Alessandro's defense.

But not for long. He'd learned too much over the past few years to ever give in to self-pity again, no matter what Dante's daughter believed. He would need time for his feelings to change . . . hopefully to whither away in light of not only the impossibility of ever meaning anything to her, but more importantly perhaps, in the wake of his disappointing discovery. Yet time was something he had. And mayhap the best thing for him would be to refuse Dante's offer—at least temporarily—until his disillusioned heart was healed.

Yet, such long-standing emotion—even infatuation—did not just die upon command. . . .

Giulietta sensed a subtle change in him. Surely she had gone too far and felt the impulse once again to take back her words. Her conscience writhed, but he had committed the first injustice. And, in her mind, it was irreparable.

"Other flaws as well?" he said quietly at last, then shrugged lightly. "So 'twould seem."

He committed to memory her beautifully animated face with one last lingering look. It was a sad and silent farewell, sadder than the farewell he'd mutely bade her the last time he'd held her in his arms, for in the bright light of day—before the lash of her animosity—she was no dream lover appearing to him like a nymph of the night.

Beau pulled at the leash at the approach of another. But for an endless-seeming moment, burning blue eyes met amber, the air between them rife with unspoken thoughts and powerful emotions.

"Your French armor is magnificent, signore!" came Leon Sarzano's voice, breaking into the seething silence.

Rodrigo dragged his gaze away first. "Your noble suitor is come," he said in a low voice as he watched Leon Sarzano approach them. His words were tinged with irony, his anger dissipating to a dull pain at the feeling of loss he was experiencing. But, then, he had experienced bitter disappointment and loss before.

*And she was never yours to lose, was she?* reminded a voice.

Rodrigo nodded in acknowledgement of Leon's compliment. "I cannot, however, take credit for the invention of such an ingenious piece of equipment." A fleeting impulse, born of sheer frustration, to plant his fist in Leon Sarzano's face came to him; but that would accomplish nothing. It wouldn't change the fact of his birth, or Giulietta de' Alessandro's enmity toward him.

Or, he thought with bleak irony, the fact that he had just witnessed one of his dreams—however unattainable—crumble to ashes.

"You are wonderful at the quintain," Giulietta said to Sarzano, suddenly feeling the words were inane in light of the

tension between her and Rodrigo da Valenti. She tried harder:
"If every man in Italy were so skilled, no one would dare say
the French army was superior, would they, Signore da Valenti?"

*Why, the little baggage,* he thought, feeling suddenly, inexplicably lighter of heart. She'd just brazenly put him in the
awkward position of having to compliment the man she obviously wished to wed. A man who looked at him—Rodrigo—
with more admiration than at her. And a man who possessed
more luck and perseverance than genuine talent as far as this
morning's competition had revealed to Rodrigo's trained eye.

"I think not," Rodrigo said graciously, fighting the urge to
laugh outright at her outrageous—and unmerited—flattery, and
thus embarrass the spoiled little minx.

Leon's face brightened at the compliment. *"Grazi,* Mona
Giulietta . . ." A light flush deepened the hue of his already
heat-pinkened cheeks as his eyes met Rodrigo's. ". . . Signore
da Valenti."

"My name is Rodrigo," he said mildly, noting the incon-
gruity of the noble Leon Sarzano addressing him so formally
after a morning spent together on a dusty tilting field.

He handed Beau's leash to Giulietta after scratching the pup
behind one ear. "And now, if you'll both excuse me, I think His
Excellence is motioning me over." He retrieved his discarded
brigandine and straightened. After a nod at Leon, who looked
suddenly disappointed, and the briefest of bows to Giulietta, he
moved away.

The old woman sat unobtrusively apart from the others, near
the end of the stands. She obviously wasn't a part of the main
group of onlookers nor was she with the *Zingari.*

Her clothing was that of a peasant, and the air around her
ripe with asafetida, a foul-smelling resin used by many of the
peasants to repel disease. In this case, however, it was meant

to ensure few would approach her—especially the nobility, even though she knew that her presence was unquestioned due to the Prince of Monteverdi's benevolence.

A loose cap concealing her hair above her dirty face, she watched the goings-on through exceedingly bright and alert eyes, all the while stroking a black cat concealed within the folds of her enveloping cape. She ignored the punishing sun and heat, her attention and all her concentration directed toward one man.

Every time he was successful at the quintain, she chuckled beneath her breath, even though she was consumed by hatred for him . . . had been every waking hour for many years now. Even her dreams were filled with images of him.

When the contests were discontinued during the hottest part of the day, she slipped from her perch quietly—and rather spryly for a bent and ancient one. No one appeared to notice as she made her way toward the trees and melted into the woods.

"But we'll be back, won't we?" she whispered to the cat. "We'll be back this eve . . ."

# Nine

After the warmest part of the day had passed . . . after a repast and rest for all, the contests of swordplay began. It was here that Rodrigo da Valenti showed his greatest skill.

The men were paired off; then as each man was eliminated, his victorious partner was matched with another winner. It came down, finally, to Bernardo and Dante, and Nicco and Rodrigo.

"At least the Alessandro family can still claim that ours are the best swordsmen instead of leaving the fighting skills to the *condottieri*," Caressa told Giulietta and Lucia.

"*Sì*," Lucia agreed. "But Angelo will have to practice more with Nardo—or *Zio* Dante—if he wishes to keep his male pride intact."

Giulietta made no comment, secretly resenting the elimination of Leon Sarzano by Rodrigo da Valenti. What right did Valenti have to be among the victorious Alessandro men?

*. . . I had some influence on Rodrigo when he was younger.* Dante's words from earlier in the day came back to Giulietta.

"Not everyone has had the benefit of an Alessandro for a tutor," she commented. Beau was in her lap, his muzzle over one knee, laying quietly as if he understood his new mistress's interest in the games. Glancing down at him, she suddenly saw the image of the animal's apparent joy at seeing Rodrigo da Valenti . . . of Beau remaining at his side until Rodrigo left.

Surely, she thought with a twinge of guilt, Beau had belonged to Rodrigo . . . and the two had formed a bond.

Why then, she wondered with a faint frown as she recalled Lucia's puzzled look earlier, had he given the dog to *her?*

The man was maddeningly difficult to understand.

The clash of steel rang through the air as Dante and his nephew dueled. The match was close, for Bernardo was twenty years younger than the uncle who had taught him many of his moves, yet Dante was still a master. When he knocked Bernardo's sword from his hand, the small crowd cheered, for it was meant that the prince be victorious.

Giulietta glanced over at the Gypsies who'd returned for the later contest. The girl whose favor Rodrigo now wore on his arm was present once more, as were the woman Giulietta assumed was Maddalena, the man who'd performed with Lily the night before, and several others. They were gaily clad, but neat-looking and clean from what she could discern. A twinge of guilt tweaked her conscience at her occasional unkind thoughts about them—especially when Rodrigo da Valenti was involved. They were no more unruly than the others in the stands, and very enthusiastic in cheering on Valenti.

Of course. He was one of their own.

Nearby, she also saw Aristo. His eyes were on the *Zingari*. More specifically, as far as Giulietta could tell, he appeared to be watching Maddalena.

Maddalena? She was a handsome woman, even from this distance. Could it be that Aristo had at long last found a lady love?

Her attention was drawn once again to the action on the field immediately before them. Dante and Rodrigo were the final duelists . . . and suddenly Giulietta was concerned about her father.

*You fear for the Prince of Monteverdi? An acknowledged*

*master of arms? A man whose participation in tournaments
was sought even outside of Tuscany when he was younger?*

Younger. That was the key word here. Giulietta glanced at
her mother. Caressa wore a slight smile as she watched her
husband speak to Rodrigo before they separated to begin. A
page offered each man a cup of water. Rodrigo took a swallow,
then grinned and poured the remainder over his head. Dante
laughed, and did the same. Giulietta could see the anticipation
in her father's eyes, even from where she sat. No one loved a
challenge more than Dante de' Alessandro.

She studied Valenti critically through narrowed eyes—and
soon forgot to look for perceived faults. His damp shirt stuck
to his torso, following the musculature of his shoulders and
chest. It was carelessly tucked into his black trunk hose, which
left little to the imagination without the fashionable hip-length
doublet, although black tended to shield with shadows, she
thought . . .

She wished his hose had been white.

And was instantly mortified by her very brazen and lusty
thought.

She glanced once more at her mother, this time guiltily. But
Caressa's attention was on her husband; and Lucia, who was
sitting beside Giulietta once again, was saying, "What a magnificent man! He's as beautiful as *Zio* Dante, but the opposite
in coloring."

"Dark devil," Giulietta muttered under her breath, then
added in a normal voice, "and Angelo should hear you!"

Lucia blushed. " 'Tis not as if we were newlyweds," she
said in her defense, then laughed. "But I'll be more prudent
with my opinions, Gietta," she said—and immediately whispered her next comment into Giulietta's ear. "Look at that
Gypsy girl watching Signor da Valenti as if he were a god.
And he still wears her ribbon. Do you think he loves her in
return?"

Giulietta glanced at Maria. Surely the expression on the girl's fine features could only be love, she realized with a start. What did it feel like to love someone outside of the family? she wondered. And, as Lucia had asked, did Valenti love the girl in return? Had he kissed her and held her in the same manner as he had Giulietta?

For some strange reason, the thought bothered her greatly.

". . . says he sings like an angel and plays the lute equally well," Lucia was saying.

Unbidden, Rodrigo da Valenti's beautiful voice echoed through Giulietta's mind. "I suppose you could say that, even if many of his songs are of French origin and sung in that language."

Lucia tore her gaze from Rodrigo to stare at her cousin. "Don't you think he's handsome?"

Giulietta shrugged. "If one likes outrageously arrogant, dark-skinned *Zingari*. Leon is more to my liking—a true gentleman with his fair good looks and—"

Dante called something to Rodrigo, snagging Giulietta's attention. The latter answered, and before his words died away, Beau scrambled from Giulietta's lap. The leash jerked from her loose grip, and before she could stop him, the pup bounded down the three benches below, dodging between a few surprised onlookers, and bounded joyfully toward Rodrigo.

As he playfully attacked Valenti's leg, the latter sent home his sword and picked up the dog. Giulietta could make out his wide grin as he held the pup toward the sky and shook him lightly with both hands. She couldn't make out his words, but the tone sounded gently admonitory.

"He but seeks to protect you," Dante called, his lips curving with good humor. "He knows who will prevail." Rodrigo's grin turned into an answering sound of mirth. "Rather he's congratulating me early, *principe*." He looked toward the stands, but the Gypsy girl came running over to him, her brightly colored skirt flaring about her bare feet and ankles.

She said something in a low voice, her eyes meeting Rodrigo's. He nodded and handed over Beau to her, then pointed toward Giulietta.

"Look," Lucia said. "She's coming to return him to you."

"He doesn't belong to me," Giulietta said without warning, her eyes on the approaching Maria. "I didn't know how close they were—how the dog was obviously Valenti's pet first." Her lips tightened as Maria came up to them—as she watched comely ankles peeking from under the *Zingara's* skirt as she stepped upon the lowest bench.

Breathlessly, the girl said, *"Perdonami, madonna,"* her olive cheeks coloring prettily, "but Rodrigo bade me return Beau to you."

Giulietta forced her lips to smile, her eyes to meet the soft, deep brown of the other girl's. She reached out reluctantly to take the pup. *"Grazi . . .* er?"

"Maria, *madonna."*

"Maria, then. *Grazi,* but I see your Rodrigo has a self-serving streak."

Lucia looked at Giulietta as if she had two heads. Maria frowned, obviously puzzled. "Mona Giulietta . . . ?"

"I had no idea Beau was so attached to Signore da Valenti . . . obviously his first master," she said in an undertone, for others—including her mother—were looking their way. "I will take him for now, but 'twas cruel of Valenti to ever give him away. I will have to return him after the games."

"Forgive my boldness—" Maria visibly drew in a deep breath, as if to gather courage—"but he wanted to give you something—His Excellence the prince told him you loved animals and hadn't had a dog of your own in years."

*And how do you know all this?* Giulietta wanted to ask. Instead, she said defensively. " 'Twas still unkind of him to

confuse Beau here, however well-intentioned he was." All the
while she spoke, she studied the Gypsy girl's face, and the
glossy dark hair hanging free about her shoulders.

*Don't stare. 'Tis rude.*

She dragged her wandering gaze upward from the smooth,
olive skin just above the bright red of Maria's simple, scoop-
necked blouse.

"The only other animal he owns is Morello," Maria explained, then looked down at her feet in obvious embarrassment for having revealed so much in Rodrigo da Valenti's
defense.

Caressa was there then, gently interceding. "Such a sacrifice
would have been beyond courtesy—or even affection," she said
to Maria with a smile. A *condottiere* is very dependent upon
his horse, is he not, Maria?"

"Aye." Giulietta watched her brighten suddenly. Caressa had
the ability to make everyone with whom she came in contact
feel comfortable with her, and important in his or her own
right. "He could havè given you Lily, *madonna,*" Maria said
guilelessly to Giulietta, breaking into her musings, "but what
would you have done with a bear?"

Caressa and Lucia laughed aloud. Under the circumstances,
Giulietta didn't see much humor in the girl's words. But she
forced a smile.

"Thank you for returning Beau," she said, "but—"

"They're beginning," Nicco's voice came to them, and suddenly Lucia was sitting forward, her eyes on the field directly
before them. With a bob of her head and a shy smile, Maria
swung away to leave them.


Rodrigo drew his sword and positioned himself across from
Dante. He faced an unexpected dilemma. Should he give his
all and, in the process, probably triumph over the prince?

Surely Dante would realize if he held back, for it was difficult to fool Monteverdi's prince. And also, if he prevailed, Rodrigo had no doubt he would earn Giulietta's further enmity . . . if such a thing were possible.

But that shouldn't even enter into it, his reasonable side reminded him as they crossed swords and awaited the signal to begin. He suspected that he couldn't arouse any more of her hostility if he tried. And it wasn't supposed to matter anymore . . . hadn't he just decided only hours earlier?

It wasn't through conceit or arrogance that Rodrigo knew he would probably win. He was more than a score of years younger than Dante, and had just returned from a place where he'd absorbed every detail of swordplay available from the finest instructors, for it was to be his way of making a living.

He became aware of Maria's red ribbon still tied to his left arm as it stirred with the breeze. He should give this contest his all—and prove to anyone who cared to acknowledge it that an illegitimate Gypsy could become a skilled *condottiere*. Among other things.

He made his decision. To hell with Dante's unsullied reputation as a splendid fighting man. And to hell with his overpampered and selfish daughter.

"First blood!" Dante called out.

Several voices raised in concern, and, in spite of his newly-made decision, Rodrigo groaned inwardly. He had no wish to wound Dante, and first blood would make the contest all the more dangerous.

"What are the stakes?" called Vittorio as they stood poised.

"The stakes are between Rodrigo and myself," Dante called back. His eyes, bright with challenge, held Rodrigo's suddenly wary gaze.

Then his low-spoken, unexpected words for Rodrigo's ears alone, were almost the younger man's undoing. "My daughter's hand in marriage, Valenti."

Rodrigo's dark brows lifted in unconcealed astonishment.

Dante nodded. "If you best me, she is yours. And all the dowry and prestige that goes with becoming her husband. . . . Do you accept?"

Before Rodrigo could even absorb this turn of events—let alone answer—the signal was given and Dante, taking advantage of his opponent's immediate surprise, applied enough pressure against Rodrigo's sword to send him stumbling backward.

The onlookers cheered their prince. Carlo's voice came from where the Gypsies stood. "A poor beginning, Rigo," he shouted. "Is that what they taught you in France? To retreat?"

His brother's deliberately taunting words were enough to jar Rodrigo from his shock. He automatically assumed a defensive position and struggled to redirect his concentration.

*All the more reason to allow him the victory. You've already decided she's the last woman you would want for your own . . .*

Or is she?

Dante came at him then, with a cleverly executed slicing motion.

Rodrigo spun away with the smooth agility of a dancer. Cheers sounded from the Gypsies, but suddenly he wasn't aware of anything save the two of them and the duel. He feinted to the right; Dante anticipated his move and leaned left to counter the swing.

"You were always good at feinting," the prince said.

"And you taught me how to do it." He lunged forward before his words died away and moved to knock Dante's weapon from his hand. The latter responded by arcing his sword upward and then circling downward and across from right to left with both hands on the hilt to create a lethal, horizontal swipe. The blades met with the resounding song of steel stopping steel.

"So you want to get fancy, eh, *principe?*" Rodrigo queried with a half-grin.

"Show me what you learned from the French masters," Dante challenged in answer as he swung his sword upward again and, circling downward to the right with a mighty *whoosh* of the blade's passage, forced Rodrigo to perform a double-footed jump to avoid the lower horizontal arc.

"This!" the latter said, and whirled about like a dervish. He performed the exact same move on the prince, who was forced to jump in turn. Then, before Dante could riposte, Rodrigo's sword continued its counterclockwise motion, this time higher, to rip Dante's shirt.

The prince jumped back with admirable nimbleness. "No blood drawn," he said, shaking his head after glancing down at his chest.

Rodrigo felt his heart sink, for he hadn't nipped the skin. He had no wish to hurt Durante de' Alessandro, however slightly. And a shallow cut inflicted merely to draw blood was difficult to perform with any kind of certainty . . . and especially with an opponent striving to put every last bit of his skill behind his moves.

But no man was invincible. Certainly advancing age guaranteed that fact. Rodrigo had to put his close relationship with his opponent aside . . . for he had not only his own reputation to establish here in Tuscany, but if for any reason he deliberately allowed Dante to win, rather than proving the measure of his love for his mentor (in spite of Dante's ensuing anger should he catch on), it would be an insult to him with his daughter's hand in marriage at stake.

But surely the prince hadn't really meant what he'd said. . . .

Dante lunged, breaking up Rodrigo's thoughts, and for moments they stood stalemated blade to blade, of equal height and, so it appeared, skill, yet nearly as opposite in coloring as two men could be.

The spectators urged them on noisily, enthusiastically, and Rodrigo read the supreme challenge in Dante's eyes: *Best your old master . . . and take his daughter as reward.*

Surely this was proof of the Prince of Monteverdi's love for him, for he obviously wanted Rodrigo to be a part of the Alessandro family.

Rodrigo suddenly felt his energy level rise with excitement, with determination. He cut everything from his thoughts save winning. If he injured Dante de Alessandro, no one could blame him, for the Lord of Monteverdi himself had called for first blood.

With a mighty shove by Rodrigo, their swords disengaged with a shrieking scrape. The steel weapons flashed in the waning sunlight of late afternoon, crisscrossing with resounding regularity, singing an irregular and dissonant song of battle, yet without either contestant drawing blood.


The sight of the two men matching swords brought unwelcome memories crashing over Giulietta. Mario di Corsini had been fair—almost as fair as her father; and she was now forced to remember and acknowledge the remarkable litheness, the promise of consummate skill, in Rodrigo da Valenti the youth as he'd employed Bernardo's sword.

"Gietta?" Caressa's soothing voice came to her. She glanced up, and saw that her mother had changed places with Lucia. Caressa's hand over her own tightly fisted fingers was calming.

"He'll kill him," Giulietta murmured. "Surely—"

" 'Tis a friendly contest, Gietta *mia,* not a duel to the death." Her hand worked over Giulietta's fingers, kneading them, loosening them. "Look how your father is enjoying it!"

But Giulietta found it impossible to view the match in the same spirit as her mother.

The faces of both men shone with sweat, their shirts clung

like second skins. Then Dante jumped for the third or fourth time (Giulietta had lost count) to avoid another scythe-like pass of Rodrigo's blade . . . and turned his ankle as he landed.

Quick to take advantage, Valenti retained his two-handed hold on the sword and swiftly drove it upward to knock Dante's weapon from his hand. The prince skipped backward, almost out of Rodrigo's range, but not quite. In a flash, Rodrigo's sword tip whistled through the suddenly quiet air and nicked the prince's upper arm. Blood blossomed over his pale yellow shirtsleeve, and the *Zingari* sent a roar of approbation ringing through the field and stands.

Rodrigo held out one hand to the prince, who accepted it and jumped to his feet with a nimbleness that belied his age. Incongruously, he wore a grin. "Do you realize what you've just accomplished, you young whelp?"

Rodrigo glanced toward where Giulietta sat, her lovely face a study in concern for, obviously, her father. He looked back at the prince, their hands still clasped. *"Dio,* but I've my work cut out for me now," he said, and threw back his head in sudden laughter, feeling inexplicably exultant, in spite of his lingering doubts. "She'd just as soon take her vows at Santa Lucia as wed me," he added under his breath when his laughter subsided.

Dante retrieved his sword, sheathed it, and put an arm about Rodrigo's shoulders. They walked toward the stands in relaxed camaraderie. "Gietta doesn't know what she wants . . . or needs," the prince told him with a grin. He ran his free arm across his sweat-streaked brow.

"You're truly serious about this?" Rodrigo asked, apprehensive about an answer either way.

"I am. This was decided, *figlio mio,* back when you first went to France. He cut a sideways glance at Rodrigo. "Giulietta won't appreciate the fact that she's been unwed for two years longer than necessary because of your obstinance."

*She won't appreciate* anything *you have to tell her this day,* Rodrigo thought, and braced himself for the worst.

Afterward, festivities were held in the great hall. As always Dante invited the participants from the games, and generously included the Gypsies as well to partake in what he called "a very special celebration."

It was a rowdy ebullient gathering, rather than a formal dinner, for the prince was, in an exceptionally exuberant mood. His turquoise eyes glowed with deviltry, and his behavior was certainly not that of a man who'd just been dethroned as the most skillful swordsman in Tuscany.

The dancing began even before some of the guests were finished eating. Giulietta watched as Rodrigo danced to the wild strains of the Tarantella with none other than Maria. In light of his lively performance, it was obvious he was far from fatigued after his participation in the earlier games. He also seemed totally attentive to the lovely Gypsy girl.

Giulietta was, against her will, fascinated by his movements. He had donned clean clothing, and beneath the deep purple and white parti-colored trunk hose he wore, his long and finely turned legs worked effortlessly as he moved across the floor. She could almost feel the power of those lean but well-defined leg muscles, and an odd feeling fluttered to life deep within her, reminding her of what had passed between them on a moon-bathed Tuscan night.

Angry with herself, Giulietta searched the hall for Leon Sarzano. Her gaze didn't wander for long, for the man she supposed was her would-be suitor had been engrossed in a conversation with two of his retainers for much of the evening. Did the man talk about anything else but his son and war? she thought peevishly.

Then Nicco grabbed her hands and pulled her from her seat.

"Come, Gietta. Show those *Zingari* that they are not the only ones who can do justice to the Tarantella."

Grateful for any action that would consume her pent-up irritation and energy, she compiled without hesitation and gave herself to the vigorous dance with a suddenly joyous abandon. She loved music and dancing, like her father, and was never the least inhibited by shyness, or even decorum. She was a good dancer, and she knew it; she also loved the compliments she inevitably received on her grace and rhythm.

However, the new salve Aristo had concocted for her could only do so much. It had worked well enough to allow Giulietta to forget about her injury—as had the new binding to protect it. The foot had begun to heal, but as she gave herself up to the dance, the salve's numbing properties began to wear off.

She gritted her teeth, kept her smile in place and continued to dance, determined not to be outdone by a Gypsy wench with bare feet and whirling skirts. Her hair came loose and flew about her shoulders as she accompanied Nicco about the floor, and her face took on the fine sheen of exertion. But she loved the activity and the attention.

And certainly the distraction . . .

Until the balm finally wore off and her foot protested beneath the weight of her body. She began to go down, and was aware of her brother grabbing for her . . .

But another pair of capable arms intervened to catch her before she hit the floor. She was swept up in a firm embrace, but it wasn't Nicco's. Oh, no, she thought with annoyance, it would have to be the *hero* of the day.

She looked up into the striking eyes of Rodrigo da Valenti . . . and wished heartily that she could have suddenly sprouted wings and escaped the infinitely unwelcome entrapment of his arms.

"You shouldn't be dancing, *cara,*" he told her as he carried her off the dance floor. Maria's anxious expression as she and

Nicco followed them only fueled her temper, which was now simmering in the wake of this newest humiliation.

"Pray tell me what right you have to use such an endearment?" she gritted, conscious of the latent strength in his neck and shoulders beneath her reluctantly clinging arms.

*"Perdonami,"* he apologized. "I forgot myself."

"It seems to be a regular habit of yours," she replied, flinging his apology back into his face. "Not asking forgiveness but, rather, taking advantage of a maiden's indisposition."

He set her down at one of the tables that had been pushed to the side of the huge hall, handling her as if she were made of the most fragile Murano glass. This was lost upon her, however, as she noted Maria's face peering over his shoulder before he straightened. "Are you hurt, Mona Giulietta?" she asked, her voice full of genuine concern.

In spite of everything, Giulietta could detect the sincerity that seemed to be part of the girl's rather simple nature, and felt unexpected guilt for her ungenerous thoughts about her.

She summoned a smile for Maria—and Nicco, who stood beside her. "I—I just turned my ankle, Maria. 'Tis nothing really."

Rodrigo noted the warmth in her eyes, the kindness in her voice, as she spoke to Maria, and instantly forgave her ungracious rejection of his lightly given apology.

Then Caressa and Aristo were there. "What is it, *nina?"* Caressa asked as Aristo bent over her, his body positioned between the injured toot and her anxious mother. She exchanged a meaningful look with the dwarf before answering.

"I just twisted my ankle," she said, and waved one hand in dismissal. "I shouldn't have jumped into the Tarantella without first trying a less strenuous dance, *si?"*

Rodrigo noted how the smile she turned on her mother animated her lovely countenance. He noticed, too, how the brightness from a sunny day outside had brought out the sprinkling

of freckles over the bridge of her tip-tilted nose . . . and
wished silently that just one time she would gift him with such
a smile.

*Romantic fool.*

The Tarantella ended just then, the musicians in the gallery
put aside their instruments, stood and stretched.

"I believe Mona Giulietta should retire briefly from the festivities so I can tend her ankle," Aristo said.

" 'Let me see," Caressa said, but Rodrigo's hand on her arm
stopped her from bending to look at her daughter's foot.

For the first time since meeting Rodrigo da Valenti, Giulietta
was grudgingly grateful for his quick thinking.

" 'Tis not so bad as that—I caught a glimpse as I lifted
her," he reassured Caressa. "And I think," he added for her
ears alone, " 'twould embarrass her unduly."

Caressa looked at her daughter's flushed cheeks and obviously realized the condition was more from embarrassment
than exertion. She straightened and nodded, with a special
smile for Rodrigo. "Then go with Aristo," she said, brushing
back an escaped lock of Giulietta's strawberry-blond hair. "You
can return after—"

"My good friends and family," thundered a voice suddenly.

All eyes went to a table that had been pushed toward the
center of the hall. The Prince of Monteverdi stood upon the
board, one hand on his hip, the other holding a gold chalice
raised high in a dramatic gesture perfectly suited to Durante
de' Alessandro.

As silence gathered in the hall, Giulietta wondered what he
could have to announce that would merit interrupting the festivities. . . . His cheeks were flushed from drinking and dancing, and he looked around until he spotted Caressa. And,
standing directly beside her, Rodrigo.

Giulietta couldn't tell that, however. She saw her father's
gaze resting on Caressa, a very natural occurrence, for he

openly shared all things with her mother and cared not one whit what others thought of it.

One by one, all eyes went to the prince. . . .

Suddenly, Giulietta thought of Leon. Her gaze sought him out from the bench where she sat, but he was impossible to see now through those milling about the hall. Tension burgeoned within her. Had this announcement aught to do with her long-awaited and much-anticipated betrothal?

*You don't really want to marry Leon, do you?* queried the unsettling voice of doubt. *He's hardly spoken to you all day, or evening for that matter* . . .

Her gaze went to Rodrigo da Valenti—why, she couldn't say. He was watching her through the tangled screen of his dark lashes—oh, yes . . . she knew how to do the same! Yet his gaze cut to Dante so quickly that she thought she might have imagined it.

"In keeping with my exceptional mood this eve, I am pleased to announce in a most exceptional—and unconventional—manner the overdue betrothal of our fair daughter, Giulietta Maria." He paused with a grin and took a swallow of his wine, then gestured with the chalice in Giulietta's direction. "Will you stand, *cara mia?*"

Suspicion gripped her as Rodrigo turned his darkly beautiful countenance toward her, this time his burning-blue gaze openly caressing her, delving into hers. . . . Not even Caressa's hand on her arm could begin to counter the premonition of disaster that suddenly loomed over her like a Damoclean sword.

"To . . ." Dante paused for effect, and Giulietta felt a roaring in her ears, ". . . Signore Rodrigo da Valenti." He lifted his chalice once again.

The roar that went up from the revelers in the hall blended with the crashing sounds in her head as Giulietta stared, stunned and disbelieving, into Rodrigo da Valenti's face.

# Ten

Rodrigo's expression softened instantly as the shock registered on her face. He held out his hand in a conciliatory offering. "He's motioning for us to join him," he said close to her ear beneath the noise surrounding them. "Can you walk?"

Can you walk? *Can you walk?* . . .

Her father had just destroyed any chance she had for happiness, and he was asking her if *she could walk?*

Concern creased his brow. "Shall I carry you?"

Oh, aye, she thought as anger purged the numbness that threatened her. Wouldn't he like *that!* Carry her to her father before all and sundry like some prize he'd won in a tournament. . . .

Tournament? Prize? For one blistering moment those words sounded an alarm in the back of her beleaguered mind.

*The stakes are between Rodrigo and myself* . . .

No, her father wouldn't do such an unthinkable thing to her. . . .

*And why not?* asked an imp. *Look at him up on the board . . . confident, beloved by all, the munificent master of Monteverdi.* And, from the glow in his eyes, the flush in his cheeks, Il Leone was recklessly heady with wine.

Rodrigo guided her from the shelter of the surrounding concerned faces: Caressa . . . Nicco . . . Aristo . . . the Gypsy girl. . . . Even Leon's face appeared unexpectedly among a host of others, his expression hardly disappointed, but rather, fixed in admiration upon his champion.

She allowed Rodrigo da Valenti to lead her like a sheep to the slaughter because she could do nothing else. She might rail and scream—tear at her hair, rake her nails down his face and open his cuts anew—but in the end it would only make her look the fool.

Because when all was said and done, Durante de' Alessandro had absolute authority over her. He could consign her to a nunnery or wed her to a frog if he so chose. He could make her scrub floors until her fingers bled, or confine her to a bolstered bed surrounded by sweets and pets and eunuch guards until she lost her mind from boredom or grew as fat as a sausage if he so chose.

Yet, Giulietta knew exactly how much her father loved her— and that she had dared much in many instances, and gotten away with the same almost as many times.

She doubted whether the betrothal papers were signed yet. And she wouldn't go along with this travesty without a fight.

She stepped heavily—savagely—upon her hurt foot, perversely welcoming the pain. Maybe her foot would fester; then her leg would shrivel and drop off . . . and even Rodrigo da Valenti wouldn't want a wife with only one leg.

As they neared the table where her father awaited them, she released Rodrigo's hand and straightened her shoulders. With a regal lift of her head, she moved toward Dante, refusing to allow her pain or her anger to show. She was an Alessandro, and she would conduct herself like one before all those present.

"Caressa!" Dante cried out then, as they approached the table. "And Niccolò! Join us!"

By the increased volume in the cheering throng around them, Giulietta guessed her mother and brother were behind them. Oh, indeed, her father knew how to play the crowd . . . how to milk the moment.

He stepped down to meet them—kissing his daughter's hand with great ceremony, then hugging Rodrigo to him enthusiastically. He hugged Nicco, and then lifted Caressa to whirl her round once before setting her on her feet again.

And the people loved it. They loved their prince. They loved his family. And they were obviously delighted that a husband had been found for the lively and lovely Giulietta de' Alessandro. . . .

"If you think for one *moment* that I'll go along with this, you're sadly mistaken!" Giulietta said under her breath to the man beside her. She was sitting on a divan in the antechamber of her parents' room, her leg propped up on a pillow beneath a light cover. Dante was speaking to a man in the corridor and arranging for the drawing up of the betrothal papers.

They were alone for a time, and Giulietta took advantage of her chance to lash out at Rodrigo da Valenti, libertine and opportunist.

He was standing beside a small writing table, a goblet of wine in one hand, his other idly tracing its way over the glass-smooth, polished top. With her words, his fingers stopped. He lifted his eyes to hers. "This was as much of a surprise to me as it was to you."

Her look turned disdainfully disbelieving. "Then tell my father you refuse!"

His brows raised slightly. "I'm not in the habit of insulting a lady, *madonna*. Even if she may deserve a dressing down." His eyes held hers, and even from across the small room she could feel his powerful pull on her senses. "And any man would be totally out of his mind," he added levelly, "to refuse the hand of the Prince of Monteverdi's daughter, even were you ugly as a crone with a razor-honed tongue to match."

She pulled in a deep, steadying breath. "Tell my father you don't wish to wed me or . . ."

His lashes lowered briefly before he delved into her gaze once again and asked softly, "Or what?"

Giulietta glanced at the partially open door of the antechamber. "Or I'll tell my father what happened the other night."

In the absolute silence that followed her threat, the voices from the passageway floated into the room. Then Rodrigo walked toward the divan until he stood within an arm's length of her. He crouched down beside her, until their eyes were almost level. "You may tell him what you like, Giulietta *mia*," he said, his breath brushing lightly across her cheek even as his lips caressed her name, "but any way you tell it, you are ruined."

He watched her mouth tighten and felt a nagging sense of regret. Yet he wouldn't allow her to turn the tables so completely as to put him on the defensive when they both knew the truth. Even Giulietta de' Alessandro had to acknowledge her part of the guilt, if only to herself. He wouldn't allow her to get away with such self-serving tactics.

He sincerely hoped her character was better than that. It had to be, for Dante and Caressa de' Alessandro could never raise so selfish a child.

*And surely you are a naive fool to fall back on normally sound judgment when your heart has more say than your head right now.*

"Perhaps," she answered, her eyes darkening, "and most especially with a lowborn man who knows naught of good manners."

Never in her seventeen years had she referred derogatorily to another human being's circumstance of birth. One part of her was appalled; but the darker, angry side firmly held the upper hand.

*"Perdonami, per favore,"* he said, his voice low and laced

with sarcasm, "but this ignorant Gypsy did not know that among some, lying is counted among good manners, as is, evidently, refusing to accept the repercussions of ones . . . behavior."

"In spite of your threat, *signore,* I can go to Santa Lucia," she interjected with vigor, "while *you* are left to deal with my father's wrath for your part in our . . . meeting."

"Then mayhap you should tell His Excellence about your very real desire to serve God. It seems to be your fondest wish, in spite of your very sensual nature."

"You are vile!" she said through set teeth. But even as her ire mounted, Giulietta found her eyes drawn to the healing gashes on his cheek.

"On the other hand," he added, obviously unperturbed by her statement, "if I tell him what happened near the camp—whether your version or mine—he could very well use that as further proof of the necessity for this union. He might even arrange for an immediate marriage."

*That* reasoning broke the spell that the sight of his cut cheek had momentarily cast over her, thus giving her the impetus to drop her gaze to the foot peeping out from the coverlet—and why was she so oddly affected by the sight of that marred flesh? For some strange reason, her toes were cold when the rest of her body was warm from anger and wine and the close proximity of Rodrigo da Valenti—much as she would have liked to deny the latter.

"Are you cold?" he asked softly. Before she could answer, he was covering her foot, the brush of his warm fingers across her toes oddly erotic. She remembered, in spite of her wish to do otherwise, how he'd ministered to that very foot not long ago, causing sensations that had nothing to do with the injury, to shoot up her leg and wreak sensual havoc.

She resisted the urge to jerk up her knee as her father entered the room. His gaze alighted on them just as Rodrigo straightened from covering Giulietta's foot. "Ah . . . I see you two are getting further acquainted," he commented with a smile. Before either of them could answer, he added, "The papers will be ready on the morrow. Shall we drink once again to the upcoming nuptials?"

Rodrigo suspected Dante knew how his daughter smoldered inside but chose to act as if nothing were amiss. He would have to remember that tactic. . . .

Dante offered Rodrigo more wine, then handed a goblet to Giulietta. " 'Twill help the pain in your ankle, daughter," he said.

She studied his face as she accepted the wine, and noted the buoyancy in his expression, his every move. Like the victor in a battle, she thought darkly. He was even more animated than usual, and the reason was no secret now.

"I hope you didn't just decide my . . . *fate* on the tourney field?" she asked sweetly.

Dante's fair brows raised momentarily then a smile curved his mouth. "Of course not, Gietta *mia*. Your secured future was too important to your mother and me to ever treat it so casually." He replaced the terra-cotta ewer back on the desk and gave her his full attention. "This was decided almost six years ago, although even Rodrigo here was unaware of my intentions." He moved toward Rodrigo and put an arm about his shoulders. His smiling eyes met the younger man's. "This match has been one of my fondest dreams, and your mother's, as well," he said with a look at Giulietta. "For many reasons, this is a great day for the House of Alessandro."

Rodrigo hid his expression as he looked down into his goblet. "You flatter a humble soldier, *principe*," he said quietly. "And, perhaps, offend Mona Giulietta."

Giulietta felt heat rise in her face, for he had hit the nail right on the head. She watched him as he drank, then lowered the goblet and met her look. For some reason she suddenly couldn't hold his gaze. Was it because of the sincerity that infused his voice, which would indicate that he was much less arrogant than she wanted to believe? Or was it because, no matter how much she might detest him, she couldn't deny that he had some strange and unwelcome hold over her physically and emotionally?

Dante squeezed Rodrigo's shoulder. "A man's occupation is in no way a true measure of his worth—I tried to instill that philosophy into both my children. Yet you displayed your skills this afternoon to the point where there can be no question that you are no mere humble soldier. I am pleased with what I've seen and heard, Rigo, and look forward to having you in our family. As for offending my daughter, how is that possible?" He looked at Giulietta, a slight frown furrowing his forehead; her eyes skittered away from his questioning look.

Rodrigo made note of that strategy, as well.

"Unless she carries some grudge from that unfortunate day when Mario di Corsini died purely by accident," Dante added.

*Tell him!* screamed a voice within Giulietta. *Tell him about the other night!*

But she couldn't bring herself to reveal either of their actions that night, for Rodrigo had been right. As much as her pride might force her to deny it, reason reminded her that she was just as guilty as he was. And, contradictorily, that shameful fact only served to deepen her animosity toward him.

"I know better than that, Papa. I was there." *But that doesn't mean I accept Valenti!* she added in silent rebellion.

"Good! Then we can sign the documents as soon as they are drawn up on the morrow, Rigo." He grinned boyishly. "I have such plans!" he exclaimed. "Nicco is my heir, *sì,* and will make a fine leader for Monteverdi one day; but my daughter's forthcoming union with the man I consider a second son has its own special importance to me." He paused, his look turning thoughtful as he studied Giulietta. "There's no reason to wait, either. You've waited long enough, haven't you, *nina?*"

"But what—what of Leon Sarzano?"

"Sarzano?" He shook his head with a moue. "You'd never suit. And whether you realize it or not, Gietta, that point is important to your mother and me. Now, shall we set the date for some time in October?"

Dismay broke over Giulietta in a tidal wave. October? It was almost September now! And Leon Sarzano had just been dismissed as a prospective bridegroom with a single shake of the head? She opened her mouth to object, but Rodrigo spoke first. "I doubt 'tis enough time for proper preparations, *principe.* And Mona Giulietta obviously needs some time to adjust to the . . . idea."

Giulietta completely missed the generosity of his gesture, the compassion that softened his face as he watched her.

"After Christmas," she blurted in a panic.

Dante nodded, but Rigo said, "Spring is the time for weddings . . . is it not, *madonna?*"

She stared at him, unable to speak for a moment.

*"Sì.* May is a beautiful month," Dante agreed while Giulietta tried to absorb the rapid decisions being made. Decisions that would be the beginning of the end for her, she was certain. . . .

*"Ebbene,"* Dante said, bending over to kiss his daughter's forehead. "The wedding will take place the beginning of May."


"So your forbidden but most cherished wish is coming true. You will take the breathtaking Giulietta to wife, and in the bargain become a part of the Alessandro family." Carlo nodded his head slowly, like an old wise man who'd pronounced some long-awaited, profound piece of wisdom to a younger disciple.

They sat beside the dying embers of one of the campfires. It was just before dawn, and Rodrigo had tired of tossing and turning on his bed in Maddalena's caravan. He'd risen and quietly left the wagon to sort out his thoughts and feelings . . . and on the way had caught sight of Giulietta's pale yellow slippers in the dimness, a poignant reminder of what had happened the other night. A brief burst of memories showered through him. They reinforced the fact that although he would one day soon possess Giulietta's hand in marriage, the less tangible but infinitely important aspects of Giulietta the woman—her love and respect—might elude him forever.

Then, too, was the consideration that he might become unhappy and disillusioned with Dante's daughter, and the prospect of such an emotionally unrewarding union was disturbing to him. He'd never entertained ideas of marrying for anything but actual love—he was that much of a romantic, he'd admitted to himself long ago. He was also disillusioned enough with the nobility to fly in the face of as many of their customs as possible; therefore wedding for love appealed to him for more than one reason.

He wasn't penniless anymore, and would have little trouble forming his own mercenary company, he knew. He also knew he would never fit in with the aristocrats for whom he had such ambivalent feelings. Therefore, even if some noblewoman were within his reach, he felt no need to wed to enhance his station in life. While Durante de' Alessandro had taught him that a man should always strive to be the best he could be, at the same time one had to learn to accept what one was and appreciate whatever one had.

Things had suddenly changed, however. Now he found himself in what many would consider a most enviable position, yet he dreaded rejection by the woman who would have enchanted him even had she been a humble farmer's daughter.

His head began to ache with his churning thoughts, and he drew up his knees, placed his elbows upon them and sat contemplating the ground with his fingers splayed through his hair.

Carlo, who knew him better than anyone, had come to him out of the shadows then, like an echo of Rodrigo's restlessness.

"You'll have everything a man could want," he said after hunkering down beside Rodrigo and allowing the silence to stretch out comfortably. "Surely you can only be happy!"

Rodrigo dropped his hands and met his friend's look head-on. "I am not *every* man. Remember, brother, what Maddalena used to tell us when we were children? *'Be careful what you wish, for you might get it.'*"

Carlo gave a low laugh. "I should have such troubles." He punched Rodrigo soundly on the shoulder. "The worst that could happen is that she won't love you, and *that,* Rigo, is minor. There are scores of women willing to give you what she might not. Once you get over your initial disappointment—if that proves to be the case—all you'll ever need from her is *bambini* with Alessandro blood running through their veins. You can get the rest elsewhere."

Rodrigo swiveled his head and stared into the darkness, his expression somber. "Don't give me advice, brother, that you wouldn't follow."

"Ahh, I see." Carlo sat and crossed his legs. "What makes you think that I wouldn't do the same were I in your position? Just because I love Laura and our children doesn't mean that I wouldn't seek solace elsewhere if things were different."

Rodrigo merely shook his head in reply.

Carlo placed one hand briefly upon Rigo's knee. "Your pride is getting in the way now. Take whatever life offers you, Rigo . . . or, in this case, the Prince of Monteverdi!" He chuckled under his breath. "What have you to lose? You can still set up your Free Company if you wish—you know the prince will let you live your life as you wish. And if you must, find a woman to fill that empty space in your heart . . . no one can condemn you for such a thing if you are discreet."

Rodrigo tossed a short stick onto the embers and watched

it smolder with narrowed eyes. "Men have strayed for less than lack of love, I suppose."

"Indeed. For much less."

The silence stretched out.

Then, without warning, Rodrigo looked back at Carlo, the curve of his mouth just visible in the deep shadows. "But we haven't taken into account the fact that I'm at heart an optimist. Dante once hinted that my father was good-natured, and so whoever he was, he unwittingly passed on a valuable trait." In the face of Carlo's expectantly raised eyebrows, he added, "Why worry when the world is being handed to me on a golden platter? I haven't really even attempted to win the lady's affections beyond a few . . . gestures."

Carlo nodded. "And I've never told you this but . . ." he lowered his voice even more, humor tingeing it, "for a man, you are most appealing in face and form . . . although certainly lacking when compared with *me*. But surely your looks and your skill with the lute will aid your cause, eh?"

"Of course. And my way with trained bears. . . . My cheek is proof."

"*Sì*. And you could charm even the hardest heart with your singing." He dramatically placed a hand over his heart and rolled his eyes. "Ah, Rigo . . . there is hope for you after all!" He threw an arm about Rodrigo's shoulders.

Their soft laughter floated through the night; and when they returned to their respective wagons, both slept soundly.

Sister Lucrezia of Santa Lucia offered the *Zingaro* a cup of cool wine. He accepted and sat across from her in a room little larger than a cell. The difference was that it was better appointed than a lowly cell, and that was because the good nun was the right hand of the aged and ailing Mother Superior.

And Sister Lucrezia, it appeared, also had her own private cache of gold.

They both sipped, eyeing each other, keeping their thoughts to themselves until either felt the time to speak was right. Two candles in iron wall brackets guttered in the draft that dodged erratically about the small room from one of the long passageways of the building. Shadows danced across the white-washed walls, which were bare except for an exquisitely carved wooden crucifix over a small table. The sounds of deepest night came to them faintly through the two high, unshuttered windows.

The Gypsy stared at the woman as she gave him her profile to gaze thoughtfully at one of the small windows. Her features were even and fine-boned, and her pensive expression held nothing of humility—was, in fact, faintly arrogant—as she sat alone with him, unobserved by others. He suspected that beneath her headpiece, she had a full, lustrous head of deepest auburn hair to match her winged brows. It would be exactly in keeping with the mysterious Sister Lucrezia. He could also picture the trouble she went to to keep her magnificent mane from the eyes of others.

What truly puzzled the man, however, was her identity . . . her origins. Who was she? Did anyone truly know? For all his contacts, the network of informants he used occasionally, he still didn't know. Neither, he suspected, did anyone else.

She reminded him of someone he'd evidently seen in the past, but he couldn't remember who. And that made him vaguely uneasy.

He'd once heard that she was close to the Dominican, Savonarola. A strange combination if there were any truth to it, for the righteous, power-drunk prior of San Marco shunned women. So it was said.

Her piercing gaze met his suddenly, catching him in his contemplations. "You have news for me?"

He nodded. "The prince has finally chosen a husband for his daughter."

"What has that to do with aught?"

He paused briefly, deliberately drawing out the moment in reaction to her contemptuous query. Did she think him beneath her? Some underling to be insulted at will? "The groom-to-be is Valenti."

Her hazel eyes widened briefly. "No!"

"Yes!"

"That cannot be." Her voice was low, husky with emotion. "He is only *Zingaro*—and an illegitimate one at that."

"How unkind . . . *un-Christian* of you, Sister." His words carried the biting edge of sarcasm. "Although we can only guess the identity of his natural father, it has always been speculated that it was a nobleman of high rank and esteem."

"I never could understand how such a secret could be kept. Somehow I think 'tis nothing more than a romantic fabrication."

The Gypsy shrugged, then lifted his wine to his lips. He drained the cup and said, "Then why would Durante de' Alessandro ever choose Valenti to wed his only daughter?"

She shrugged. "The son will inherit the title—not the son-by-marriage. And Alessandro is a fool—in spite of everything." She looked at him. "When is the wedding?"

"Early May . . . immediately after Lent. Considering Giulietta de' Alessandro's pique, however, with her father's long overdue arrangements, I wouldn't be surprised if it took place even sooner."

She frowned, her eyes trained unseeingly on the far wall. "He cannot become a part of the Alessandro family," she mused aloud. "That would bring the prince and his relatives into it, and others have tried to bring about their downfall . . . and failed. I am not so self-deluding as that."

She reached into her robes, then slid one palm across the

table. She quickly withdrew her hand as his larger one moved to cover the glinting coin that briefly reflected the candlelight.

It was obvious, he thought with annoyance, that she didn't want their fingers to touch. She wouldn't dare hold herself so aloof were the Mother Superior—or anyone else, for that matter—present. But then, neither would she be consulting with him. He kept his irritation to himself, deciding that one day he would make Sister Lucrezia regret her dismissal of him as nothing more than a lackey.

First, however, he would continue to accept her gold for as long as she cared to use his services.

Her glance met his and held. Beauty and baseness, he thought with one objective part of his mind as he stared, every bit as mesmerized as if she were a coiled cobra.

Her lips moved, the sound of her words pulling him from his thoughts. "What of the Gypsy girl? Are they as close as they were as children?"

"Maria? *Sì*. He looks upon her as a sister, or so he says, although the entire camp knows she would prefer more." He kept his voice carefully modulated here, lest she suspect more than he wished her to know. "But she is a sweet and simple soul, and will hide her pain to spare Rodrigo."

"If she loves him that much, she won't be able to hide it," came the blunt reply. "Poor fool. But is he attached to her? Enough so that it would cause him great pain if she were to . . . die?"

The *Zingaro's* head reared up. There was something in the tone of her question. . . . "You aren't thinking of—"

She unexpectedly slapped another coin upon the table and leaned toward him, her eyes a-glitter. "You aren't getting paid handsomely for trying to guess what I'm thinking! If you persist in doing so, you can easily be replaced. And," she added with soft menace, "don't even *consider* blackmail, for no one will ever believe the word of a *Zingaro* over that of a soon-to-be abbess."

He didn't doubt her for one moment.

# Eleven

Giulietta held her breath and carefully pushed open the heavy wooden door. It slowly swung inward, its hinges emitting a single sharp squeak, then settling into a soft, scraping noise with the unaccustomed movement. From within came the smell of dust and disuse . . . and something more.

Her heart was throbbing at the base of her throat from apprehension, for not only was she defying her father, but she was also picturing in her mind the daring abduction of her mother through that very room nineteen years ago by hirelings of the late Bishop of Florence, Stefano Ruggerio. She could still hear Caressa's voice as she'd revealed those fateful events: *". . . a small, vacant room beside the granary with a long-forgotten tunnel beneath it . . . led outside the wall of the keep and to the edge of the forest . . ."*

Her mother would be appalled if she knew what Giulietta intended to do.

But she mustn't allow echoes of the past to frighten her . . . or thoughts of her mother to swerve her from her purpose. She had to concentrate on using what she had learned from Caressa to aid her with her own plans.

She entered the chamber and carefully pushed the door closed behind her. She stood unmoving before it then, listening and allowing her eyes to adjust to the pitch-black room after the flambeaux in the passageways of the keep that had guided her to this lower level of Monteverdi. A sliver of moonlight edged the closed shutters over the high-set, single window. As her eyes searched the small room, she could just make out the narrow bed against one wall, perpendicular to the window wall.

Drawing in a calming breath, Giulietta walked over to it. She had to move it—no mean feat, she suspected—for the entrance to the tunnel lay concealed by the fitted stone floor beneath it. Doubt assailed her. How could she ever move a heavy bed? And even if she could, it would surely make noise as it scraped across the floor. Yet what choice did she have?

She knelt beside it and gingerly poked her head beneath. A sneeze gathered in her nose and throat, and she quickly stifled it with the cupped palm of her hand. When it had passed, she peered farther beneath the impenetrable-seeming shadows of the crawl space, straining to see. The bed was high enough for her to crawl beneath it. . . . Perhaps she wouldn't have to move it.

Something slithered across the floor behind her, raising the hair along her neck. It would take more than a mouse to deter her, she thought as she reached out with one hand and felt for the loosely fitted stones Caressa had told her of. She tested the alignment of the closest ones and realized with rising excitement that those directly beneath her questing fingers could be dislodged.

Quickly, she began prying them loose, one at a time. She worked by touch. Breaking nails and scraping the pads of her fingers in the process. As she set the stones aside, one by one, her thoughts moved to the man responsible for her flight: Rodrigo da Valenti. A month had passed since the signing of their betrothal papers, but Giulietta had seen very little of him. When he was at Castello Monteverdi, he was either closeted with her father or drilling the Alessandro *condottieri* in ways of war. He seemed to be deliberately avoiding her, yet when they were thrown together, he was the epitome of courtesy.

Giulietta made a face in the dark, then winced aloud as one

of the stones slipped and fell back into place, pinching two fingers. At other times, he was purported to be in Florence, although the reasons were unknown to Giulietta.

*No doubt,* she thought with acerbity, sucking on her injured fingers, *he was having himself a rousing time in the* tavernas, *drinking and wenching and making up for the time he's been away* . . .

She felt an unwelcome warmth creep into her face at the thought of another woman, even a prostitute, in Rodrigo da Valenti's arms, and doubled her efforts to clear the trapdoor of stones. Her back began to ache from her awkward position, her bruised fingers stung. She suddenly wondered whether she would be able to lift the door high enough to slip through it.

And what if there was no ladder within? Or mayhap it had rotted over the years, or even been removed. . . .

It was late as Rodrigo left Castello Monteverdi. He'd just finished conferring with Dante—relating all he'd seen and heard in Florence during the past few days. He silently saluted the guard at the small door beside the drawbridge and portcullis, then exited as swiftly and silently as a shadow.

Snatches of his conversation with the prince ran through his head as he moved around the south wall of the castle and toward the east forest. . . .

" 'Tis a more somber Firenze then I remembered," he'd told the prince earlier. "Thanks to the monk's influence, they say."

Dante had nodded, his fingers visibly tightening about the quill with which he'd been writing when Rodrigo had entered his library. He'd obviously been going over Monteverdi accounts. In the wake of Rodrigo's words, he'd dropped the implement, his eyes narrowing as they moved from Rodrigo's face to the painting of his late father. "No one from my father's generation would recognize the city now." His words were sour.

"Oh, the physical aspects have changed little, but the spirit is subdued—like a dog with its tail between its legs—as too many of the citizens try to please that self-inflated, miserable excuse of a holy man!"

Rodrigo nodded and continued. "I managed to befriend some of the *Compagnacci* while I was there. You've heard of them?"

Dante's eyes met his. "*Sì.* A group of young men, mostly from rich families, bent upon causing Girolamo Savonarola as much inconvenience and embarrassment as possible."

"Indeed. They're bent upon discrediting the prior and sending him packing from Florence once and for all. But no one has heard from him since he fled to San Marco in June."

"I'm surprised he has enough sense to stay out of sight . . . even in the wake of excommunication." Dante's lips twisted into a grimace. "Can you imagine our Sandro adding some of what that lunatic monk calls his more *lascivious* paintings to the huge pyres built and burned by those Florentines who'd taken leave of their senses?"

"Botticelli?"

"*Sì!*" He smacked the desk with one closed fist. "Lorenzo should be alive to flay the monk with his own rhetoric! Sandro's paintings are beautiful, not lewd!" He frowned darkly. "A tragic and irretrievable loss."

Rodrigo had had no chance to actually see the Dominican who had held much of Florence in thrall for so long with his dire warnings and promises of redemption. . . .

"I'd like to see him . . ." He shrugged. "Which means I must find a reason to seek him out at San Marco."

Their eyes met and held. Dante's frown eased; and suddenly their mouths curved slowly with, obviously, the same thoughts. "Did you go by your real name among the *Compagnacci?*" the prince asked.

"No."

Dante nodded. "Nor should you if and when you go to San Marco. I seem to remember that Salvatore Corsini's family gave large amounts of money to the monastery. It would be unwise, I think, to reveal your identity, even though those of the family who were spared by the plague scattered to the winds."

" 'Twas an accident," Rodrigo stated firmly, his grin fading, "and I'll challenge any man who says otherwise."

Dante stood and moved around the desk. He put one hand on Rodrigo's shoulder. "Rein in your pride, Rigo. You are in a position to defend your name and honor now, *sì*, but don't risk your future by failing to use a bit of common sense." Rodrigo opened his mouth to speak, but Dante squeezed his shoulder and added, "Caution is a wise man's weapon. Don't ever underestimate its importance, or judge it a coward's defense . . ."

Of course Dante had been right. Rodrigo knew very well the importance of caution and practiced it, he thought now as he rounded the southeast tower and headed toward the trees across the way. He glanced up at the keep as he neared the woods, thinking of Giulietta, his reluctant bride-to-be. What had Dante said about his daughter? *"Be patient with her, Rigo. She can be willful at times, and bolder than might be seemly for a young woman her age . . ."*

*That* was certainly no exaggeration.

*". . . but she hasn't had the benefit of the influence of convent life—I wouldn't allow it. Caressa lived at home until she was wed, and we decided to do the same for Gietta. A convent would stifle her spirit . . ."*

Rodrigo had hidden his reaction behind a cough in the wake of those last words—and had earned a suspicious look from the prince. But he'd managed to control himself and nodded in the face of this newly perceived flaw in his idol. It was obvious that Durante de' Alessandro's famed judgment was clouded when it came to his daughter.

Before Rodrigo had taken his leave, he'd mentioned it was

believed that Savonarola's supporters were steadily losing
ground in Florence. "The harvests were poor this year in Tuscany—as you undoubtedly know." His gaze touched the open
ledger on the desk. "Starving people still walk the streets . . ."
He shook his head. "I saw a man fall dead outside the gates
of the *Signoria*—he looked like a skeleton. And plague . . .
the outbreak of plague this past summer didn't help."

"Nor did Savonarola's hero, the French king, keep his promise to return Pisa to Florence," Dante said. "That surely is a
sign to many that the prior isn't all he claims to be—cannot
do all he's claimed he can." He folded his arms across his
chest, a thoughtful look settling over his face. " 'Tis surely
not winning him new support, or even strengthening the support he already has."

"His opponents are gaining in number," Rodrigo said, then
nodded slowly. "As I said before, if you still wish me to continue with what I began in Florence, I think the time is right
to consider seeking him out in his lair . . ."

The ladder was there . . . rotting and creaky from years in
the dank hole, but it held Giulietta's weight. Just as she reached
the bottom, the last rung snapped, however, jarring her as her
foot landed on the tunnel floor; but she was unhurt, and just
grateful it was the lowest one that had disintegrated beneath her
rather than one higher up. She would have been in dire straits
had she injured herself while trying to flee Monteverdi in a
little-used room, and through an even less-used, ancient cavern.

In the inky darkness she swung away from the ladder and
reached tentatively toward one side. Her hand encountered a
dirt wall. Using it as a guide, Giulietta made her way forward
with careful steps, her breath caught in her throat. She had no
way of knowing what was ahead of her—a blockage of some
kind, perhaps even an animal. . . .

She tried to put that last thought from her mind with a light shudder, having no wish to encounter any denizens of the crude passageway before making her exit.

A sudden thought struck her. What if the other end was blocked? What if it had been deliberately sealed years ago? No, that couldn't be, logic told her, for it would defeat the purpose of the tunnel. The Italian city-states were still involved in enough political turmoil to necessitate such an emergency escape route.

What was the Alessandro credo? she thought in an attempt to reassure herself that her efforts weren't for naught. *To lower the vigil is to die.* The words flared through her mind like a burst of pyrotechnics, as clearly as they appeared beneath her grandfather's portrait. Surely, even in the most peaceful of times, being prepared for any contingency was wise, and her father was no fool

She blundered head-on into an enormous spiderweb. More surprised than afraid, Giulietta began flailing her arms to fling it off . . . and encountered what felt like a multitude of small— and not so small—objects imprisoned within the engulfing silken strands. The thought of what those things might be caused a sound of distress to burst from her lips. "Ugh!" she exclaimed in acute distaste, and plunged forward in an attempt to put it behind her.

It worked. She felt the kiss of empty air and freedom, and swiped at the remaining clinging threads. Placing her hand on the wall for guidance once again, she moved forward, hoping the other end would be free of obstacles. . . .

Dirt rained down around her as Giulietta scrabbled at the solid-seeming wall of debris that blocked her exit. To come so far and fail, she thought in frustration, was unthinkable.

Suddenly, as if in answer to her thoughts, the barrier gave way, dropping dirt into her uplifted face—her open mouth as she gasped for air . . . her eyes, her nostrils. She began to choke on it, coughing to clear her throat and spitting out dirt as she fought her way with clawed hands to the exit that *had* to be there.

She thrust one hand forward through the opening she was creating, only to encounter a tangle of attacking thistles. A soft cry of surprise and pain escaped her as the thorns bit into her tender flesh. She tried to draw back her bleeding hand, but that only hurt more.

Suddenly, the undergrowth was being torn away. A man's voice mumbled soft expletives as he obviously encountered the same vicious thistles.

Giulietta didn't have time to wonder who her savior was— honest man or thief. Or worse. She'd always taken for granted the assumption that Monteverdi lands were well enough patrolled to prevent easy access to any brigands. For a few panic-stricken moments her escape plans were pushed aside for the more immediate need of extrication as she grabbed on to one helping hand and scrambled through hindering, pinching underbrush onto her knees in the open air. Blessedly cool and pure night air. . . .

Gulping in several lungsful of purging breath she was unmindful of anything in those brief moments but the fact that she was free. She felt cool hanks of her loosened hair brush against the warm, stinging flesh of her scratched face; her hands and arms throbbed with pain.

She opened her eyes, now adjusted to the tarry blackness of the tunnel, and perceived a figure before her, limned by the bright contrast of moonlight. Before she could speak or act, hands were upon her elbows, drawing her upward and to her feet.

*"Madre di Dio!"* exclaimed a deep, shocked voice. "Giulietta?"

Her eyes widened, and she whipped her head up to meet

the man's look, all discomfort forgotten in the face of her instant recognition of her "rescuer." *Of all the foul luck!* she thought in angry dismay, her ordeal already receding with the shock of this newest—and most unwelcome—turn of events.

She didn't answer him, *couldn't* answer him, feeling anger and frustration and disappointment and humiliation wrench through her all at the same time. *He* was the very reason she was in this sorry predicament, and here he was, foiling her plans!

She turned her head aside to cough once again, and when she'd subsided, in a totally unexpected move, Rodrigo brushed her tangled hair from her face, then tilted it back gently to examine the cuts and scratches. "Giulietta *mia . . . ,*" he said in a low, husky voice. "Are you hurt?"

Before she could answer, his arms were about her, drawing her close. The magic he seemed to work over her when he so chose enfolded her, warmed her from within, until Giulietta felt herself leaning into him. Sensations showered through her like spring rain. Her knees turned weak. . . .

"Whatever are you about this time, eh?" he murmured against her hair, deciding to take advantage of his unexpected good fortune, even if he suspected her motives were anything but romantic. "Once again you materialize before me, like a lovely fantasy of the night. Surely you need not employ such unconventional means to gain my attention?"

The laughter in his voice brought her back to her senses. She bridled beneath his touch and tried to pull away. "Get away . . . Let me go!" she said heatedly. "Where I go and what I do are none of your concern." She tried to use her haughtiest tones, yet deep down despised the way she sounded.

Somehow Rodrigo da Valenti managed to bring out the very worst in her, forcing her to act like an absolute shrew in his presence rather than the daughter of the Prince of Monteverdi. These past months had been the most confusing and emotion-

fraught in all her seventeen years. And this only added to her
irritation, her deep resentment of him. She stubbornly refused
to look beyond his behavior during their first encounter for
the reason for her anger.

The fact that he should also elicit such a powerful sexual
response from her, she refused to attribute to anything but
being well into marriageable age and, therefore, extremely vulnerable to almost any eligible and halfway attractive man who
chanced to cross her path.

*Not Leon Sarzano,* reminded a demon. *He left you cold as
a lump of congealed fat. Or have you forgotten?*

"But you are very much my concern now, *cara,*" he was
saying softly against her ear, his arms remaining firmly about
her. The scent of earth and autumn and saddle leather teased
her nostrils, along with his own individual masculine essence,
a combination as beguiling as the most potent fragrance. . . .
"And this is so reminiscent of our first meeting, I can only
hope that you mayhap used this tunnel in an attempt to . . .
*rendezvous* with me again."

She stared up at him, once again rendered momentarily
speechless, this time by his audacity.

Her lips were half-parted, an impossible temptation for him
to resist. After all, he had the advantage, didn't he? What man
in his right mind wouldn't use it to steal a kiss from the woman
who was to become his wife? And to prove a point? For surely
it would serve his purpose if he ever needed or chose to confront her with her own responses to him. If she considered
him a rogue and a knave, why not act the part?

*Because you are no such thing.* The words crept through
his mind.

He ignored them.

"And," he added as his lips descended toward hers, his head
blocking out everything but his shadowed visage and midnight-
dark eyes, "since my *Zingaro* heart is flawed . . ."

As his lips hovered over hers, guilt pounded through her like an unexpected blow from a battering ram at the mention of her unforgivable words to him at the tourney. But she had little time to ponder the significance of that guilt, for his mouth was touching hers then, his tongue immediately encountering hers. Curling heat flared low in her abdomen—raced like quicksilver through her loins and limbs—making her like warm clay in his arms.

She couldn't allow him to do this . . .

Yet she would soon be rid of him for good. She would be safely behind the walls of Santa Lucia, with his blessing or without it. So why not enjoy the forbidden fruit of this impossible liaison? Even as she thought the thought, her mouth relaxed beneath his in offering, and she ignored a faint warning that she was stoking the embers of forbidden fire.

*Or are you trying to make up for your cruel words?* asked another voice. *Is it only pity?*

As she succumbed to the maelstrom of sensations taking over her body, paralyzing her very thought processes, her last coherent thought was that she could never pity *him*. . . .

Rodrigo felt his desire rise like a rampaging river, spilling through him with incredible speed and sweetness, and intuition told him that this encounter would be even more intense than the first for both of them. He could only hope that Giulietta was responding to him with more than physical desire, but there was no guarantee. His own soul-shaking response was the result of the depth of his feelings—feelings that he had wanted to wither away like the disintegrating leaves of autumn.

Or so he'd told himself.

He'd always prided himself on his rigid control when it came to women. Not that he'd led a monk's life by any means, but he'd preferred to expend his energy when possible on the rigors of training and practice . . . participating in tournaments to earn his gold, then falling into bed, exhausted, at night. Not sowing his seed all over France.

Until he'd left Italy, Rodrigo had had Durante de' Alessandro as a rare example of fidelity to one woman, and although he'd never been wed, he couldn't forget his own bastardy. He'd promised himself long ago that he would never do to any child what had been done to him, however unwittingly.

One of the few times he'd asked Dante about his father, the prince had said simply. "He's dead . . ." Then added, "And he never knew about you. Shut him from your mind, Rigo."

Perhaps his natural sire *would* have revealed himself to Rodrigo, but there was no guarantee anything would have been different had the man lived. Rodrigo wouldn't make the same mistake. Even loving adoptive parents couldn't ease the pain caused by his father's obvious promiscuity, which had resulted in the death of his mother and his own illegitimacy.

But now . . . Now Giulietta de' Alessandro was in his arms once again and altogether too willing. Why not give in to his raging desire for her? Why not act the scoundrel she thought he was and take her? She would soon be his wife anyway.

*You think a man becomes noble through taking advantage of a woman?* sneered a voice. *Suddenly your own code of behavior has been modified just because you will marry into the Alessandros . . . and now you'll treat the woman to whom you've secretly compared all others like you've never even treated a peasant woman?*

He tried to wrestle with his contradictory feelings as his hands, seemingly of their own volition, glided down her ribs to her waist, then back upward, his thumbs grazing the sides of her softly rounded breasts. Her skin seemed to burn his fingers through the light silk of her gown, and as their tongues clashed and played to the thunder in their blood, he wanted nothing more than to brand her as his own—to become a part of her, and make her a part of him. Inseparable.

He pressed her closer, their hips all but fused, as were their seeking mouths, and he deliberately ignored the echoes of *Fool! Fool! You are lost* . . . in one lingering, logical part of his mind.

Indeed he *was* lost, for with every beat of his hammering heart, a riptide of emotion was rushing him farther away from any restraint that still lingered. . . .

Giulietta felt his hot, pulsing need for her through their clothing. A frisson of intense desire—edged with a sliver of fear at her evident influence over him—moved through her. She had never been so intimate with a man save for one moonlit night this past August when she would have given her maidenhead to a dark and tender stranger.

She began to tremble, wanting more, needing more. She longed to press her naked flesh against his, feel the steely length of his body against hers, and the solid scepter of his masculinity within her. God in Heaven, she thought dimly, she was surely losing her sanity . . . as surely as she had lost control of her will.

Wave upon wave of liquid heat poured through her, and moisture bathed the most feminine of recesses of her body as she instinctively strove for the glorious promise that seemed to hover just out of reach. She dug her fingernails into his broad, solid back with a soft moan of ecstasy . . . and frustration.

Suddenly he pulled the hot adhesion of his mouth from hers. He drew her head to his chest and held it there for a long, pounding moment, fighting for self-control. His sense of honor, instilled to a large degree by Dante de' Alessandro, rose to the fore after all . . . past his selfish desires, his physical needs. His respect for and loyalty to the Lord of Monteverdi were too deep-seated to throw it all away in a moment of passion, no matter how intense. Unwilling to ever make another impulsive mistake like the one that had taken him away from all he knew and loved, Rodrigo da Valenti had honed his self-control to an admirable degree. It served him well now, or he would have been unable to end their loveplay.

Giulietta, however, was at first dismayed by the abrupt change in his behavior. Her quest for that tantalizing and most elusive of fulfillments was foiled by Rodrigo da Valenti's unexpected actions. On the heels of dismay, however, came humiliation. *He* had pulled away from *her,* no doubt in the same manner he might shun some street woman whose services he was refusing.

Her embarrassment grew like wildfire, until it overrode her dwindling desire. Anger swept through her in shame's wake, and she jerked from Rodrigo's firm but careful grip, unmindful of anything but her own burning sense of degradation. When he finally looked at her, he should have been warned by her eyes: they were slightly narrowed, and brass-bright with fury.

"Giulietta *mia,*" he began in a low, husky voice, searching for words that could even begin to explain the complexity of his feelings, begin to penetrate her obvious anger and salve her trampled pride.

With whiplash speed, she struck him with her open palm full in the cheek.

# Twelve

The contact reverberated like thunder in the quiet of the night. Rodrigo's head jerked to the side, his only outward reaction save the tightening of his fingers upon her shoulders.

But anger was boiling up from deep within him . . . anger at her need to preserve her pride when she'd sought to destroy his on more than one occasion. Surely her face-saving anger had gone on long enough! And if she was still blaming him for Mario di Corsini's death, not only would it be impossible, but it wouldn't be worth the effort to attempt to convince her otherwise.

"How *dare* you!" she threw at him in a shaking voice.

His mouth tightened into a thin line, and even in the moonglow she could see his skin darken to an angry red where she'd struck him.

"How dare I kiss you? Or *stop* kissing you?"

She raised her hand again, but this time he was ready. He caught her wrist and stilled her midmotion. Both their arms raised, they glared at each other in a stalemate.

"*You*, madame, for all your claim to blue blood, are rude and insensitive. Not only am I extremely disappointed in the daughter of my mentor, but I've met serfs with more manners and sensitivity than you."

Before she could answer, he pressed home his attack, "Just *what* are you doing here in the middle of the night . . . and at the mouth of a secret tunnel created for clandestine activities or desperate escapes?"

She wrenched her wrist from the vise of his fingers, opened her mouth to retort, and was stopped cold by his next question. "Exactly where were you going, my eager bride-to-be? Surely you of all people know of the dangers of wandering the woodlands at night and unescorted?"

The ironic emphasis of his last few words was not lost upon Giulietta, and suddenly her anger began to give way to a genuine fear that he would stand between her and the haven of Santa Lucia. No matter what story she told him.

This was a firm, unrelenting side of Rodrigo da Valenti she hadn't encountered before, and it gave her pause, for she'd thought to possibly bully her way past him—hold something over his head, mayhap, to ensure his cooperation, although that "something" would incriminate her, as well. Even if he revealed nothing of *her* shameful behavior that night. . . .

With all the dignity of an empress, Giulietta threw back her shoulders and lifted her chin, unaware of the dirt streaking her face, the dead leaves and briars lacing her untidy locks. She looked him straight in the eye and said, "I am going to Santa Lucia to take my vows. And neither you—nor anyone else—can stop me. If you try, I'll escape again—and eventually succeed." *Or perish in the process!* she added to herself.

A tense silence ensued, and Rodrigo didn't know whether to laugh aloud or take her over his knee. Finally, he said, "And what makes you think even the good sisters at Santa Lucia would accept an unmannered ingrate like yourself? Other than your father's money, of course . . ."

She was totally unprepared for his question. Rather, she'd expected outright disagreement. "You'll let me go, then?" she asked, trying to ignore the queer feelings stirring inside her at his openly insulting words. And the impression that she'd finally managed to slip more than a few rungs down the ladder of his esteem.

*It doesn't matter!*

"I not only wholeheartedly endorse your idea, *bambina,* but I would be happy to take you there myself."

And without further ado, he bent forward, grabbed her around the waist, and tossed her over his shoulder like a farmer would a sack of wheat destined for the *mercato*.

In the face of the swiftness and unexpectedness of his move, Giulietta was too stunned, at first, to struggle. Then, the slamming of her stomach against his shoulder literally knocked the breath from her.

As his long strides took them into the forest, she fought to pull air into her lungs. The blood rushed to her face, which only added to her acute discomfort. In a panic, she tried to pound her fists against his backside—not the most effective place to aim blows, she quickly discovered. Branches slashed at her face and exposed hands, tore at her hair and scalp.

Rodrigo pushed aside his guilt and tightened his grip. His arms banded about her hips like iron manacles, for angry as he was, he didn't want her to fall headfirst over his shoulder and onto the ground. If she suffered from scrape, and scratches, so be it. But any more serious injury was unthinkable.

"Let me go!" Her words sounded strangled, breathless.

"Hush!" he warned over his shoulder, noting briefly the nicely rounded rump so close to his cheek. Unable to resist the temptation, he patted her beneath her bunched cloak and dress, ostensibly to emphasize his command, and not purely out of the temptation to take advantage of the situation.

A muffled cry of outrage was her response—hardly loud enough to register as anything more than a choked gurgle.

He smacked her backside with more force, this time in real warning. "You're putting your escape in jeopardy," he warned. "Or is that what you want? Are you willing to end up back at Castello Monteverdi should someone hear your caterwauling? To make me look the miscreant . . . and salve your pride?"

Caterwauling? How dare he? "I don't need you to get where I'm going!" she answered indignantly, and hit his solid flank ineffectively with her fist for emphasis. Her words, however, held nothing of authority from her awkward position. And while she may have been furious and humiliated, she was smart enough to realize that he was right. If her cries alerted someone from the castle, she would have to answer to her father—not from the sanctuary of Santa Lucia, but rather while standing before him in his own keep. And then she'd *never* be able to get away from Rodrigo da Valenti.

"I can walk, signore!" she hissed, straining to cant her head upward. But to no avail. All she could see was the back of his head . . . between the black spots that were appearing as a result of being upside down. Obviously the rogue was dead serious about taking her to Santa Lucia—on his terms.

She'd never been more humiliated in her life . . . and decided, as she bit back a string of expletives she'd learned from Nicco and Bernardo in bygone days, that if Rodrigo da Valenti had ever had the slightest chance of winning her acceptance, that prospect had just been dashed into oblivion.

Rather than joy, Sister Lucrezia—now Mother Superior—felt a sense of justice about her triumph. After all, she was meant to be the head of Santa Lucia . . . it was the least God could do for her in the wake of all the misfortune he'd thrown her way. Testing her, some would say. But she'd finally come to the conclusion that God was vengeful, and only came to the aid of those who were strong within themselves, in spite of adversity. If you didn't take what you wanted from life, chances were you wouldn't get it.

She was bright and beautiful, with noble blood running through her veins. She deserved better than the drudgery she would reap if she followed the example of the blindly accepting majority.

And her latest discovery and credo had resulted in good things for her recently. Hadn't the ailing Sister Ana, Mother Superior, taken Lucrezia under her wing—granted her her full trust (which enabled Lucrezia to occasionally skim the convent coffers and increase her own secret cache) and seen that the leadership of Santa Lucia was passed to her after the old nun was gone? And hadn't she stumbled onto a *Zingaro* who was willing to keep her informed of certain things in exchange for gold? And he appeared to be trustworthy, as well, even against his own kind. A rarity, she mused, among Gypsies.

Her mother, an auburn-haired beauty who'd made the mistake of falling in love with and bearing the child of her own half brother, Salvatore di Corsini, had always told Lucrezia that she was special . . . destined for special things. *You are a Corsini—whether they will acknowledge you or nay. You only need to exercise patience and use your intelligence, and all will come to you in time . . .*

And how right her mother had been! First to demand a hefty sum of gold from her lover in exchange for a promise to abort the child, then to keep secret that child's birth (for those righteous Corsinis would have shunned any child who bore the taint of incest); she had also told her daughter that the day would come when Lucrezia would have the chance to stoke the embers of vendetta even as she satisfied the very need for revenge. She would avenge the death of her half brother, Mario di Corsini.

Lucrezia had since then come to her own conclusions, and plotted her own course of action. When the time was right, she would go to Rome and present Gabriella di Corsini with the head of her son's murderer on a platter . . . just like Salome had been presented with the head of John the Baptist.

Oh, yes! She had ambitious plans, like her mother before her, who was somehow able to portend these things; and who had secretly worshipped, some said, the Dark One.

Then, too, there was the powerful Girolamo Savonarola, who was so eager to accept her sympathy and support—and occasionally lend her his own. Did he suspect her background? And was he therefore showing his own type of gratitude for the Corsini family's substantial contributions to San Marco in the past? If so, he no doubt would have been shocked to learn of her clandestine correspondence with the Borgia Pope, Alexander, who in turn was extremely interested in the prior's activities. His Holiness would in all likelihood consider himself well rid of the Dominican thorn in his side if Lucrezia's ultimate plan was successful.

A knock on her office door intruded into her thoughts. "Reverend Mother?" queried a low, agitated voice.

Who would be disturbing her at this hour of the night? she wondered briefly, suddenly annoyed at the interruption. "Yes?" she asked, her annoyance quickly tamped.

The door swung open to reveal an agitated Sister Sophia, the porteress. A small, sallow-skinned woman, Sister Sophia was normally not easily flustered. Now, however, her wimple was askew, and the rosary and crucifix normally worn in the middle of the waist were a-dangle inappropriately close to her backside.

It was clear that something was amiss. "Forgive me, Sis—, er, Reverend Mother, but we have . . . visitors."

"Visitors? At this hour?" Lucrezia asked in a calm voice, her auburn brows raised in surprise.

*"Ebbene,* they are—they are . . ." She trailed off, obviously at a loss for words.

Lucrezia stood and moved toward the door. "Come, Sister.

Let's greet these . . . *visitors.*" She followed the bewildered
nun from the chamber down the stone-floored corridors of
Santa Lucia. Like two spirits in their cream-colored robes, they
moved through the halls. The whispers of their soft leather
shoes were the only sound in the quiet of deep night within
the cool dimness of the convent walls. A thousand feet had
traversed those passageways in private quests for inner peace;
a thousand more would walk those very halls seeking a similar
tranquility and refuge from the bitter disappointments of life.

But Lucrezia wouldn't be there to witness their comings
and goings. Something deep within her was quickening, coming to life with a force that threatened to rend her very heart.
She knew suddenly, somehow, that whoever had come to Santa
Lucia this time would have a direct bearing on her future. . . .

As they approached the entrance, with its locked grill gate,
Sister Sophia removed a long-shanked key from within the
draped folds of her habit. Lucrezia's hand upon her arm stopped
her in midmotion as she essayed to adjust her eyes to the darkness of the night that surrounded them and make out the two
figures on the other side of the gate.

The night wind caught the bell's clapper, and it clanked
softly, forlornly, in the quiet. The bell rope undulated in the
breeze like a serpent, and with a hiss and snap the flame from
the single brand that illuminated the immediate area of the
gate danced fitfully.

Sister Lucrezia didn't notice. Her eyes were trained upon
the two figures before her as they stood in silence, agitation
emanating from them both. Angry red lines streaked the man's
left cheek, as if he'd been slapped. . . .

God above! Why would any woman ever want or need to
slap such a man? came the unexpected thought.

In the next instant, she recognized them. The tall man whose
image she had committed to memory not long ago . . . the
woman, too, she would have known anywhere. But *she* wasn't

important in the scheme of things. *Her* presence wasn't making Lucrezia's heart thrash like a landed trout within her breast.

For whatever reason, as if conjured up, here was Rodrigo da Valenti at her doorstep. Hard on recognition's heels, another thought came rushing through her mind in the wake of meeting Valenti face-to-face: What a pity it was that angry and disheveled as he appeared, he was such a magnificent man. So beautifully male, in fact, that the mere sight of him close up literally took her breath away. He was almost too fine a specimen to meet an early death.

Almost.

Rodrigo watched the shorter nun insert the great iron key into the lock of the gate and turn it. As it soundlessly swung open on well-oiled hinges, he spoke to the more imposing of the two women, assuming she was in authority. "Forgive the intrusion, er . . . Reverend Mother?"

At her nod he continued, his agitation at first drowning out the faint, instinctive warning that began to sound in the back of his mind. "Mona Giulietta here was attempting to seek sanctuary at Santa Lucia, and I happened upon her . . ."

He glanced sideways through his lashes at Giulietta, who was silently fuming. Her gaze, however, wasn't on him but, rather, the Mother Superior in whose hands she was about to place herself. It was obvious she was struggling to calm herself before the two nuns. Her lips parted in awe, even as his glance touched her, adding to the effect of that innocently enchanting profile he ached to trace with gentle fingers . . . then with his lips . . .

When she wasn't pushing him to the brink of madness.

Obviously recovering herself before Rodrigo could continue, Giulietta blurted, "This man *abducted* me, Reverend Mother! He—"

"I thought I had rescued you from suffocating to death," he interrupted, his look now openly sardonic, "from beneath the dirt and debris you encountered at the mouth of the tunnel in your escape efforts. Why, I could have easily dispatched you with my dagger, mistaking you for a brigand emerging from his hiding place."

With uncharacteristic satisfaction, he watched her face pale at his words before he returned his gaze to Sister Lucrezia, who seemed to be waiting for him to continue. "I took it upon myself to *escort* her here," he added firmly. "She wishes to take her vows, although her intentions were unknown to her father, Prince of Monteverdi, and her betrothed, as well." He gave Lucrezia a brief bow. "Rodrigo da Valenti, Reverend Mother, at your service."

As he straightened, she spoke with a smile that didn't quite reach her almond-shaped, hazel eyes: "I am Sister Lucrezia, and this is Sister Sophia. We welcome you to Santa Lucia. None of God's children are turned away from here, no matter the time of day or night. Come in and take some refreshment while we talk this over."

Giulietta had been expecting an ancient and cantankerous woman to introduce herself as the Mother Superior, and was pleasantly surprised to discover this fairly young nun was the spiritual leader of Santa Lucia. Surely this was a place where she could be happy, and forever out of reach of her domineering father, as well as Rodrigo da Valenti.

Jeering laughter rang out in the back of her mind as they followed Sister Lucrezia into the sanctuary of the convent. Giulietta tried to ignore it, but a voice whispered, *Domineering father? He loved you enough to keep you at home while you grew to womanhood—turned his head a hundred times when you did things most other young girls wouldn't dare. He worships the ground beneath your feet! Nor does he know what transpired that night you lost your shoes—and almost your*

*virginity! And even if he did, you cannot entirely blame Va-
lenti . . .*

". . . some cool cider?" Sister Lucrezia was asking her politely.

Giulietta numbly nodded her head, half-wishing that the entire episode would turn out to be only a bad dream. Here she
was, filthy and disheveled (and for once Valenti didn't look
exactly cool and immaculate, either), with *him* trailing in her
wake—both of them looking fresh from some furtive tryst in
the forest. Dear God, but the man was a nuisance! She couldn't
get away from him!

As Sister Sophia handed her a cup of cider, Giulietta threw
Rodrigo a fulminating glance, then drank.

There was a brief silence, as they both slaked their thirst,
but the air was charged with tension. All too soon for Giulietta,
Sister Lucrezia asked her, "Now, what is this about Signore
da Valenti abducting you?"

Giulietta sat straighter in the austere wooden chair and met
the nun's look. "I was trying to leave Monteverdi without my
father's knowledge . . ." Color flared in her face. "He wants
me to wed—" her eyes narrowed and went to Rodrigo, who
was watching her—*"him."*

Lucrezia's brows lifted, but it was Rodrigo who spoke. "I
want no such thing, Reverend Mother, now that I see how . . .
*unsuitable* Mona Giulietta would be as a wife."

Just as he expected, Giulietta's anger intensified at the insult. She threw him a murderous look, but he continued evenly,
" 'Twas Durante de' Alessandro's decision, and I agreed—for
the obvious reasons. Her father's wealth," he said bluntly and
unnecessarily, "and, of course, her considerable . . . er, *attributes* for an over-cosseted and spoiled child." (The sharp sibi-
lance of Giulietta's indrawn breath was ear-piercing, but he
ignored it.) "But it seems that the lady would rather wed Leon
Sarzano, Reverend Mother. She would never have attempted

to run away had the prince wished to give her in marriage to *him*."

Sister Sophia stepped discreetly aside as Lucrezia looked at Giulietta. "And is this true, Giulietta de' Alessandro? Is this the reason you were trying to leave Castello Monteverdi? To avoid carrying out your fathers wishes?"

Giulietta opened her mouth to answer, then closed it. Suddenly Sister Lucrezia wasn't seeing Giulietta's actions in a favorable light. She couldn't bring herself to lie, but she had to say something in her own defense. "Rather, to dedicate my life to God," she said, lowering her lashes in what she thought to be a show of humility.

It was all Rodrigo could do to swallow the last bit of cider in his cup. He coughed behind his free hand and cleared his throat. "I think, Reverend Mother, rather to avoid marriage to me." To Giulietta he said, "Don't add lying to Reverend Mother to the list of your transgressions, *bambina*. I'm sure you have more than enough sins to confess before you can even don the habit of a novice."

Giulietta's cup fell to the stone floor as her hands clenched at her knees.

"Children, children!" Lucrezia finally said, obviously fearing a physical altercation. "Why don't you go with Sister Sophia, Giulietta, and wash and undress for bed. Mayhap 'twould be better if I speak in private with Signor da Valenti. You and I will speak on the morrow, child."

Giulietta chose to be gracious and ignore the word "child"— which was fast becoming a sore spot with her—and leaned to retrieve the empty cup. Her hand encountered Rodrigo's, and she pulled away as if singed.

As she straightened and looked at his dark head, then encountered his laughing blue eyes as he also straightened, for the second time in less than an hour, she wanted to slap him silly. Uncharacteristic and unladylike as was the urge, it was

also so overwhelming that she stood, in spite of her resentment
of Sister Lucrezia's dismissal of her, and said through stiff
lips, "As you wish, Reverend Mother."

It didn't matter how she arrived at Santa Lucia, she thought
as she followed in the diminutive Sister Sophia's wake, completely ignoring the man who rose to his feet and watched her
silently as she left the room. She was *here* now, and that had
been her goal.

At the door Giulietta paused and swung back, noting that
Sister Lucrezia's eyes were narrowed slightly . . . and, oddly,
riveted to Valenti. Unease touched her and was almost imme-
diately gone. Even a nun could be affected by one such as
Valenti, she supposed. "You will send a message to Castello
Monteverdi, Reverend Mother?"

The nun cut short her silent contemplation and met Giulietta's look. She nodded. "After morning prayer, a messenger
will be sent."


"You realize, do you not, that her father will not tolerate
this for long?"

Rodrigo considered his crossed ankles with a frown. "He
won't like it, but as her betrothed I have a say in the matter."
He looked over at Lucrezia. "We are to be married in the
spring. I think 'twill do wonders for Giulietta de' Alessandro
to live at Santa Lucia until just before the wedding."

The nun nodded. "And what if Alessandro demands she
return home?"

Rodrigo was quiet a moment. Then, "I would think, for
enough recompense from me, you would be willing to remind
him of the sanctuary in any house of God. I intend to speak
to him first to smooth the way, but the understanding will be
that I will donate funds to Santa Lucia over and above what

is needed for her stay, and the only visitor she may receive is myself."

She hesitated, and he added, "And I will donate generously and regularly to Santa Lucia every year after our marriage as a token of my . . . gratitude."

As if his last statement were of little concern to her, Sister Lucrezia said, "Although we are short-handed at this time, I will require the presence of one of our sisters at your meetings."

Rodrigo had the distinct impression that she was plumbing the depths of his mind . . . and soul. He shook his head. "That won't be necessary. She'll come to no harm by my hand before May . . ." His lips curved with rue. "As you can doubtless see by the hand print on my face, if anything, *I* will be the one risking bodily harm. The lady has a temper."

Sister Lucrezia looked down at the table before her for a moment, then steepled her fingers beneath her chin as she regarded him with her catlike gray-green eyes.

Rodrigo would have given much to be able to read her mind just then. And there was something elusively familiar about her features. Where had he seen her before? Or did she merely resemble someone else?

"If I agree to your terms, you must give me your solemn oath as a Christian that you will not compromise her in any way while she is in our midst."

"You have my word, Sister, but I also have a condition that must be met."

She just stared at him, revealing nothing of her thoughts. No frown of surprise at his boldness—no flattening of her eyebrows in annoyance. Yet he got the feeling that much was at work behind those mysterious eyes. Sister Lucrezia was more than she would have him believe, he strongly suspected; and he no longer wondered how such a relatively young woman had managed to be elected Mother Superior of Santa Lucia.

He *did* wonder, however, if she had guessed how much he cared for Giulietta de' Alessandro, in spite of his deliberately taunting remarks earlier. "As I said before," he told her, "I think 'twill do wonders for Giulietta to live here for a few months . . . to practice obedience and learn humility, two qualities she has not developed fully because of a doting father. I would ask you to accord her no better treatment than any of the others. In fact . . ." He paused meaningfully. "Well, since we only have a few months to persuade her that marriage to me is preferable to life in a cloister . . ." He shrugged. "I think you understand."

She stood slowly, walked around the table, and stood facing a simple but beautifully wrought gold crucifix on one wall, her back to Rodrigo for a moment. "Signor da Valenti, being a novice is not easy under the best of circumstances. One must prepare to serve God to the exclusion of all other pursuits—"

A vague uneasiness crawled up his spine. Had she even been listening to him?

She turned to him suddenly. "And how could you ever know that marriage to you would be preferable to serving God?" she asked as she looked away again.

"Giulietta will live here until the month of our wedding," he said calmly, ignoring her last question. "As I said before, she will benefit from a rigorous regimen, but under no circumstances will she remain here and take her final vows—although she may be allowed to believe otherwise for now. I am certain the prince would be in full agreement at least with that."

She spun around, her eyes flashing. But almost at once, that most unholy light extinguished. Not, however, before Rodrigo had seen it; not before he'd caught the hint of derision in the momentary curl of one corner of her mouth. He suspected that beneath that wimple she had a luxurious crown of auburn hair to match her fine eyebrows, and therefore was still very much aware of herself as a woman. He made up his mind then and there to make inquiries about her.

But for now, he'd managed to offend her, and he could not afford to do so with Giulietta in her care.

Her next words confirmed it. "I am not obtuse, *condottiere*. But neither do I wish to lock horns with one of the most powerful men in Tuscany. This method of persuasion has been used before by a few of the more lenient patriarchs—although I must admit, never in my experience by the betrothed."

He wasn't quite certain *how* he'd alienated her, but Rodrigo intuitively knew that Sister Lucrezia, Mother Superior of Santa Lucia, could be a formidable enemy if crossed. Beneath her pious exterior ran strange and dark currents. And a whisper of contempt for men that had managed briefly to crack her steady facade.

"Forgive me, Reverend Mother, if in any way I've offended you," he apologized. He gave her a hint of a smile. "And leave Durante de' Alessandro to me. If anything should go awry, I will take the full blame, you have my word." He stood. "I will send a gesture of good faith in the morning; then I'll visit in a fortnight. Is that agreeable?"

She stepped toward him and reached up one hand to touch his cheek, a gesture that reminded him of Giulietta, although compared to this comely but enigmatic she-spider, Giulietta de' Alessandro was an uninitiated babe.

Her fingers were chill, and reminded him unexpectedly of the coldness of a day-old corpse. "Allow me to tend your face . . . perhaps a cool compress for your cheek?"

"Thank you, no," he said, and immediately, as if she'd realized what she was doing, her hand fell away. "I can see myself out," he added.

He bowed formally from the waist, his blue and gold brocade doublet sighing with the movement in the quiet of the room, then turned toward the partially open door and exited.

As he strode through the hallway and toward the inner door to the small courtyard, he suddenly wondered how she had known that he was a *condottiere*.

Indeed, for a cloistered nun, she was well-informed.

# Thirteen

"You escorted her *where?*"

Rodrigo faced the Prince of Monteverdi. It was barely dawn, and they were in the antechamber of Dante and Caressa's bedchamber. Dante's golden hair was rumpled, his feet were bare, and he was clad only in obviously hastily donned trunk hose as he stared in bemusement at Rodrigo.

And reminded Rodrigo poignantly of Giulietta caught off guard.

"Santa Lucia. And 'twas her own idea. After I left you last night, I ran smack into her as she was burrowing her way out of the end of the tunnel beneath the keep."

Dante ran his fingers through his tousled mane and shook his head. "Why in God's name would she be using *that*? And going to Santa Lucia?" He looked genuinely perplexed.

"To avoid marriage."

Dante's eyes met his. He opened his mouth to speak.

"Specifically, to me."

Dante waved one hand in dismissal, sank down onto the divan. "I don't believe she would still hold you responsible for the Corsini boy's death. She—"

"Perhaps not," Rodrigo interrupted, "but she no doubt holds me responsible for what she considers her embarrassingly late marriage. Her pride is smarting, and I'm the most convenient scapegoat in her mind."

Dante shook his head again, but Rodrigo pressed home his

point, for he wouldn't reveal the other reason for Giulietta's animosity. "Yes! Don't you see? She never dreamed you were awaiting my return to Tuscany to become her husband . . . not only the man responsible for her unmarried state, but a Gypsy bastard. I don't find it surprising that she expected more. Forgive my bluntness, Excellence, but she *is* the daughter of a prince."

Some of Dante's bewilderment disappeared, and his look hardened. "She knows naught of your background—your father could have been an emperor for all she knows!"

"Or a woodcutter."

"Bah! Furthermore, Giulietta knows better than to judge a man by his birth."

He clapped his hands, and a birdlike little man, immaculately dressed in the latest fashion, appeared at the antechamber door. "Pico," Dante said, "my clothes, please. Something appropriate to wear to visit Santa Lucia." He looked back at Rodrigo. "We'll straighten this out before the day is done!"

Rodrigo placed a hand on his arm. "I think we should let her be. Until, perhaps, a fortnight before the wedding."

Dante looked at him as if he'd gone mad. "Let her *be*? Remain at Santa Lucia for six months?"

"Aye. Let her have what she thinks she wants. A few lessons in humility certainly wouldn't hurt her."

Rodrigo knew he was treading touchy ground here. Obviously, Dante de' Alessandro's weak spot was his daughter.

The prince pulled his arm away. "My Giulietta in a stuffy convent? Why, she would wither away from boredom!"

Rodrigo repressed a smile at the thought of Giulietta withering away from *anything*.

". . . can you even think such a thing?" Dante was demanding. He allowed Pico to adjust his bright blue, twisted trunk hose, but his angry gaze was still on Rodrigo.

Determination settled over Rodrigo's features. He drew a

deep breath, crossed his arms over his rib cage, and said, "I'm afraid I must insist upon it, Excellence. As her betrothed, I surely have some say in the matter, and I think she would benefit from the . . . experience."

*To put it mildly,* he added to himself.

Just then, Caressa emerged from the bedchamber, fully dressed compared to her husband, yet obviously having had her toilette interrupted. Her long, black hair hung down her back, and with it loose, Rodrigo could discern strands of silver among the thick, dark tresses. Something in her expression reminded him unexpectedly of Giulietta. Although the latter was generally acknowledged as favoring her father. Was it the frown that threaded across her brow? he wondered. . . .

"I couldn't help but overhear, Dante," she said, "and I think you might want to seriously consider what Rodrigo recommends."

Dante's expression immediately softened at her appearance. "What? You, too, *cara?*"

"I ask only that you listen." She looked at Rodrigo. "Will you break the fast with us?" she asked. He nodded, and she addressed her husband in a quiet but confident tone. "Don't you think we could discuss this at length at the board?"

"Neither one of us may even *be* here for the meal if I have any say," he mumbled in answer as Pico lifted a fine silk shirt over his master's head.

As he shrugged into it, Caressa, who was obviously unruffled by his words, pressed him further. "Then we'll discuss it right here. Surely you can see that she must be allowed to learn a lesson . . . the hard way?"

"I don't want Gietta in that convent one moment more than I can help!" he said as the shirt settled over his torso. "You can accompany me or nay, as you will," he told Rodrigo as Pico helped him into his blue and yellow doublet.

"Then I'm afraid I must renege on the betrothal contract."

As if she'd been anticipating Rodrigo's declaration, Caressa swiftly responded. But her words were for Dante. "Giulietta has threatened many times over the years to run to Santa Lucia, when less doting parents would have threatened *her* with banishment to a convent. Now she's actually done so and she must suffer the consequences. It only makes sense! Rodrigo sees that . . . I see that. Why don't you take the blinders from your eyes?" she beseeched him, "before all your well-laid plans for Gietta's future—and Rodrigo's as well—are ruined?"

Dante looked up at his wife, his fingers falling away from the belt he'd been fastening at his waist. When she'd finished speaking, he met Rodrigo's bleak look. Their eyes locked.

Without waiting for dismissal, Pico quietly slipped from the room.

"Think you, Valenti, that mayhap the Lion has lost his bite?" Dante's voice was low, menacing. "Or mayhap getting so long in the tooth that you dare threaten him?"

Caressa bit her lower lip, but was silent.

Rodrigo shook his head. "I'm not threatening you, *principe*. Rather exercising my rights as Giulietta's betrothed. If you are so protective of her now, flying in the face of my decision, then I suspect you will take it upon yourself to set up house within our very bedchamber after the wedding to ensure her well-being. And *that* I will not tolerate."

Color flooded the prince's face. "You dare much," he said in a low voice.

"There is much at stake."

Rodrigo stood his ground, fearing the worst—that he would lose Giulietta and his opportunity to join the Alessandro family—yet unable to retract his words, for he believed his way was right. And he was prepared to live his life without the Prince of Monteverdi's help. He still had plans to start his own company of mercenaries. He had men who were eager to join him, including Carlo. And he had enough money already to build his own home—a small villa somewhere in Tuscany. That, too, had been one of his dreams.

Meanwhile, he could live temporarily in Florence if need be, for the *Zingari* were planning to move on for the winter.

No, he didn't need Durante de' Alessandro—or his daughter—to live a good life; to attain the few things he'd always thought important.

"Very well," Dante said, breaking into Rodrigo's thoughts. "We'll do it your way." His back was to Valenti, for he'd been stoking the coals in the fireplace, his jerky movements indicating his anger. As the embers flared to life, he added kindling, then a fragrant cedar log from the shining brass bin beside the hearth. Brushing the dust from his hands, he swung back to Rodrigo, who couldn't believe he'd heard right. "Until mid-April, Giulietta will remain at Santa Lucia . . . on one condition."

Rodrigo held his breath, praying he could meet the condition without compromising his position. "Which is?"

"You say she was attempting to go to Santa Lucia on her own?"

Rodrigo nodded, thinking that Dante knew very well she wouldn't have gone to the trouble of traversing an old and possibly dangerous tunnel merely to get some fresh air. The temptation to say that she'd tried it before danced across his mind, but he held his silence, as he knew his sense of honor would command until he breathed his last.

*"Ebbene,* if she wishes to leave the convent before April, you will allow her to return to Monteverdi. That is my condition. Agreed?"

Rodrigo hesitated a moment. Giulietta was far too proud to ever admit she'd made the wrong choice, therefore it would obviously be most humiliating to her to find herself begging to leave the confines of Santa Lucia. And Rodrigo had no intention of allowing her to believe anything but that eventually she would take her final vows.

"Agreed."

But he knew his relationship with Durante de' Alessandro had been severely strained once again, only this time by their difference in opinion over Giulietta. Dante was, obviously, reluctant to acknowledge the faults of his daughter, and his own part in indulging her over the years.

"And, of course, she will be allowed to come for visits as often—"

"No." It was Caressa who spoke now, echoing Rodrigo's very thoughts. "If she chose to leave her home, she can't come running back to us every time she gets lonely . . . or objects to something at Santa Lucia."

Dante turned to her, his look troubled. "But she will be there for six *months,* Caressa! She's never been away from us for more than a few hours."

Caressa moved toward him, her silk skirts rustling softly, and placed one hand upon his arm. "If you welcome her with open arms any time she wishes to visit Monteverdi, what lesson has she learned?"

"That she is better off here!"

But to Rodrigo's relief, the prince only shook his head in defeat—for the logic in Caressa's and Rodrigo's reasoning was right before him. And although he was often unduly partial toward his daughter, Dante was no fool. "And so you are both against me, I see," he said darkly before he swung away. "My own wife . . . and the man I've taken to my heart as a son."

He strode toward the door, and Caressa threw Rodrigo an apologetic look. He felt badly for her, yet he was certain his way was best where Giulietta was concerned. He graciously offered Caressa his arm, and a corner of his mouth lifted with a rueful half-smile as he attempted to lighten the mood, for he'd learned in the last few months that it was unusual for Dante to be angry with his wife . . . or her opinions.

As they followed a stiff-backed prince from the antechamber, Rodrigo acknowledged that Caressa was definitely a more likely ally where Giulietta was concerned than her husband; and with a soft but genuine sigh of resignation, he mutely mourned the disappearance of a younger, more flexible Prince of Monteverdi.


Although Giulietta wouldn't admit it for weeks, the prospect of marriage to Rodrigo da Valenti grew in appeal with each day she spent at Santa Lucia. As the weather grew chill and damp, she dreaded traversing the drafty corridors in the clumsy open sandals novices were required to wear—no cape or cloak to pull snugly about her for added warmth. Although the heavy habits were warm in and of themselves, Giulietta would have welcomed the added protection of a good cloak, especially when she was sent outdoors.

The autumn weather wasn't severe, but Giulietta was accustomed to Castello Monteverdi's glowing braziers and crackling fires in huge, hooded hearths to chase away the chill. At Santa Lucia, she quickly discovered that little consideration was given to physical comfort, and especially that of the novices. Things like fires and extra clothing for warmth weren't a primary consideration in convent life, and having been pampered from the day she was born, Giulietta had a real problem accepting and adjusting.

"I would not love God any less were I warm and well-fed," she informed another postulant, Sister Luigia, soon after her unorthodox and humiliating arrival. They were in the refectory for the evening meal, and talking among the postulants was forbidden. Nonetheless, talk she did, under her breath, for Luigia's ears alone.

Luigia, who nurtured a healthy respect for the convent rules—and a fear of the nuns—did not acknowledge her friend's comment beyond a slight tightening of her mouth, her eyes upon her bowl of *polenta,* a thick porridge, and a tap against Giulietta's ankle beneath the board with her sandaled foot. The light kick was obviously a warning, which Giulietta ignored.

The smell of roasted sausage floated past her nose, and she cast a veiled glance at the veritable feast set before Sister Lucrezia and the other nuns at the next table. Indeed, she caught a tantalizing glimpse of sausage and cooked vegetables. And what looked like some kind of fowl. Plumes of steam spiraled upward from a tureen of sauce set at either end of the head table.

Fairly simple, yet a veritable banquet compared to what the postulants were given. And the final outrage, at least to Giulietta, was the rich, dark wine they poured from terra-cotta pitchers set out along their table . . . a far cry from watered-down cider.

Luigia kicked Giulietta yet again, this time more emphatically. But it was too late. Sister Elena, who was responsible for Giulietta and watched her like a hawk watching for a sign of weakness in its prey, caught sight of Giulietta's roving eyes, even as the latter was attributing her diluted cider to the good sister's extraordinary talent for economy. The nun stared straight at Giulietta, who, by now, was looking with undisguised longing at the food at the head table.

Luigia gave Giulietta a third kick—sharp enough to drag the latter's hungry gaze from the forbidden. Giulietta narrowed her eyes at the young woman beside her, then realized that someone from the head table was staring at her. She knew, without looking again, who it was, and hid the sudden, rebellious light in her eyes by assuming the same attitude as the other postulants.

She quickly lifted her spoon to begin eating. . . .

* * *

During the first week, Luigia had shown her the herb garden and taught her to recognize the herbs that Sister Margherita used in the kitchen. The two nuns who were normally in charge of the herb and vegetable gardens were in conference with Sister Lucrezia, and Giulietta and Luigia had had a heretofore unprecedented opportunity to talk softly as one young woman ostensibly instructed the other.

"My family lives in Florence. My father is a weaver, but after three other daughters, my parents had no dowry left for me," Luigia informed Giulietta. "I hate it here, but what else can I do except, mayhap, become a prostitute." Bitterness filled her voice with her last words.

Giulietta instantly felt sympathy for the girl. Guilt flooded through her at the difference in their circumstances. "I—I chose to enter the order," she said in honesty, yet feeling like a hypocrite. "But I don't like it here either," she admitted.

Luigia, a tall, lissome girl about Giulietta's age, briefly turned puzzled gray eyes upon her new friend. "But you are beautiful, Giulietta, and the daughter of a prince. Why ever would you *choose* to become a nun?"

Before Giulietta could concoct an answer, Luigia raised one hand to her mouth. Her fingers had been working to free a bulb from the earth, and the gesture left a streak of dirt across one cheek. "Forgive me for prying. 'Tis none of my con—"

Giulietta took up where Luigia left off, her fingers breaking up the clods of earth, her eyes on her task. *"Grazi,"* she said softly, "but beauty comes from within, so my mother tells me . . . and according to my father, a healthy curiosity can do no harm. Even if you *are* a female."

At Luigia's silence, Giulietta looked up. Their eyes met. Suddenly they both grinned at Giulietta's cheeky quote. "Suffice it to say," she added, "that I didn't want to marry the man

my father chose for me. I'm here of my own volition and—
*Dio!*—'tis nothing like I imagined."

"If Sister Elena heard you . . . why, she'd make you prostrate yourself before the chapel altar for a week!" Luigia said,
one corner of her mouth bowing with mirth.

"Cristo al cielo!" Giulietta swore under her breath in exaggerated shock, "you jest!"

"A fortnight, now, Sister Giulietta!" Luigia admonished
with sham severity. "But you are in for a treat, didn't you
know?" she teased, as Giulietta swiped the edge of one sleeve
across Luigia's dirt-smudged cheek. "You haven't milked the
cows yet, have you?"

"Milk the cows?"

"*Sì.* They are meaner than some of the nuns. Beware the
second brindle . . ."

Within the constraints of the convent rules, they managed
to form a friendship, and it was the one bright spot in the
dreary routine that became Giulietta's life. She missed her family terribly, thought about them constantly. And, yes, if she
were absolutely honest with herself, her thoughts strayed too
often to Rodrigo da Valenti . . . and the very potent memories
of his kisses.

Yet she stubbornly attributed her thoughts of him to the life
she was leading. Any daydreams that distracted her from the
drudgery of Santa Lucia were welcome . . . even if they were
of the man her father had chosen for her to wed. The man
she'd convinced herself she despised.

She would discipline herself to concentrate on her devotions. She just needed time to adjust to her new life. She would
find everything she needed here at Santa Lucia. . . .


One day of the second week, Giulietta was "meditating" in
her cell after the midafternoon service. In fact, she was ad-

*Linda Lang Bartell*

miring the illuminated pages of a religious manuscript Sister Lucrezia had loaned her, for Giulietta had long been a lover of art. It was a genuine pleasure to peruse the pages of brightly colored religious scenes, for the monk who had labored over this particular work had been extremely talented.

She thought back to her request of Sister Lucrezia—and the nun's unexpected consent. And her even more surprising comment: *"I applaud a woman who is interested in reading scripture for herself, for women are no less than men."*

A strange remark, Giulietta had thought at the time, but the more she pondered the Mother Superior's words, the more she realized she agreed. She hadn't volunteered the fact that she was more interested in the artwork . . . some things were better left unsaid.

Now, as she admired the illuminations, she could picture some obscure monk shut up in his sterile cloister, laboring ceaselessly, and going unrecognized for his talents.

What a shame. . . .

The faint strains of a lute came to her unexpectedly. She raised her head, her heart turning over in her chest. No, it couldn't be.

She closed her eyes and willed away the music, but it wasn't her imagination. She stood and peeked out from her cell. The hall that ran past was empty. She stepped out and moved toward the sound; the closer she got to the source, the more identifiable the music became. The dirgelike strains were certainly not being created by the lute player to whose music she'd recently become accustomed.

Suddenly the music stopped . . . and Giulietta halted in her tracks near the parlor door where guests were received. Fearing discovery, she quietly retreated one step, then another. She was about to swing away when a figure emerged from the room: a dark-robed figure—a monk, she saw immediately.

He didn't speak at first, didn't even acknowledge her except to stare directly into her eyes. His own were the oddest shade of green, and as mesmerizing as any she'd seen in her lifetime, although not because of their beauty but, rather, their intensity.

Giulietta felt pinned to the spot as those glowing green eyes, seemingly lit from some inner source, plumbed her heart . . . her soul. She felt her breath catch in her throat, and a chill of premonition ghosted over her as she realized who he was.

She'd never seen the Prior of San Marco before, but she'd heard plenty about him—and none of it good, according to her father, who'd been close to the Medicis. Girolamo Savonarola, she knew, despised the Medici family and all they represented. . . .

"Who are *you?*" he asked without warning in a hard voice.

"Giul—er, Sister Giulietta," she murmured, more afraid of attracting attention than incurring Savonarola's displeasure. "M-may I fetch Reverend Mother for you?" she asked in an attempt to appear useful in a place where, to some, simple curiosity was considered the equivalent of sloth.

He didn't seem to hear her, and reached out one hand. As her eyes darted to that hand, it jerked away as if yanked by a string. "Giulietta?" he mumbled.

*"Sì."* She frowned in growing bemusement at his odd behavior.

"Giulietta who?"

"De' Alessandro."

By this time she was making note of the pallor of his face, which emphasized his dark and heavy brows, his ugly nose and thick, fleshy lips. He was thin, too, and small—not much taller than she was. His habit was worn and patched.

"Was that you playing the lute?" she asked, feeling extremely uncomfortable now, and hoping to elicit a response from him other than terse queries.

He nodded as he continued to study her face, a storm brew-

ing on his brow. "The Lord may be worshiped through simple
and unadorned music."

*Aye,* she thought, *but certainly not the plaintive chords with
which you were lauding Him.* She only nodded, however.

"Devil's daughter!" he blurted.

Giulietta looked sharply at him, feeling suddenly swept
along on a powerful tide of consternation. Women had been
burnt at the stake for witchcraft in the face of such accusations.
And here was a religious of great importance—to some, anyway—accusing her of ungodliness.

Giulietta stepped back, offended and confused by his words.
And suddenly fearful. She didn't dare laugh in his face, even
though that was the initial reaction this ludicrous man had
inspired within her. He'd defied Pope Alexander and been excommunicated. Surely he feared nothing—not even her father's
wrath should he harm her.

In the blink of an eye, Santa Lucia lost its status as a
haven. The walls closed in on her as threateningly as those
of a prison—or a tomb.

*He's only a man.*

Some of her trepidation turned to anger, and with a burst
of boldness, she asked, "Why did you call me such a thing,
Fra Girolamo?"

He lifted one arm, his heavy brows meeting in anger, and
pointed a thin finger at her. His eyes seemed to shoot red from
their glowing green depths. "You are a mirage . . . sent by the
Devil, to remind me of my greatest temptation in this life:
Laodamia."

Bewildered, Giulietta searched her memory for a clue to the
name Laodamia. Laodamia . . . Laodamia . . . Then she remembered. Laodamia Strozzi, natural daughter of a Florentine
exile, who'd loftily rejected the friar's love some years before.

Did he somehow think she was the Strozzi woman?

Giulietta lifted her chin, her own expression hardening as

the Alessandro pride rose within her to shore her up. She shook her head. "No. You are mistaken. I'm no one but Giulietta de' Alessandro. Ask anyone here—"

"Fra Girolamo? Giulietta?" came Sister Lucrezia's voice from behind the prior.

His gaze didn't leave Giulietta, even as he canted his head to one side. "Indeed, Sister Lucrezia," he answered, " 'tis I. But, pray tell, who is this . . . creature?"

Giulietta bristled, her fear completely gone now. *Creature?* And if that weren't bad enough, the condescension in his voice was untenable. Why, the Prior of San Marco was the one who looked creaturelike! He could have passed for a gargoyle glaring down upon the unsuspecting crowds from his perch atop some cathedral.

She opened her mouth to speak, forgetting what she'd learned of humility, but Sister Lucrezia intervened. "This is Sister Giulietta. Sister, this is Fra Girolamo Savonarola, Prior of San Marco." Before either could say a word, she added, "Giulietta is one of our postulants, and has been with us only a few short weeks. Pray excuse her ignorance, Fra Girolamo," she soothed, "if she has in any way offended you. Her family is steeped in the ways of the worldly."

*"Sì."* His features seemed to relax slightly, his eyes cleared. "The Alessandros are a godless lot, full of vanity and lust; a family that epitomizes the heathen love of material things and pleasures. They are no different than the Medici tyrants with whom they trafficked."

*At least none of my family has managed to invoke the Pope's wrath,* she told him silently, her eyes alight with real anger. *None of us has been excommunicated!*

But his thoughts seemed already to have been diverted, for he turned abruptly to face Lucrezia, rudely giving his back to Giulietta. "I have several matters I would discuss with you,

Sister," he said to her, and proceeded past her toward her office, his worn robes swirling about his ankles.

Sister Lucrezia gave Giulietta a nod, a warning in her eyes. "Back to your devotions, Sister," she instructed, then swung away to follow the Dominican.

As a final act of defiance, Giulietta remained right where she was and watched them walk away, coming to the conclusion that the man was truly the fanatic so many called him. He appeared not the least bit humbled by His Holiness' interdict.

A chill pricked the flesh on the back of her neck, for the Scourge of Florence, she thought, was only a man after all. And one, she had heard, who had already touched off the chain of events that would lead to his own destruction.

# Fourteen

*"Sister Giulietta!"*

Giulietta woke with a start at the low but stringent voice in her ear. The sight of the prune-faced Sister Elena made her forget herself and groan softly. The woman surely would be the cause of her ignominious death at Santa Lucia, where she would most likely be found in the exact spot where she expired beside a newly cleaned chamber pot, starved to death and exhausted.

And reeking, no doubt, like a noxious chamber pot herself.

"What do you *here,* Sister?" the older nun hissed into her ear again, causing Giulietta to sit up on the hard floor with alacrity to escape further auditory abuse. "Night is for sleeping—the day to toil and pray!"

"Yes, Sister," she mumbled, her eyes downcast as she wondered if Sister Elena had ever smiled or laughed in her life.

"Do you realize where you are?"

*Of course I do,* she thought with ire. *After one month I know every corner of this convent!* But she glanced about, perversely feigning disorientation, a ploy she often used lately on Sister Elena.

The nun spoke before Giulietta could seemingly get her bearings. "The parlor—where we receive visitors! Imagine Sister Lucrezia receiving someone in this very room and discovering *you* curled in the corner like some sleeping mongrel."

Mortification flooded Giulietta's face at the reprimand.

"Your lack of industry is a disgrace to Santa Lucia. And to your family, as well."

In spite of her good intentions, fire flashed in Giulietta's gem gold eyes. She couldn't tolerate the thought of shaming the House of Alessandro. Yet, by curling up in a corner and succumbing to sleep, mayhap she *was* disgracing her family. And especially since it had been *her* wish to enter Santa Lucia.

She bit her tongue, choked back her pride. "Yes, Sister," she said in her most humble voice. "I'll try harder."

Out of the blue, her stomach rumbled, sounding like Lily's roar in the stillness of the room.

"And your appetite is shameful," the whip-thin Sister Elena added. "You're plump as a partridge and you eat enough for five. You must curb your self-indulgent tendencies and take more interest in your spiritual needs."

*You eat enough for five* . . . Giulietta fought the unholy urge to lob the newly cleaned pot right at Sister Elena's head. Instead, with her gaze demurely downcast, she hurled a less-than-subtle verbal missile at the nun. "You're absolutely right, Sister. And if more of the good nuns at Santa Lucia eschewed food and drink as you do, we wouldn't even *need* chamber pots, would we?"

She sneaked a peek at Sister Elena through her lashes . . . just in time to catch the look of startled suspicion that entered the nun's expression. Her mouth pursed even more tightly, and her small, dark eyes narrowed. Giulietta kept her expression bland, however, lest the good sister come up with some punishment that would make cleaning chamber pots an enjoyable task in comparison.

Just as Sister Elena began to speak, the bell rang out to signal vespers. Giulietta inwardly sighed with relief, for it heralded the end of her toil and the coming evening meal. True she must first endure one last hour of prayer and devotion, during which it was exceedingly difficult not to nod off. The thought of food afterward, however, was a powerful incentive to stay awake. And the thought of retiring after that to her hard and narrow pallet was also a welcome prospect.

"The cows are lowing—Sisters Isabella and Francesca heard them while in the herb garden a short while ago. You should have been milking them instead of napping."

Giulietta sighed audibly at the thought of milking the four cows in the small barn. They were the most recalcitrant animals she'd ever encountered, and what should have been (according to the ever-present Sister Elena) no more than an hour and a half task, lasted at least three for Giulietta. Even after almost a sennight of performing this latest task, Giulietta found that the wretched animals still refused to give their milk with anything remotely resembling cooperation.

Sister Elena's tone suddenly softened. "I know 'tis difficult for you, child, but everyone must share the load—especially in light of having recently lost some of our beloved order this past summer to plague."

At the mention of death among the nuns at Santa Lucia— something that had only been whispered about up until now— Giulietta evinced a pang of contrition. After all, it had been *her* decision to come to the convent; she was young and healthy and certainly could contribute more than some of the aging sisters who'd lived there for their entire lives.

"Forgive me, Sister," she said in all sincerity. "I will tend to the cows after vespers."

Sister Elena nodded. "And if you are quick about it, you can get something to eat from the kitchen before it gets too cold," she said gruffly. "I'll ask Sister Margherita to put aside a portion for you."

Before the word "thank-you" could even form on Giulietta's lips, the nun had swung toward the door and disappeared.

\* \* \*

After an hour of prayer, Giulietta roused herself to go to the barn. The thought of food—which she'd nurtured all during vespers—fired her determination to milk the cows in short order. After all, she reasoned as she walked across the walled courtyard and toward the byre, lantern in hand, she loved animals, and the creatures had always responded positively to her.

That is . . . until she'd encountered the cows of Santa Lucia.

The barn door stood open, and upon entering Giulietta was immediately assaulted by the smell of bovines, hay, and manure . . . in particular the malodorous cow droppings. She wrinkled her nose and hung her lantern on a protruding nail just above the stall divider between the first two cows. All four animals were lowing, a definite indication that they were past due for milking.

Speed was of the essence, she thought, if she were to have at least a luke-warm meal. She rolled up the full sleeves of her habit, grabbed a clean milk pail, and slid the milking stool in place just forward of the first cow's bony hip. What was the animal's name? she thought suddenly. It was a brindle, as was the one in the second stall, but she couldn't recall its name. After all, she thought with rue, she had only just learned each of the sisters' names. Four milch cows were certainly not high on her list of priorities.

She sat upon the stool and set to work, hoping that she could somehow communicate a sense of urgency to the animal to help the process along. She tugged at the teats in the manner Sister Elena had taught her, knowing it might take a few minutes for the milk to come.

But as the minutes multiplied, Giulietta grew frustrated. "*Will* you cooperate?" she said through set teeth to the cow. "Lest I leave you full to bursting 'til morn!"

Evidently the creature was unaffected by threats, for it only swung its head about and cast a jaundiced eye at Giulietta, chewing its cud in seeming contentment.

But then, a thin stream of milk began spraying the sides of the pail. Giulietta was jubilant. Her dinner was only an hour and a half away. . . .

Reverend Mother's pet black cat came prowling around her stiff skirts, obviously at the sound of milk flowing into the pail. Giulietta sent him skittering away with a movement of one foot, afraid he would disturb the cow. But he was not to be denied.

She tried ignoring him, which worked for a while, and concentrated on her task. The sight and smell of fresh, frothy milk set her stomach a-growl once again, and before she knew it, her head was resting against the cow's flank as she became mesmerized by the stream of milk slowly filling the pail. How she longed for a cup of milk. . . .

The cows manure-matted tail switched suddenly, swiping Giulietta in the side of the face. Between the sting and the stench, she found herself straightening with alacrity. The pail jumped as her foot hit it, sending the precious milk sloshing dangerously close to the lip. She finished with the first brindle while sitting as straight as a soldier and eyeing the innocuous-looking tail from time to time as if it had a will of its own.

When she'd taken all the milk the animal had to give, Giulietta carefully moved the pail out of the stall and to a corner where it would be out of the way. She stood and stretched her arms toward the ceiling, arching her cramped back, and wondering why—aside from the cost—nuns never wore habits made from more comfortable material like silk. Surely Sister Lucrezia's habits were easier on the skin, for Giulietta had noticed the Reverend Mother's clothing appeared to be of better quality than that of the other nuns.

With a feeling of accomplishment—and growing confidence that the second cow would be as cooperative—Giulietta picked up the milking stool and moved it into position. She sat down and spoke to the cow in what she considered amiable tones, then took hold of two teats. As she did so, it occurred to her that she'd neglected to get another pail to catch the milk. Uttering a soft expletive she'd learned from Nicco, she quickly stood and began to swing away from the brindle.

Without warning, the cow lashed out at her with one hind leg. Pain exploded through her hip, startling her and taking her breath away. She lurched backward, hit the wall behind her, and slid to a sitting position in the hay, dazed. Her wimple edged over her forehead and came to rest just over her eyebrows.

It was then that Luigia's warning about the second brindle came to her . . . belatedly.

When her mind cleared, she wondered if she looked as ludicrous as she felt. Of course it didn't matter, for only the cows were there to see her.

Annoyed, she ripped the wimple off her head and tossed it aside. She struggled to her feet, ready to do battle with the brindle. As she limped toward the stack of empty milk pails, the faint strains of a lute came to her from outside the barn.

Surely her mind was playing tricks on her. No doubt the lack of food. Or (God forbid!) mayhap it was the prior again.

But as she paused and strained to listen, the soft music continued, its allure overpowering. It was beautiful, not like that which Savonarola played, and, like a sleepwalker, Giulietta moved toward the open door, momentarily forgetting the cows, the milk . . . and her dinner.

There on the low stone wall surrounding the cloister sat a man, strumming his lute as if it were the most natural thing in the world to do on convent grounds. His legs were folded, ankles crossed, and the pear-shaped body of the instrument rested in his lap. His face was raised to the deep cobalt of the twilight sky.

His music had attracted her; now the sight of his familiar silhouette clutched at something deep within her and roused a myriad of conflicting emotions. Not the least of which was gratitude. Gratitude for a welcome diversion, even though it came from *him*. Gratitude for a respite, however brief it might prove to be, from the drudgery to which she'd willingly consigned herself. Even if it came from *him*.

After a month at Santa Lucia, even Rodrigo da Valenti was a welcome visitor.

Among other things, whether Giulietta liked it or not, the *condottiere* possessed the power to lure her forth with his music; and she found herself moving toward him as unerringly as a trained falcon homing to its master's wrist.

She had the presence of mind to acknowledge that even had he played as poorly as Girolamo Savonarola, she would have followed the sound.

He looked down at her then, the movement of her pale skirts obviously catching his attention. His look was unreadable for a moment, as much from the deepening dusk as undoubtedly his own self-control, before he smiled that soul-shaking smile. In the dimness she caught the flash of healthy white teeth against his shadow-shrouded visage.

*"Buona notte,"* he murmured, the lute's sweet notes fading away as his fingers stilled. He laid it aside and narrowed his eyes slightly.

*"Per piacere, signore,* don't stop," she beseeched in quiet tones. She glanced furtively over her shoulder toward the convent building, then back to him.

Her reaction to his presence was totally unexpected. He had hoped she'd perhaps had time to think about her precipitate actions and had, in the process, felt the beginnings of regret. But this almost *eager* reception both surprised him . . . and aroused a hint of suspicion.

He studied her intently without leaving his seat upon the wall. There was no need to alarm or offend her and send her

fleeing . . . although the idea of Giulietta de Alessandro fleeing anyone was hard to imagine.

Her face looked wan and thinner, its fine bone structure
more prominent. It lent her an ethereal look. He supposed she
could have suffered a significant weight loss in a month, and
felt sudden concern. She was slight of frame to begin with,
so of course it would be more obvious on her than on a larger
woman.

He reached for the lute again at her request, and absently
strummed a few chords as he studied her features in the waning
light.

"Can you play the tune you played . . . at the camp that
first night?"

He couldn't tell if she blushed with her words, but he did
notice a faint sway before she seemed to recover herself. She
put her fingers briefly to her brow, as if to massage away
dizziness or pain, then almost immediately allowed her hand
to fall back to her side.

Fearing to offend her—it had never been difficult for him
to do so, he thought wryly—he played, very softly, the French
love song she'd requested, disinclined to attract unwanted attention from the convent, especially now that he'd found her.
He assumed Sister Lucrezia would remember their agreement
if and when his presence was reported, but one could never
be certain. And, above all, he didn't want some purse-lipped
nun standing sentinel over them.

He didn't sing, although singing was almost as natural for
him as breathing. Still, Giulietta seemed content and didn't
move until the last notes faded away. Her chest rose slightly
with a sigh; then her eyes met his as she stepped toward him.

"How are you, Giulietta?" he asked, half-afraid of breaking
the spell.

She seemed suddenly distracted, and responded by asking
in a whisper, "Do you know aught of milking cows?" Again,

she threw an anxious glance over her shoulder, then drew
nearer in obvious anticipation of his answer.

"Cows?" He set his lute aside and slid down from the wall.
He flashed her another smile. *"Ebbene,* enough, I suppose, for
a mercenary."

"Forgive me," she said on another sigh of what sounded
this time like disappointment. "What would a *condottiere*
know of cows?" She swung away with obvious reluctance. "I
have unfinished tasks to—"

"Wait." He stepped closer and put one hand on her shoulder.
"The *Zingari* normally keep a cow or two, especially when
there are infants or young children among us. Do you need
help?"

She raised her face to his, hope lighting her eyes. *"Sì!* I
cannot eat until the cows are taken care of and they—" a trace
of the old Giulietta entered her voice here—"they are the most
obstinate beasts in all of Christendom!"

"You cannot eat?" he echoed, irked by the thought. *Dio mio,*
she'd only been here four weeks! How could anyone withhold
food from her when a little help from one experienced nun
would have easily solved the problem?

"Show me," he said, then smiled inwardly as he caught the
faint smell of barn animals and manure wafting upward from
her shoes and shirts.

She did, then pointed to the second brindle after they entered
the byre and said darkly, *"That* beast has surely been trained
by Sister Elena to thwart me. And she has the devil's own
disposition, too!"

"I'm not surprised. Cows are stupid animals, *cara,* and stubborn as well. But they still respond to a kind word or even
more to a song. You'll learn that over the years." He was unable
to resist the temptation of reminding her of her wish to live
out her life at Santa Lucia.

She looked from the cow to Rodrigo with unguarded dismay. He felt his spirits lighten considerably. Perhaps there was hope for a willing bride after all.

"So she's holding back, is she?" he asked in an attempt to erase that heart-wrenching look. He was such a soft-hearted fool where she was concerned.

Giulietta's look turned puzzled. "I don't know. The good nun who saw to the cows perished during the past summer and we're shorthanded. No one explained such things to me."

Her expression turned hopeful as she looked up at him, and she reminded him of Giulietta the child, six years past. She absently rubbed at one hip as he examined the cow's swollen udder. He caught the gesture out of the corner of his eye. "Did she kick you?" he asked with a frown.

She shook her head. " 'Tis nothing." She narrowed her eyes at the cow's hind legs. "In fact, 'tis my own fault . . . I forgot to tie her legs."

Rodrigo nodded, and Giulietta reached for the length of rope used to control a cow's back legs, which was hanging from a nail in the stall divider. "First," he advised her, "stand back." As Giulietta backed away from the stall, he bent over and drove one shoulder into the brindle's ribs. The animal released a gruntlike sound, but continued to chew her cud.

Rodrigo held out one hand for the rope from Giulietta and swiftly looped it about the animal's back legs. Dragging the milking stool into position, he grinned up at her as he sat. "Now let's see how cooperative she is."

Within moments the welcome sound of milk hitting the pail met Giulietta's ears, and her stomach began to churn in anticipation of her coming meal. She found herself crouched beside Rodrigo, watching in fascination as his nimble fingers coaxed the milk from each teat.

Her father had told her that the *Zingari* had a way with animals—and this she had seen with her own eyes. Yet she wondered if there was anything Rodrigo da Valenti couldn't do.

"I wonder if 'tis because you're a man," she mused aloud. He glanced at her with raised eyebrows, then back to his moving hands. "Surely these cows," she explained, "if they were born in this barn, have never been touched by a man . . ."

Giulietta's eyes flew to his as she realized what she'd said. The words sounded like sacrilege in a barn owned and run by women who considered themselves brides of Christ. Color climbed her cheeks and proceeded upward to the roots of her sunset-blond hair.

His hands stilled; his face moved ever so slowly closer to hers. Of course her theory was wrong. The cow had responded to what felt like a calf butting its head against her side in its demand for milk. But Giulietta couldn't know that. . . .

Their eyes locked. "Is that what *you* want, Giulietta?" he murmured, his breath fanning the tendrils of hair curling about her cheeks and forehead. "To live out your life here? Without children? Without the love and companionship of a husband for the rest of your natural life?"

She waited in sudden, intense anticipation as his lips hovered a heartbeat away from hers. His breath was warm and sweet, unexpectedly erotic in the unlikely surroundings of a stable.

She unconsciously ran the tip of her tongue over her parted lips, wondering if she'd become so caught up in her rigid pride where Rodrigo da Valenti was concerned that she was giving up marriage to this beautiful and maddeningly alluring man for a life of kneeling on hard, cold chapel floors . . . and milking cows. Surely she must be mad. And surely God was reminding her of that very madness by placing Rodrigo de Valenti within her reach like this, in stark and startling contrast to the day to day, mind-dulling routine she'd been living the last month.

Suddenly, her life stretched endlessly before her, and one of God's commandments came to mind: *Honor thy father and thy mother.* She certainly hadn't honored her father by blatant disobedience. She'd defied him to escape marriage to this man. And why? Because of pride.

And ever since Mario di Corsini's death, she'd been threatening to go to Santa Lucia. Now that she was there, she knew she'd made a mistake; yet she couldn't admit her mistake . . . her pride wouldn't allow it.

Pride, again. Her pride was as great and unyielding as any man's.

Rodrigo's lips touched hers with exquisite tenderness. His tongue traced the delicate line of her lower lip, and a host of involuntary sensations showered through her.

"Do you, Giulietta?" he whispered against her mouth, scattering her thoughts like leaves before the wind.

The brindle shifted her weight, wrenching Giulietta back to her senses. Suddenly she was more apprehensive of the prospect of being discovered in the barn kissing Rodrigo da Valenti than the possibility of eternal damnation by breaking God's fifth commandment.

Difficult as it was, she managed to dredge up enough indignation to attempt an admonishing frown, still very much aware of him as a vital and virile male bursting like a breath of fresh air into her stultifying surroundings. "You take extraordinary liberties, *signore,*" she managed, but her traitorous voice held little of censure.

"You're my betrothed, *cara.* How can a simple kiss be considered an extraordinary liberty?"

She raised her chin slightly, essaying to ignore the steadily strengthening belief that marriage to Rodrigo da Valenti would be preferable to taking her vows. "I am betrothed to Christ," she countered, feeling like a hypocrite. A lifetime of monotonous repetition and deprivation had been steadily losing its

appeal for her over the weeks, even as images of Rodrigo da
Valenti seemed to creep more and more frequently into her
thoughts—her very dreams.

And now here he was before her, under the most unlikely
of circumstances, having stunned her emotionally and physically with the sweetest, most tentative of kisses . . . and after
he'd come to her rescue like some knight errant.

Indeed, she thought as the Alessandro sense of humor threatened to overcome her, a *condottiere* in gleaming armor, to
rescue her from an uncooperative cow.

She watched him resume milking the brindle, and a smile
curved her mouth. Then a bubble of laughter worked its way
up her throat and emerged from her lips, ringing through the
quiet stable like soft, melodic chimes.

Rodrigo's eyes met hers questioningly, but they were also
bright with answering humor. He returned her smile. "If 'tis
my skill at cow milking that moves you to laughter, you're
truly ungrateful. I don't make a habit of rescuing maidens
from . . . milch cows." He cocked one dark eyebrow. "And
were anyone to discover our secret, I would be the laughing-
stock of Tuscany."

"I won't tell a soul," she promised when she could speak
without laughing. "But hurry, won't you? I'm afraid Sister
Elena will eat my portion of supper if I tarry."

His look sobered. He nodded and renewed his efforts at
milking the brindle. Giulietta couldn't help but notice the
healthy bronze of his long fingers against the cow's pale pink
udder.

He quickly finished, placed the pail beside the first one,
and deftly removed the rope from the brindle's hind legs. As
he secured the legs of the third cow, a fawn-colored animal,
Giulietta said, "I'll milk the last one."

"Are you so eager to be rid of me?" he asked. "And after
I came to your rescue?"

She looked over at him, suddenly so concerned she'd offended him that she failed to catch the teasing note in his voice. Why had she ever thought him *dark? Dark as the Devil,* a voice reminded her. And unappealing in looks? "Oh, 'tisn't that," she said hastily, flushing with confusion in the wake of her unexpectedly physical thoughts, "only . . . I'm so hungry!"

"Then come sit beside me and I'll not only milk these last two in record time, but I'll sing you a song."

Her look brightened.

"And," he added at her reaction, wanting in the worst way to keep her smiling, "I'll give you as much milk as you can drink and no one will be the wiser."

The thought of fresh, creamy milk made her mouth water. And the thought of putting one over on the omniscient Sister Elena was almost as inviting.

He offered her the milking stool, then dropped to one knee to finish his task while Giulietta had time to relax . . . and study him surreptitiously.

Rodrigo da Valenti was, for all his gentleness and apparent good humor, quintessentially masculine. The sound of his voice, the size and obvious strength of his form, the confidence he exuded even in his lighter moments—his very scent. . . .

Somehow, in those quiet moments they spent while he performed Giulietta's task, he was more fascinating than anyone she had ever met in her relatively sheltered life. More interesting by far than what she remembered of Mario di Corsini (although a memory couldn't compete with a man in the flesh), or even Leon Sarzano. No doubt it had to do with Rodrigo da Valenti being the only male at Santa Lucia—even the cows were female. Giulietta could only imagine how masculine *any* man would appear to her after year upon year spent among the nuns.

Yet if she were truthful with herself, Maddalena's grandson

had never been any less. She'd seen him pitted against other men of skill upon a tournament field, including her own father, and had born witness to his victories.

She'd heard him explain the merits of French armor, weapons, and methods, influencing men of battle with his knowledge and experience.

And, of course, she herself had fallen completely under the spell of his devastating maleness on that very first night of stolen bliss . . . and several other times since then.

Ah, yes . . . that first night, when she'd fled Castello Monteverdi in anger because her father had failed to find her a husband. Now, here she was, a novice at Santa Lucia because she refused to wed the man her father finally *had* chosen for her.

Doubts assailed her. Doubts about her rash actions one month ago, and also about her obstinate resistance to the idea of marriage to Rodrigo da Valenti. . . .

*But he took advantage of you that first night . . .* reminded an echo of her pride.

No, she admitted for the first time with brutal honesty. She had been just as guilty as he—had been looking to spite her father in any way she could that night, and had taken advantage of the situation as much as Rodrigo da Valenti.

Very softly, he began to sing the words to the French song she'd requested earlier. The strange allure of the language appealed powerfully to the part of her that enthusiastically embraced beauty in anything, and without warning, Giulietta was moved to tears.

Confused and embarrassed by her reaction, she lowered her gaze to the stable floor lest the man singing to her interpret her tear-filled eyes as a sign of weakness. She was an Alessandro, and *that* would be unthinkable.

She was just exhausted . . . and famished.

Yet, even the fawn cow seemed to be enjoying Valenti's dulcet singing, for its milk came faster, and the white cow on the end had ceased its lowing.

He finished his song, and Giulietta felt his gaze upon her. She'd brought her tears under control and dared meet his eyes for a brief eternity. Surely, she thought, God had given Rodrigo da Valenti the most magnificent eyes in all of Italy . . . wide and deep-set and heavily lashed beneath dark, winged brows surely like those of the proud and beautiful Lucifer before his fall from grace. And their deep blue was so intense that she began to feel as if he were drawing out her very soul.

Her mouth went dry, her breath caught in her lungs for a moment, and her heart somersaulted within her breast. . . .

# Fifteen

"Come, *cara*," he murmured. "One more and our task is finished."

She nodded, dragging her thoughts away from his features. "How—how is my family?" she asked as he straightened. She missed them so!

He swung away to place the pail beside those already filled. "They are all well—and miss you."

Fresh tears threatened, and Giulietta turned away so Rodrigo wouldn't see her distress. "And . . . and Beau?" she asked over her shoulder in an attempt at lightness.

"Beau?" he repeated as he turned back with a fourth pail. "Why, he's growing by leaps and bounds—and he still knows your name."

He watched as she fought emotion, her back straight and shoulders rigid, and remembered her steadfast insistence that he take back the dog. Her concern and affection for the pup was obvious in her actions—she'd told him she just couldn't keep a dog who was already so attached to one master.

"When we're wed, he'll belong to both of us anyway," he'd offered at the time as consolation. But now he remembered with rue that Giulietta had bristled at the reminder . . . taking it in an entirely different spirit than that in which it had been given.

"My name?" She turned back to him.

"*Sì.*" Too late, Rodrigo realized what he was about to reveal, and it wasn't time yet. "I—well, I said to him as he was romping with some of the children at the camp . . . trying to get his attention, you see . . ." He trailed off, hating even the thought of lying to her. *"Ebbene,* I asked him where you were. *'Dov'ĕ* Giulietta?' I said, and he turned and trotted over to me, his ears forward . . ."

Giulietta watched in bemusement as a faint blush tinted his face. She didn't know he was fibbing about the presence of children—couldn't know that Beau was often the only one to whom he mentioned her name, as if the dog understood Rodrigo's feelings for her.

"You're his master," she said with a light shrug. "He belongs with you." She turned toward the last cow and dragged the milking stool in place.

"Giulietta?"

She hesitated a moment, before turning back to him. He'd taken a dipper from its nail on the wall and had filled it from one of the pails. As he stepped toward her and held it out in offering, he smiled. "Here . . . I promised you this."

Giulietta took it from him gratefully and drank without question, her umber lashes sweeping downward to shadow her high cheekbones. The sweet, foamy milk tasted heavenly, and she downed it with uninhibited enthusiasm. When she'd finished, she held the ladle toward him in mute appeal, like a child begging for more. A streak of milk followed the line of her full top lip.

His smile still in place, Rodrigo took the dipper and refilled it. This time, however, when she drank, Giulietta's eyes locked with his over the rim of the ladle. She drank more slowly, remembering her manners, in spite of her hunger.

*"Grazi,"* she said softly as she handed it back to him. She was tempted to use her billowing habit sleeve to dab at her mouth, but she knew better.

Then suddenly there was no need, because he was gently

sliding the pad of one thumb over her upper lip. His long, swordsman's fingers lingered along her jawline, then fell away. With deliberate slowness, he brought his thumb up to his own lips and tasted the trace of milk there.

A flame of arousal fired deep within Giulietta at the sight of his lips pressed momentarily to the place where hers had touched. Raw desire raced along her limbs, accelerated the beat of her heart, and settled low in her abdomen. Her eyes became riveted to his mouth, and she watched, powerless as he reached for her and drew her into his arms.

If he hadn't, surely she would have collapsed in a boneless heap, for the languor that claimed her was sapping her strength with alarming speed—to say nothing of her will. . . .

Was he that forgiving? one part of her wondered. Or was he still hoping to gain wealth and prestige through marriage to her?

*You'll learn that over the years* . . . His words came back to her. If he believed she would remain at Santa Lucia for the rest of her life, as his words had indicated, then no doubt he was only trifling with her. . . .

Her thoughts dissolved, and the dipper slipped from her relaxed fingers and dropped to the straw-covered floor. Neither noticed. The white cow recommenced its lowing. Neither noticed.

Rodrigo felt her slender body through her habit, and one part of his mind noted with irony that even French armor couldn't have protected her any more successfully than the ells of wool enshrouding her form. How very difficult, he thought, it would be for any man to intimately caress one of the good sisters of Santa Lucia. And rightly so.

His last coherent thought was that Giulietta de' Alessandro was as much his own Achilles heel as she was her father's. And then he succumbed to the incredibly heady experience of having her willingly in his arms and responding to his kisses. . . .

*"God's mercy!"* exclaimed a shrill voice.

Rodrigo raised his head. But it was Giulietta who recognized that voice through the mists of ecstasy veiling her mind. She pulled away from him, cheeks fiery, lips rosy. And even through the haze of desire, she felt her conscience begin to writhe in an agony of embarrassment and guilt as she met Sister Elena's outraged look.

"What is the meaning of this? Giulietta? You were to milk the cows, not . . . not . . ." She sputtered to a halt, obviously at a loss for words strong enough to describe this blasphemy in the barn.

"I am to blame for this," Rodrigo said calmly, stepping away from Giulietta to fully face the outraged nun.

"Indeed you are," agreed Sister Lucrezia as she stepped from the shadows behind Sister Elena.

Giulietta's eyes widened at the sight of the Mother Superior, but Rodrigo's expression registered no surprise.

"But—well, he is my betrothed, Reverend Mother," Giulietta said in Rodrigo's defense when she found her tongue, "as you already know. And I am just as guilty as—"

"He *was* your betrothed," Sister Lucrezia interrupted, "but not now. You came here to serve Christ, and there will be no more of . . . *this.*"

She gestured toward Sister Elena then, the wide, scarlet sleeve cuffs of her altar attire standing in sharp contrast to the ivory of her habit. The older nun began removing the pails containing milk, glancing from the corner of her eye at Rodrigo as if he were the Devil himself.

To Giulietta, the red embroidered cross that emblazoned Sister Lucrezia's chest seemed to quiver with censure in the deeply shadowed byre, and she caught the faint whiff of candle wax and incense.

"I assume full responsibility—" Rodrigo began.

"Now," Lucrezia interrupted, as if he hadn't spoken, "you will finish your task, Sister Giulietta, and then go straight to your cell."

Giulietta opened her mouth to object, for she needed in the worst way to eat, but then thought better of it. She looked at Rodrigo.

"I'll see to this," he said to her soberly, but his eyes held a message of reassurance . . . and something much more profound that set her pulses racing again.

She nodded. *"Grazi* . . . for your help, signore," she said, then retrieved her mangled wimple from the corner where it lay, and brushed the straw from its folds. As she fixed it in place, Rodrigo unexpectedly thought of a hood being placed over the sun.

"Come with me," Sister Lucrezia commanded Rodrigo.

He balked at her tone for a moment and caught Giulietta's look of concern as she glanced at him, then at Sister Lucrezia. He was not about to be intimidated by the Abbess of Santa Lucia—or any other self-righteous cleric . . . especially one who sounded more like a soldier than a nun.

Normally a patient man, Rodrigo called upon that very patience to bite back an acerbic retort. "I would humbly ask, Reverend Mother, that you permit me to milk the last cow so that Giulietta may eat her dinner. I'll drop off the last pail in the kitchen on the way to your office."

Sister Lucrezia studied him for a long moment. "First of all, we don't allow the laity to wander about the halls and rooms of Santa Lucia—and most especially *men.* Secondly, I doubt if you are capable of humility, Signore da Valenti . . . considering your profession."

Giulietta straightened swiftly from beside the fourth cow and stared at Sister Lucrezia as if the nun had lost her mind. She didn't bother to stifle her soft but audible gasp of surprise.

Yet Rodrigo wasn't surprised at Sister Lucrezia's barbed reply, nor would he allow himself to take offense. This woman was a viper in a habit, and had Giulietta not been under her supervision, he would have responded in an equally curt manner. But something sinister and secretive was afoot here, and he suspected it involved himself rather than Giulietta.

What it could be, he hadn't the slightest idea, but he knew intuitively that he had to tread carefully.

"That may be, Reverend Mother, but again, I ask you with all due respect to allow me to finish here in Giulietta's stead. I'll leave the milk pail anywhere you like—*outside* the building. Afterward I would be happy to speak to you alone—and accept the penalty, if need be, regarding any breach of convent rules."

He watched her eyes narrow at him consideringly. "And will you clean out the stalls as well, *condottiere,* for your lady love?"

It was a direct challenge. Yet Rodrigo still didn't perceive the situation as unsalvageable. It would be easier for him to shovel out four stalls—and quicker—than for Giulietta to do so. He'd performed such menial tasks before in his life, and had no aversion to honest labor.

He also acknowledged that had he wished to end this increasingly confrontational situation with Sister Lucrezia, he could have easily gained the upper hand—forcibly removing Giulietta from Santa Lucia and thereby putting a halt to his generous payments.

He wondered if the abbess realized just how close she was to cutting off her nose to spite her face. But he merely nodded. "If my doing so would allow Giulietta to eat and then go directly to bed."

He heard Giulietta's sharply indrawn breath and glanced over at her. The heat of battle lit her eyes, and although he was warmed by the thought of her coming to his defense, he didn't need her interference right now, however well-intentioned. Nor did *she* need to arouse Sister Lucrezia's anger.

"And one more thing," he added. "Again, with all due respect, Reverend Mother, Giulietta is only human, as am I; but she should never be considered anyone's mere 'lady love.' By calling her such, you do an injustice not only to her, but to the depth of my affection and respect for her, as well."

He glanced up at Giulietta. "Please do as you are bid, Giulietta," he said then, and looked back at Lucrezia before Giulietta could react. "When I finish here, I would like a word with you, if I may."

Just then, a black cat emerged from the shadows and went straight to Lucrezia. It arched its back in feline contentment as it rubbed across her robe-shrouded ankles, and she bent to lift the creature into her arms. Her eyes met Rodrigo's over the cat's dark fur as she nuzzled it. The hazel orbs were murky with ire. And something more. "I have an important . . . meeting soon, and therefore, Signore da Valenti, will be unavailable. You may come to me—*directly* to me—mayhap on the morrow or the day after."

He watched Giulietta walk stiffly from the stable without a backward glance. She was irked at being dismissed like a child by him—he could read it in her movements. But then, it couldn't be helped. And he had long ago grown accustomed to being the recipient of Giulietta de' Alessandro's irritation.

He nodded at Sister Lucrezia. "As you wish, Reverend Mother." But as Giulietta disappeared from sight, the nun stepped up to him and placed one hand on his arm. "Surely, my son," she said softly, her up-tilted hazel eyes clear now and reflecting the green in those of the feline resting in her embrace, "you will forgive me if I am abrupt at times? My heart is troubled these days, and I am seeking counsel to . . . er, remedy the problem. You will find it in your heart to be patient with me, *sì?*"

Her expression turned suddenly guileless, something he wouldn't have thought possible for her. But it was too late. His keen insight and leader's instincts had already confirmed it in his mind: Sister Lucrezia was a chameleon—capable of lightning mood changes and swiftly altering facades. She had, obviously, mastered the art of deception.

"Of course, Reverend Mother," he said, allowing a suggestion of a smile to curve his mouth. "No harm done."


But Rodrigo wasted no time milking the white cow, then shoveling out the four stalls. He met Sister Elena at the back door to the convent and set the last pail at her feet. He winced inwardly at her blatant look of remonstrance, for he had no wish to unsettle her further, or give her the impression that he intended to desecrate the inner sanctum of Santa Lucia with his unwanted presence. Nor did he wish her to vent her spleen on Giulietta because of what she'd seen in the byre.

He backed away with a solemn, respectful nod, turned and strode toward the front of the convent and the gate. He retrieved his lute and made a nonchalant but direct retreat.

However, instead of going to where Morello was tethered out of sight, Rodrigo chose a large spreading oak across from the front entrance of main building, hid his lute among some hardy foliage at its base, and climbed to a height from which he could command a view of the grilled gate and, therefore, anyone who might leave or enter the compound.

It was dark now, and the wind had picked up. Marauding clouds, ash gray against the Stygian heavens, rushed across the sky, obliterating the moon and stars. From somewhere within the convent a bell tolled. Compline. The final canonical hour. The good sisters would be retiring after the service—if one was held.

Still Rodrigo waited, wondering exactly who was coming

to "counsel" Sister Lucrezia. The Mother Superior's heart wasn't her problem, he suspected. Rather it went deeper . . . down into her very soul.

He had no problem imagining exactly how she'd managed to fool others—had gained the trust of those who had a direct say in who would assume the head position at the convent of Santa Lucia when it was time. And the Church was full of corruption—from the lowliest cleric to the Pope himself.

But the woman reminded him of someone else, and more importantly, Giulietta was in her care. Rodrigo surely had no wish to endanger his betrothed in any way by leaving her at Santa Lucia. Nor, even if all his suspicions were unfounded, did he want Dante to discover Giulietta wasn't exactly thriving.

There was a difference, he thought with bleak irony, between persuading a young novice that convent life wasn't for her . . . and outright abuse.

Within an hour, Rodrigo heard the soft clop of hooves. He'd been studying the small, high windows of the main building, essaying to guess which room was Giulietta's. In the process, he'd finally dozed off, having pulled his cape about him against the increasingly chill night wind. He dreamt of a bath—for he was damp with sweat and reeked of cows—and clean clothing . . . and Giulietta in his arms. He came instantly alert at the sound, however, noting that the animal's gait sounded like that of a donkey rather than a horse. A donkey, which a humble cleric might ride.

He sat up, bracing his right foot firmly against another branch for better purchase, and with narrowed eyes studied the forest edge across from the gate in the convent wall. Within moments, a figure emerged from the trees: an unprepossessing figure, with thin legs sticking out from his clerics skirts and dangling just above the ground. His dark robe flapped in the wind, and just before he dismounted at the gate, his hands momentarily occupied with the reins and saddle, a gust of air caught his cowl and whipped it back from his head.

Rodrigo had never seen this man before, but he'd heard descriptions of him from various sources. Yet the night shadows played tricks upon even the best eyes, and he couldn't be certain . . .

Until a break in the clouds allowed a beam of moonlight to slant earthward. Like a beacon from God, it bathed the profile of the figure on the donkey as clearly as if it had been the middle of the day.

The man paused in the act of dismounting and looked up, as if in silent acknowledgement of the unexpected illumination from the heavens. Then his feet touched solid ground, and he quickly pulled his cowl back over his head, concealing his face once again.

But Rodrigo had caught the huge, hooked nose, the fleshy lips . . . a heavy black brow against a pale face . . .

And he knew.

The slight figure with the unpleasantly distinctive profile could be none other than the man who'd declared his words divinely inspired and himself the instrument through which Florence and its church would be scourged and regenerated. The man who had dared urge death to those who advocated the restoration of power to the exiled Medici family. The man who'd declared himself above even the Pope . . .

The Prior of San Marco: Girolamo Savonarola.


*"La Dama Fortuna* seems to delight in flinging trouble your way," Carlo told Rodrigo, "when you are in Tuscany."

The words were spoken lightly enough, but Rodrigo caught the concern that flared in his brother's dark eyes.

"If you are so suspicious of the abbess after your visit last night—if you fear for Giulietta's safety—then why don't you tell the prince and have her removed from Santa Lucia?"

Rodrigo, who had just returned from a lengthy morning meeting with Dante at Castello Monteverdi, dismounted Morello and began walking toward the rise ahead. Carlo did the same, staying close on his friend's heels. The afternoon was brisk, with the sun peeping now and then from behind sweeping gray clouds before a rushing, cheek-stinging wind.

"You cannot avoid the answer by walking ahead of me, Rigo . . . or changing the subject," Carlo continued, lowering his voice so that Rodrigo had to turn his head to catch his words—an indication that, indeed, he heard everything Carlo said.

Rodrigo halted his steps and gazed at the rise ahead. They were in the middle of a good-sized piece of land, which Rodrigo had obtained from a minor—and financially strapped—nobleman. It was by no means vast, but he had plans to build his villa here . . . one of his childhood dreams.

Carlo fell silent, in obvious appreciation of the beauty of the land around them. The meadow behind and on either side of them was surrounded by lightly wooded forests, and a stream gurgled past at the base of the hillock just ahead, its soothing melody seeming to embody the promise of all the good and simple pleasures an honest life offered.

Rodrigo raised an arm and pointed toward the crest of the rise. "That is where I will build Casa Valenti, Carlo," he said softly, his voice full of emotion. "Not so large or formidable as Castello Monteverdi—nor so forbidding—but rather light and airy, a place to raise children and live out a good life."

Carlo nodded. "Like Casa Chiari?"

"Sì . . . similar to Caressa's family seat, although not so grandiose."

"And what will Dante say to that?"

Rodrigo looked at him. "What can he say? Monteverdi will

go to Niccolò. We surely can live there part of the year if Giulietta wishes it so. But Casa Valenti will be mine. *Ours.* Built at my bidding, with my gold, and for my wife and children." He smiled suddenly. "You and Laura and the children will be most welcome to make it your home as well. If you expect to work for me, you won't need to travel—or live in a wagon—and there will be plenty of room."

Carlo frowned and stroked his chin thoughtfully. "The idea will take some getting used to . . . And do I detect a certain dissatisfaction with our caravans on your part?" He gave Rodrigo an arch look. "Yet I cannot just ignore generations of *Zingari* blood running through my veins. On the other hand, 'tis easier for you to settle in one place. You're only half-Gypsy . . . even less if Maddalena's sire was *gorgio.*" He drew a breath, then added on a more serious note, "But what of Giulietta?"

Rodrigo's look sobered. "Giulietta." The whispered word fell from his lips like a prayer. His expression hardened as he met his friend's look. In a normal voice he said, "There isn't a moment that goes by that she is not in my thoughts. But I can't go running to Dante and tell him of my suspicions regarding the abbess, for I can't prove anything yet. And surely Savonarola may be many things, but not a killer—although he may preach of death for the Medicis. Even were he so inclined, however, he wouldn't dare harm the Prince of Monteverdi's daughter." He shook his head, his eyes narrowing in thought. "Especially now that his popularity is declining. . . . I believe 'tis time for him to make some desperate move to regain his following."

"Then he will have to defy His Holiness himself," Carlo said.

"Exactly." Rodrigo sighed. "So it's back to Florence . . . I want to be there when Savonarola acts."

Carlo nodded.

"I do think, however, that although our infamous prior is no killer. Sister Lucrezia, on the other hand, is quite capable of hurting someone. I sense a hidden malevolence in her . . . and an intense dislike. 'Tis directed, specifically, at me."

A frown pulled down the corners of Carlo's mouth. "I cannot imagine why. Yet if it's true, she might try to get at you through Giulietta."

Rodrigo shook his head again. "I don't think so. She wouldn't deliberately pull the Lion of Monteverdi's tail any more than would Savonarola, let alone harm his daughter."

Carlo pulled his cape more securely about his body in the brisk November wind. "I don't know, Rigo . . ."

"And if Dante dragged Giulietta back home," Rodrigo added firmly, seeming impervious to the chill, "she would be furious with me. The whole point of allowing her to remain at Santa Lucia is to give her time to discover for herself just exactly what she is sacrificing for the life of a religious."

Carlo threw back his head and laughed heartily. "Coming from anyone else, that would have smacked suspiciously of conceit. But I know you better than that. The lady Giulietta, however, would surely view your words as blatant self-inflation and male arrogance."

Rodrigo moved forward again, leading Morello. He grinned suddenly. "Of a certainty. But I know you would never repeat our conversation to anyone." He slanted a meaningful look at Carlo.

"Never! But as a precaution, you may want to visit Santa Lucia more often . . . intensify your methods of, er, persuasion."

Rodrigo nodded allowing his features to soften. "My thoughts exactly. Her attitude toward me last eve was unexpected and heart-warming. To be perfectly frank, it was near miraculous, and I'll not allow this opportunity to slip by. If I have any success at all, she'll be begging to leave Santa Lucia by Christmas at the latest." One corner of his mouth lifted wryly. *"Ebbene* . . . mayhap not exactly begging, but surely wishing it."

His look turned thoughtful then, and he braced a foot against a rock along the streambed while Morello lowered his head to drink. His unfocused gaze upon the foaming waters of the swift-moving brook, he asked, "What of Maria, Carlo? Have you heard aught?"

"I was hoping *you* might have, since you spend so much time in Florence. Laura wanted to go search for the girl, but I wouldn't allow it. Marco and Giorgio have done so twice, and her mother has all but given up hope. Either she's vanished . . . or she's dead."

Dante's fingers tightened about Morello's slack reins. " 'Tis all my fault. I'll look for her myself before she gets hurt—or worse. Her mother is too old and fragile, and I have no faith in the bumbling work of either Marco or Giorgio . . . who'll be gone with the others on the morrow anyway. Who knows? Searching for Maria may help me in my work for Dante." His dark brows had drawn together over his eyes in concentration.

"Marco feels you are to blame, but he's a jealous and spurned suitor. He'll place blame wherever he can, except on himself. And Giorgio has never been a friend to her. He's always been thick with Marco . . ." He trailed off, drawing Rodrigo's eye.

"And?" Valenti pressed.

"The latest rumor is that she's found a benefactor, which could be the reason she seems to have disappeared into thin air."

Rodrigo looked again at the rise, his features tightening to bedrock. If he hadn't become so close to Maria years ago, perhaps this could have been avoided. But the only child of the ailing widow Clarice had aroused all that was compassionate within him. As it was, he'd been surprised that she wasn't married by the time he had returned from France. And more than a little concerned. But how do you tell a woman who'd been like a sister to you since childhood that it could never be anything more? That you loved her, but not in the way she wanted?

He'd underestimated the affections of the sweet and simple Maria.

". . . can't take this upon your shoulders, Rigo," Carlo was saying. "She refused Marco's offer of marriage a while back, and yet he managed to keep others away from her. Anyone who cared to look past Maria's starry eyes when you were around could see that you never felt the same way about her. You have enough on your mind without adding unnecessary responsibility."

Rodrigo's gaze clashed with that of his brother. "I cannot believe my ears. I had thought you more sensitive than that."

Carlo, obviously seeing that he'd made a mistake, added with a touch of annoyance, "You cannot be responsible for the whole world!"

Rodrigo threw Morello's reins back over the horse's head and mounted. He stared down at Carlo, feeling his sudden anger fade. "Nay, I can't. No one can or should. But Maria is my friend. The fact that she is a woman changes nothing." He leaned toward Carlo, his eyes intense, determined. "I would do nothing less for you, brother, or Dante, or Maddalena . . ."

"But where are you going now? They're breaking camp in the morn. Don't you want—"

"If I'm not back by the time they leave, you'll have to say my goodbyes for me," he said grimly. "The *Zingari* will return—they always do—and I have urgent business to attend to in Florence." He reached to adjust one stirrup.

"And Giulietta?"

"I won't be gone long . . . and she's safe enough for the moment." The wind threatened to sweep the cap from his head as he added, "Mayhap you can keep an eye on the comings and goings at Santa Lucia for a few days, *sì?*"

Knowing his friend wouldn't refuse him, Rodrigo wheeled Morello about. Carlo called out, "I'll be taking my wagon to Verdi, as you asked. But find Maria . . . and hurry back. I don't like the idea of skulking about a convent, for God's sake!"

"*Grazi, amico!*" Rodrigo saluted in acknowledgement. "Just don't let the abbess catch you . . . or Sister Elena!" He touched his heels to the stallion's great sides and sped away before Carlo could say another word.

# Sixteen

The sleek, ebony stallion pounded down the road to Florence, shaking the very earth beneath its hooves. Dark clods of dirt hurtled through the air in its wake. The figure astride the horse loomed low over its neck, as if urging it forward even faster; his dark cape billowed behind him like an onyx furl of smoke in the slashing wind.

The woman in the ditch to the side of the road flattened herself against the rime-coated grass. Her body was by turns on fire—the cold dampness soothing to her heated flesh—and frigid, the prickly weeds and grass beneath her feeling like a bed of ice. She was ill, and she knew it; but she didn't dare risk revealing herself to just anyone.

As the hoofbeats receded, she raised her head and peered over the edge of the road. There was something vaguely familiar about both man and horse, but in the gathering darkness, with her eyes playing tricks on her and the blood pounding through her head, she couldn't seem to focus her thoughts in that direction.

Then a sudden memory spurted through her mind. Rodrigo. Something about the figure who'd ridden past her brought Rodrigo da Valenti to mind; and that memory filled her with an anguish equal to the pain wracking her body. It also gave her the impetus to push herself to her feet, to stand in the purple shadows of twilight that cloaked the countryside and climb with unsteady steps from the depression alongside the road.

As she stood in confusion, trying to marshal her thoughts, the swollen bites on her arms and legs seemed to come alive and throb with a life of their own. She moved to touch her arm, then stilled just before her fingers came in contact with her hot skin. Touching them wouldn't alleviate the pain, but rather cause more of it . . . adding to the ache beneath her arms and about her neck. She'd had flea bites before, but not like these. . . .

Sweet Mary, she hurt! She had to get help, for surely she was going mad.

*There are physicians in Florence,* reminded a voice.

No . . . she'd had no money, and hadn't dared take the chance of encountering the very man she was fleeing . . . Alberto Palmieri. Tall, dark and handsome—so some would say—he'd reminded her in a way of Rodrigo da Valenti. And, in her state of crippling disappointment, she had believed his lies and allowed him to lure her to Florence.

He was the one to whom she'd foolishly entrusted herself, with the desperate hope that he could soothe the gaping wound that was her heart . . . and had ended up his prisoner in a filthy room near the docks beside the Arno.

*Zingara puttana!* he'd called her once he'd had his way with her.

Shame washed over her, and derisive laughter crashed discordantly through her mind.

With an effort, she pushed her chaotic thoughts aside and commanded her legs to carry her toward the woods. Toward the one place where she dared to go. . . . Not the Gypsy camp. She had disgraced herself—and therefore her people—and could be stoned for her sins. Nor could she go to the great *castello* of Monteverdi. Rodrigo was there much of the time now, and she would rather die than face him.

Mayhap she would be better off dead.

Yet the instinct to survive was still strong within her. Cold beads of rain began to pelt her through the bare boughs of the trees overhead. Goose bumps spread over her suddenly chill skin, and she began to shiver. *Keep going,* a voice urged. *Keep going . . . 'tis your only hope.*

The cry of a lone animal came to her on the wind—a seeming lament in accord with her own despair. Rain spattered into her eyes, blurring her vision. Mindlessly she plunged onward, essaying to maintain her bearings—and the picture in her mind of the one place where she might find shelter. . . .

She somehow knew that if she didn't find it, she would die.

A cold rain was falling—big, fat droplets of frigid water that beat against Giulietta's exposed face like stinging pebbles whenever she raised her head.

A bucket full of milk in each hand, she clumsily made her way toward the kitchen door of the main building, wishing for once that she were still among the cows in the haven of the barn. At least it was warm and dry there.

She was late this eve. Most of the nuns were abed already, but at least she'd eaten.

The wind whipped her heavy skirts about her ankles, blew her wimple straight out behind her like a banner. The flapping noise it made sounded like thunder in her ears, yet didn't quite drown out the faint stirrings of the bell at the compound gate. It chimed erratically, as if ghostly fingers were playfully batting the clapper about, but Giulietta didn't spare a glance in its direction.

Her foot hit a shallow, water-filled depression, and she shifted to the right, off balance. The milk in the pail sloshed over the rim, streaked down the side, and fell to the muddied earth at her feet. She stopped in her tracks, suddenly unmindful of the deluge, and set down both buckets. If Sister Elena noticed the streaks of milk that painted the wooden side of the pail, Giulietta would no doubt earn a lecture about carelessness and waste. At the least.

She vigorously rubbed her palms over the coarse wool of her habit in an attempt to dry them, then bent to readjust her grip on the handles. As she straightened she heard a faint, mewling sound beneath the scream of the wind and rain. At first she thought she was imagining it—or that mayhap it was the bell or, she hoped nastily, Reverend Mother's cat drenched by the pitiless downpour.

The wind blew one end of her headdress into her face, the corner slapping her in the cheek. She jerked her head to the right in reaction and heard the sound again. Squinting against the rain, she looked toward the entrance and what appeared to be pale hands clutching the iron grillwork of the gate.

The buckets hit the ground even harder this time, and she ran toward the gate. Supplicants often came to Santa Lucia for food or healing, and Giulietta's first concern was to get the poor creature, whoever it was, inside and out of the elements.

She slowed, however, as she approached the gate itself, a thread of suspicion weaving through her suddenly. She was alone, and Sister Elena had warned her of tricksters and brigands who might pose as beggars to gain access to the cloister.

It also dawned on her that only the porteress and Sister Lucrezia had keys for the gate's lock.

Giulietta bent and peered through the grillwork, close enough to see who was on the other side, yet out of reach should one of those clinging hands come alive unexpectedly and thrust through the bars to grab at her . . .

And was immediately ashamed of her suspicions. The figure was a woman with long, tangled dark hair; she was half-prone, her head drooping lifelessly between her slender arms. A sodden cloak hid the rest of her from Giulietta's gaze. Even as she stared, the fingers began to slide down the iron bars, and a moan sounded from the woman.

"Who are you?" Giulietta asked through the noise of the wind and rain, and pushed back the bothersome wimple that insisted on flinging itself in her face and obscuring her view.

The woman slowly, and with obvious effort, raised her head. *"Buona suora,"* she wheezed, *"perdonami . . ."*

Familiar brown eyes met Giulietta's. Beautiful eyes that were now glazed with fever. "Maria?" She formed the name with her lips, a strange foreboding filling her. "Is that you, Maria?" she added in a stronger voice.

The woman's lids lowered, but she answered with a weak *"Sì.* Help me . . . I beg . . ."

Giulietta scrambled to her feet in a mad jumble of hampering skirts just as Maria trailed off. Before she turned away to fetch Sister Sophia, she watched helplessly as the Gypsy girl's fingers slipped farther down the iron bars. The image of Maria's cheek hitting the muddy earth seared across her mind's eye like a cauterizing iron, and Giulietta stumbled past the milk pails and back toward the kitchen entrance, where she knew Sister Margherita—or someone—would still be at work cleaning up.

Sister Lucrezia stood to the side as Sister Sophia unlocked the gate and pulled it open. Giulietta rushed to the stricken Maria's side. Sister Francesca, who ran the infirmary as well as the herb garden, and Luigia followed right behind her.

Giulietta knelt in the mud and, with Luigia's help, turned the girl over. Sister Francesca bent to examine her. The downpour had let up to a drizzle, but the wind still whistled around them.

Giulietta watched anxiously as Sister Francesca pushed aside Maria's drenched cloak and examined her arms. Then her neck. The nun straightened with a spryness that belied her age and faced Lucrezia, who was standing clad only in cloak and shift, hanks of her long, exposed auburn hair flying in the wind.

" 'Tis plague, Reverend Mother. A Gypsy girl struck down by the plague."

Giulietta caught Luigia's gasp from behind her, but it was the look on the abbess's face that took her by surprise. Stark terror streaked across Lucrezia's features before she could recover and take refuge in anger. She backed away, and for a moment Giulietta thought she was going to slam the gate in their faces.

"She cannot enter Santa Lucia!" Lucrezia said through stiff lips. *"Zingari* are not welcome here . . . and I will not lose any more to plague."

"But Reverend Mother," Giulietta began, appalled at what she had just heard, "we cannot just leave her here to—"

"And why not?" Lucrezia snapped. "As Mother Superior I am responsible for the well-being of every woman within the cloister. 'Twould be madness to take her in!" She moved to swing away, and Giulietta stepped toward her.

"Please, Reverend Mother . . . I'll care for her—"

"That's not the point! She cannot be allowed to contaminate the rest of us." She jerked her arm from Giulietta's beseeching hand. "Have you not heard of entire convents and monasteries being wiped out by plague?"

"Then I'll—I'll care for her in the barn . . . no one else need enter or come in contact with either one of us until she's well."

A sly light entered her hazel eyes as Lucrezia stared at Giulietta de' Alessandro.

Finally she said, "Very well. *You* may tend to her in the barn. You alone. Your meals will be brought to you, and you will be forbidden to enter any part of the convent until she is well. Do you understand?"

Sister Francesca looked troubled and opened her mouth to

speak, then evidently changed her mind as she backed away from the figure at her feet.

"And if she dies?" Giulietta asked.

Lucrezia shrugged in utter dismissal. "It matters not. The souls of the *Zingari* are damned anyway."

In spite of every unkind thought she'd ever had about Rodrigo or any of his people, Giulietta felt only outrage surge through her at the nun's reply. "And if she survives?" she managed through stiff lips.

"There's little chance of that, you can be sure," Lucrezia answered. "But if by some miracle she does, then you yourself will be forced to remain quarantined for a fortnight to be certain you don't carry the disease either." She nodded at Luigia. "Help your friend take the *Zingara* to the barn." Then, holding a corner of her cloak to her mouth and nose, the abbess directed Sister Sophia to take in the two pails of milk still sitting where Giulietta had left them, and beat a hasty retreat back to the building entrance.

"Help me, Luigia," Giulietta implored her friend. The other novice took Maria's ankles while Giulietta struggled with her head and shoulders. Sister Francesca came to her aid, and Giulietta murmured, *"Grazi, suora."*

As the trio struggled toward the byre, none noticed the porteress return to the gate from the shelter of the convent to close and lock it. She scurried back inside, like a mouse to its hole, and slammed the door.

They lay the stricken Maria upon a prickly bed of hay, and Giulietta fumbled with the lantern she had just extinguished. As the light flared, Sister Francesca backed toward the door. "Come, Sister Luigia," the older nun instructed the novice, "I'll give you medicaments to ease the girl's suffering . . . and some dry bedding also. You may leave them outside the door for Sister Giulietta, but do not enter the barn again, lest you, too, are quarantined."

*"Sì,"* Giulietta said. "And please, Luigia, fetch me a dry cape and some blankets for myself."

Luigia nodded, looking frightened yet obviously reluctant to leave her friend.

*"Go,* Luigia," Giulietta urged her, just as Maria began mumbling something unintelligible. " 'Tis the only way you can help us without endangering yourself."

Luigia turned and followed Sister Francesca out into the rainy night.

Slowly, Maria's eyes opened and focused on Giulietta. "Where . . . where am I?"

"Santa Lucia, Maria. Don't worry now, I'll tend you." She mustered what she hoped was a convincing smile.

"How . . . ?" She struggled to her elbows and squinted at Giulietta. "Giulietta?" she asked, disbelief entering her voice and expression.

Giulietta nodded. "Sister Giulietta now." She gently pressed Maria onto her back. "Don't talk. You need water and dry clothing and rest—"

"What do you *here?"* the other girl asked as if Giulietta hadn't even spoken. "You were to . . . wed Rodrigo. How could you . . . ?" She trailed off, her eyelids suddenly drifting shut.

Giulietta pushed a lock of tangled wet hair from the girl's flushed cheek. She couldn't help but notice that it was as smooth as velvet.

*Do you suppose he loves her in return?*

Her cousin Lucia's words came to her suddenly. Obviously, she loved Rodrigo, and would never say anything against him. Suspicion snaked through her. Could their betrothal possibly have had anything to do with Maria's present predicament? But, no. Rodrigo would have told her. . . .

*Why should he confide anything in you?* whispered a voice.

Jerking her thoughts back to the question still hanging in the air between them, Giulietta said, "I would rather serve God."

*Liar! Hypocrite!*

For the first time, a frown pulled down the corners of Maria's mouth. Her lashes fluttered, then lifted with obvious effort. "Forgive me . . . but surely you jest. What woman in her right mind . . . would prefer a nunnery to . . . to Rodrigo da Valenti's arms?"

Her dark eyes filled, and she turned her head, as if she couldn't bear the sight of Giulietta. "He is all things a man should be . . . and more." Her voice was weak, but her words held the strength of conviction.

"Indeed," Giulietta found herself agreeing, and her cheeks grew as warm as Maria's—though not from fever. "But tell me, Maria, how you came here. Why aren't you at the camp and—"

*"Palmieri,"* the Gypsy girl whispered. Giulietta barely caught the name, and leaned closer to her. . . .

Just then, Luigia reentered the barn and caught Giulietta's attention. As the girl stepped toward them, Giulietta held up one hand. "That's far enough, Luigia. Just set everything down right there. And . . . *grazi,* my friend."

Luigia nodded, her look distressed. "Take care of yourself, Giulietta," she said. "Please don't get sick!"

Giulietta smiled a little in reassurance. "I have no intention of getting sick. But pray for us, will you?"

"You know I will. And God bless you," Luigia said, doubt edging her words. She backed away then, obviously torn, turned and left.

As Luigia disappeared the enormity of her undertaking struck Giulietta. She knew a little of healing, but not much. She also knew that the plague was lethal—certain strains more deadly than others.

Maria, who was either asleep or unconscious, groaned and listlessly rocked her head from side to side. An inborn, profound compassion moved within Dante de' Alessandro's daughter, and pushing aside her fears, she set her mind to the task at hand.

She undressed her charge and covered her with two blankets. The wet clothing she laid in a heap near the door, for she had no way of drying it, and wondered if, somehow, the disease could be carried in Maria's garments.

As she worked, the abbess's condemnation of Gypsies came back to her—and the revulsion on the woman's face. Giulietta couldn't blame her for fearing the plague, but her reaction had been extreme for a nun. And certainly unfairly prejudicial. . . .

Yet why had Maria come to Santa Lucia instead of the Gypsy camp? Unless they'd shunned her or turned her out. Somehow Giulietta couldn't believe Maddalena would ever refuse to tend one of their own.

A sudden thought struck her. Of course. The *Zingari* were probably moving to a warmer place for the winter, as they often did. They were, no doubt, gone by now. But if that were true, then why hadn't they taken Maria? Surely they just hadn't abandoned her?

Perhaps Maria herself could enlighten her eventually. . . .

As Giulietta worked, her own clothing became damp in places, but she wanted Maria to be as comfortable as possible before she saw to her own needs. She dried the girl's dark hair with her discarded wimple as best she could, and noticed the beginnings of dark splotches under Maria's skin.

Sister Francesca was right. There was no mistaking the very distinctive marks of plague.

Shaking off her morbid thoughts, she stood to fill a pail from the water trough and returned to Maria's side. She began to apply wet cloths to the Gypsy girl's heated body, even though, despite her best efforts, the sight of the ugly splotches filled her with trepidation. Could Maria possibly be saved? she thought. And especially by her?

She wouldn't give up, however, and could only pray for a miracle. She knew for a fact that plague wasn't always fatal—some lived to tell about it and never be stricken again.

When she was satisfied that Maria was asleep, and as comfortable as Giulietta could make her, she dropped the cloth back into the bucket of water and examined the bottles of medicine sent by Sister Francesca.

One of the cows lowed, and unease drifted through her once again at their utter isolation. A barn was no place for a sick woman.

*Jesus was born in a stable, and slept in a manger,* a voice reminded her.

True, she thought, but neither mother, father, nor child were ill.

Sister Luigia's black cat appeared at her side without warning, and for once the creature was a welcome distraction. Aristo had once told her that cats seemed to hold the plague at bay. How they accomplished this was a mystery, but others believed it was true, as well—including her mother.

She looked down at the cat. "I wish for once that you were ten instead of one," she told it, and took the time to run one hand over its back and the length of its tail. The feline arched with obvious pleasure and rubbed against Giulietta's hip as she knelt in the hay.

"But, even more," she whispered, "I wish you were Beau, and I was back at Castello Monteverdi. Preparing for my wedding . . ."


Rodrigo had no luck finding Maria, but it wasn't for lack of effort. He bitterly acknowledged that a young woman could easily disappear in a city the size of Florence—especially if she didn't *want* to be discovered.

And for all he knew, she could be dead. But he refused to allow himself to evince any more than a niggling of guilt, for he had never given Maria any reason to believe he wanted to marry her.

That Sunday, he was seriously considering visiting Santa Lucia again, but guilt over what he considered his role in Maria's decision to run away to Florence held him back. Then, as luck would have it, early Sunday morning he ran into Andrea Lenzi, one of the spirited young men of the *Compagnacci,* who told him that the Prior of San Marco himself was to celebrate High Mass at Santa Maria del Fiore—the first public sign of the Dominican since he'd been excommunicated in June.

Of all the *Compagnacci* Rodrigo knew, he was closest to Andrea, had even been to his family's country home outside Florence once . . . where he'd run into Father Antoine, an exiled French priest he'd met in France.

Shortly before noon, Rodrigo, Lenzi, and two others strode across the Piazza Giovanni toward the front of the great cathedral. As always, Rodrigo was awed by the magnificent church with its revolutionary duomo, designed and built by Filippo Brunelleschi earlier in the century. Even with so many things on his mind, he couldn't help but feel humbled by the imposing edifice. In spite of what he knew was about to happen inside, a deep sense of peace moved over him as they continued toward one of the three sets of great double doors. But this time, however, he only glanced at the intricate pattern of the white, pink and green marble exterior that shone beneath the winter sun, the beautifully carved bronze doors, and Giotto's soaring bell tower at one corner.

As they mounted the four stone steps leading directly from the *piazza,* Rodrigo redirected his thoughts to the fact that

Girolamo Savonarola, fanatic and now excommunicant, actually had the temerity to defile this magnificent house of God by saying mass. If it was true, it confirmed everything that Rodrigo had heard about the man since he'd returned from France.

"I think you'll enjoy what we have in store for the Prior of San Marco," Lenzi said to Rodrigo as they entered the cathedral.

Rodrigo cast him a look askance, then grinned. "Sly devils—all of you. Why didn't you enlist my help?"

Lenzi, a tall, thin young man with lank brown hair that hung stick straight beneath his red velvet cap, answered, " 'Twas a last minute thing . . . we had only learned of the Dominican's intentions last eve." He winked at Rodrigo and murmured, "Next time—if there is one—we'll be sure to include you."

"Let's hope there will be no time after this," commented a third man, Berto Cavalli, sourly.

"You'll not believe this until you see it, Valenti," added Taddeo, the other young man, in spite of his companion's words. "Enjoy the surprise . . . along with the good Dominican, eh?"

Rodrigo nodded, and they situated themselves well toward the front of the church, before the low, veined marble walls of the choir. The altar loomed above and behind it. The crowd was sparse—an obvious sign that Savonarola's supporters were not only losing ground, but were also dwindling in number.

"Mayhap His Holiness will send troops to arrest him and we'll be rid of him once and for all," Lenzi grumbled. Then his expression brightened. "Or we could put him on display with the lions in the pit beside the Palazzo Vecchio." Rodrigo's eyes met his, one dark brow raised. "Surely if he converted them," Lenzi added, "even the Pope couldn't deny he was sent by God."

"And if they ate him?" Rodrigo asked, one side of his mouth curving wryly.

"They will have done the Republic a great favor!"

"Not if the monk begins preaching through one of the lions!" said Taddeo.

Low laughter sounded among them.

"You can be sure," Lenzi told them, "that no beast could stomach that stringy, sour-faced cleric. He would give even a lion indigestion."

"What is that stench?" Rodrigo asked suddenly. He wrinkled his nose, for it seemed to come from the altar area. Or was it from somewhere else?

" 'Tis the Dominican. 'Tis doubtful he's ever taken a bath," answered Taddeo.

As his words died off, as their renewed laughter quieted, a hush fell over the congregation. Expectation tightened the air—along with the stench—and grew until Savonarola himself emerged from one side of the altar and stepped up to the pulpit.

"What's that draped around the pulpit?" Rodrigo asked, his eyes narrowing to study what appeared to be a gray-brown hide of some sort hanging about the front and sides of the raised structure behind which Savonarola now stood. "What . . . ?"

And then he knew. He glanced at the others—who were all watching him, various degrees of deviltry in their expressions. He glanced at the pulpit, from which Savonarola was now beginning to speak, then back to his three companions. "The foul smell?"

Three heads nodded in unison.

"An animal hide?"

They nodded again. "The putrid skin of an ass," explained Andrea Lenzi. "Perfectly fitting, don't you think?"

"*Sì,*" said Cavalli. "As they say . . . if the shoe—in this case the *hide*—fits, wear it! And look . . . he hasn't even noticed. He obviously has no sense of smell, even with that great beak of his!"

But Rodrigo had his own theory. The Dominican no doubt

wasn't giving the culprits who'd set out to ridicule him the satisfaction of calling attention to the skin *or* the smell.

Fra Girolamo Savonarola almost immediately captured his audience's attention. His green eyes seemed to glow within their sockets. Rail-thin he was, his skin almost translucent, his robes patched and hanging on his gaunt frame like from a scarecrow. Even his movements were awkward; yet the content of his sermon was extraordinary, and the passionate, urgent sincerity could not be denied.

". . . must repent, O Florence, before the wrath of God is further visited upon you . . ."

A chill of premonition crawled up Rodrigo's spine, and he pulled his cape about him more tightly, even though he knew his discomfort had nothing to do with the temperature.

"We've heard this before," Lenzi said in his ear. He rolled his eyes dramatically.

"He's so small-statured," Rodrigo mused aloud, his gaze never leaving the friar. "And awkward. 'Tis hard to believe he has so many followers . . . and has incurred the wrath of Pope Alexander."

Lenzi grunted. "And he's ugly as the day is long. But if you listen long enough, you'll understand his allure, although his influence is dwindling."

"Even Sandro Botticelli has come under his influence." Rodrigo echoed Dante de' Alessandro's words to that effect. "He threw one of his precious paintings atop a pyre before 'twas set aflame, so I've been told."

"*Sì.* It happened during one carnival. He called the pyre his 'sacrificial bonfire.' But his days are numbered, surely, and if *we* have aught to do with it, his downfall will be sooner than later."

Cavalli leaned over and hissed, "They should have *stoned* him when they had the chance!"

". . . God's displeasure!" Savonarola intoned. "Poor harvests and an outbreak of plague are surely signs of His anger with His Holiness in Rome. I can no longer place any faith in Alexander, but must trust myself wholly to Him who chooses the weak things of this world to confound the strong. His Holiness is well-advised to make immediate provisions for his own salvation . . ."

"He's brazen—I'll give him that much," Rodrigo commented as his eyes slowly roved the sparse congregation. Many were obviously enthralled by the Prior of San Marco—in spite of his state of disfavor and state of excommunication. Others, interspersed among the gathering, looked more irritated than spellbound, and many of the younger men—some of whom Rodrigo recognized as other *Compagnacci*—looked ready to pounce upon the Dominican and toss him out onto the *piazza*.

A few even dared to heckle him; then someone began to beat a drum. Just as Rodrigo picked out the culprit, several of the Dominican's supporters started an altercation with the drummer and his companions.

Someone shouted, "Crawl back into your hole, prayer mumbler! *Piagnone* . . . sniveller!"

A woman shrieked—a child began to cry loudly. Others attempted to separate and quiet the men.

"Look!" Andrea Lenzi exclaimed suddenly.

And Rodrigo lifted his gaze from the growing fracas to the vaulted ceiling directly over the pulpit. . . .

# Seventeen

Aristo headed for Santa Lucia with more than a little trepidation. He wasn't so much afraid as repulsed by the thought of entering a bastion of Christianity. The trappings of the religion reminded him too vividly of Stefano Ruggerio, late Bishop of Florence, the man who'd raised him. And had attempted to crush his very soul in his twisted iron grip.

The only reason Aristo was going anywhere near the convent was because the woman he'd worshiped for years, Caressa Chiari de' Alessandro, had expressed a need to hear about her daughter from a trusted family member. Someone with whom she was better acquainted than Rodrigo da Valenti. She'd not asked Aristo, but had been unsuccessful in her attempts to hide her distress from him. Or the prince.

And so, when Dante had swallowed his pride and grudgingly announced his intentions to visit his disobedient daughter, Aristo had gallantly stepped in and offered to do it in his stead.

At first, the prince wouldn't hear of it. But when Aristo hinted that it would be less compromising to Dante to keep his vow not to visit any daughter of his while she was locked up like "some damned martyr in a stuffy cloister" (and in direct defiance of his wishes), he'd relented.

And so, once again, Aristo found himself bouncing uncomfortably atop a horse that perversely seemed to seek out every rut and depression along the path to Santa Lucia.

The faint sound of other hoofbeats suddenly came to him, dragging him from his musings. He sawed mightily on the reins with his short arms, almost toppling backward over the animal's rump because he'd carelessly allowed too much slack. His short legs spoke-wheeled into the air, exposing his small leather-shod feet and pale, hairy ankles before he finally managed to regain his balance and force the nag to a jolting halt.

Aristo canted his head and listened, but the animal beneath him picked that precise moment to throw a snorting fit, thus shattering the silence of the woods. If his legs had been longer, the dwarf would have kicked the creature in the jaw to quiet it. As it was, he could only grit his teeth and wait until the animal subsided.

The definite sound of another approaching horse was closing the distance between them from behind, and with one hand going to the hilt of his dagger, Aristo clumsily heeled his mount into an about-face. And waited.

"Who goes there?" he called just as the bare branches of a sapling edging a bend in the path quivered and the movement of a large animal became discernible.

A chestnut horse rounded the bend, and a man called out in answer, "Carlo of the *Zingari.*" He halted and narrowed his eyes at Aristo.

Relief wafted through the dwarf, and he relaxed his hold on his dagger. Carlo. Rodrigo da Valenti's brother.

"What are you doing here, *maestro?*" Carlo asked as he heeled the mare forward once again before Aristo could speak. "You wish to join the nuns, perhaps?" He winked, then offered Aristo a grin of amusement as he pulled his mount to a halt before the smaller man.

"Only if you'll join me," the dwarf replied, his dark eyes suddenly glinting with a spark of answering good humor. He liked Carlo, for the man had always treated him like an equal.

"Then you think we could take them all?"

Aristo sighed, as if the weight of the world were upon his already hunched shoulders. "No doubt most of them aren't worth the trouble . . . save for Madonna Giulietta."

"Of course." Carlo shrugged. "But I hear the abbess isn't bad . . ."

"You didn't answer my question, *Zingaro,*" Aristo interrupted him, suddenly feeling anxious to see Giulietta de' Alessandro for himself. "Are you mayhap—" He halted in midsentence as a thought struck him. "Why aren't you gone with the rest?"

Carlo shrugged again, then shifted in the well-worn saddle. "I moved to Verdi, *maestro,* and anticipate working in my brother's Free Company one day." He glanced down a moment, as if debating whether to speak further. "And Rigo asked me to keep an eye on Santa Lucia . . . and Madonna Giulietta."

Aristo frowned, alarm skittering through him, even though he was warmed by the man's apparent willingness to confide in him. "He has reason to be concerned?"

Carlo's lips tightened; his expression turned bleak.

Aristo leaned forward expectantly, his frown so virulent now that it twisted his simianlike features. He'd been uncomfortable with the thought of Giulietta de' Alessandro staying at Santa Lucia from the very first, but had not voiced his feelings to anyone. "Well?"

"Rigo has seen Savonarola at the convent. It could be nothing, but he plans to be in Florence for mayhap a little longer than usual and merely asked me—"

"Why?"

Carlo, obviously bridling at Aristo's demanding tone, said tersely, "He is in the prince's employ, is he not? You would know more about it than I."

But like Carlo, Aristo was *Zingaro.* He knew of a Gypsy's affinity for lying if the occasion called for it. "It cannot be for the prince, for Valenti missed an appointment with His

Excellence yesterday and wasn't to return to Florence until some final instructions had been given. 'Tisn't like Rodrigo, so my master says, and he's both annoyed and concerned."

Carlo adjusted his woolen cloak about him with studied nonchalance before gathering up the reins. His dark eyes met Aristo's, his expression uncompromising. "I'm not privy to Rigo's business."

"Somehow I don't believe that. If you don't tell me exactly what I wish to know, I'll march right back to Castello Monteverdi and tell His Excellence of Rodrigo's concerns—of your mission to, er, *keep an eye* on things at Santa Lucia because Savonarola is evidently trafficking with the abbess. And you can be sure that the prince will pull Mona Giulietta out of that convent faster than you can blink . . . which, I understand, would be contrary to Valenti's desire to teach the young lady a lesson in humility."

Carlo's jaw began to drop. He managed to snap it closed, however, just in time to rescue his dignity. He obviously recognized when he'd been outmaneuvered. *"Ebbene,* Rigo is in Florence searching for the girl Maria. She ran away some weeks ago and hasn't been seen or heard from since. Rigo feels he's responsible—although I pointed out the absurdity of such reasoning." Annoyance moved over his face like a shadow.

Aristo nodded. "Come then. Between the two of us, surely we can, ah . . . *persuade* the abbess to allow us to see and speak to Mona Giulietta for ourselves, *si?* After all, I am the prince's trusted servant, and you the brother of the lady's betrothed." He shook his head, suddenly feeling a chill waft over his heart at the mention of the Gypsy girl's name. "I have a bad feeling about the girl—Maria, that is. And I also have a bad feeling about Giulietta . . . as if somehow the two were related."

Without another word between them, the two continued on toward Santa Lucia.

* * *

A wooden chest came plummeting earthward. . . .

Rodrigo's heart turned over beneath his ribs as the object seemed to hover menacingly above the congregation. Yet in reality the seemingly slow motion was in his mind, and there wasn't time to do anything.

The heavy chest crashed resoundingly onto the stone floor of the nave. Panic-stricken people scattered from the front of the cathedral and broke for the doors, the urgency of their flight emphasized by the whisper and scrape of hundreds of leather shoes over the tesselated marble floor.

Rodrigo and his friends were among the last to exit—his three companions obviously to savor the results of their latest prank, and Rodrigo to make certain no one was injured.

The last image he had of Fra Girolamo Savonarola was the dawning of anger across his pale features as he stood utterly alone before the pulpit in the cavernous cathedral.

Shouts and laughter from a number of youths emerged from the hubbub outside on the *piazza*. "So that's what you've been up to," Rodrigo accused Andrea Lenzi and the others. "Frightening the good people of *Firenze*." He shook his head. "Someone could have been hurt."

"The *good* people of Florence," said Cavalli, "either attended mass at another church . . . or stayed home!"

"Except for us, of course," added Lenzi, looking pleased with what he and his cronies had accomplished.

"Mayhap 'twill keep him from lecturing again, eh?" Rodrigo mused with a lift of his eyebrows as they strolled away from Santa Maria del Fiore and the dispersing crowd. "Mayhap he fears physical injury more than Alexander's interdict?"

Taddeo snorted. "The fool fears naught . . . and our rigged chest could have saved everyone a lot of trouble by squashing him like a bug!"

"My father told me the *Signoria* has just decided that he must be asked to preach no more," Berto Cavalli said to Rodrigo.

In recent weeks, Rodrigo had learned that the elder Cavalli was a member of the *Signoria,* the ruling body of Florence, and therefore his son, Berto, a reliable source of information.

"Rigo?" Cavalli said suddenly, as if the thought had just struck him. "Come for dinner, why don't you? A few others you know will be there and—"

"And we'll decide what to do next," Taddeo added with a sly look.

Rodrigo quickly considered his options. He'd not found Maria—but he suspected that a few hours spent at the Cavalli home could only prove informative, advantageous in his work for Dante. And also help establish himself further in their confidence.

Surely a few hours couldn't hurt. He ached to see Giulietta once again, but then he might even be able to learn something of Maria.

"Well?" Berto pressed. "What do you say?"

Rodrigo managed a grin, and hoped Carlo was keeping his word about watching Santa Lucia. "Of course, *amico.* And *grazi.* I wouldn't miss planning more mayhem for anything."


Carlo rang the bell while Aristo watched from where the horses stood. It was a while before a light-robed figure emerged from the convent and hurried across the yard to the gate.

*"Buona sera,"* Sister Sophia greeted Carlo. She looked anything but happy to receive a visitor.

*"Buona sera,* good Sister," Carlo returned. "I'm here to visit Sister Giulietta. May I see her?" He gave her his most charming smile. "Er, Sister—?"

The nun paled. "Sophia," she supplied distractedly. She cast an uneasy glance over her shoulder and toward the small barn before she finally answered, "Sister Giulietta is indisposed and cannot receive visitors just now."

Carlo's eyebrows shot upward in surprise. "Indisposed?"

"*Sì.* She's . . . ill. Come back another time, signore." She turned away abruptly, which immediately aroused his suspicions.

He looked askance at Aristo, who was loping toward him with his peculiar, wheeling gait, obviously agitated. "I—I've brought someone who can mayhap prescribe the proper tonic for her, then," he said, hoping that Aristo would overcome his aversion to the place for Giulietta de' Alessandro's sake. The dwarf was a master in alchemy and on occasion had been consulted by Maddalena.

But the nun did not turn back.

"I demand to see Mona Giulietta!" Aristo commanded in his raspy voice at Sister Sophia's retreating form. "If you don't wish the Prince of Monteverdi to raze the very walls of the convent, you'd better speak to the abbess immediately!"

At the sound of his voice, she swung back. She took a few steps toward the gate, where Aristo had wrapped his skewed fingers tightly about the bars. She peered at the little man beneath the weak afternoon sun. His hood had fallen back, revealing his homely features, now contorted with anger. "I . . . I just explained the situation to you! Sister Giulietta is ill. When she is better, she can receive visitors. But not now."

She turned and scurried toward the building. Another nun emerged from what appeared to be a root cellar under one side of the barn. In her haste, and preoccupied with an apron full of whatever she'd retrieved from the cellar, she neglected to close the near ground-level door. She followed the porteress into the main building with no more than a glance in their direction.

Aristo beat on the bars in frustration. "Thick-headed women! I'll find a way to get into that henhouse—just watch!"

Carlo looked up at the sky. The day was growing old. " 'Tisn't so long until dark. Mayhap we can scale the wall then and speak to the abbess herself . . . convince her how important it is to let you see the lady Giulietta."

"I doubt whether I can get these old, malformed bones over the wall," Aristo grumbled. "Besides, something's not right here. I can feel it." He shook his head and gazed at the main building as if he could will the porteress to return and unlock the gate. "His Excellency must be told."

Carlo knew that if Dante de' Alessandro came to Santa Lucia and found his daughter gravely ill, Rodrigo's relationship with him, which was already strained, would be in serious jeopardy. And (God forbid!) if she should die . . .

The consequences would be unthinkable—for when all was said and done, blood *was* thicker than water. No matter how much Dante loved Rodrigo, he surely loved his own flesh and blood more. And it was Rodrigo, after all, who'd taken the young woman to Santa Lucia against the prince's wishes.

"You cannot tell His Excellency," Carlo began, then trailed off at the look Aristo gave him. "At least not yet . . . I mean, how serious an illness can anyone contract here in a cloister, with almost no contact with the outside world?"

"Nothing much . . . only plague."

The blood drained from Carlo's face.

"However 'tis brought into such a place, the disease can wipe out an entire cloister," Aristo added.

"Rodrigo wouldn't consign his betrothed to an unhealthy place!"

"No one said it was done deliberately. And she's been here for weeks now. Whatever she has could have been brought in since she first entered this place."

"Surely you are making too much of this! Why don't we

wait until dusk, then scale the wall—I'll do it alone if you cannot. Nothing will keep me from getting in there once I'm over the wall." He tapped the hilt of his sword.

Aristo gave him a look of disdain. "Of course. The armed warrior against a flock of sheep." He walked over to the horses, and Carlo thought surely he was going to mount and ride off to Castello Monteverdi and ruin Rodrigo da Valenti's life.

But instead, the dwarf reached into a saddlebag and withdrew a small jar. He unstoppered it, pushed back his sleeves, and began smearing the contents over his arms, neck and face.

As Carlo watched, perplexed, the breeze shifted. And carried the revolting stench of the concoction to Carlo's nose. "Sweet *Gesù!*" he swore. "What's *that?*"

"Asafetida."

His senses reeling, Carlo said in a scathing voice, " 'Tis what the superstitious peasants use. You're a man of learning."

Aristo moved toward him, to his dismay, and held out the offending jar. Carlo had nowhere to retreat but up the grilled gate. "If you're smart, you'll apply it as well, *Zingaro*. We don't know what we're dealing with here, and it cannot hurt."

*"That* depends on your sense of smell," Carlo mumbled as he vigorously waved the jar away. "Get that stinking stuff away from me!" He held his breath until Aristo recorked the jar and slid it into the folds of his dark robes. It *was* enough, he had to admit, to keep just about anything or anyone from approaching the wearer, so offensive was the smell. Possibly even plague. . . .

"Does this mean you'll stay here with me and move at dusk?" Carlo asked.

*"Sì.* But against my better judgment." He turned his head toward the woods, and the direction of Castello Monteverdi. "And I just hope His Excellence doesn't become alarmed at my lengthy absence and come to Santa Lucia himself. With an army."

* * *

Inexplicable unease crawled up Rodrigo's spine in the middle of dinner.

In the midst of other wealthy young men his age, with food and wine aplenty at the board, and Signore Cavalli recounting the vote in the *Signoria* to inform Girolamo Savonarola that he was to cease his preaching, Rodrigo felt a sudden, debilitating fear rise up within him.

Someone asked him a question, and he fought to concentrate on his answer. *"Perdonami,"* he apologized to the female servant standing beside him and offering a bowl of lightly perfumed water in which to cleanse his hands after the dish of quail in rich sauce he'd consumed. He had no idea how long she'd been waiting.

As he dried his fingers on the proffered linen cloth, Giulietta's image came to him. He frowned unconsciously, the discussion around him a meaningless babble of sound. And with the image came the sudden realization that his premonition while in the cathedral earlier had had nothing to do with Girolamo Savonarola, but rather with Giulietta.

He had to return to Santa Lucia at the first opportunity without alarming his host . . . just to make certain all was well.


"Get your *foot* out of my *face*," Carlo growled, "or I'll drop you and your precious asafetida!"

In the deepening shadows of dusk, the two men had set in motion their plan to breach the convent walls. However, Carlo hadn't forgiven the dwarf for dousing himself with the foul-smelling gum resin used by the more superstitious peasants to ward off evil spirits and disease. With every breath Carlo drew, the stench of asafetida seemed to intensify and sear the inside of his nose.

"Damn it, man! I *said,* get your—"

The small foot that had been digging into his cheekbone suddenly dislodged, slid down his neck, and came to rest on his shoulder. Carlo could feel the little man scrabble for purchase upon the top of the stone wall. Then, with a grunt, Aristo pulled his foot from its mooring and heaved himself atop the wall.

Carlo followed with ease, and immediately felt some of his irritation with the dwarf dissipate. The latter's face was beaded with sweat, in spite of the cold; unmistakable pain twisted his features. In spite of his age—at least two score years, Carlo guessed—the dwarf was still stronger than several normal men. He'd been the one to roll the boulder against the sturdy wall. But his malformed body—even more bent now with age— surely was protesting against the stretching and twisting necessary to scale the wall.

As Carlo scrambled up beside him, he asked in a low voice, "Are you all right, *maestro?*"

Aristo nodded, but said nothing, his breathing labored. A half-moon shone down on them, the subtle play of moon glow and shadows accenting the agony imprinted upon his heavy-browed countenance. "Hard to breathe," he gasped in explanation. "Just give me a moment . . ."

The sound of a closing door came to them. "Flatten yourself and stay still," Carlo ordered. His eyes briefly met Aristo's, and he realized that it would be impossible for the hunchback to flatten his body. "Just don't move," he said, and turned his gaze to the compound below.

Two figures hurried toward the barn—the first with a lantern in one hand and a bundle under the other arm. The second nun carried what appeared to be a tray of food. They didn't disappear completely into the stable, but Carlo couldn't see the door from his position. By the speed of their reappearance, with only the torch between them now, he guessed that they had dropped off the bundle and the tray without even entering the small building.

Their hurried, furtive movements reminded Carlo of the behavior of the porteress who'd refused to grant them entry earlier.

When they'd disappeared into the convent, Aristo said, "Someone's obviously in the barn and, from their actions—" his eyes moved to where the two nuns had disappeared—"very ill. Ill enough to be isolated."

"Mayhap they harbor a fugitive."

Aristo shook his head. "Not likely."

"Then I know what you're thinking," Carlo whispered, "but it just couldn't be!"

His breathing having eased, Aristo pushed himself into a sitting position. "Help me get off this damned wall and we'll find out."

Carlo shook his head. "Stay here. I'll go alone and—"

"Nay!" came the fierce reply. "What if it's Mona Giulietta?"

"In a *stable?* That would be unthinkable!"

Aristo shifted over to the edge of the wall and looked down. "Naught is unthinkable under the guise of Christianity, my *Zingaro* brother." His mouth tightened, his expression turned bleak. "Now, you go first and I'll follow."


In spite of Giulietta's constant attention and ministering, Maria was near death. Giulietta knew it, even though her experiences with sickness and death had been limited.

She was exhausted from her efforts, and also bitterly disappointed in her inability to save Maria's life. The girl was sleeping—or unconscious—her breathing very shallow. Giulietta laid a cool, wet cloth on her forehead, made certain she was covered, and retreated to her own bed in the hay.

She began to burrow deep into the straw and woolen blankets, too cold and weary to even retrieve the food set just inside the door for her. Something inside her, however, warned, *Eat! You must eat or you'll die, too.*

With the greatest of efforts, she thrust aside the blankets and got to her feet. As she bent to lift the tray, she heard a sound outside the door. "Luigia?" she called softly into the shadows outside. "Is that you?"

When no one answered, she sighed, transferred the tray to her left hand, and moved to close the half-open door against the cold . . . and encountered two pairs of eyes looking directly at her, one head above the other, around the edge of the door.

She started, tipping the tray, then steadied it. Rather than being frightened, however, she found herself fighting the incongruous urge to giggle at the sight.

*"Gesù Cristo!"* swore a familiar, raspy voice. "Mona Giulietta!" And Aristo lurched through the doorway with Carlo right behind him.

Relief and joy swept through Giulietta at the sight of the dwarf—until she belatedly remembered Maria and the disease she carried. She held up her right hand. "No! Don't come in here—either of you. There's plague here!"

Both men stopped in their tracks, and it was at that point that Giulietta noticed the smell. Emanating from Aristo. A far cry from his usual rose water. But she didn't even wrinkle her nose, for there were other, more important considerations than the dwarf's peculiar odor . . .

And his companion—one of the *Zingari,* and a handsome one, too. She wasn't too tired to notice that.

"What do you here?" she asked Aristo.

"We were looking for you—the porteress said you were

ill and couldn't receive visitors. *La principessa* was so concerned about you, *madonna,* that your father offered to come to Santa Lucia. But I . . . persuaded him to send me instead." He motioned toward his companion. "This is Carlo, Rodrigo's brother."

Carlo nodded. "My lady . . . er, Sister Giulietta," he said and bowed briefly. He didn't feel an explanation was necessary at that point.

"You must leave here," the dwarf said before she could do more than give Carlo a tired smile. He stepped toward her, despite her warning.

Giulietta backed away. "No. I—I can't just leave her."

"Leave who?" Carlo asked from the doorway. He thought how beautiful she was, even though obviously exhausted—and mayhap sick, if her color were any indication. He hoped to God not! Her cream-hued habit was soiled and wrinkled. Her wimple had been discarded and her hair a mass of red-gold silken snarls.

She swung toward the blanket-covered figure across the room, and her voice was suddenly pain-filled. "Maria."

*"Our* Maria?" Carlo asked in bewilderment.

*"Sì."* She faced him again, frustration written across her lovely features. "I tried everything I knew! But 'twasn't enough." She shook her head. "I couldn't let them turn her away. Mayhap if they'd allowed her a more suitable shelter . . ."

"Go outside with Carlo, *per favore,"* Aristo cut in. "Let me see the girl."

"Naught can be done for her now," Giulietta said, distress darkening her eyes, "and you mustn't risk exposing yourself."

"And what about you?" the dwarf said as he ignored her warning and sidled toward Maria.

Giulietta shook her head angrily. "No one else would help her—Sister Lucrezia wanted to leave her outside the gate in the wind and rain in her condition. I told her I would tend the girl in the barn myself."

"The woman sounds like the epitome of Christian charity," Aristo flung over his shoulder.

"I don't know why she wasn't with the other *Zingari,* but I surely couldn't refuse to help her."

"Maria ran away to Florence," Carlo enlightened her, "a fortnight after . . . your betrothal." He took a step inside the door and held one corner of his cape over his mouth and nose.

"Leave us," Aristo repeated as he removed part of the blankets and looked at Maria, "both of you."

"Not without you," Giulietta said stubbornly. "You need not risk your life."

Aristo swung awkwardly toward her, his look fierce. "I've *had* the plague," he rasped. " 'Tis unlikely I'll get it again." He looked at Carlo. "Take her outside, please."

Carlo stepped toward her, and unwilling for him to jeopardize himself further, Giulietta moved toward him. Reluctance made her drag her feet.

When he'd firmly guided her outside, the crisp night air hit her like a blow. Cold and clean it was, and invigorating it should have been, too. But she hadn't eaten much or slept well over the last few days and evinced a deep and constant chill, right down to her very bones, that only hours before a roaring fire could dissipate.

She hesitated in the face of the brisk breeze and hugged herself.

"Have you a cloak?" Carlo asked, his fingers already moving toward the fastening of his own.

"Inside."

"Here . . ." He removed his cape and covered her shaking shoulders.

He looked toward the convent. "You surely don't want to

**return to the selfish women hiding like timid rabbits behind**
those walls?" he asked, half to himself.

Giulietta shook her head.

"Rodrigo will be furious at them . . . to say nothing of your
father. *Madre di Dio!"*

"Why did she run away?" Giulietta asked, her mind on Maria's motives rather than her father's reaction. She hugged his
warm cloak to her body and turned her back to the wind.

Carlo pulled her against the lee of the barn wall before he
answered. "We can talk about that later. But for now, I'd like
to know why Maria was refused care here. Why they forced
you to remain alone with her—in a cold barn—and treated the
two of you like outcasts!"

Aristo came through the door just then and obviously caught
Carlo's last words. "Plague victims are normally ostracized,"
he said. "And many Christians believe Gypsies are damned
anyway. Why bother with a mere *Zingara?"*

"But that's barbaric," Giulietta said, her eyes lighting with
anger.

Aristo shrugged. "She's dead, anyway. There was nothing
more anyone could do."

Carlo shook his head, his fists clenching at his sides. Giulietta averted her face, obviously miserable. And cold. And
perhaps ill herself.

Suddenly the bell at the entrance jangled loudly, insistently,
a discordant screech that shattered the moment—and communicated an ominous urgency.

# Eighteen

Giulietta turned her gaze toward the gate. A tall figure was pulling the bell rope and . . .

*Rodrigo.* Dear God, it was Rodrigo! Mixed emotions tumbled through her—joy, dismay, fear.

"Rigo," Carlo exclaimed softly. Then, loud enough to be heard, "Rigo!"

Rodrigo caught the sound in a split-second pause between the bell's reverberations, and narrowed his eyes at the shadows around the barn on the left. His fingers released the rope as his gaze came to rest on three figures moving toward him: Carlo, Aristo of Monteverdi . . . and Giulietta.

"What in God's name . . . ?" he began. "Carlo? What's going on here? And where's the porteress? Open this damned gate!" He rattled the bars in frustration.

Giulietta ran forward, then stopped short of the gate, his safety uppermost in her mind. "Get away from here, Rodrigo! Please . . . there's *plague* here."

*"Sì,"* Carlo added. "We'll help her over the wall, and . . ."

For an instant, Rodrigo froze. His heart jumped to his throat. *Plague?* At the very place he'd thought to incarcerate Giulietta and teach her a lesson?

*She was on her way to Santa Lucia of her own volition when you met her that night . . .*

He ignored the reminder. This was *his* doing.

"Giulietta!" Her name was torn from his lips, a low, anguished cry of denial. He seized the lathered Morello's reins, and quickly positioned the stallion beside the wall. He climbed onto the saddle, then vaulted to the top of the wall.

"No, Rigo!" Carlo called to him. "Stay away!"

But it was too late. He dropped to the ground, his flexed knees absorbing the shock and was before them in a few long strides. His arms went about Giulietta in a fierce embrace, his lips against her forehead. *"Cara . . . cara mia,* what's going on here?"

"We must leave this place," Aristo said. "The woman in the barn—the *Zingara* girl Maria—is dead of plague."

Rodrigo's head snapped up. "Dead? Here?"

"Aye," Carlo answered as he began urging them all over toward the wall. "The good sisters have been cowering within their cloister while the lady Giulietta tended her. Alone."

For the first time in his life, Rodrigo was frightened. But not for himself. The raw fear that clawed at his insides was for the woman he loved. "Giulietta?" he whispered, and stopped in his tracks. He looked down into her face. Even by the meager light of a half-moon and a handful of stars, he could tell she was pale. And the shadows beneath her eyes were darker than the last time he'd seen her. Her face looked thinner and—

Desperation moved him. "The key?" he demanded, jerking his chin toward the convent.

Carlo nodded. "They wouldn't let us in."

His features taut with anger, he thrust Giulietta toward Carlo and spun on his heel. He assaulted the stout wooden door with a fist. "The key!" he shouted. "This is Valenti . . . do you *hear* me in there? Sister Lucrezia? Give me the gate key or I'll break down the door!" He pounded again, with both fists this time, the force of the blows sounding like thunder in the otherwise quiet night.

For a brief eternity, no one answered. Then, after he'd called out again, his threats even more dire, he heard someone fumble with the crossbar. The door inched open, and the great metal key was nudged across the stone threshold. Rodrigo stuck his foot between the door and the jamb. "If aught happens to my lady Giulietta, your abbess's life will be forfeit. Do you hear me?" he snarled. "No cloister walls will keep me from her then. Tell her *that!*"

He removed his foot with a jerk, scraping the key toward him in the process. He bent and retrieved it and swung back toward the other three.

"She must go to the castle," Aristo said as they quickly followed Rodrigo to the entrance gate.

"No!" He turned the key in the lock, and the gate swung outward. "She belongs with me . . ."

"What if I have the plague?" Giulietta protested. "I can't let you—"

"Hush," Rodrigo said as he lifted her into his arms. *Dio!* she felt as weightless as a wasted invalid.

"You cannot carry her off like some prize!" Aristo objected.

Rodrigo ignored him and looked at Carlo. "Will you attend to Maria's burial?"

*"Sì.* But where will you take her?"

"If you don't know, you cannot tell Dante, can you?" Rodrigo answered. He looked briefly at Aristo, who'd opened his mouth to object again. "And will you . . . ?" He trailed off suggestively, cutting a glance toward the open cellar door as it rested against the side of the barn in mute invitation. "Will you see to our friend here, as well, brother? I only need a few hours . . ."

Understanding dawned across Carlo's features. And Aristo's, as well. *"Maledizione!* Don't you touch me!" he warned.

"Aristo!" Giulietta appealed to him in a weak voice. She pushed halfheartedly against Rodrigo's chest. But it was too late. And the dwarf was outnumbered.

Carlo nodded at Rodrigo in answer. "God be with you both," he said, and quickly moved toward Aristo. Rodrigo swung away with his precious burden, his dark cape billowing in the wind like the wide swoop of a raven's wing.

Aristo launched himself at Rodrigo, but Carlo was faster. Knowing how strong the diminutive man was in his upper body, he bent low and plowed one shoulder into Aristo's mid-section. Caught by surprise, the dwarf expelled a puff of breath and collapsed over Carlo's shoulder, stunned.

Carlo's last glimpse of Rodrigo was his brother striding swiftly through the open gate and disappearing around the wall.

Aristo kicked his short legs violently, almost bringing Carlo to his knees. But he renewed his grip on the struggling dwarf and marched toward the root cellar. Surely he could ease Rigo's burden by doing these two small things for him. Surely he could deposit Dante de' Alessandro's faithful servant in the cellar for a few hours to buy Rodrigo some time. And then he could bury Maria.

Aristo's cursing surely would hold the nuns of Santa Lucia at bay for a while, Carlo thought as he neared the cellar door. And meanwhile he could lay Maria to rest without further commotion or interference.

He wondered if he would ever see Rodrigo again . . . alive.

Rodrigo held Giulietta close, glancing down at her often, but seeing nothing beneath Carlo's enveloping cloak. As Morello's distance-eating pace carried them away from Santa Lucia, he combed his mind for a safe place to take her. He considered, then discarded each idea, like a man sifting through sand, seeking an elusive jewel.

He couldn't take her to his apartment in Florence, for Dante knew exactly where it was located. And he needed someplace close—for Giulietta needed to be in a warm bed and cared for immediately. Every moment that slipped by was precious.

The small town of Verdi was nearby . . . and he knew Carlo and Laura would take them in. Yet as part of his principality, it was right under Dante's nose. But Rodrigo would never expose Carlo's family to plague. He knew of no other place to stay save the small *taverna* with its handful of rooms upstairs. Surely in such a small place, he or Giulietta would be recognized. And although the best hiding place was often the audaciously obvious, he was extremely reluctant to chance it.

Without warning an image appeared in his mind. A French priest who'd been exiled for his "heretical" studies in medicine in the East. Father Antoine. If anyone could heal Giulietta—if anyone was more knowledgeable in medicine than Maddalena or Aristo—it was Father Antoine, whom Rodrigo had known in France.

And not only was the priest an exceptional healer, but he had had the extreme good fortune to have met and come under the protection of Rinaldo Lenzi, scion of Andrea's wealthy family. He'd taken up residence near the Lenzi country villa between Monteverdi and Florence, which was used only in the hot summer months. Rodrigo had been there once just before the family had moved back to Florence in September.

Relief flared within him. And hope, for he and Giulietta could remain safely hidden at the villa, with no one the wiser but perhaps a skeleton staff of two or three local villagers. And Father Antoine.

His mouth set in a grim line, he thought of how he'd brought tragedy to Maria, and now Giulietta. Guilt flailed him, for had he stayed in France none of this would have happened. After all, who was he to dare what he had in the last few months? To dare believe he could ever be part of the House of Alessandro? To deceive Giulietta and deal with the abbess behind her back just to teach her a lesson in humility? Who was he to go against the Prince of Monteverdi's express wishes and escort her to Santa Lucia himself—to even *dream* of setting his sights on the prince's daughter when the sweet and simple Maria, one of his own, had loved him?

He glanced down at Giulietta. The wind had blown one corner of Carlo's cape from her face and head. She appeared to be asleep—if that was possible at the breakneck pace he'd set for the stallion. She was either ill, or exhausted. Or both. The deep chill of the night invaded his heart, for he couldn't bear the thought of losing her. Even if he couldn't have her for his own—for whatever reason—the world would be an emptier place without her bright smile and her oft-outrageous behavior. And her courage and convictions, as well, for without a doubt, he knew now that he'd not misjudged her. A secret, silent part of him had always known that beneath the outer facade of pampered daughter, Giulietta de' Alessandro was everything Rodrigo would have expected of any child of Dante and Caressa. The weeks at Santa Lucia had brought out the best in her—matured her in a way nothing else might ever have done.

And also placed her life in jeopardy.

He urged Morello onward, ignoring the possibility of doing irreparable harm to the magnificent stallion Dante had given him. The horse's life was nothing when compared to that of the woman in his arms.

He found Father Antoine in a small cottage on the east side of the Lenzi villa. The exiled clergyman welcomed him into his home, with Giulietta still resting in his arms.

*"Père Antoine!"* he breathed, daring to hope and lapsing into the language he'd learned and then spoken for six years. "I fear she has plague," Rodrigo said, hesitating at the thresh-

old. "She was tending a young woman who died of it, and if you don't wish to tend her, I'll—"

"Come in, come in . . . ," the priest interrupted him, and took hold of Rodrigo's elbow to draw him into the warmth of the room.

"But I'm warning you, Father . . . you'll be exposed as well," Rodrigo said, still balking. However reluctantly, he was giving the clergyman a chance to withdraw his offer and, possibly, save his own life. "I'm prepared to care for her myself; we but need shelter and . . . anonymity."

"Plague holds no terror for me," the Frenchman said quietly. "I've been to hell and back." His last words hinted at a profound anguish, and Rodrigo ceased his halfhearted protestations before the priest's obvious pain.

Father Antoine was perhaps ten years older than Rodrigo, with a full head of thick, dark hair. He was tall and handsome, his features even, his bearing proud for a man of God. He exuded vigor and intelligence, and his origins were obviously aristocratic.

An aura of mystique had surrounded him in France. Men had been drawn to him by his natural magnetism, and women by rumors of his tragic past and exotic tales of his life among the Arabs. Even after he'd been exiled by the French king, he'd shown little humility or remorse, and had continued to condemn many of the practices of the physicians in France . . . including those employed by King Charles.

Those who turned to him for help, however, were his firmest supporters.

Father Antoine led the way to a bed in one corner of the cottage. "Put her here," he said, and drew back the bedclothes as Rodrigo bent to lay her down. "Your lady wife?" he asked as Rodrigo straightened, his eyes still on Giulietta's pale, but peaceful features.

"No, Father. My betrothed." He looked at the clergyman. "Can you help her?"

Father Antoine moved to sit beside Giulietta. "Bring the lantern here," he instructed Rodrigo as he gently pushed back her hair and examined her face, then her neck. Rodrigo did as he was bid and remained at the foot of the bed, watching the priest as he pushed up her habit sleeves and examined each arm. "Do you love her?" he asked unexpectedly.

Emotion banded Rodrigo's chest. For a moment, it hurt to draw breath. "Love is a pale word for what I feel," he said in a husky voice.

"Then I would suggest, *mon fils,* that you marry her . . . immediately." He took the lantern from Rodrigo and set it on a small table beside the bed.

The words knifed through Rodrigo's heart. She was going to die. . . .

"From the way you brought her here, I would guess you are keeping her from her family."

Rodrigo nodded. "She is the Prince of Monteverdi's daughter."

Father Antoine reached for an extra blanket that lay folded at the bottom of the narrow bed and spread it over Giulietta's still form. "Because you aren't wed, you're ruining her reputation even as we speak. And her father will have your heart on a platter whether she lives or dies. If he cares enough, that is. But if she is your wife, you're accountable only to yourself." He looked at Rodrigo then, his expressive dark eyes probing.

Rodrigo had the distinct impression that the renegade clergyman was testing him. . . . "Then do it," he said without hesitation. He looked at Giulietta, fighting the despair that threatened to tear him apart, and whispered, "I'd wed her a hundred times if 'twould save her life."

Father Antoine was silent a moment. "You know there are many who question my right to wear the collar."

Rodrigo shook his head emphatically. "I'm not one of them."

The priest nodded. "Then give me your hand . . ."


After what seemed like an eternity, Aristo quieted. His throat ached; his entire body ached. And he was exhausted. By now, he reasoned, not even the prince could find Rodrigo and the lady Giulietta . . . they'd had too long a head start.

He knew, deep down, that Giulietta de' Alessandro was in good hands. Valenti loved her, there was no doubting that. Surely the man would move mountains to save her life . . . although to Aristo's trained eye, Giulietta had shown no symptoms of plague. Mayhap things were not as bad as they appeared.

At any rate, he reasoned tiredly, some things were just out of his hands. All he could do was wait for Dante or his men to discover him, which was only a matter of time.

He dozed. . . .

The screech of hinges wakened him with a start. He narrowed his eyes and made out a pale figure above him against the dark background of night.

"Who's there?" he croaked, and was immediately frustrated by his inability to project his voice.

The figure appeared to fumble; then the dwarf saw a spark and the flare of a candle flame. A young nun peered down at him. She looked little more than a child. *"Maestro?"* she whispered. "Aristo of Monteverdi?"

*"Sì,"* he hissed.

With a flurry of skirts she climbed onto a short ladder and descended toward where he sat with bound hands. Watching her movements, he felt renewed anger at Carlo, who hadn't bothered to use the ladder when disposing of him earlier. The scoundrel! the dwarf thought darkly. Carlo had been almost gentle with the gag and bonds, but either hadn't seen the ladder in the dark or had been in too much of a hurry to guide his captive into his temporary prison. Pain had shot along his mal-formed spine, then splintered out into his hump and shoulders as Aristo had landed upon his backside on the hard-packed dirt floor.

The candle was thrust into his face, the light making his eyes narrow and then blink rapidly in reaction. "I'm Sister Luigia," she said. "And I—"

She stopped and wrinkled her nose at him. Good manners obviously prevailed, however, and she valiantly tried to continue. "Sister Giulietta was my friend."

Aristo thought her eyes looked dangerously close to crossing, and then remembered the asafetida he wore. " 'Tis asafetida," he growled. "To fight evil spirits and disease."

Luigia nodded and set the candle in its small holder on the floor. She worked to untie his wrists. "How long was the sick girl at Santa Lucia?" he asked.

"Four days . . . almost five." She released his wrists, and the rope fell away. Distress filled her gray eyes. "Do you think Sister Giulietta will die?"

Aristo shook his head. "I don't know. But I saw no signs of the disease on her person." He leaned one hand against the dirt wall, grabbed the girl's offered arm with the other, and levered himself awkwardly to his feet. "If you could just get me to my horse," he murmured with a grimace, the pain in his cramped joints robbing him of his breath.

Sister Luigia shook her head. "I think Reverend Mother took your horse."

His mouth tightened in anger. "Then be so kind, Sister Luigia, as to help me out of this hole . . . and over the convent wall. If I must, I'll walk to Monteverdi to tell His Excellence what happened."

She carefully helped him to his feet. "If I had the gate key, I would loan you a mule . . ."

She trailed off as the thunder of hoofbeats shook the ground above them. Debris sifted down from the dirt ceiling. Sister Luigia glanced upward, squinting against the dust.

"That won't be necessary," Aristo muttered. "The Prince of Monteverdi is come."


Giulietta dreamed of Rodrigo—swooping her into his arms and riding away from the convent with her. She felt incredibly warm and secure. And loved. But so tired. Something tragic had happened, but she couldn't remember what it was. . . .

She awakened to the sound of a crackling fire and low male voices nearby. With great effort, she lifted her weighted eyelids . . .

And looked into the intense gaze of Rodrigo da Valenti. How beautiful his midnight blue eyes were, she thought, and a sweet joy suffused her at the sight of him. She tried to speak, to say his name, but couldn't summon her voice.

His lips curved in a beautiful smile. He was holding her hand. Another man, with dark eyes and hair—a priest—was speaking, and Rodrigo answered, "I will."

Why had she fought this man for all these months? she wondered as she watched his lips form words that sounded familiar.

The priest leaned toward her, and spoke low and soothingly: "Will you, Giulietta, take this man . . ."

"I'll answer for her," Rodrigo said softly.

Why, they were being married! She was actually being wed to Rodrigo da Valenti without any farther ado. Simple and straightforward. Surely she was dreaming . . . or was she in Heaven? She tried to smile, and managed a slight, sweet curving of the corners of her mouth. Oh, yes, this time she wouldn't allow her silly pride to interfere—or anything else. She wanted this, she'd come to realize over the past weeks, as badly as she'd ever wanted anything in her life.

Now she could die happy, if that was God's wish. . . .

"I will . . . take Rodrigo . . . husband . . . ," she murmured, fighting to keep her eyes from closing. She was so happy, but so tired. Her aching body was cradled by a mattress of some heavenly substance . . . not prickly straw in a barn. . . .

An image of tragedy pushed at the walls of her memory, but didn't break through.

". . . kiss of peace," the priest was saying.

Rodrigo leaned toward her, his eyes pulling her into his very soul. Why had she ever thought she hated him? Why . . . ? His lips touched hers as softly as the brush of a gentle spring zephyr, but against her will Giulietta slipped back into slumber.

Rodrigo looked at Father Antoine, his expression turning bleak and questioning. "She but sleeps now," the priest assured him. "Stoke the fire and place a pail of clean water on the grate. We need to wash away the taint of disease. First I'll give her some broth to help strengthen her. Then she needs rest to build her resistance."

Rodrigo nodded, a fist of apprehension forming in the pit of his stomach, then strode toward the hearth and the stack of wood beside it. As he bent to lift a cut branch, Father Antoine's voice came to him once more: "Plague isn't always fatal," he said. "Eastern physicians believe some types are more virulent than others, and in this case, there's no sign of a respiratory problem—which is good."

Rodrigo rearranged the wood in the hearth with a poker, replaced it, then set a pail of clean water on the grate and returned to the bed.

"She was in a convent?" the priest asked.

"Aye." He couldn't keep the bitterness from his voice. "Because of me—I'd thought to teach her a lesson. In humility."

The corners of his mouth turned down. "I should have consigned myself to Santa Lucia right along with her—as another soul in need of acquiring that very virtue."

Father Antoine looked as if he would comment, then evidently changed his mind and asked instead, "And she was tending a girl who died of plague?"

Rodrigo nodded his head. "*Sì.* A young Gypsy woman from outside the cloister who sought their help. The abbess refused to admit her, and consented only to isolating the two of them in the stable. The girl died a few hours ago."

Father Antoine's eyes narrowed fractionally. "How charitable. Did you see the body? Close up?"

"No. Why?"

"It might have told me something about the kind of plague your lady wife may have." He looked down at Giulietta. And for the first time gave Rodrigo a glimmer of hope. "She doesn't appear to have the symptoms yet. Do you know how long she tended the girl?"

Rodrigo mentally counted the days since he'd been at Santa Lucia. "At the very most, five days." He wanted to hold her in his arms, will her to get better. Take her illness onto himself if there were any possible way. . . .

"Your stallion was hard-ridden," Father Antoine said. "Why don't you tend to him while I bathe her—'tis important, despite what many of our physicians say. If you have no objection, that is . . ."

"Of course not," Rodrigo answered without hesitation. He dragged one palm over his mouth and chin in agitation, and shook his head. "I'd completely forgotten about Morello."

"The Lenzi stables are just over the hill to the east. There's a youth who tends to them every day. Alfonso. Tell him Padre Antonio sent you." His lips curved slightly. "But don't give him your real name."

"But—"

"Take heart, *mon fils*. She's exhausted, not ill from plague. At least not yet."


In the smoky, noisy *taverna,* Carlo felt like a man waiting for the executioner's ax to fall. He tried to drown his troubles in the wine served him, along with a score of other kindred souls. It was inevitable: Any moment, Dante de' Alessandro's men—or even the prince himself—would come bursting through the *taverna* door to question him about the dwarf and, more importantly, Giulietta de' Alessandro.

It was only a matter of time before they found Aristo, if they hadn't already, and learned that Carlo and his family were in Verdi. Even though Aristo had heard Rodrigo refuse to tell Carlo where he was taking Giulietta, the prince would grill him, pick his brain apart in an effort to discover *something*. After all, his daughter might very well be dying. . . .

Therefore, every time the door to the outside opened, Carlo stiffened in expectation of the Prince of Monteverdi's mercenaries marching through it . . . with the outraged Aristo at their head.

He sighed heavily and stared into his half-empty wine cup. The deep ruby wine reminded him of blood. His own blood, he thought with a grimace, if the Prince of Monteverdi decided to be merciless.

He wasn't so worried about his own skin as he was about what would happen to his family. And as much as he loved Rodrigo, he acknowledged that he should have taken Laura and the children and left with the Gypsy band earlier. There was no reason he couldn't have waited to begin training for Rigo's Free Company a little longer. . . .

"Carlo."

Carlo looked up with a start. His eyes widened further as instant recognition hit him. "Marco . . . ?" He was genuinely surprised. Perhaps everyone had underestimated the man's feelings for Maria, for Carlo could think of no other reason for Marco's failure to have left with the other *Zingari*.

"Where is she, Carlo? Or does Valenti know? I lost track in Florence, but I believe some *briccone* lured her there for his own pleasure—took advantage of her vulnerability." He motioned to the owner, and asked for San Gimignano. He sat beside Carlo and sank his head into his hands. "I cannot fault Valenti anymore. He didn't encourage her—he treated her with respect." He raised his head, and stared unseeingly, his eyes bloodshot.

As preoccupied with his own problems as Carlo was, he suddenly pitied the man before him. Obviously he'd cared enough for Maria to stay behind and search for her . . . even though he suspected that she'd been with another man. But what Carlo knew would be a crushing blow; of that he was now certain.

The *taverna* owner set down a mug before Marco. Marco lifted it to his lips and drank.

"Marco," he began, glad for the steadying effects of the wine he'd imbibed, "Maria is dead. I just buried her at Santa Lucia."

# Nineteen

*Maria's skin was turning dark before Giulietta's eyes. The girl was bleeding to death internally, and there was no way Giulietta could stop it.*

*She looked frantically toward the barn door, which was closed against the cold. Rising on stiff legs, she stood and stumbled to the portal. Surely someone could help her! Surely Sister Francesca would give her more medicines . . . or even come herself when Giulietta told her how bad things looked for Maria.*

*"Don't leave me . . . please don't leave me," Maria said in a weak voice.*

*Giulietta hesitated, then turned back toward the Gypsy girl. To her horror, Maria had transformed to a gleaming, bony skeleton, with only her long black hair hanging in patches from her skull to indicate who or what she'd been only moments before. She began to sit up, and extended one pale, skeletal arm toward Giulietta in supplication. "Join me, Giulietta . . . come with me . . ."*

*Giulietta opened her mouth to scream. . . .*

"Hush, *cara mia*," a deep voice bade her softly. " 'Tis only a dream. You're here with me. And safe."

Giulietta struggled to sit up and opened her eyes. She met Rodrigo da Valenti's concerned gaze. "But—but Maria? What—?"

"She's at peace now, Giulietta. She died in the stable just before I came for you."

A frown of genuine distress darkened her lovely brow. "I'm so sorry," she murmured.

He put his arms around her and pulled her gently, firmly against his chest. "It wasn't your fault. Nothing can hurt her again. . . . Now, I want you to concentrate on regaining your strength. Will you do that for me?"

She felt suddenly chilled, for a light sheen of perspiration had broken out over her body beneath the bedclothes. She shivered. Would she ever be warm again? As if reading her thoughts, with one hand Rodrigo tucked the blankets more snugly about her.

" 'Tis from weakness, Father Antoine said," Rodrigo reassured her against her hair. "Not fever . . . not plague."

"You shouldn't be here," she told him, weakly attempting to push him away. But her voice utterly lacked conviction. She was secretly happy to be with him, wherever they were. "I don't want you . . . to get sick."

"I'm fine, *dolce*. And you will be, too."

She wasn't sure he was being truthful; but she wanted to please him, so she attempted a smile. "Where am I?" she asked, her eyelids getting heavy once again.

"At the home of a friend. Are you ready for more broth?"

She shook her head against his solid chest. "Later . . . ," she said in a muffled voice. "I'm just tired."

He carefully laid her back against the pillows then. *"Ebbene,* rest and get well, *amore mio*. And I promise, you'll never be cold again."

By the end of the third day, Rodrigo was jubilant. Father Antoine had told him that if Giulietta hadn't exhibited signs of plague by then, she had successfully cheated the dread disease.

"Soldiers from Monteverdi inquired at the Lenzi villa," Father Antoine later told Rodrigo. "Fortunately, they didn't go to the stable." Some of Rodrigo's euphoria faded, for he still had to deal with Giulietta's family. More specifically, Dante.

Guilt tainted his happiness.

"But even if they had, Alfonso doesn't know your real name," the priest added.

"They'd know my Morello. It won't be long," he predicted bleakly. "I've worked with some of those men—they're among the best in Tuscany."

Father Antoine shrugged, his dark, Gallic eyes unreadable. "God works in mysterious ways. It isn't for us to question. Besides, if you take the lady Giulietta to Monteverdi *before* they can find you, you'll have the advantage."

Both men looked at Giulietta. "Two or three days and she'll be ready to leave." At Rodrigo's skeptical look, he added, "Not quite herself, mayhap, but ready for the trip to Monteverdi . . . considering you don't have the luxury of time."

Rodrigo suddenly realized he hadn't thanked Father Antoine for taking them in and keeping their secret. "I owe you much, Father," he said. "And I vow there will be a day when I'll be in a position to help you in any way you may need. Don't hesitate to ask."

The Frenchman waved a hand in dismissal and allowed a smile to light his eyes. "I'm a romantic as well as a clergyman, Rodrigo. How could I refuse two people in love—healthy or otherwise?" He stared into the middle distance thoughtfully. "There mayhap will come a time when I need your support." He shrugged. "Who knows but God? That isn't, however, why I helped you."

The next morning he was gone, supposedly on his "rounds" to the tiny village nearby, and then to visit the Lenzi retainers who remained at the villa year round. Rodrigo thought about the priest's confession to being a romantic. Surely it was true, for Antoine had made a point of letting Rodrigo know that he would be gone for the night. And possibly the next, as well. He'd also chosen to begin his rounds on a day that dawned with a drenching downpour. From the look of the contusive skies, it promised nothing better for hours.

After a more substantial lunch of broth, bread and a bit of cheese washed down by wine, Giulietta slept again. Rodrigo wondered if she would ever again remain awake for more than an hour or so.

By dusk, he picked up his lute, and began to strum softly.


The notes of a beautiful, haunting melody beckoned to Giulietta. They were foreign, yet familiar, and reminded her vividly of an enchanting time in her life in the recent past.

Her lashes fluttered, then lifted as she came fully awake in the shadows of the one-room cottage. She recognized the instrument as a lute . . . its player Rodrigo da Valenti.

Memories surged back to her as her eyes sought his form. Memories of a moonlit summer night when that same melody had called to her—and awakened a flood of new feelings— propelling her into a world she'd previously only dreamed of. She knew now why she had responded so ardently to his music and his kisses. And acknowledged herself a fool for denying what had been before her nose.

"Rodrigo . . ." She whispered his name, savoring the sound of it on her lips before her gaze alighted on him. He sat to one side of the fire, his dark head bent over the lute, smaller than the one he owned, but an instrument that nonetheless responded to his touch as magically as his own.

Giulietta pushed herself to a sitting position and for the first time realized she was nude beneath the blankets. Color touched her cheeks, and an unexpected warmth wended through her at the thought of being so near Rodrigo . . . and completely naked at the same time. She was clean, too. Even her hair, which hung loose, was clean and brushed. She felt marvelously clean, and warm . . . and alive.

*And you're married now,* whispered a voice.

Were they really? she thought as she absorbed every visible detail of the man who sat across the room and brought the lute to life so skillfully. Or had it all been a dream? Perhaps a happy dream to counteract the ugly reality of sickness and death?

Please, God, don't let it be a dream.

Rodrigo lifted his head and looked over at her. Their eyes met, and Giulietta felt her heart tumble through her chest at the smile he gave her. "So you're awake finally, are you?" He set aside the lute and stood.

Giulietta watched his every movement, and her mouth turned suddenly dry as he walked slowly toward her. If they were wed. . . . And they were alone. . . . Where was the priest? one part of her wondered.

Another part didn't care. She was too caught up in the suspended moment as he sat down beside her, her breath trapped in her lungs in anticipation. Surely he could read what was in her heart?

*After the way you've treated him?* sneered her conscience. *After the things you've said?*

She felt her face grow even warmer at the reminder, and dropped her gaze.

"Giulietta, *sposa mia,*" he entreated softly as he lifted her chin with one lean, callused finger. "Don't look away, *cara.* I came too close to losing you to ever let anything get in the way again—including your sudden shyness."

The lilt of laughter touched his voice, and as Giulietta's eyes met his, his own mirrored the same rich emotion. She smiled tentatively in return, still hesitant to ask if they were really married, in spite of the way he'd just addressed her. "Are you teasing me, *signore?*" she asked, one dimple showing.

The query reminded him of the old Giulietta, and that was good, for she was truly feeling better if she could conjure up some of her natural sauciness.

"I have every right now, you know." His mouth moved toward hers, his eyes never leaving her face. "You're my wife."

Evidently it hadn't been a dream, one small part of her thought before all thought fled. "Why?" she asked, her innate curiosity getting the better of her, even as his lips hovered a breath away from hers.

"Because I almost lost you," he whispered before his lips touched hers. The contact was brief, light, but promised so much more. Giulietta felt desire flutter to life deep within her, and her arms automatically twined about his neck in innocent abandon.

"Are you hungry?" he said against her mouth, surprising her. He began to pull away. "I'm forgetting myself, *cara*. You need to build your strength."

"I'm not hungry for food." She pressed against him, feeling the sheet over her breasts begin to slip downward, but also feeling a titillating tingle on her skin where she came up against his tunic.

"At least have some wine," he coaxed, and with obvious reluctance pulled away. "Father Antoine said 'tis good for the blood . . ." He reached over to the small table beside the bed, where a single candle burned beside a ewer of red wine. He poured some of the ruby liquid into a cup and handed it to her. "Drink, love."

"Father Antoine?" she repeated, then raised the cup to her lips. He watched the luxuriant sweep of her sable lashes lower momentarily, before she peeked at him over the cup's rim.

He nodded. Smiled faintly. "A priest I'd met while in France. He lives here now, and married us. He also saved your life."

"I must thank him," she said, handing him the half-empty

cup. "And you, too. You took me away from Santa Lucia"—a look of distress crossed her features—"and brought me here."

"Don't think about it now." He brushed the pad of his thumb over her lower lip, catching a droplet of wine. Her skin was like cool silk, and he felt renewed desire move through him. She looked beautiful and fragile at the same time. Healthy color touched her cheeks and mouth, and her tawny eyes were clear and alert; her coppery tresses framed her head and shoulders, draping down over her collarbone and beckoning his fingers to caress the shining, sunset gold strands. He reached out to touch her hair and allowed the backs of his fingers to glide over the flawless flesh of her shoulders, then down to the firm roundness of the tops of her breasts.

Their gazes fused, and her eyes turned liquid. He would have been a fool to ignore the shy invitation in them. He was only human, after all, and had loved her for so long.

He leaned toward her; their mouths met again, this time with more urgency. He tasted the wine on her lips, then stroked his tongue over their delicate flesh, thinking her honeyed mouth as intoxicating as any wine, and fast losing himself in the eagerness of her response. . . .

He tasted faintly of woodsmoke and cologne, and his own unique scent—a most heady combination, Giulietta thought as they renewed their kiss. It reminded her of that first night near the Gypsy camp, which only served to heighten her excitement. Her fingers splayed over the corded muscles in his neck and moved upward through his hair.

Groaning softly against her lips, he slid his tongue into her mouth.

Fire shot through her abdomen, leapt along her veins, invaded her limbs. Her mouth opened in response; their tongues met, twined, retreated, then met again. She reveled in the rough velvet of his tongue, explored the warm slickness of his mouth and thought she wanted to go on like this forever.

She felt disappointment as he pulled the moist adhesion of his mouth from hers and strung a filament of exquisitely gentle kisses across her cheek . . . until his questing tongue delved into her ear and sent desire, hot and pulsing, roaring through her belly. Giulietta's hands sought his skin beneath his tunic as the need to press flesh to flesh—and some unidentifiable urge that was even more primal—overcame her and threatened to send her sanity spinning into oblivion.

Rodrigo obliged her and slipped out of his shirt. She caught a glimpse of upraised arms and sleek, powerful musculature as splendidly hewn as any Maestro Donatello had wrought from Cararra marble. He reached for her with one arm. The other hand drew down the coverlet as his eyes delved deeply into hers, a question in their midnight depths.

"Love me," she murmured, suddenly barely able to lift her free arm and plant one hand over his, for an insidious languor was spreading through her like quicksilver. She pushed on his fingers, and the coverlet obligingly gaped away from her body before Rodrigo pressed it down to her waist.

"Are you chilled?" he whispered, a crease chasing across his brow.

"I'm on fire," she whispered back, and leaned against his supporting arm until he lowered her to her back and captured her mouth once more—deeply, hungrily, but all too briefly. He slowly dragged his lips down her chin, her throat, pausing at the hollow where fluttered her heartbeat. His tongue laved that delicate depression, then followed the sweet and satiny valley down between her breasts.

As he took one nipple gently between his teeth, Giulietta felt a corresponding warm wetness bathe the silken and sensitive folds between her thighs. He tugged lovingly at the taut bud, and Giulietta gasped softly at the distinct spurt of flame his action caused deep inside her.

The fire coughed and cackled like an ancient old woman.

The steady rain droned on, dancing on the cottage roof like thousands of tiny feet. Giulietta barely noticed for the thunderous tattoo sounding beneath her ribs in reaction to Rodrigo's lovemaking. This was better than she'd ever dreamed, and from the dim recesses of the rational part of her mind, she knew why.

She loved this man. Had loved him for many weeks, and wouldn't acknowledge it. "Rigo," she murmured, and drew him upward, her desire steadily rising. She laced her fingers through his hair. "Undress, my love, and make me yours . . ."

He gazed deeply into her eyes, feeling the threat of tears behind his own. *My love.* God in Heaven, he'd never thought to hear her use those words to him. What had he ever done, he thought humbly, fighting the emotion that threatened to choke him, to deserve this?

"Are you certain you're—" he began.

Impatiently, Giulietta reached downward toward the waist of his trunk hose. "You exhibited no such concern that first night," she reminded him with surprising impertinence.

Low, rich laughter formed in his chest, bubbled up his throat and made him grin with pure joy. And deviltry. "You hadn't just recovered from exhaustion then," he teased. "Why, as a matter of fact—"

*"Briccone!"* she whispered on a ragged breath. "I'd cut my foot!"

"But it didn't hamper your . . . ardor."

Her eyes suddenly closed, and he went still. "Giulietta?" he asked in a low, concerned voice. His hands came up to cradle her face. "Giulietta?"

Her eyes flew open then, the haze of desire diluted by unmistakable Alessandro pique. "If you don't do what a husband is supposed to, I swear, Valenti, I'll go to sleep again . . . for a sennight! And you'll have to make love to that lute!"

"At least the lute won't fall asleep," he said, his voice gruff with relief . . . and much, much more.

Rodrigo struggled out of his tights and shoes, then turned back to Giulietta. She wasn't sleeping. She was staring at him, at every part of his body she could see from her vantage point. *"Che bello,"* she breathed. *"Mio bello Zingaro."* The unmistakable awe and appreciation in her voice made the words sound like the most reverent tribute.

Rodrigo felt his cheeks warm and removed the remaining blankets from about her. "No, *bellissima, you* are the beautiful one."

Before she could answer, his mouth was over hers, his fingers threading through the silken skein of her hair, caressing her scalp . . . reaffirming the fact that she was alive and well, and his at last.

Giulietta reveled in the feel of his skin against hers, from lips down to thighs, and melted anew inside at the insistent pressure of his manhood against her leg.

*"Ti amo, Giulietta mia,"* he said against her mouth. *"Dio mio,* you'll never know how much . . . and for how long."

She moved invitingly against him, causing him to draw in his breath sharply. "Long?" she echoed dreamily, naughtily. "How long, husband?"

"You don't deserve to know," he teased, and Giulietta gasped. But not from his words. The fingers of one hand had found their way to the hot, slick core of her femininity, and stroked steadily.

As if to deliberately torture her, she thought through the fog of runaway passion, and began to move against his hand. An unbearable pressure gathered within her, increasing until Giulietta thought she would go mad.

"Since I was eighteen," he answered her question in a husky voice against her ear, "and you were eleven . . ."

He entered her then, with a lithe and precise movement of

his hips, then stilled. Giulietta moaned with pleasure, but he remained unmoving, watching her, gauging her reaction. He wanted nothing more in this world than to spare her further discomfort, in any form. In spite of his own driving need; in spite of the incredible lure of the final sheathing.

She lifted her lashes then, and regarded him with ecstasy-sheened eyes, expectation and invitation in their gilded depths.

He drove into her fully then, and she met his thrust with only a slight wince. Immediately she moved against him, not allowing him to pause inside her, and began a lusty rhythm that was as old as time and natural to every woman since Eve.

They rose swiftly, joyously on gossamer wings of glory . . . until the pitch of their tension was an exquisite agony. And heedless of the drum of the rain, the distant growling of thunder, the whine of the wind.

Giulietta's release was quick and wondrous. She felt their small and secure bower silently explode into a thousand bright shards of purest pleasure, in exact concurrence with the implosion within her body, setting every nerve atingle and bringing every fiber of her body to an exquisite quickening.

Rodrigo watched her through loving eyes, his own fulfillment secondary. Her soft cry of surcease was music to him, but it also unexpectedly hastened his own climax. He held her tightly as ecstasy showered through him, spewing his essence into her and bonding her to him forever.

All too aware of her fragility, Rodrigo shifted his weight aside immediately. He looked down at her, a tender smile illuminating his beautifully masculine features.

Giulietta had made good her threat, however unwittingly. Sated and content, she had succumbed to sleep.

In the chapel at the monastery of San Marco, Sister Lucrezia's thoughts kept returning, as they inevitably did now, to the humiliation she'd been obliged to suffer because of an insignificant Gypsy girl's blunder.

And Rodrigo da Valenti's meddling.

If she'd had cause to hate Valenti before, the need for revenge had increased one hundredfold. And if she couldn't obtain Savonarola's help, she would surely be forced to flee empty-handed to Rome, instead of triumphantly presenting herself at Gabriella Corsini's door bearing proof of Rodrigo da Valenti's death.

The familiar scent of burning incense came to her as she raised her head and stared at the crucifix above the altar in the candlelit chapel. Her eyes narrowed slightly, but not in concentration. Rather in anger as she conjured up the events of that last hellish night when she had ben forced to leave Santa Lucia. . . .

After Valenti had whisked away Giulietta de' Alessandro, they'd all been forced to listen to the dwarf's caterwauling (after he'd obviously worked the gag free) for what seemed like forever. All the while the remaining Gypsy had worked at digging a grave for the dead girl—and had the gaul to bury her in the cloister cemetery! Even after he'd completed his task and left, there had been no volunteers from among the nuns to release the imprisoned dwarf—no doubt for fear of the lingering taint of plague. Yet Lucrezia knew that if she hadn't ordered it otherwise, someone would have eventually let him out. If for no other reason than to assure the nuns of a decent night's sleep.

"The longer he's in there, mayhap the better, for now," Sister Sophia had ventured to say to the abbess. They'd both covertly observed everything that had transpired in the yard below from the window in the second-floor dormitory. "The moment he is released, he'll ride to Monteverdi and raise the hue and cry. If his first loyalty is to the prince, he surely won't remain silent about Sister Giulietta's illness and her abduction by Valenti."

Lucrezia had nodded her agreement, suspecting that his daughter's exposure to plague would infuriate the prince far more than Valenti's actions. And Alessandro would hold her responsible for Giulietta's illness and, more than likely, death. But the porteress's words had given Lucrezia an idea. . . .

When the *Zingaro* who was evidently Valenti's friend (he obviously wasn't on Aristo's side if he'd imprisoned the little man in the root cellar) had finished his task and ridden off, Lucrezia had discerned the sounds of a single horse cantering away. The dwarf's horse was more than likely still on the other side of the wall. And Lucrezia knew that she had to flee. No matter what her excuse, no matter how she lied and the other sisters might corroborate her story, the prince would, at the least, toss her into his deepest, darkest dungeon. From Abbess of Santa Lucia to denizen of Monteverdi's dungeons, she thought bitterly, like a fallen angel.

She hadn't quite been able to come to grips with the fact that her well-ordered and plotted-out life had turned into complete pandemonium. And if Giulietta de' Alessandro died of plague . . .

It was just too disturbing to contemplate.

Wrenching her morbid thoughts to safer ground, she had reasoned that surely Aristo of Monteverdi's horse would better serve her during her flight than either of the two mules owned by the order.

And so, when Aristo's voice had finally dwindled to an unintelligible croak, and the other nuns had taken to their beds, Lucrezia had sneaked from the convent and managed to climb the wall beside the gate to make an ungraceful but hopefully unnoticed getaway. There were only two keys to the heavy grilled gate, and Sister Sophia had placed one under her pillow.

Rodrigo da Valenti—damn his Gypsy soul to hell!—had the other.

With nothing but a pouchful of coins (a few to bribe a gatekeeper to allow her to enter the walled city of Florence after curfew), Lucrezia had ridden away, feeling the Prince of Monteverdi breathing down her neck the entire way. And not least of her worries was the fact that she was being forced to throw herself at the mercy of the man who was considered a raving fanatic by many. A man who might conveniently forget how she'd patiently listened to his complaints and grievances, and then had consoled him, soothed his feelings and encouraged his ambitions to retrieve lost ground in his influence over the pleasure-loving Florentines. Even to defy His Holiness.

A man who might conveniently forget the generous financial support the Corsinis had given San Marco before their downfall.

But what if the unpredictable Savonarola interpreted her flight as contrary to God's will? Mayhap even turned her over to Alessandro in some unexpected bid to win Dante de' Alessandro's favor?

Again, she had deliberately diverted her thoughts, essaying to concentrate on her immediate goal: escape.

The faint shuffling of feet near the altar intruded into Lucrezia's musings. She lowered her gaze from its seeming contemplation of the great crucifix to see Fra Domenico, a handsome, strapping man, replacing several candles and straightening the altar cloth.

Lucrezia lowered her head until the sides of her wimple touched her cheeks. And planned. No one at San Marco had openly objected to her presence, yet she felt lost . . . adrift. She had to tether herself more tightly to Savonarola; that was the only answer.

She knew of only one way to do it, and it might prove difficult indeed, for Savonarola shunned women. Yet Lucrezia's mother had been a seductress, and had passed certain knowledge on to her daughter.

The refugee Abbess of Santa Lucia thought of all the ways in which a woman might subtly lure and entrap a man sexually. After all, Girolamo Savonarola was only human . . . with human needs. And she was considered very comely, although she'd taken pains to hide her attributes behind the concealing folds of a habit and the accompanying stiff and severe headpiece.

Lucrezia thought of her shapely body beneath the voluminous robes; her beautiful auburn hair beneath the coif and wimple. She thought of perfumes and pomades she might secretly obtain from the *mercato* right there in Florence. Certainly she couldn't be obvious, for not only was she already an intruder among the brothers of the monastery, but it wouldn't do to have any of them condemn her for overtly exhibiting worldly wiles while among them. Or even succumb to her charms when she had only one man in mind. And if she couldn't earn his dependence upon her in some way—*any* way—she was doomed.

Rodrigo da Valenti, in that case, would once again be responsible for the destruction of a Corsini; and she would never allow that to happen.

# Twenty

"We've combed the countryside and no sign of them." Dante's voice was dulled with defeat.

Caressa watched her husband run his long fingers through his silvering hair as he sat at his desk in the library. She pushed her own worries aside, even the threatening anguish that hovered on the edges of her mind. This was the first time since they'd heard Aristo's story that Dante had taken on this uncharacteristic attitude of defeat.

His head came to rest in the cradle of his hands, the slight slump of his shoulders reaffirming his despair. "First, and most important, is the distinct possibility that Giulietta is . . . dead. Secondly, I obviously made a monumental mistake in my judgment of Rodrigo da Valenti." He looked over at his wife, his normally bright eyes as dull now as his voice. "Not only did he spirit her away when she was in grave need of a physician, but *he* was the one who escorted her to Santa Lucia. And then insisted upon her remaining there against our wishes." Anger flared within the turquoise depths of his eyes as he slammed one open palm against the desk top. "God *damn* him!"

Caressa came to stand behind him. Her hands automatically went to the tense muscles of his shoulders. "Aristo said she'd shown no outward signs of plague," she reminded him for what seemed the hundredth time. "And surely if Giulietta were dead, Rodrigo would have notified us."

The prince's muscles tensed beneath her fingers. "Not necessarily. Coward that he is, he could have left her somewhere and fled to France."

Rare irritation rose in Caressa. "Then why would he have taken her in the first place?" Her hands fell away from her husband's shoulders, and she swung toward the window. "His actions weren't those of a coward," she said in clipped tones, "and neither are you so poor a judge of men. Surely, in your heart of hearts, you know Rodrigo is incapable of such behavior." She stared out the window, not really seeing anything before her. "He loves her. I think he has since the first time he saw her. Put yourself in his place." She swung back to him. "Put your anger aside for a moment, Dante. What would *you* have done were you in his shoes?"

His eyes narrowed. "If I loved you beyond all things, and I thought I was going to lose you, I would have . . ." He trailed off, his voice turning husky with emotion. "I would have done the same thing. And then I would have wed you—if only to call you mine for a few precious hours."

Caressa fought back her tears. "And wed or not, you would have taken me to the best physician you could find, sought the best care available, wouldn't you?"

He rose in the face of her distress, and moved toward her. Pulling her into his arms, he pressed his lips against the dark, fragrant fall of her hair. *"Perdonami, amore mio.* Forgive me, my love, for allowing my fears to add to your burden. 'Tis just that I . . ."

"If Giulietta were dead, I would know it!"

He fell silent, and rested his chin atop her head. He directed his gaze through the window, to the winter-dreary countryside beyond the stone wall surrounding Castello Monteverdi. "I'll go out again this morn. We evidently haven't done a thorough job if we cannot even pick up their trail."

Suddenly, as if conjured up, three figures emerged from the

woods across the way, two riding double on a magnificent and familiar ebony stallion.

At the same time, like a shriek of portent, the blast of the signal horn shattered the peaceful quiet of the late morn.

Caressa started, then followed her husband's gaze. Hope filled her heart at the sight that greeted her eyes.

Rodrigo knew even before the horn sounded that watchmen in the towers would be on the alert. He therefore wasn't the least bit surprised when troops in sapphire and silver Alessandro livery moved in on the three of them almost immediately after they left the shelter of the trees.

He felt Giulietta tense within his arms, and murmured against her ear, "Easy, *cara mia.*"

Guards closed in behind them, cutting off any retreat into the forest.

"The warmest of welcomes," observed Father Antoine dryly as they were forced to come to a halt before the leader.

It was Paolo.

"Paolo!" Giulietta cried in delight, in spite of the forbidding expression on the guard's features.

Despite the gravity of the situation, Paolo obviously couldn't hide the relief that lit his eyes. "Mona Giulietta," he said, his voice rough with emotion. *"Grazi a Dio!"*

He looked at Rodrigo, concealing what had to be his uncertainty, in the face of Giulietta's safe return, with more success than he'd hidden his happiness. He nodded stiffly, then threw an unreadable glance at Father Antoine.

"The lady Giulietta is in good health, as you can see," Rodrigo said to Paolo without ceremony, although one side of his mouth lifted. "I would like an audience with the prince, Paolo. Is that possible?"

"From the dungeons *sì*," Paolo answered. "My orders are to incarcerate you on sight."

Rodrigo felt Giulietta draw in her breath sharply, and gave her waist a light, reassuring squeeze. He had no intention of languishing in Monteverdi's dungeon.

"You can't do that to Rodrigo," she said in affront. "He's my—"

The sound of hoofbeats cut across her words.

"I think you can soon take that up with your father," Rodrigo said, his gaze moving to the figure riding toward them on a snow-white charger. He lowered his voice and added, "If he doesn't run me through first."

"You've brought his daughter home safely," Father Antoine said unexpectedly. "Any reasonable man would forgive old grievances in light of that."

Giulietta looked at the priest. "My father can be most unreasonable when it comes to me."

As the men immediately before them parted for the prince, Father Antoine said, "Had I a daughter like you, *mon enfant,* I would more than likely be the same."

Rodrigo detected a wistful note in the priest's voice, but had no time to wonder about it. Durante de' Alessandro, Prince of Monteverdi, was before him, his handsome face a study in displeasure.

"I should cut you down where you stand!" he said with soft menace. "No matter what happened after you left Santa Lucia, your black heart should be decorating my battlements!"

" 'Tis a poor way of showing gratitude, Papa, and you would also make me a widow," Giulietta said. She slipped from Morello's back before Rodrigo could object. As she approached Dante, he dismounted to meet her. They embraced, and Rodrigo saw Dante close his eyes momentarily in obvious relief, and hoped it would soften the prince's ire—at least for Giulietta's sake.

Dante held her away from him, looking her over from head to toe. "A pale nun's habit ill-becomes you," he told her gruffly, "and you are thin as a rail. And colorless as a wraith. Why are you traipsing about the countryside if you aren't yet hale?" He looked at Rodrigo before she could answer. "She has recovered, has she not?"

"She never had plague, Excellence," Father Antoine answered for him, "but suffered from exhaustion."

Dante gave the priest a disparaging look. "And who are you?"

"This is Father Antoine," Rodrigo said. "He saved Giulietta's life."

"A priest? Are you a physician, as well?"

The Frenchman shrugged. "Of sorts."

Dante frowned, obviously at the enigmatic answer, then looked down at Giulietta. Comprehension abruptly spilled over his features. "Widow? This charlatan clergyman married the two of you?"

"That is uncalled for," Rodrigo said with soft menace.

"Immediately upon their arrival," Father Antoine added with equanimity in the face of the prince's insult, "to spare the lady's reputation."

"My wife is tired, *principe,* as you can see," Rodrigo interjected. "May we offer her—and Father Antoine—some refreshment? And mayhap a bed for Giulietta?"

"Ready to take over Monteverdi, are you?" Dante asked softly, ominously. "You abduct my sick daughter, wed her while in hiding, then dare to return and dictate to me?"

"Papa, please!" Giulietta pleaded. "You were going to give my hand in marriage to Rodrigo in the first place. Why can't you see that what he did was for my sake?"

Dante frowned down at her. " 'Twas purely for his own selfish reasons, *nina,* but I wouldn't expect you to understand that yet. You still have stars in your eyes—mayhap fever in your brain, in spite of this priest's assertions that you never had plague. Your lady mother anxiously awaits. Let's not make her suffer another moment." He lifted her by the waist and firmly planted her atop his horse.

Rodrigo opened his mouth to object, then thought better of it. No matter what Dante did, Giulietta was his legal wife—had been his legally betrothed before that—and there was nothing the prince could do about it now.

Rodrigo's features settled into bleak lines. He was prepared to do battle with the prince, if need be, to ensure that nothing came between him and Giulietta again. Not illness, not harsh words, not even family.

Father Antoine leaned over and spoke in a low voice as the entire party moved toward the castle. " 'Tisn't as bad as it seems, *mon fils*. Just his damaged pride. Alessandro will get over his anger at you, you'll see."


Dante carried Giulietta into the great hall of Monteverdi, and word spread like wildfire that she'd returned safely. Servants and retainers alike filled the hall to welcome her back.

Messengers were immediately dispatched to Vittorio and Gianna in Florence, Bernardo and Lucia and their families; troops were called back to Monteverdi from all over Tuscany.

Nicco gave his sister a huge hug, then sheepishly loosened his grip at his new brother-in-law's words of caution.

Beau came bounding into the room—appearing twice as big to Giulietta as when she had fled to Santa Lucia. He wore a path between Rodrigo and Giulietta, obviously torn between his master and mistress, and causing all kinds of calamity in his enthusiastic wake. No one seemed to mind.

And Caressa . . . Caressa hugged her daughter joyously, tears streaking her cheeks. "I knew you would come home afely," she murmured in Giulietta's ear. "I had faith in God . . . nd Rodrigo."

Giulietta laughed happily. "I'm sorry for the worry I caused you, but when Rodrigo thought I had the plague . . . that I might die, he stormed the convent single-handedly to obtain he gate key and swept me away on Morello. He's a wonderful man and I love him terribly."

"I know, *nina*. I've known for quite a while."

Mother and daughter exchanged a meaningful look, and Giulietta felt her face grow warm in embarrassment. "I treated him abominably, *Mamina*," she said in a low voice.

"That's behind you now, *cara*. You have your life. And your love. Thank God for both . . ."

In the middle of the short, impromptu celebration, Giulietta made a request to Rodrigo. He promptly relayed it to the prince, who held up his hand for silence. "Would you say a few words, Father Antoine, for Maria's soul?"

"She was a beautiful and sweet girl," Giulietta said to Caressa, her smile fading, her expression sobering. "She didn't deserve to die . . . and in a stable."

"She'll be avenged, I swear," Rodrigo promised. He looked at Dante.

"Oh, indeed, one day soon the abbess will pay for her callous treatment of both Maria and my daughter. We will continue to search for her—all of Italy, if necessary."

Murmurs of agreement sounded here and there, and in his heavily accented Italian, Father Antoine asked for bowed heads while he recited a short prayer. His voice was deep and resonant, and made up for his French lilt. When he'd finished, he said, "Vengeance must come from God. Remember that, *mon prince*, lest the double-sided blade of revenge turn on him who wields it."

"Where's Aristo?" Giulietta asked Caressa as she sat upon a stool, Rodrigo's hand resting lightly on one shoulder.

"*Sì*. Where is he?" Rodrigo repeated. "I owe him an apology. . . . He wasn't injured, was he?"

"I believe he's in the dungeon . . . visiting your friend Carlo. Aristo has become very forgiving lately," Dante answered from beside Caressa. "No doubt due to the influence of my wife."

Giulietta frowned, but Rodrigo went suddenly still. "You imprisoned my brother?" he said through stiff lips, fighting disbelief.

"Indeed. And another man called Marco. You cannot tell me they knew nothing of your whereabouts."

Rodrigo's hand tightened on Giulietta's shoulder. Her hand went to cover his, but from the expression on his normally composed features, it was too late. "Aristo is not the only one who has changed over the years," he said. "But your change, *principe,* is not for the better. You took a man from his family? A man who knew nothing? And Marco . . . Marco wasn't even there!"

A sudden hush fell around them at Rodrigo's reprimand.

"I imprisoned a man who locked my servant in a cellar so he couldn't come to me with his story. That is collusion of the basest kind."

Rodrigo pulled his hand from beneath Giulietta's and went to stand directly before Dante. "It was no such thing! He did it out of love for me . . ." He clenched his fists in anger. "I insist you release him—and Marco, as well. Immediately."

Dante's lips thinned, and Giulietta thought with dismay that they might come to blows. The Prince of Monteverdi wasn't accustomed to taking orders from anyone. "Go yourself, since you seem so determined to take over as *padrone* here. Tell the guard I said to give you the key."

"I'll take him, Father," Nicco said, and stepped up to stand between them. He gave his father a brief look of appeal before he motioned to Rodrigo to follow him.

As they left, Giulietta moved to stand. Dante's firm hand on her shoulder where Rodrigo's had just been kept her still. "You surely don't need to visit a dank and drafty dungeon, daughter, so soon out of your sickbed."

She looked over at Caressa, who shook her head in warning.

The prince turned to Father Antoine, who was examining the bandage on a minor wound suffered by one of Dante's watchmen. *"Ebbene,* tell me, good Father," he directed the priest as a servant offered him wine from a heavy silver tray balanced on one shoulder, "how you came to be in Tuscany. How it is you are so well-versed in the art of healing . . .

"And exactly where you and Valenti managed to hide Giulietta while we fruitlessly searched the entire area—not knowing if she was dead or alive."


The dungeons beneath Castello Monteverdi were better than most, for the castle had been built within the last century and, therefore, not as airless and forbidding inside. It had also been well-maintained, even the underground prison.

Still, the very thought of Carlo being incarcerated *any-where* . . . and because of him, was extremely disturbing to Rodrigo. Nicco had obtained the key from the guard, Vincente, without incident, and at first Rodrigo spoke little to the young man beyond monosyllabic answers, his mind on other things besides explaining to the younger man how he'd eluded Dante and his men.

". . . well-treated," Nicco was saying, breaking into Rodrigo's dark thoughts. His look was apologetic in the wavering light of the torch he held.

Rodrigo managed a half-smile. His new brother-by-marriage was obviously still in awe of him and attempting to make amends for Dante's actions. He was a fine figure of a man— with his good looks and tall, lithe build. Even though his hair was sandy, his eyes gray, his features vividly reminded Rodrigo of Giulietta. Although he seemed to have less of a temper than his sister, Rodrigo detected signs of the same, irrepressible nature.

Nicco was also forgiving, which was important, Rodrigo silently acknowledged. If inner strength and intelligence were an integral part of a man's nature—and especially a man destined to be a leader—the ability to forgive was an asset, as well.

"I'm certain they were given the basic necessities," Rodrigo allowed, "but that isn't the point."

As they walked down the cool, damp main passageway, Niccolò added, "My father was furious—beside himself with rage and frustration. I don't remember the last time I saw him so angry . . . and only Mother and Aristo could even begin to convince him that you'd never do aught that wasn't in Gietta's best interests."

"I thought she had plague," Rodrigo said shortly. "I sincerely believed you would all have been exposed had I brought her here."

Their footsteps echoed along the silent corridor, adding to the building tension, the unease, for Rodrigo had a real aversion to dungeons. Any below-ground prison was unacceptable to him. His conscience still bothered him for having directed Carlo to lock Aristo in that dank root cellar—away from fresh air and light. Like a crypt. But there had been no other quick solution, and time had been of the essence.

Now, in the face of what Dante had done to Carlo—and Marco, who'd not even been involved—Rodrigo couldn't bring himself to say anything reassuring to his new brother-by-marriage. His anger was too close to the surface. . . .

"There." Nicco had slowed, and was pointing to a cell on the right. He held the torch higher, and Rodrigo strained to see into the small, square grill in the wooden door.

There was no guard outside the door, and as Rodrigo said Carlo's name, Niccolò placed a heavy-shanked metal key into the lock and turned it. The door swung inward, allowing the torchlight to illuminate the interior.

A small, hand-hewn table appeared, with two men seated at either side of it. A chessboard between them indicated what the prisoners were doing.

"No candle or torch?" Rodrigo asked tersely. "How can you play chess in the dark?"

"My candle just went out," said a familiar, raspy voice. Aristo came forward and into the light.

"I see. In his generosity, the Prince of Monteverdi granted you the luxury of a single candle. Remind me to thank him." His words were weighted with sarcasm.

Carlo stood then, squinting against the sudden, bright light, and stepped toward Rodrigo. "Rigo!"

Rodrigo embraced him, then held him back to inspect him from head to toe. He looked as if he'd lost some weight, but by no means appeared mistreated. Neither did Marco, who moved to stand behind his cellmate.

Rodrigo nodded at Marco, then said, "Let's get out of here. We can talk upstairs, away from this tomb. In the light of day, and among others." He motioned Nicco to lead them out into the passageway.

Once the men had retired to the study, to Rodrigo's surprise, Dante apologized to Carlo and Marco for their incarceration. "If you knew naught, imprisoning you served no purpose. I thought you would change your mind and give me the information I wanted."

He looked at Rodrigo. "I should have known that my . . . son-by-marriage wouldn't have burdened you with that knowledge." His glance alighted on Carlo. "As for your family,

Carlo, they were told that you were imprisoned here; that you would be released as soon as Rodrigo da Valenti returned to Castello Monteverdi with our daughter."

Rodrigo slanted a look at Marco. He was normally sullen, a man Rodrigo had never trusted. He looked miserable, however, and subdued. Exactly like a man who'd lost the woman he loved, no matter who he was, and for the first time since he'd returned from France, Rodrigo felt sympathy for the young *Zingaro*. Gone—at least for now—was the hot temper, the rashness, the tendency to blame others when things didn't go his way.

"As for you"—Dante's gaze went to Marco—"I—"

"I have no family here," Marco said dully. He was of medium build, but solid, with dark hair and eyes in an even-featured face. "I loved Maria, the girl my lady Giulietta tended at risk to her own life." He drew in a deep, steadying breath. "I would thank her, *mio principe,* if I may."

Dante nodded. "Of course you may. I sincerely regret that Gietta couldn't save your Maria."

Rodrigo cast Dante a look askance, but could detect nothing in his voice or expression that indicated the prince was anything but sincere.

"You will find, once you know the Alessandro family," Rodrigo told Marco, "that valor runs naturally in their blood. That the lady Giulietta risked her life in an effort to save Maria is not surprising."

Aristo stood quietly in the shadows, listening. He spoke then, virulence adding to the natural rasp of his voice. "But the question remains: Where is that she-spider of an abbess? She has much to account for. 'Twas His Excellency who summoned a physician to visit the other women within the cloister in case the disease had spread—certainly not that scheming succubus!"

Four pairs of eyes went to him.

"I've felt uneasy about Santa Lucia for weeks," he added. "No doubt since Lucrezia became abbess. I said naught, Excellence, not wishing to unduly alarm you. And then, 'twas too late."

"We'll find her," Dante vowed. "If we have to comb all of Italy, we'll find the woman."

"And if she seeks the Pope's protection in Rome?" Carlo asked.

"Not likely," Rodrigo said. "I've seen Savonarola at Santa Lucia myself. I doubt if even Alexander would help her in any way, considering her relationship with the prior."

"What if she turned on Savonarola?" Dante asked. "The woman is obviously capable of anything. In return for Alexander's protection, she could give him valuable information— mayhap even help him lure the prior to Rome, something the Pope's been trying to do for months."

" 'Twouldn't surprise me," Marco said unexpectedly. "There is no level to which she will not stoop."

Rodrigo looked at him sharply. "You know her, then?"

There was a moment of silence. "Let's say I've made her . . . acquaintance."

"Know you aught of her background?" Rodrigo pressed.

Marco shook his head, but Rodrigo noted the faint flush beneath his skin. "Only that she has gold to spend."

There was a brief hesitation in the conversation as unspoken questions hovered in the air.

"She could have been skimming the convent's coffers for years," Dante said.

Marco shrugged.

"Sì," Rodrigo reasoned. "But she might also have a wealthy sponsor . . . or family somewhere." He took a draught of wine, his eyes meeting Dante's over the rim. He replaced the empty goblet upon the desk. "There's a distinct possibility she might have taken refuge at San Marco," he said. "In fact, 'tis my belief."

"But why would a fanatic who shuns women take her in?" Dante mused aloud.

"Every man has his weakness," Carlo said with a suggestive waggle of his eyebrows. "Rodrigo told me the abbess is very fair."

"Aye," Rodrigo replied with irony, glad his good-natured brother held no ill feelings toward the Prince of Monteverdi. "But there are also beautiful snakes populating the earth. Ofttimes, the more beautiful, the more deadly. Given her looks and obviously sly disposition, my guess is they are lovers . . . or fellow conspirators. Or both."

A knock at the door interrupted their discussion. At Dante's bidding, a servant entered with a fresh tray of cheese, slices of cold sausage and balogna, five more Murano glass goblets and two terra-cotta pitchers of wine. She set the tray down upon the desk, then poured wine into each of the goblets and passed them out.

"I wouldn't put such a thing past her—being the prior's lover," Marco growled from the depths of his misery.

The girl quickly collected the used goblets and empty pitchers. When she'd gone, Carlo said, "From what Rodrigo told me of their exchange when he first escorted Mona Giulietta to Santa Lucia, the abbess seems to bear him some poorly hidden grudge."

Dante looked at Rodrigo, his fair brows drawn together.

"I cannot fathom why," Rodrigo explained, "but when we find her, she will have more than enough reason to hate me."

Dante helped himself to a piece of sausage, and chewed slowly, thoughtfully, his unseeing gaze trained on the middle distance. But not for long. "You cannot guess," he suddenly asked Rodrigo, his voice dropping in pitch, "why anyone would harbor enmity toward you?"

Rodrigo met his bright, expectant gaze. "Of course I can. But what connection would *she* have to what happened six years past?"

Carlo asked, "What kind of man was the elder Corsini? Mayhap he'd sown his seed in a few places besides the marriage bed and . . ." He lifted his shoulders, leaving the unfinished statement hanging in the air like undispersed smoke.

Rodrigo looked at Dante, feeling a strange clenching deep within him. To think Giulietta had been in the woman's care—his Giulietta, who the abbess knew, by his own admission, was his betrothed. And he had been so confident the nun wouldn't dare harm her. . . .

"And we know nothing of her background?" he asked softly.

"Naught . . . yet," Dante answered "But I am by no means finished with my search: for her identity . . . and her person."

"We can dispatch men to cover the main roads leading out of Florence and its immediate environs," Rodrigo said, "and can only hope we're not too late."

"*Sì*. Some of the men we just called in were looking for you and Giulietta, not a runaway abbess . . . and more than likely in disguise. We'll send fresh troops out, and you can go to Florence," Dante said, "to continue your work for me." His eyes narrowed, a subtle challenge within their depths. "If you can keep from playing any more tricks . . . Unobtrusively keeping a watch over San Marco and its prior is more important than ever now, for 'twill serve two purposes."

Rodrigo twisted his lips slightly at Dante's jibe, but he wasn't about to open up the argument again, especially when he could understand a father's concern for his daughter. For now, an unspoken, tentative truce had been established between him and his father-by-marriage.

He nodded at Dante's words. "As you wish."

"I'd like to join you," Carlo said. "I'm beginning to enjoy

the excitement . . . but after I'm reunited with Laura and the children, of course."

"Another day or so won't make a difference as long as the roads are watched," Rodrigo said glancing at the prince for affirmation.

"And the monastery of San Marco, as well," Dante added.

"I would like my mare back, too," Aristo added from his place in the shadows. Dante gestured for him to come forward and handed him a goblet of wine. "Although it pains me to ride her," he added with a small sigh.

"Your rose water becomes you better than asafetida," Carlo said, and grinned at the dwarf.

"One never knows when one will need extra protection," the diminutive man defended his actions. "Was that why you pitched me so energetically into that cellar?"

"*Sì*. And I'm sorry if I hurt you, *maestro*, but the stench made me . . . eager to seal you away."

The others laughed, and even Aristo had to grin.

Only Marco failed to register any amusement on his saturnine features.

# Twenty-one

Before a blazing fire in her bedchamber hearth, Giulietta reveled in the soothing warm water of her bath. She was tired, but happy. In fact, she was so very happy, she feared she was only dreaming—that her newfound joy as Rodrigo da Valenti's wife was only a wonderful dream formed from her secretly harbored wishes at Santa Lucia. A state as sweet and fragile as marzipan, and every bit as ephemeral as the airy confection . . . Or a dream.

The ornate figures on the hood over the fireplace danced before her eyes. Her lids began to get heavy as the warmth from the water relaxed her further and weighted her limbs.

As her lashes drifted shut, Giulietta allowed herself the luxury of thinking back to the very first time she'd met him. Of course he hadn't killed Mario di Corsini, she'd realized that years later. But it would have appeared that way to a child, and she had held that for as long as possible between her and Rodrigo as an insurmountable obstacle.

What had galled her when she'd finally met him as an adult was just as much—probably more—her doing as his. She had had no business running off to Santa Lucia in defiance of her father (and had even less of an idea of what the life of a religious was like!). She'd hurt her foot, then run into Rodrigo . . . And gone along with—even encouraged—his lovemaking, in further defiance of Dante, and out of her own curiosity and long-denied needs.

*There is nothing common about you, Mona Giulietta, nor was there anything in the least bit common about our meeting . . .*

It hadn't been flattery, she knew that now, and her conscience squirmed at the memory of her disdainful treatment of him. Unthinkingly, she raised her hands to her ears to drown out the sound of her own haughty words not so long ago.

Elsewhere in the room, she became aware of Caressa and Lisa fussing about, and the sudden splash of the water in the tub must have caught Caressa's attention. Instantly, she was at Giulietta's side, leaning over her daughter, the scent of her jasmine perfume familiar and comforting to Giulietta. *Dio!* but she couldn't even remember when last she'd worn perfume. . . .

"What is it, *nina?*" Concern furrowed Caressa's ivory brow, shadowed her clear, gray eyes. "Are you finished? Do you—?"

"No." Giulietta managed a wan smile in the wake of her disturbing thoughts, and lifted her lashes to meet her mother's anxious gaze. "I want you to pinch me, so I know this is real."

Caressa smiled, relief relaxing her features. " 'Tis real enough, Gietta."

Giulietta frowned suddenly, a sliver of guilt unexpectedly lancing through her to taint her euphoria. "I was so wretched to him," she said, a tremor in her voice. "I don't deserve to be so happy. I don't deserve him."

"Hush," Caressa said. "No more talk like that. You're his wife now, and he loves you as you love him—a rare commodity in any marriage. And, *cara,* love forgives all."

Giulietta was silent a moment, pondering her mother's words. "I'll make it up to him, I swear it. I'll never give him reason to regret making me his wife." She looked at Caressa earnestly. "He was under no obligation to wed me—in fact he *couldn't* have after I chose to become a nun. Can you imagine a man so in love with you that he defied a prince's wrath and married you, even though he thought you might die in his arms?"

Caressa smiled lovingly at her daughter. "I can think of only one other man so romantically inclined."

Giulietta sighed, and closed her eyes again. "Papa, of course. Your courtship and marriage have been part of the legend that is Il Leone. Everything noble about the Alessandro family . . ."

Caressa raised her eyebrows. "None of us is perfect, and there have been some less than noble Alessandros in the family. Your father, however, was not one of them. Nor was your grandfather Alessandro.

"Are you ready to dry off now? You don't need to catch a chill."

Giulietta sat up, reluctant to leave her bath, but eager to see her new husband again. A cool, black nose touched her elbow, and she started. "Beau! You rascal!" she chided as the half-grown pup eyed her over the lip of the slatted wood tub with his intelligent, amber-brown eyes. He hefted his front paws onto the edge, the pristine plume of his tail whipping the air above his hindquarters. His long pink tongue swiped at Giulietta's flushed cheek barely missing her.

"Kiss me, will you?" she admonished him. "Rodrigo will be so jealous he'll throw you in the dungeon!"

At the name Rodrigo, the dog's ears moved forward alertly. He whined softly, and turned his head toward the door.

"Now see what you've done, Mona Giulietta," Lisa said from across the room. "He'll be scratching at the door to seek out Signor Rodrigo, and you'll catch a chill from the cold draft."

But Beau dropped his paws from the tub, and instead of going to the door, he went to Giulietta's wooden wardrobe, the doors of which stood open. He poked his head inside and began sniffing the bottom, tail still waving.

Caressa held out a length of linen toweling, and Giulietta stood. Just like when she'd been a child, she allowed her mother to wrap her in the towel before she stepped out and onto the lush mat used to absorb extra water and cushion the feet.

*"Grazi, Mamina,"* she murmured with a dreamy smile as Caressa rubbed her skin with vigor. "You always did this best."

Caressa returned her daughter's smile. " 'Tis a mother's greatest pleasure, caring for her children."

Lisa's squeak of surprise snagged Giulietta's attention. She turned toward the sound, and saw Lisa standing frozen in horror. Beau was pulling out Giulietta's soiled and wrinkled jonquil silk dress. The dress Lisa had been instructed to clean and repair . . . to try and salvage. The dress that Giulietta had worn the night she'd encountered Rodrigo da Valenti outside the Gypsy camp and. . . .

A slow flush began at her neck, spread up into her face and to the roots of her hair. She'd forgotten all about it. And so, evidently, had Lisa.

*"Maledetto, animale!"* the girl exclaimed as she attempted to take the dress from the dog. "Wretched animal!" But Beau, evidently thinking she meant to play, began tugging at the rumpled hemline, while Lisa pulled the bodice in the opposite direction—thus inadvertently exposing the entire front of the gown to anyone who cared to notice.

Giulietta closed her eyes and sent a silent appeal heavenward, afraid to look at Caressa. A knock on her door, however, claimed her mother's attention.

"Giulietta?" It was Rodrigo.

Caressa hastily wrapped her daughter in the toweling and straightened. "Come in," she called. Beau instantly released the garment at the sound of Rodrigo's voce and bounded to the door. But it was Dante who entered first.

Giulietta's heart tumbled to her feet. Even now, she feared

her father's wrath if he discovered their amorous encounter that night—and the fact that she had been fleeing to Santa Lucia. He was a powerful man. Could he somehow have the marriage annulled in light of what had happened months ago?

The two men came in, Rodrigo holding back. "If now is a bad time . . . ," he began apologetically.

Dante answered for him, with a negligent wave of one hand. "Look at the color you bring to my Gietta's cheeks, Rigo. Now is quite the right time, I would think. After all, you *are* her husband now."

The blush to which Dante referred had more to do with him catching sight of the telltale gown than any embarrassment she might have felt before Rodrigo. He had, after all, cared for her while she was suffering from exhaustion.

They'd also had two glorious days and nights alone together.

Out of the corner of her eye she saw Lisa ball up the incriminating gown, shove it back into the wardrobe and all but slam the doors. Fortunately, both men appeared more concerned with Giulietta than the activities of a servant.

Rodrigo paused to scratch Beau behind the ears, his eyes on his wife. A slow, appreciative smile curved his mouth, and one demon-winged eyebrow arched rakishly. He had changed his clothes and was wearing his sapphire and scarlet doublet— the one that made his eyes as deep a blue as the semi-precious lapis lazuli the ancient Egyptians used in their jewelry.

"How are you feeling, *nina?*" Dante asked as he moved right up to her and planted a kiss upon her forehead.

"Well, Papa," she answered, feeling a sudden chill from the partially open door. An involuntary tremor moved through her, but she couldn't say if it was from the draught . . . or the look in Rodrigo's eyes.

Rodrigo, ever perceptive where she was concerned, swung back to close the portal, and Dante glanced around the chamber. His gaze alighted on Lisa, who stood planted before the narrow wooden wardrobe like a hired mercenary. He nodded in acknowledgement. "I think, *bellezza mia,*" he said to Caressa, "that 'tis time to leave Giulietta alone with her husband, don't you agree?"

Giulietta lowered her gaze, suddenly shy before her parents in light of her new status. And what her father had just implied.

"But she's not dry," the well-meaning Lisa blurted from her post before the wardrobe, "and her hair is still wet!" She instantly clapped one hand over her mouth, as if regretting her outburst before the prince.

Caressa threw her a placating look. "You're right, Lisa. Will you finish helping Gietta?"

Dante took Caressa's hand and looked over at Rodrigo, who was absently stroking Beau's head, his eyes still upon Giulietta. "Mayhap you wish Lisa to finish your wife's ablutions, as well, son-in-law?"

Rodrigo met Dante's look as Lisa draped more toweling about Giulietta's shoulders. He read a distinct challenge in those bright, blue-green eyes, and silently accepted. *"Grazi, principe,* but no. I prefer to do it myself. I have been doing just that the last sennight or so, and enjoy every moment."

In spite of his natural self-confidence, Giulietta thought she detected the rise of color that tinged his cheeks.

*"Ebbene,* then we'll leave you."

"I'll send up a supper tray later," Caressa told Giulietta and gave her a light kiss on the cheek.

"Unless you wish to join us for a late repast?" Dante added innocently.

"Giulietta is still very tired," Rodrigo said simply.

Dante nodded. "And Giulietta . . . ?"

*"Sì,* Papa?"

"I told your Rigo that I would consider forgiving him for spiriting you away if he would consent to a proper wedding for you in May. Does that meet with your approval?"

Her face lit up. "How could it not?" she said, delighted, and stepped toward him and stood on tiptoe to plant a kiss upon his cheek. He lay his blond head against her damp auburn tresses for the briefest of moments, the fingers of one hand still laced through Caressa's, then swung toward the door.

Evidently needing no further hints, Lisa followed Dante and Caressa to the door, then closed it carefully behind her.

Rodrigo approached her with those long, lithe strides she'd always admired, if unconsciously. His smile faded, but at first she didn't notice. She was too busy covertly admiring the sleek turn of his calves and thighs beneath deep blue hose . . . and the unassailable proof of his masculinity, outlined and accented beneath his scarlet silk codpiece.

Her face warmed a few degrees . . . and so did her body.

"Surely you are cold, *cara*. How could Lisa allow you to stand thusly for any longer than it would take to retrieve a shift or gown from the wardrobe?"

Giulietta laughed softly, as he took her in his arms. "She was apparently afraid to open it in the presence of my parents after what happened just before you arrived."

He held her close, imparting the warmth of his own body to her. "And what does *that* mean?" He began to briskly run his hands up and down her back.

She'd been wrong, one part of her mind acknowledged. Mamma never did it like *this*. . . .

She began to tingle, but from more than just increased circulation. "Lisa forgot to clean and sew the dress I wore the night I met you. Beau pulled it from the bottom of the wardrobe while Mother was here."

He glanced at the closed wardrobe, then at Beau, who was now exploring the area around it. "Are you still so afraid of their learning of our encounter?"

Giulietta, feeling absolutely soothed and secure within his embrace, with his heart beating steadily beneath her ear, said, "Not Mamma. She would keep my secret—especially now that we're wed. But I don't know if my father wouldn't be furious even now . . ."

He pressed his lips against her forehead. "I was completely to blame, and will take full responsibility, *dolce mia*. As far as I'm concerned, all you did was take a walk after a disagreement with your father. You hurt your foot; I came across you and insisted that you bathe it in the stream, then took you right back to the keep. There's no need to be concerned. Not now, not ever again."

She closed her eyes, feeling desire wend through her as his stroking slowed and became more intimate. One length of toweling fell, but Giulietta didn't miss it.

"Your hair," he murmured. "We can't have you go to bed with wet hair." He scooped her into his arm and carried her to a spot directly before the fire. He set her down, pulled over a carved walnut chair, then seated himself and took her onto his lap. He began to dry her hair. The feel of him so close to her, with only a towel about her body, made Giulietta feel giddy. She reveled in the feel of his strong but gentle fingers beneath the towel as they massaged her scalp, and from time to time threaded through her long tresses.

It appeared that he had more control than she, for he seemed content with his task and smiled deeply into her eyes when they met now and again. Or so she thought until, in shifting her weight, she felt his arousal beneath the laced codpiece in his trunk hose.

She felt him stiffen, and gazed at him through her lashes. He was holding his lower lip between his teeth, and Giulietta felt a devilish thought dance through her head.

She nonchalantly moved again, turning far enough to one side to allow her hip to settle against his arousal. "Pray don't neglect this side, *condottiere*," she said sweetly, her lashes donwcast as she fingered the edge of the linen towel resting across her thigh.

Without warning, his lips came against the sweet softness where her neck met her shoulder, his tongue sending frissons of pleasure up her spine.

"Rodrigo," she murmured from deep within her throat. " 'Tis no way to dry a lady's hair."

"Nor, my little witch, is teasing a man any way to encourage him in his task. If you're curious, by all means, indulge yourself." He slowly placed her hand over his full codpiece, and Giulietta felt a curling warmth bloom in her belly at the feel of heat and hardness beneath her fingers. It traveled up her arm like quicksilver, swept in a tidal wave through her entire body until she could only moan softly and lean against him.

Her hand still in place, acutely sensitive to what lay beneath the fine, cool silk, she whispered, "Does this please you, my lord *condottiere*? Do *I* please you?"

"I'm no lord, *carissima*," he murmured, "but *sì*, you please me more than you'll ever know . . . anything you *do* pleases me . . ."

His lips moved to the sensitive area beneath her ear lobe, before he nipped it gently with his teeth. She smelled of jasmine on a late summer day, and of her own particular scent that set her apart from every other woman alive. And she tasted better, felt better, than in any of his paltry dreams, for the real woman made even the most vivid fantasy a mirage in comparison.

She splayed the fingers of her free hand over his cheek and brought his face back to hers. "You are lord of my heart, Rodrigo da Valenti, and always will be. Remember that."

She sealed her pledge with another kiss, open-mouthed and hungry, and found herself breathing in short little bursts, breathless from her own boldness and his answering loveplay.

She moved to turn farther, and to her surprise, he slid her bent knee across his lap and over his other leg, until they were sitting face-to-face.

"Since you're so fascinated with my codpiece, wife, mayhap you'll have better access from this position." The slow, sensual spreading of his beautifully molded lips was in complete accord with the unholy glint in his eyes.

The last towel had slipped to the floor, but the warmth from the hearth heated her back as did, even more, the consuming fire that came from within. She shivered when his mouth returned to her ear and his tongue slipped into that delicate aperture. She felt herself bathed in sudden, heated moisture between her thighs—a feeling so languorous and intense at the same time that she was driven to even bolder measures.

"I accept your invitation, *bello mio,*" she whispered huskily, and tentatively began to loosen the lacings that held the now-taut silk of his codpiece in place. "But only on one condition . . ."

"*Sì?*" he murmured from the area of her shoulder.

"That you wear your tunics longer, for I would have no other woman see what is mine and mine alone."

She felt rather than heard the laughter rumble upward from his chest. "I see. I am to look unfashionable to please my possessive wife. But if—"

His words died midsentence as his manhood sprang free and filled Giulietta's hands. Fire erupted along his veins, through his entire body, to settle, hot and pulsing, within his loins. The feel of her hands upon him threatened his control, and he let his head fall back, steeping in the pure sensation of her sweet touch.

Giulietta pressed her mouth against the corded column of his neck, her lips trembling even as were her fingers against the satin-sheathed steel of him. She dragged her tongue down his throat to the depression where his neck joined his chest, reveling in the powerful pulse that danced an erratic rhythm there, proof of her effect on him. "Take me," she murmured against him. "Take me here, now . . . like this, *sposo mio*. My husband."

" 'Twill hurt," he answered, bringing his lips down to hers, pulling her hips even closer. "My little virgin wife, it might hurt and—"

But at the brush of the downy entrance to her womanhood against his desire, his protests died. He slid one finger into the hot, silken folds of her in preparation; but she was ready. God in heaven, she felt like liquid fire spasming about his finger.

"You cannot hurt me," she said, beginning to stroke him. "Please, Rigo . . ."

He placed one hand on either side of her hips in answer, and guided her readiness to the tip of his tumescent shaft. Giulietta moved against him, eagerly taking him in, inch by inch at first, and whimpering softly with undiluted pleasure as he moved, then, into her more fully.

The feeling of being united as they sat upright was new to her; Giulietta felt as if his manhood were within a hair's breadth of her heart. She welcomed his rock-hard fullness, even as she wondered if she could sheath all of him.

She moved against him greedily, wanting to absorb him . . . and gasped with unexpected pain. He stilled immediately. "You're practically a virgin, my Gietta," he murmured, "let's go to the bed . . ."

She shook her head, her eyes luminous with love, and looked deeply into his. "I can't wait," she answered. "Take me here, *amore mio*, please!"

Before she could protest, he caught her more firmly to his chest and stood, maintaining their bond of rapture. Giulietta automatically wrapped her legs about his waist, and slowly, carefully, he moved to lower them both to the bright Oriental rug before the blazing hearth.

Their eyes locked, amber and sapphire, as Rodrigo once more began a slow, steady rhythm that took her breath away with its promise of heaven on earth. He levered himself above her and let his head drop back, softly calling her name, once, twice. In fascination, Giulietta watched the place where their bodies were joined in love; allowed her gaze to lift and briefly admire the superb spread of his shoulders, the beautifully sculpted musculature of his torso, rippling bronze in the fire-light as he moved with fluid, animal grace, guiding her toward that pinnacle of all physical pleasures.

Then he lowered himself, until they were chest to breast, and the exquisitely gathering tension within Giulietta drove all thought from her mind but fulfillment.

"I've loved you forever, *amore mio . . . anima mia*," he rasped softly in her ear. "You are my heart . . . my soul. You've been my most beautiful dream, my brightest hope, and my only salvation. Not even death can ever part us, for its power is a pathetic illusion compared to the strength of my love."

In the recesses of his mind, where dwelt the last of all rational thought, his declaration sounded akin to blasphemy. But in those moments, Rodrigo didn't care, for he meant every word. Every word, even as the movements of his body reinforced through physical expression all that his lips had proclaimed. He bared himself on the altar of his love for her, as he had longed to do for what had seemed like forever.

His words, the cadence of his sweetly potent strokes, brought the quickening deep within Giulietta to an unbearable pitch, crested, then imploded into thousands of shards of sensation throughout her entire body. And in the middle of her mind-stripping ecstasy, Rodrigo cried out her name, spewing forth into her womb his molten seed, the very essence of his maleness—

claiming her, branding her, committing himself to her for all of this life and the next. . . .


Marco sat in a corner of the crowded *taverna,* unobtrusively watching through seemingly heavy-lidded eyes. And listening. Not necessarily to the young prostitute on his knee . . . except when he caught something of interest, of course. He was in no hurry, for he had all the time in the world now.

He was also in Rodrigo da Valenti's employ, at least for the time being.

"I'll pay you to try and discover the identity of the man who was responsible for luring Maria to Florence," Valenti had told Marco a week earlier. " 'Tis the least I can do for a sister *Zingara,* and my Giulietta, who was fond of her as well."

His last words had convinced Marco to go along with the idea, even though he'd never had any liking for Valenti . . . and especially after Maria had exhibited a sudden and very real reluctance to wed him in the wake of Rodrigo's return from France.

But Giulietta de' Alessandro was now like a saint to Marco, for she had tended his Maria. When no one else would, and at great risk to her own life. Marco had also had time to talk further to Valenti's brother, Carlo, while they were incarcerated at Monteverdi, and had admitted to himself that any amorous interest had been only on Maria's part. Even before Rodrigo fled Italy.

"Maria was like a sister to me," Rodrigo had told Marco, genuine anger darkening his eyes, "and I would see her murderer pay for his crime. My lady wife said the girl mentioned the name *Palmieri* . . ."

It hadn't even bothered Marco to enter into a pact with the very man about whom he'd previously given information to Sister Lucrezia. God had punished him one hundredfold for that, he'd decided, and it was enough for now that he was tracking Maria's murderer.

". . . so handsome, and so wicked!" the girl on his knee was saying. Her long, dyed blond hair hung lankly down her back, and the hair around her forehead was plucked, as was the style in Florence, to make her rather low forehead look higher.

The word "wicked" caught Marco's attention. "Who's wicked?" he said blearily.

The girl in his lap—Cristina was her name—dropped her chin into her hand in an attitude of thoughtfulness, and said, "Palmieri. Alberto Palmieri."

Like magnet to metal, his eyes were immediately drawn to a tall, well-dressed son of the aristocracy. He had a woman on each knee and was engaged in pouring wine down the low-cut bodice of first one, then the other.

". . . from *Venezia,* they say. Chased away by the Venetian authorities for his sins."

*Palmieri.*

Marco narrowed his eyes at the man as the latter began to lick the enticing valley between one of the girl's breasts, to her squeals of delight. When the other girl wanted equal treatment, she pummeled his arm playfully to retrieve his attention . . .

And earned a sharp slap across one cheek for her efforts. The girl immediately stilled, a dazed look moving across her face; and just before Palmieri returned to nuzzling and tonguing the tops of the first girl's large breasts in full view of the entire *taverna,* his dark eyes quickly scanned the taproom . . . and briefly encountered Marco's.

Marco felt his heart stutter beneath his ribs. He was reminded of a deadly cobra, and a frigid finger of foreboding slid along his spine.

"Why wicked?" he asked with feigned nonchalance as Cristina stared moodily at the threesome.

She shrugged. "They say he's contemptuous of prostitutes— luring them with promises of gold, then brutalizing them and turning them into the street without a *scudo.*" She looked at him suddenly, suspicion flaring in her brown eyes. "You aren't like that, *signore,* are you?"

Marco gave her an innocuous grin and said, "I *love* women. Why would I abuse those who give a man such pleasure, eh?"

She nodded, grinned lasciviously, and slid one hand up his thigh. His fingers over hers stilled her. "First things first, *nina,*" he said, and pressed a shiny gold florin into the hand that he'd removed from between his thighs. "This is to ensure your, er— discretion, eh? Now, tell me more about this Palmieri . . ."

# Twenty-two

"They say just recently he lured a young *Zingara* to his home," Cristina had confided to Marco, "who was supposedly an innocent."

Marco had had to fight for calm. "What happened to her?" he'd asked.

Cristina had shrugged. "No one knows."

Palmieri left the *taverna* with one of the two women just as the taproom began to empty out—and just as Marco thought he couldn't bear the noise any longer, or the smoke, or the stale stench of many unwashed bodies unrelieved by cloying perfumes in a warm and closed-in area.

He was, after all, a Gypsy, accustomed to spending much time outdoors as he traveled with his small group. And he was tired of the girl perched on his numb knee, and her endless attempts to arouse him, as though she had to do more than talk to earn her florin. Nonetheless, she had gained his gratitude for what she'd revealed.

The bracing night air was just what Marco needed to chase away the echoes and smells of the *taverna* and clear his mind to plan. He'd intended to follow Palmieri home and confront him. Even if it cost him his life, he didn't care now. His sweet Maria was dead, and if he had to die in the act of avenging her, so be it.

But Palmieri got rough with his female companion, and when she stubbornly refused to move up the street with him, trying at the same time to wrench free of his grip, he backed her into a narrow alleyway.

Marco heard her cries, as did several others. He plunged into the space between the two buildings and paused, letting his eyes adjust to the blackness. "Where is that knave?" muttered a voice in his ear.

*"Sì,"* rasped a second man. "I've a score to settle with him for hitting Francesca in the taproom."

If there were three of them against Palmieri, Marco thought, so much the better. He didn't care how the job was done—just so it was done. And Palmieri wore a sword, a definite advantage against Marco's dagger.

The girl whimpered from somewhere ahead of them, and Marco cautiously moved forward, knife in hand. He felt rather than heard the other two men close behind him. The night air felt even colder in the dampness of the alley, which never saw sunlight, and the smell of rotting garbage and urine prevailed.

"You think I want you to soil my bed?" Palmieri's contemptuous voice rasped from the dimness. His slurred speech told Marco that he'd had plenty to drink this night. "You'll yield to me now, *puttana,* or regret it."

"No! *Per piacere,* you're hurting me . . ."

One of the men from behind Marco evidently couldn't contain himself any longer in the wake of the prostitute's cry. He lunged around Marco. A scraping of shoe leather along the alley floor, and then the thud of bodies sounded dully in the airless corridor; a grunt of pain followed, and a woman's stifled cry again.

Marco felt the passage of air from what had to be a sword blade, although Palmieri didn't have much room to wield it. He retreated one step, two steps, bumping into the remaining man behind him.

"Daniello?" the second man called out boldly.

"Daniello is dead," snarled Palmieri, "and so will you be if you don't get out of here!"

The tip of his sword shot past Marco's middle, missing him by a hair's breadth and, from the gasp of pain that echoed along the alleyway, evidently catching the man behind him. Marco, wiry-framed and agile, flattened himself against the wall behind him, praying for a chance to use the knife any *Zingaro* could wield so well. One chance only. . . .

He could see Palmieri's outline in the gloom—saw him jerk his sword from the second man, who had sunk to his knees, cursing Palmieri and groaning softly. Another whimper sounded from Marco's left, where this Francesca evidently remained, no doubt frozen in fear.

Palmieri turned, a pale blur in his light-colored doublet. With sword still unsheathed, he lunged past Marco . . .

And threw himself squarely into the latter's razor-honed, up-turned dagger, the momentum from his own movement impaling him all the way up to the weapon's hilt, protruding now from his chest.

*"This,"* Marco hissed, "is for my Maria, you filthy cur!" and twisted the weapon with all the strength of his grief and rage, ensuring the man's death. As Palmieri began to sink to his knees, a death rattle issuing from his lips, Marco pulled the dagger from his belly with both hands, feeling a savage satisfaction at the ominous sucking sound of sharp steel retracting from organ and bone and blood.

He backed toward the entrance and flung away the bloodied blade with his lips twisted in purest contempt. Swinging about, he encountered a small group of men who were evidently debating whether to enter the fray or not. Marco jerked his chin toward the alley, drawing his cape more securely about him. "There's a woman in there . . . and several wounded men."

Before anyone could question him, he turned and melted into the night.

\* \* \*

Father Antoine relented and stayed at Castello Monteverdi for a sennight, entertaining them with stories of his travels, and his escape from France.

"My name is anathema in some parts of France," he told them at dinner the evening before his departure, "yet I chose not to give up my own faith, but rather to accept the beliefs of others as well . . . and the methods of healing that I've seen with my own eyes, and now practice with my own hands." He shook his head and stared at the wine goblet before him at the table. The flame from a nearby candle branch bathed his face in gold. "Some would call me a heretic—just like some are beginning to call your Savonarola."

"He's not *our* Savonarola," Dante said darkly. "He's originally from Ferrara. And from what I've seen and heard, you do yourself a great injustice by mentioning yourself in the same breath."

Rodrigo was only half-listening, for he already knew much of his story. His thoughts were occupied by his new wife, the sight of whom never failed to accelerate his heartbeat, induce a rush of tender feelings within him. And especially tonight, for he was leaving in the morning, with Father Antoine, for Florence: the priest to consult with the Lenzis, and Rodrigo to continue his acquaintance with the *Compagnacci*. Christmas was approaching and Savonarola was expected to mayhap outwardly defy the Pope's interdict. Equally important, also, was Rodrigo's intention of discovering the whereabouts of Sister Lucrezia, even if he had to ride to Rome itself.

Tonight Giulietta wore an overgown in a beautiful shade of rose satin, embroidered with delicate yellow flowers. Her undergown was of pale yellow damask and cut modestly across the tops of her breasts. Rodrigo noted the way the warm rose of her gown suited her fair countenance . . . the way her eyes sparkled with good humor and happiness. And, thank God, perfect health.

Her eyes met his briefly, and Rodrigo decided the word "radiant" was the only suitable description for her. She'd rapidly regained most of the weight she'd lost at Santa Lucia and, to Rodrigo's delight, much of her sauciness.

*"Per favore, Padre,"* Nicco asked Father Antoine, "tell us how you came to meet Rodrigo, won't you?"

His name spoken by Nicco, and the fact that Giulietta's entire face brightened even further with interest, jarred Rodrigo from his warm contemplation of her, and alerted him to the fact that something had really caught her full attention.

He glanced over at Father Antoine, who was looking directly at him. "Rodrigo, tell Nicco here how we met, lest I make you out to be so great a hero that I embarrass you." Amusement shone in his handsome brown eyes.

Rodrigo closed his eyes briefly in good-natured resignation. "How can I refuse either you or my new brother-by-marriage?" he asked with an affected sigh. "If I refuse, I suspect I'll never hear the end of it, even after you leave here, Father"

"And if Nicco doesn't hound you, Rigo, I will," Giulietta told him with an impish smile. She rested her chin in one hand and fixed her gaze on him in expectation.

He glanced about the board. All eyes were on him: Vittorio and Gianna, their son Bernardo and daughter Lucia, along with their own spouses. The prince had even included Carlo and his Laura, since, he'd told them with a smile, they had been "adopted" into the family by marriage.

And, of course, the faithful Aristo, who sat near the sideboard, ready to help with the serving if necessary, also appeared interested in the tale. Rodrigo briefly wondered if Aristo realized just how much Dante de' Alessandro loved him, for in an age when the favored fools and buffoons of noble families were most often dwarfs or those who suffered other deformities, the Prince of Monteverdi held Aristo above such ridicule. The little man's opinions were respected, his knowledge and experience valued. It was typical of Dante to measure a man by his heart and mind, rather than his birth or appearance, and Rodrigo believed the prince had sought over time to make up for all the dwarf's years under the rigid control of the former Bishop of Florence.

"I'm outnumbered, I see," Rodrigo sighed at last, feeling the expectation in the dining room rise to a palpable pitch. He sat back in his chair. "Two friends and I had traveled to southern France to enter a tourney in a town at the base of the Pyrenees. One of the men, however, Jacques, was so taken with the beauty of the mountains that he insisted we engage in some mountain climbing after the tournament. It was late autumn and—"

"And dangerous!" Giulietta added, frowning. "Is there not snow in the mountains at that time of the year?"

Rodrigo gave her an indulgent smile. *"Cara,* there is always snow in the Pyrenees, only more so at that time of year."

"But 'tis so magnificent," Father Antoine added, "clear and brisk and pristine, like a paradise."

"A frigid paradise," Rodrigo said wryly, "and dangerous, as well, especially if one is not dressed for it, or loses his way. Or if one doesn't respect the mountains."

"Tuscany is cold enough for me," Lucia said with a delicate shiver. "Although the snow, I'm sure, must be beautiful."

"Unbeknownst to us," Rodrigo continued, "there had been a small avalanche during the night."

"Young and arrogant," Father Antoine added, "they didn't even bother to hire a guide . . ."

"Young and ignorant," Rodrigo corrected mildly. "But God was, in this instance, our guide. For he led us to you, *Père* Antoine."

The priest nodded, his expression somber. "Indeed. I was

buried beneath a deep layer of snow. Even *mon chien* couldn't reach me."

"The dog is what attracted our attention," Rodrigo explained. He smoothed one hand over the white linen tablecloth with its embroidered lilies, a thoughtful look crossing his features. "The most beautiful dog I'd ever seen, almost as white as the snow around him, was digging furiously. He approached us and began to bark, not in warning, but more as if trying to communicate something of urgency to Jacques and me. It was a frenetic barking, and he continued, even as he ran between us and the spot where he'd been digging."

*"Sieur de Bijou,"* said Father Antoine, his eyes misting. "He was an intelligent animal and valiant, as well. I miss him."

"What happened to him?" Giulietta asked with a slight frown.

"Can't you wait, Gietta?" Nicco said in mild male exasperation. "Let Rigo tell the story!"

In the face of Nicco's scolding, Giulietta subsided with a tightening of her lips in obvious annoyance with her sibling. Rodrigo could tell, however, that she wouldn't remain quiet for long . . . he could sense a host of questions simmering just beneath the surface, and smiled inwardly.

"And then what?" Nicco urged.

"We began digging in the snow. Our progress was aided by the sun, which melted some of it, but also made it heavy—dangerous to anyone who was trapped beneath."

"Suffice it to say," Father interjected, "that they found me—half dead, *bien sûr*—but I'm tougher than I look. Later, I gave Rodrigo one of Bijou's pups."

"So Beau is the son of a real hero!" the exuberant Lucia exclaimed. "I knew he was special when I first saw him at *Zio* Dante's tourney."

Obviously at the sound of his name, the dog emerged from beneath the table beside Rodrigo. He stuck his nose into his master's lap, bumping the board, and sending one shining brass candelabrum skittering over the table in a drunken dance. One of its two tall, pale candles fell to the tablecloth, and was quickly rescued by Vittorio de' Alessandro before the cloth could ignite.

"Where are your manners?" Rodrigo chided the dog, and ordered him down.

"He's more rambunctious than his sire," Father Antoine observed. "But then, he's still a pup. He'll come around."

"If not, perhaps you'll take him back?" Rodrigo asked with a straight face.

"I wouldn't think so," Carlo interjected. "The animal would eat the good Father out of house and home."

"You mean to say Lenzi is stingy in providing for you?" Dante asked, leaning forward. The priest chuckled, but before he could answer, Dante offered him a lazy smile. "In that case, you can come and work for me. I'll keep you better than Rinaldo Lenzi ever could, *Padre,* especially after saving my Giulietta."

"God saved your Giulietta," Father Antoine answered, sobering. Silence fell along the board at his words. "He obviously never intended for her to contract plague." He looked at Rodrigo. "And then He sent Rodrigo here to take her from that wretched place."

There was a brief, awkward silence before Caressa said with a troubled frown, "Surely all the women at Santa Lucia weren't like the abbess." She looked at Giulietta

"No, *Mamina.* Only a few . . ." She thought of Sister Elena, but there was no vindictiveness in Giulietta. None of the sisters were bad people, just strict or misguided. "And even they weren't evil." She wondered about Sister Luigia, and looked at her father.

As if reading her mind, Dante assured her, "I've sent Father Michele from the church at Verdi and another representative of mine to help with counseling and reorganization at the cloister. If the nuns need aught, they have only to ask."

The name of Father Michele brought on a sudden thought. Giulietta looked at Father Antoine. "Would you . . . please, *Padre,* say the mass at our wedding in May?" She looked appealingly at Dante, seeking confirmation, but it was more out of respect than a need. Giulietta already knew he would grant her her request.

She also threw a glance at Rodrigo, but there was only approval in his eyes. And something so tender that her heart stumbled in its steady cadence.

"I would be honored," the priest replied, "if your village priest has no objections."

"Practice makes perfect," Carlo threw in with a wry grin. His dark-haired Laura smiled shyly, color rising in her cheeks. "You've already wed them once."

Light laughter sounded along the board.

"Oh, I think Father Michele can bear the disappointment," Dante answered. "He's been planning it for all these weeks, but he's a most generous soul. I'm certain he won't mind sharing the ceremony with you, Father."

"And it wouldn't be complete without Messer Magaldi of Verdi, also, as magistrate," Vittorio added. "He was quite impressive at your own wedding, brother." One corner of his mouth quirked.

"What's more impressive is that he's still alive," Dante replied. "The man consumes enough wine for five."

"He wasn't drunk at our wedding, was he?" Caressa asked her husband with a feigned look of shock.

Giulietta smiled automatically, but she didn't hear the rest. She was thinking about what her father had said. Something didn't sit quite right—something at first vague and indefinable . . .

Until she remembered his exact words. *He's been planning it for all these weeks . . .*

An innocuous enough statement, and in keeping with her father's personality. In the presence of a roomful of guests and family he wouldn't cause any embarrassment by mentioning the fact that for six weeks or so the wedding had been cancelled.

Or had it? Knowing her father, and his absolute refusal to visit her at Santa Lucia as a way of showing his disapproval. . . .

She glanced at Rodrigo, her brows drawn together thoughtfully. He was heart-stoppingly splendid in his rich, white silk shirt, his bright green and black velvet doublet with its slashed sleeves. Tufts of white silk peeped out from the slashes in striking contrast, and ordinarily Giulietta would have envisioned his long legs, now hidden from view beneath the table, encased in black trunk hose. And the frivolous and flimsy scrap of green velvet that would, even in the presence of others, unerringly draw her hungry, if covert gaze. . . .

But she reined in her lusty thoughts, trying to ease the disquietude forming in the back of her mind. It didn't help, either, that her husband was watching her through his lashes. It was a guarded look, the fingers of his right hand, she noticed, uncharactically tensed about the stem of his crystal goblet.

The look, the slight tautness in his demeanor, snagged her attention, deepened her vague unease, to suspicion. Giulietta was reminded of someone anticipating something unpleasant. . . .

No! How ungracious of her to think such things about Rodrigo. She wouldn't allow anything to spoil her happiness. She would wed Rodrigo da Valenti a hundred times over if necessary, no matter what, and with no regrets. She loved him, had unknowingly for weeks. It was as simple as that.

"Papa?" she blurted unthinkingly, interrupting the conversation.

The sense of urgency in her voice must have communicated itself to Dante, for he looked over at her with an indulgent smile. "You interrupted us, Gietta. It must be important."

Feeling heat rise in her face at the mild rebuke, Giulietta couldn't seem to help herself. "Didn't you tell Father Michele of my plans to take my vows at Santa Lucia?"

Dante looked at Caressa, his face blank for a moment, then back to his daughter. "Well, actually, *cara,* I didn't. You see, I was hoping you would change your mind after spending some time at Santa Lucia. I could never allow you to become a nun when the Alessandro line needed to continue."

"But what of Nicco? He's betrothed . . . he'll wed and have children."

Caressa came to the rescue. "This is not the place to discuss such things, Gietta. Why not speak to your father in privacy if you feel the need to clarify anything?"

"What if I am killed in battle, Gietta?" Nicco asked unexpectedly—and obviously to his mother's dismay. "Your children would then be the heirs to Monteverdi." He grinned naughtily. "And you certainly couldn't produce any heirs from behind the walls of Santa Lucia!"

"Of a certainty she could . . . and 'twouldn't be the first time," Aristo muttered under his breath. "A pox on all those devious frauds."

A few snickers sprinkled the air at his words, in spite of the dwarf's low tone, for everyone present knew of Aristo's aversion to the trappings of Christianity. Giulietta forced herself to drink some fortifying wine. Much as she was irritated by her father's high-handedness, she had no wish to cause her mother distress or embarrassment at the board. Of course her father wouldn't have allowed her to become a nun, she thought with bitterness. Her entire life had always been held in the palm of his hand—it couldn't have been any other way.

"Or what if I produced only girl children?" Nicco pressed.

"Then a woman would rule Monteverdi," Lucia answered firmly. " 'Tisn't so unusual, you know. And we are certainly capable."

"You seem to be enjoying my best Trebbiano," Dante told Aristo, a mischievous grin curving his mouth.

"The wine eases my aches and pains, Excellence." He hiccuped.

"I thought Maddalena gave you something for that," Rodrigo said with a lift of his eyebrows.

"I think Maddalena gave him more than tonic," Carlo said, and the dwarf actually flushed to the roots of his dark hair.

"Whatever 'twas," Rodrigo said in an attempt to draw attention away from the subject of Aristo's embarrassing incident with the love philter, "it seems to have worked. You are spryer than when I left for France, *maestro.*"

Aristo ambled forth from the shadows beside the carved cypress sideboard and reached for an empty terra cotta wine pitcher. *"Grazi,* signore. You are most kind to notice." He hiccuped again and sent a sly glance Carlo's way. "Whatever Maddalena gave me, *Zingaro,* 'twas better than any aphrodisiac."

To Rodrigo's surprise, the dwarf's face split in a lusty grin, and everyone had to laugh at that, especially Carlo, who said, "In that case, mayhap when Maddalena returns in the spring, she can give you lessons in climbing convent walls, as well." But his voice was playful, not critical.

Aristo let out a hearty sigh, as if at the memory, shook his head and turned to the sideboard to refill the wine pitcher.

"Leave the poor man alone, Carlo," Laura admonished softly.

She reminded Giulietta poignantly of Maria with her looks and coloring, her soft voice, but her thoughts were unexpectedly pulled back to Aristo. "Were you injured coming to my aid?" she asked, concern darkening her eyes, all other thought banished for the moment. She was extremely fond of the dwarf and, along with Caressa, always his champion.

"Only, I fear," Carlo answered before Aristo could reply, "when I tossed him into the root cellar. But I had little choice at the time." Amusement shone in his dark eyes as he looked first at Giulietta, then back to the dwarf, who was replacing the newly filled pitcher on the table. "Although I must admit to feeling the score was evened, *maestro,* after you stepped on my face while scaling the wall."

Lucia clapped her hands gleefully, her eyes alight, and Rodrigo thought of Giulietta, six years earlier. What a pair they would have made had Giulietta been born at the same time! He suspected they would have turned Castello Monteverdi upside down.

Nicco leaned forward expectantly, obviously with the same thought as his effervescent cousin. "Do tell us the tale," Lucia begged Carlo. "If, that is," she added repentently, " 'twill not offend Maestro Aristo." She looked at Dante. *"Zio?"*

Dante looked at Aristo, a question in his eyes. The dwarf shrugged noncommittally, and the prince said, "By all means, Carlo, regale us with the events of that night while we catch our breaths before dancing, *sì?"*

Rodrigo resisted the urge to roll his eyes as Carlo, with his innate Gypsy love for storytelling—and natural propensity for exaggeration—began, *"Ebbene,* 'twas definitely the asafetida that warned me a most malodorous person was also heading toward Santa Lucia. At first I was certain that only the hook-nosed Prior of San Marco would emit so foul a smell . . ."

Rodrigo leaned against the closed door behind him and watched as Giulietta whirled about on light feet before the fireplace. The firelight caught and reflected the rose of her gown, and alternated with the shadows dancing about her slender form. Part of her hair had come loose during the dancing earlier in the great hall, and now she kicked off her slippers, still obviously caught up in the music of the lively Tarantella.

She looked like a copper-maned Gypsy girl dancing before a campfire, and Rodrigo smiled as he lifted one hand and worked the castanets he'd borrowed from one of the musicians.

Giulietta flashed him a look of surprise, and called over her shoulder, "Am I more graceful than Lily, my lord husband?"

"Definitely." He stilled the castanets. "And infinitely more beautiful." He walked up to her, caught her about the waist, and lifted her high, twirling her about once. Then, in a deliberately slow and sensual movement, he pressed her body to his and allowed her to slide downward to the floor, their bodies touching intimately the entire, deliciously drawn-out time.

Giulietta gasped softly. "My lord, you steal my breath away."

"I think, *carissima,* that you mayhap tax your own strength with your exertions," he murmured into her ear. You're done with dancing for now."

"I wonder what Sister Elena would say if she could have seen me." Soft, sweet laughter erupted from her, and Rodrigo nuzzled the jasmine-scented flesh beneath her ear. Her father's Trebbiano definitely agreed with her.

"She'd no doubt prostrate herself before the altar and pray for your wicked soul," he murmured, then pressed closer, feeling the quick, steady beat of her heart.

She looked up into his eyes. "Of a certainty," she said, her own expression suddenly, strangely, somber. And slightly troubled.

He should have been warned . . . but he had other things on his mind just then. "Shouldn't you be in bed now, *preziosa mia?*"

"*Sì.* With you. But first . . . I must ask you something."

His grip tightened about her. "And what might that be, wife?" he asked softly, seductively, nuzzling her once again.

The gentle gust of his warm, sweet breath sent a frisson of pleasure through her as it misted her cheek, teased her ear.

Rodrigo was unprepared, however, for the question that followed.

"If my father had no intentions of allowing me to remain at Santa Lucia, why did you tell me in the stable that time—when we were milking the cows—that over the years I would learn how stupid and stubborn they are? As if I would spend the rest of my life in that cloister?"

# Twenty-three

The cadence of his breathing altered, just the smallest bit. If his lips hadn't been so close to such a sensitive area of her neck, she wouldn't have noticed. His grip tautened almost imperceptibly, too; then he held her away from him and **looked** into her eyes.

"You deliberately let me believe you had accepted the fact that I would be allowed to take my vows and become a nun. Why didn't you tell me the truth?"

"You didn't ask. And what was the point? If you had asked, I would have answered truthfully." His look turned wary. "And you would have been furious."

"All the while you were wheedling your way into my trust, you were deceiving me!" Her eyes turned as dull as tarnished brass with pain. "Do you always speak the truth, Rodrigo da Valenti? Like when you told me you loved me? That you'd loved me since I was eleven and—"

"I don't recall 'wheedling' myself into anyone's trust," he cut her off. "Ever. And I don't lie, Giulietta. But there are some things better left unsaid."

"Then you *do* lie, signore. You lie by omission."

"Giulietta—"

She pulled away and presented him with her back. "If you had truly loved me, you wouldn't have deceived me. You would have taken me back to my father, rather than to Santa Lucia. You would have convinced me that—"

"That what? That I hadn't really killed Mario di Corsini that day in the woods? That I wasn't a Gypsy bastard, unfit to touch your hem? That I would have died before admitting to anyone that we met that night near the campsite and shared something rare and beautiful?" He shook his head in frustration, but she didn't see it. "I seriously doubt it."

"So you let me go to that dreadful place . . ." She whirled back to him, understanding dawning in her face. "Of course! Marriage to *anyone* would have been preferable to a lifetime at Santa Lucia!"

He took a step closer, his expression full of regret, but also steady. *"You* chose to flee to a cloister . . . 'twasn't my idea, or your father's. You reaped the consequences of your actions—and rightly so. A month and a half in a convent did you a world of good, Giulietta de' Alessandro. Or so I thought."

"And if you thought so little of me, how could you have loved me?"

"No one's perfect . . . and mayhap I'm a bigger fool than most, for I thought to teach you a little humility, if you want me to be brutally honest—"

A scratching at the door caught Rodrigo's attention. He turned to open it, and Beau came bounding in. As if sensing her distress, the dog went right to Giulietta. She stooped and buried her face in his thick, white coat, which felt cool against her flushed cheeks.

Teach her a little humility? By God, he was as bad as any high-handed, arrogant male, including her father! She thought back to the humiliation she'd suffered in that barn with those wretched cows . . . and all the while he'd been laughing at her, no doubt enjoying watching her learn her lesson in humility. Of course he'd been able to be generous at the time and take over her tasks. He knew in the end he would get exactly what he wanted.

Unexpectedly, tears filled her eyes, and she was glad for

the momentary shield of Beau's body. Her image of Rodrigo the gentle, the sweet, the honorable man she'd come to love suddenly shattered into a thousand pieces.

"Giulietta," his voice came to her from close by, "you're being unreasonable, *cara*." His sudden proximity, his hand gently stroking her hair, was proof of his willingness to yield, to mend things between them; yet pride wouldn't allow her to banish the picture in her mind's eye of a soiled habit, manure-caked shoes, and a crushed wimple lying discarded in the corner of the stable, evidence of her undignified struggle to milk four cows so she could get her meager supper.

And all because *he* thought she needed a lesson in humility.

*Is this what you want, Giulietta?* his question came back to her. *To live out your life here? Without children? Without the love and companionship of a husband for the rest of your natural life?*

He'd been rubbing it in, all the while knowing she would become his wife in May after all.

And then her ludicrous answer: *I am betrothed to Christ.*

Shame washed over her like a high tide; reopened old wounds, and shoved all reason aside like so much insignificant driftwood. "You knew exactly what you were doing that first night I met you," she said, her face still half-buried in Beau's coat. "Any gentleman would have taken me right back to Castello Monteverdi . . . would have never done the things you did to me! But you—"

"I did them *with* you, not to you." His voice was low, strained, and if she hadn't been so steeped in her own misery, if she'd allowed herself to really hear him, she would have recognized the reverence in his voice—the depth of his feelings for her.

But she didn't hear it. "A gentleman would have—"

He suddenly couldn't bear to hear it again from her. From

anyone else, it would have rolled off harmlessly, but not from Giulietta . . . again.

He struck back, cutting across her words: "And you were the perfect lady, as I recall."

The cutting edge of his voice ripped through her like a blade. She wasn't accustomed to such sarcasm from him.

And should have been warned.

But his answer only fueled her ire, propelled her to lash out at him harder. She raised her face to his, deliberately pushing aside all other emotions in the face of her humiliation, then stood and stepped away. One shaking finger pointed at him in accusation. "You're nothing more than an opportunist! A Gypsy bastard who had the extremely good fortune to somehow worm your way into my father's graces."

One darker part of her felt satisfaction at the way he flinched, as if she'd dealt him a blow. Then another thought struck her, spurred her on. "And now I know that you wed me because you thought you were losing me, *si*, but it had naught to do with love! You panicked. You envisioned my hefty dowry—and the prestige of being a part of my family—slipping right through your greedy fingers."

It came to him then, that all along he'd feared this reaction, half hoping she would put the entire episode behind her in light of all that had happened. But he hadn't anticipated anger to this degree. Surely she knew her father well enough to reason out that he would never have allowed her to take her final vows. She had been deluding herself if that was what she truly believed. Now she was blaming him for her own gullibility.

It seemed he'd made a monumental mistake in believing they could be happy together, in spite of the obvious obstacles. He could never gain her freely given love, for she would forever be erecting walls between them because she didn't believe him worthy of her.

In one last, desperate attempt, he asked in a low voice, "And if I apologize for the deception?" He sent a silent prayer heavenward that she would prove him wrong. That she would accept his apology and put all this aside once and for all.

"Does that include attempting to teach me a lesson in humility?"

He shook his head, his expression turning bleak as defeat pressed down on him. "You're absolutely right, of course. About everything. In the morn I leave for Florence, and you can prettily plead your case to your father . . . obtain an annulment if 'tis what you wish. Father Antoine can say he insisted we wed. You can use that fact to obtain an annulment. We were married . . . under duress." His expression was unnaturally grim, his voice not quite steady as he said the last two words. "I'll not live out my life with a wife who constantly flings my birth in my face, Giulietta. And my honor."

He turned on his heel and strode from the room, with the fickle Beau trotting behind him.

When the door had closed with finality behind him, some of Giulietta's anger turned to bewilderment. Never had he been so angry with her—treated her so coldly and matter-of-factly. Even in the face of her unkind words at previous times. . . .

She threw herself upon the great bed and buried her face in the pillow, allowing the tears to flow freely. How *could* he have deceived her so? she thought, deliberately stoking her anger as a defense against her hurt at his unexpected actions. And now he had the nerve to tell her she could obtain an annulment! As if their marriage—as if *she*—had never really meant aught to him.

And to add insult to injury, he'd said he'd married her under duress! So much for love.

Well, he certainly could go on his merry way and establish his own Free Company. He had money of his own—he'd told her that, and so had her father. Prestige he could build on his own, even if he couldn't change the fact that he was part Gypsy.

*You know his Gypsy blood means nothing. He's a man, just like any other—more than many,* her irksome conscience whispered. The principles her father and mother had taught her, reinforced by her weeks at Santa Lucia, fought her obstinance and pricked female pride.

Like a stubborn child, however, she refused to acknowledge those principles.

She stared across the room at the hearth for a long, long time, even thinking briefly when she heard faint steps in the corridor that Rodrigo was returning. Her heart jarred within her chest, and she sat up, her eyes red and swollen, but feeling unexpected hope spurt through her . . .

And was bitterly disappointed. She tossed and turned most of the night, having quickly grown used to his warm body next to hers, entwined with hers, in intimacy and love.

The fact that he didn't return deepened her frustration more than anything, although she would never have admitted it, and Giulietta didn't fall into an exhausted slumber until near dawn.


Rodrigo *had* walked past the bedchamber they'd shared. He'd intended to apologize for withholding the truth from her when he'd thought to teach her a lesson. But common sense told him it wouldn't matter now. The damage was done, and Giulietta de' Alessandro had rarely been reasonable or forgiving when it came to him.

But still, he shouldn't have mentioned something as drastic as ending their marriage. He could have told her how spoiled she was—how she'd supposedly learned a well-needed lesson at Santa Lucia.

The thought of her tending Maria, however, threatened to dissipate most of his irritation.

It was odd, he thought as he lay awake much of the night in the room he shared this once with Father Antoine, that he still thought of her as Giulietta de' Alessandro, not Valenti. Evidently his head was more perceptive than his romantic Gypsy heart. Surely that was the reason he still loved her. That streak of *Zingaro* whimsy—a romanticism inherited no doubt from his mother. Mayhap even his great-grandmother, Maddalena's mother. Hadn't she been involved with a blue-eyed *gorgio?*

Maybe she would see things differently after he'd been gone a few days. He would apologize when he returned, then put all this nonsense to rest for good. He hoped.

He listened to the sleeping priest's soft snores, and envied him his peace of mind.

When Rodrigo was ready to leave in the morn and Giulietta hadn't joined the family to break the fast, he'd gone to her.

Not, however, before he'd had to answer to Dante. "I—we had a disagreement last night," he'd explained evenly. At the prince's raised eyebrows, he'd added, "She's hurt and angry that I let her believe she would be taking her final vows."

Dante's mouth had twisted. "Silly child," he'd surprised Rodrigo by saying. "She wouldn't have accepted anything less. You had no choice."

But as Rodrigo knocked softly upon her closed door, he felt a sense of unease when there was no answer. He knocked again, harder, and when he met continued silence, he opened the door. Lisa was nowhere to be seen, and as he moved quietly through the doorway, he discerned Giulietta's form, her hair spilled out from beneath the covers in a bright pool of auburn-gold.

Beau raised his head, his tail thumped against the mattress, but he remained where he was. Devil, Rodrigo thought. He'd wondered where the dog had spent the night. He must have somehow sneaked back into her room and now lay curled up at the foot of the bed.

Rodrigo approached her and saw that she was sound asleep. Her cheeks were flushed, her eyes swollen from tears. Something twisted beneath his ribs. Maybe he *was* a knave. How could any man of compassion leave his bride alone during the first fortnight of their marriage like this? Obviously, her night had been as bad as his.

He leaned over her and touched his lips to her warm cheek, half hoping she would awaken. He allowed his mouth to linger against her velvet flesh, inhaling jasmine and Giulietta . . . a potent combination. But she didn't stir.

Finally, with a sigh that brushed her cheek as softly as the sweep of a moth's wing, he straightened. And noticed a teardrop hovering at the end of the cinnamon sweep of her lashes. *"Ti amo,"* he whispered. I love you. *"Per sempre . . ."* Forever.


Rodrigo faced Marco across a table in his rented home in Florence. He wondered what the taciturn Gypsy had to tell him, after having related the details of Alberto Palmieri's death.

"I'm leaving Florence," Marco said, as if reading Rodrigo's thoughts. "There is nothing for me here—I don't belong in a city. I'm *Zingaro.*"

Rodrigo nodded. " 'Tis for the best, anyway, lest some of Palmieri's cronies discover your identity and come after you. If they are anything like him, from what you've told me, they wouldn't hesitate to retaliate."

Marco shrugged, as if he doubted the fact that a man like Palmieri had any cronies. His dark eyes studied the tabletop between them. He hadn't touched his wine yet, but bad as he

ooked—tired and unkempt—in addition to his obvious grief,
he exuded an aura of peace that Rodrigo could not remember
having noticed before. There were bloodstains on the sleeves
of his tunic, and Rodrigo suspected they were Palmieri's. The
Gypsy wore them like trophies.

"I was in the right—there were witnesses who survived the
attack in the alley. But even should any of his acquaintances
seek revenge, I'll be gone from here shortly. I just wanted to
tell you one thing more . . ." He trailed off, his gaze meeting
Rodrigo's and then skittering away.

Carlo, who sat in the shadows sipping his own wine without
hesitation, remained silent, only the soft sound of his breathing
revealing his presence.

"I think Abbess Lucrezia is part of the surviving Corsini
family . . . born on the wrong side of the blanket, but a Corsini
nonetheless."

If someone had hit Rodrigo over the head with a sledge-
hammer, he couldn't have been more shocked. He sucked in
his breath sharply. The sound of the front legs of Carlo's chair
hitting the floor with a loud thump sounded like a cannon shot
in the silence.

"But how—"

"I never had any liking for you, Valenti, even though deep
down I knew you did nothing to encourage my Maria to fall
in love with you. But I'm doing this for Madonna Giulietta.
I don't want to see her a young widow because of any hidden
threat to you."

He picked up his wine at last and drank deeply, then wiped
his mouth with one bloodstained sleeve. Rodrigo let him drink,
too stunned to say anything yet, but also knowing that Marco
wasn't finished.

"Up until you first returned from France, I served as her
informer."

Carlo choked on his wine.

"I couldn't tell her much, but her questions always concerned you specifically. She paid me well—in gold—and I believe she intended to have you murdered, whether by my hand or someone else's. And still does, more than ever after her humiliation."

"How could you *do* such a thing to anyone, let alone one of your own?" Carlo said through set teeth, his outrage apparent.

Marco's gaze clashed with Rodrigo's as he answered Carlo. "Valenti isn't truly one of our own. Everyone knows that—no prince would ever take a ne'er-do-well *Zingaro* under his wing . . . offer him his own daughter in marriage!" He glanced at Carlo, then back at Rodrigo. "And Maria couldn't stay away from you. She even talked about you incessantly while you were gone. I just wanted to take the gold and convince Maria that I could provide for her as well as you . . . or anyone else. I didn't say I would have agreed to kill you." He grimaced. "I mayhap would have taken the money to perform the deed, and then left Tuscany with Maria."

"But why do you say she's a Corsini?" Rodrigo asked with a frown.

"Doesn't she resemble Mario di Corsini?" Marco asked in answer. "The hair and eye color are different, as I remember—I only saw Corsini once or twice—but there's a resemblance in the features. And her arrogance . . . No *contadina* carries herself like that, and the Corsini boy was arrogant, as I remember. Along with her unusual interest in you specifically . . . *Ebbene,* why couldn't it be true?"

Carlo scraped his chair backward and stood. "The entire aristocracy is unconscionably arrogant," he muttered; then, with more enthusiasm, he added, "But don't you remember, Rigo? The sire—I forget his surname—was haughty as the day was long. And a flagrant lover of women. 'Twas rumored at one time that he'd sired half the bastards in Tuscany!"

"Salvatore," Rodrigo said softly, remembering how Dante had once mentioned the names of Giulietta's future in-laws. "Salvatore di Corsini."

He stood and walked toward the single open-shuttered window that looked out onto the narrow lane. It was empty, save for two dogs frolicking between the orange tile-roofed town houses.

Now he had a reason for his suspicions regarding the abbess's animosity toward him. If what Marco suspected was true, he had, indeed, a real adversary from the Corsini family. When he thought about Giulietta having been under her protection, his blood ran cold.

"The mother—Gabriella, I believe—was very fair. Mario favored her. But the father had auburn hair—I saw him," Rodrigo mused aloud.

"Sister Lucrezia has auburn eyebrows and lashes," Marco added, "and a full head of flaming hair to match beneath her wimple, I would wager anything."

Rodrigo swung back to Marco. "I appreciate this information—whatever your reason for telling me. I had intended to pay a visit to San Marco, if only to try to establish whether she'd fled to Savonarola or not. Both Dante and I would see her punished in some way." He stroked his clean-shaven chin, a thoughtful frown creasing his forehead. "Now I've more reason than ever to confront her . . . if I can find her."


Rodrigo studied the exterior of San Marco as he approached, wondering what Cosimo de' Medici would think if he were alive to see who headed the monastery he had generously endowed in the first half of the century. His son, Lorenzo the Magnificent, had been patient and tolerant with the Dominican, and even requested the monk's blessing upon his deathbed. But the irascible Cosimo, no doubt, would have thrown the man into the Arno long before the latter had acquired such power and influence.

Rodrigo dismounted and lifted the knocker on the door of one of the front wings of the building. After a few moments, a black-robed figure appeared. Rodrigo requested an audience with the prior, and was led through a corridor. At its intersection with another passageway, he recognized a fresco of the crucifixion by Fra Angelico. They turned and passed a number of high-and-narrow arched doors before entering one, obviously a waiting room. It was very Spartan, the weak winter sun spilling through windows set just under the ceiling for adequate illumination, and furnished with a handful of backless scissors chairs.

Before the monk left, he said, "You will surrender your weapons to me, signore. 'Tis the rule of San Marco."

Reluctantly Rodrigo unbuckled his sword belt and handed it over.

"And your dagger."

Rodrigo complied, annoyance rising within him, even though he had a smaller dagger tucked secretly in his boot. Even in a monastery—this monastery—he felt vulnerable without the tools of his trade.

As the monk swung toward the door, Rodrigo could just discern the soft drone of chanting voices somewhere within the building. He hoped he wouldn't be kept forever awaiting the prior. Of course, if Savonarola were to be so inconsiderate, he could always do some investigating on his own . . . using the excuse that he was most curious about cloister life, having considered serving God in the past.

He smiled inwardly at such a sorry excuse for snooping, and Giulietta came to mind. Not the Giulietta who had spurned him after he'd told her the truth the other night, but rather an image of the impish novice bent upon serving God and taking on the cows of Santa Lucia.

He wondered if she would ever accept him as he was. Bitter disappointment moved through him once again as he acknowledged how shallow were her feelings for him if she could hold his minor deception between them like one of Castello Monteverdi's thick, solid walls. Surely it was a sign of a more deep-seated problem. Mayhap she had never really possessed the character traits he'd expected her to acquire from her parents . . . one of them being acceptance of a man or woman for things more important than birth and background.

And that meant if he could never meet her expectations, then neither, conversely, could she ever meet his.

*Of course not, fool* whispered a scathing voice in his head. *Your expectations were born of memories . . . memories enhanced by time and distance and dreams. You love a phantom, romantic Gypsy fool . . .*

A form moved through the open doorway, catching Rodrigo's attention. He stood automatically, not out of respect (among other things, Savonarola had been excommunicated), but rather in preparation for an unpleasant meeting.

"Valenti," the prior pronounced without ceremony in a harsh voice.

Rodrigo nodded, noting the intense green eyes beneath the monk's dark, bushy brows. Small, thin and ugly, he thought with one assessing part of his mind, even as he carefully chose his words. "I am looking for a nun—specifically, the Abbess of Santa Lucia."

Savonarola stopped halfway between Rodrigo and the door behind him. "Nuns reside in convents, not monasteries," he said with a touch of disdain. "You are confused, and of a certainty, in the wrong house of God."

"Harboring a criminal in your cloister does not enhance your reputation," Rodrigo replied. "And were Sister Lucrezia not a criminal, she would yet be among the women of Santa

Lucia who looked to her for guidance—spiritual and otherwise—and owning up to her sins."

Savonarola was silent a moment. Rodrigo took advantage
of that moment for his follow-up salvo, "Forgive my bluntness,
Fra Girolamo, but your influence in Florence is on the decline—as you witnessed during your last sermon in the cathedral. However, as an excommunicant, you no doubt consider
yourself above the laws of both man *and* God." He paused
briefly for effect. "Yet mayhap the threat of the Prince of Monteverdi going directly to the *Signoria* to intercede by force
might convince you to cooperate."

"No one can enter this monastery by force! Nor remove
any person from sanctuary." The green of his eyes intensified;
his thin body trembled visibly with righteous anger. "Not Durante de' Alessandro, nor any member of the *Signoria!*"

"But what of the people of Florence themselves? If you
keep a mistress beneath your very roof, they have every right
to be outraged. Haven't you warned them of the consequences
of their sinful ways? And yet you—"

"She's not my mistress!" the monk hissed. "Even *she* cannot violate my celibacy! I am God's vessel—pure and unsullied."

Rather than argue, for he'd merely been fishing for information, Rodrigo tried a different tack. "Whatever she is to
you, I would speak with her. Nothing more for now . . ."

Rodrigo's unexpected retreat evidently took Savonarola off
guard. His eyes widened, and for a moment, words seemed to
desert him. Then, "You wish to pass judgment on her for what
you consider her sins against the rich and corrupt, *Zingaro.*
You, who are damned for all eternity."

Rodrigo's eyes narrowed slightly. He remained calm outwardly, his experience having taught him it was the best way
to deal with a zealot. "A young Gypsy girl in need of tending
is hardly what anyone could call rich . . . or corrupt. And my

chances of going to *paradiso* are much better than yours, Prior, at this point. Certainly His Holiness would concur."

Savonarola's entire body went rigid, the blood left his face. "You dare to—"

"And let's pursue the matter at hand rather than the state of my soul, shall we?" Rodrigo cut across his words, then shook his head. "Tsk, tsk, Fra Girolamo," he chided, "I would have thought you above such superstition—against Gypsies or any others. You, the spiritual leader of the brothers of San Marco . . . the self-proclaimed *savior* of Florence."

"Get out of here, you blasphemer, else I have you carried out bodily!"

"Blasphemy is against God, not the prior of a monastery."

Savonarola raised one arm, as if he would strike Rodrigo, and took one menacing step toward him.

"I would be happy to depart this place, Fra Girolamo," Rodrigo said with all sincerity, for he felt a sudden, inexplicable chill creep over the back of his neck. "But first, I would speak to Sister Lucrezia." He crossed his arms over his chest, allowing his face to settle into determined lines. "I don't wish to remove her from your, er, protection, merely to speak with her, as I said before. It seems she bears me a grudge because of a misconception. I would like to clear the air and tell her the truth. Especially since she sought to take out her anger on an innocent Gypsy girl . . . and my wife."

Savonarola glowered at him, but Rodrigo was unaffected. He could see why some had been drawn to this man and his sermons over the past years, but also sensed a desperation within him; Rodrigo was unintimidated by either his reputation or his frenetic energy. If only he could keep his mind on the man before him, rather than Giulietta. . . .

"She's not here, I tell you." The monk's voice burst into his wayward thoughts.

"And I say you lie."

An antagonistic silence swirled around them, filling the very room, and bonding them in enmity . . .

Until, without warning, Savonarola relented and said tersely, "You may speak to her briefly in the chapel." Before Rodrigo could react, the prior turned away with a swish of his worn robes and exited the room.

He should have been warned by the unexpectedness of Savonarola's actions. But his thoughts kept flitting back to Giulietta and the problems she insisted on keeping between them.

As Rodrigo strode through the door and followed him out into the passageway, once again he felt the icy breath of premonition waft across his neck . . . and the eerie sound of Maddalena's voice in his mind . . . *Rigo! Rigo, beware . . . !*

A hard object came crashing down onto the back of his head, sending pain splintering through his cranium. Darkness closed over him as he slumped heavily to the floor . . . and sank into a swirling, shadowed void.

# Twenty-four

Voices called to her, warning her, frightening her. Maddalena's image appeared before her. *Where's my Rigo?* she demanded in a terrible voice, her long, silver-threaded dark hair billowing in the frigid wind. *You've sent him away hurting. You've sent him away to his death . . . It's too late, spoiled girl . . . too late . . .* Her deep blue eyes stabbed Giulietta with their intensity.

Where *was* Rodrigo? Giulietta thought in a panic. She reached out for him, but she was alone. Terribly alone. In the cold wind and darkness.

A clicking sound came to her . . . Closer, closer, then receding, then closer again. What *was* it? And where *was* everyone?

*Click, click, click . . .*

She put her hands over her ears to shut out the sound, but she couldn't. Then a soft whine came to her, not that of a human, but—

She sat straight up, chilled to the bone and shaking, but from the iciness within her, not any winter draught, for the embers still glowed brightly in the hearth.

"Lisa?" she called softly. "Lisa?"

The clicking recommenced, and for one horrible moment Giulietta thought her dream had followed her into reality. A large white form appeared beside the bed, then rose up on its hind legs and plopped two pale paws upon the mattress beside her. . . .

Beau. His nails had been clicking against the tiled floor. It was his whine she'd heard. His cool nose touched her cheek. He whimpered again, dropped to all fours, and loped toward the door. Giulietta gripped the covers and pressed them to her breastbone in an effort to still her trembling, her eyes narrowing against the gloom as her gaze followed the dog. He stretched to his full height against the portal, then dropped, his nails scraping softly against the wood, and trotted back to the bed.

"Beau?" she said. "Is it Rodrigo? Is Rigo here?"

But this time when he bounded toward the door, Giulietta scrambled from the bed and snatched a shift from the wardrobe. She was close behind when he reached the door, dragging the garment over her head and shoulders. As they emerged into the passageway, lit dimly by evenly spaced oil-burning lamps, Giulietta suddenly had second thoughts. If indeed Rodrigo had returned from Florence, it wouldn't do to fling herself into his arms as if everything—

*And why not? You're his bride. You had a disagreement. What better way to welcome him home and to show him you've had a change of heart? That you've reconsidered and—*

"And decided that he was justified in escorting me and consigning me to Santa Lucia after the way I'd treated him?" she muttered as she lightly treaded down the hall behind Beau. What she would undoubtedly feel if he were back in the castle—and rightly so—was embarrassment for her behavior.

*I thought to teach you a little humility* . . . His words returned with all the force of a slap in the face to stir the sense of humiliation and betrayal she'd tried so hard to tamp.

But old habits die hard, and before she realized what she was about, the thought flashed through her mind: Who was *he* to teach her humility?

Even worse, her father had revealed that Rodrigo had told him he would break off the betrothal if Dante didn't go along with Rodrigo's wishes. Even her father hadn't wanted her to remain at Santa Lucia—not for even a few months. Only Rodrigo.

Her thoughts dredged up even more conflicting feelings, serving only to unsettle her further. Familiar butterflies invaded her stomach, and her heart hammered against her breastbone with an incongruous mixture of eagerness and dread . . . and newly awakened anger. As she followed Beau toward the dungeons, she realized she would *never* sleep now and—

Dungeons?

She slowed her steps as the thought registered. Even if Rodrigo had returned, what business would he possibly have in the nether regions of Castello Monteverdi?

"Nay," she said softly to the dog. "Here, Beau," she whispered, and turned toward the wing that housed the servants' quarters. When the dog didn't follow, Giulietta dismissed his behavior as typical of a half-grown, overeager pup. . . .

She would ask Aristo for a mild sleeping draught. That would make her sleep, chase away her nightmares. She walked faster, for she realized that her feet were cold. Of course, she thought, glancing down. She'd forgotten shoes. And all because of a bad dream . . . and Beau's nocturnal antics.

But Aristo didn't answer her knock. She pushed open his door. Aside from a single candle on a small table, the small chamber was dark, the bed empty.

Giulietta frowned. Where could he be when the entire castle was abed? She glanced in the direction Beau had taken, and the thought of the dungeons brought to mind Aristo's workroom below the keep. He often worked there, mixing his salves and elixirs and powders. When Giulietta was younger, she and Nicco spent many fascinating hours with the dwarf, listening to him answer their endless questions about his medicinals and his astrology charts.

As she moved to close the door, a pair of his small, pointed shoes caught her eye. She stepped into the room and slipped on the brown leather shoes, for her feet were freezing, and warmth was more important at this point than fashion. They were just a smidgeon too snug, but definitely warmer.

She closed the door softly and hurried down first one passageway, then another, and toward the great wooden door at the head of the stairway leading below the castle. Beau stood before it, sniffing vigorously along the crack between the stone floor and the bottom. He snorted, then lifted his head at the sound of Giulietta's steps.

"What's so interesting down there?" she asked him, and reached to open the door. A current of air rushed over her, smelling of must and dust and disuse, but the pitch torches on either side of the stone stairs had been lit.

Someone was down there.

As far as she knew, the only prisoners Dante had held recently were Carlo and Marco of the Gypsy band. Mayhap Aristo was the one down below. . . .

The door to his laboratory was slightly ajar, and voices came to Giulietta from within. She made a grab for Beau's collar before he could go bursting into the room, for she was curious to discover just who was present.

"Quiet," she whispered into the dog's ear, hoping he would understand and obey while she attempted to eavesdrop.

". . . traveling south, I tell you! To Rome!" said a woman's voice emphatically. "My Sight has guided me this far, dwarf, and Carlo says Rigo's a prisoner of Savonarola. I feel his pain—he's been injured. Incapacitated, and no doubt handed over to the Corsini woman. Look for yourself!"

"But—"

"Never have I been more certain of aught!" the woman said. "I've had visions of Salome . . . of a man's head on a platter. But not here—farther south. In Rome. It makes sense!"

"But what has that to do with Rigo?" a man asked, obviously perplexed.

"She'll present his head to the Corsinis—or at least that's what she plans . . . aberrant creature! I *feel* this!"

Giulietta couldn't believe her ears. Rigo a prisoner? Injured? Corsini woman? Unease fluttered to life within her, and before she could even contemplate the rest of the woman's horrible prediction, she placed one hand on the door to the room and slowly pushed it open.

The hinges sang a discordant song. The noise sounded clear and crisp as a clarion in the sudden silence. It caught their attention, and for a moment the figures revealed to her within the room were frozen in a bizarre tableau: a tall female who'd just straightened from gazing into a crystal ball, the small and hunched Aristo beside her, and Rodrigo's brother looking on.

Only peripherally did she receive impressions of the well-remembered chamber that had fascinated her so as a child: shelves bearing books and a multitude of medicinals, a table covered with astrological charts, another with heavy tomes, distilling alembics and retorts hanging from the beams overhead along with dried herbs, roots, the skull and claws of a small animal, and other paraphernalia . . . the sharp, acrid smell of the alchemist's ingredients. . . .

She wrinkled her delicate nose unconsciously as the latter invaded her nostrils, and the fingers wrapped around Beau's collar went slack. The mountain dog tumbled into the room, like an avalanche of virgin snow, and right to Carlo.

"Madonna Giulietta," Aristo mumbled, obviously stunned. "What do you here?"

"Nay, Aristo," she said, stepping into the room, and locking eyes with Maddalena. "Rather, what do *you* here with your . . . friends? And what about Rodrigo? What's wrong?" She couldn't keep the alarm from her voice.

*"Everything* is wrong!" Maddalena said, stepping toward Giulietta. "If you hadn't decided to hie yourself off to Santa Lucia, my grandson's life wouldn't be in danger!"

Giulietta was struck by the anger and urgency in the woman's voice. And her presence. She stood tall and proud, like a queen, and obviously commanded the respect of the two men present.

She also didn't bother to conceal her disdain as she stared at Giulietta, and the latter felt unprepared to meet this woman straight from her bed. Her hair, no doubt, was a wild mess, her hastily donned shift could have been on backward for all she'd noticed (but she refused to glance down at it beneath the Gypsy woman's glare), and she wore Aristo's brown leather shoes with their curled and pointed tips.

Giulietta felt her face suffuse with heat, but wouldn't give Maddalena the satisfaction of seeing her squirm. Generations of Alessandro princes flowed through her blood, and the very pride that had caused such conflict between her and the man she loved came to her aid as she faced his regal Gypsy grandmother.

She straightened her shoulders and lifted her chin "I did nothing to deliberately jeopardize my husband's life, I can assure you, signora," she said levelly. "And if Rodrigo's in danger, I want to help, not stand here dredging up past mistakes."

Maddalena raised a dark brow at her, but her expression didn't alter beyond that.

"We need to tell my father," Giulietta said.

"He's not expected back from Pisa for another two days," Aristo reminded her.

"We can send a messenger—"

"No! We don't need Alessandro's help!" Maddalena said.

"Rigo's in trouble because of his very connections with this family. He needs no more interference."

Giulietta bristled. "A messenger will be sent, whether you wish it or nay," she said steadily. "He is my husband now—part of 'this family'—and he can only benefit from Monteverdi's might."

"Enough arguing. We're wasting precious time," Carlo said.

"Where *is* he?" Giulietta asked, stepping farther into the room and throwing a curious glance at the crystal ball on the table amidst Aristo's astrological charts. "San Marco?"

" 'Tis where he started out," Carlo said, "but Maddalena believes Sister Lucrezia plans to take him south . . . possibly to Rome." He paused. "We think the nun is a Corsini, *madonna,* and Rome is the seat of the Corsini family."

Undiluted fear clawed at Giulietta with razor-honed talons. If this was true, surely Lucrezia was taking him there for the twisted purpose of avenging Mario di Corsini's death.

"We *must* hurry," Carlo insisted. "Marco met Maddalena on the way out of Florence and agreed to return and watch the monastery while she sought me out. I was here, explaining the situation to Aristo."

"Will you send a message to the prince, *madonna?*" Aristo asked her in spite of Maddalena's earlier objections.

"Indeed, we can tell Paolo on the way out—"

"What if he insists upon sending a contingent with us?" Carlo asked.

"So much the better . . . we need all the help we can get."

"We?" Aristo asked with a worried frown. "What if he won't let you leave here?"

"Paolo is not my keeper. I am a married woman now, and not my father's responsibility. I'll tell him I'm going to Florence with three escorts."

Maddalena pulled her cape about her and moved past Giulietta toward the door. "We need no *gorgio* to frustrate our efforts to rescue one of our own. Nor an escort of bumbling outsiders."

Giulietta put a hand on Maddalena's arm. The woman's eyes delved deeply into hers, as if she were scouring Giulietta's very soul. The muscles in the Gypsy's arm tensed beneath Giulietta's fingers. "I *will* go with you, signora, you can be sure of that."

Maddalena looked down at Giulietta's hand, then back to her face. "As you wish," she said, then turned away and threw over her shoulder as she headed for the door, "but we don't need a thundering army to alert the culprits and further endanger Rigo . . . if he is yet alive."

*If he is yet alive* . . . The words rang ominously through her mind, conjuring up images of the vitality and animation—the essence of Rodrigo da Valenti—stolen by that utterly indifferent master of all thieves, death.

Carlo looked as if he might disagree with Maddalena, but held his tongue. Giulietta didn't notice.

Handing Giulietta a dark, hooded cape, Aristo said, "I don't approve of this, *madonna* . . . and His Excellency will have my head when he finds out. But I know you will have your way unless physically restrained."

Giulietta was taken aback by his words, for in the past, he'd never implied that she was headstrong or willful. *Mayhap he's always considered me so,* came the disturbing thought. It gave her something to ponder, to momentarily divert her mind from Rodrigo and his imminent danger, as she followed him through the door. Carlo brought up the end . . . with Beau trotting beside him.

Lucrezia stood beside the pallet and stared down at Rodrigo da Valenti. His dark hair was sticky with blood, some of which had run down onto his white shirt and doublet. The right side of his forehead, his right eyelid and cheek held dried streaks, as did the side of his neck.

But he was still breathing, she noted as she placed one hand upon his chest. He looked as if he were merely sleeping, except for the incriminating bloodstains. And the sight of him lying upon her pallet, his dark hair and rich-toned skin in stark contrast to the pale bedding, was erotically arousing, even though he was her enemy. He seemed to fill the tiny cell, even unconscious, and the thrill of having him within her grasp at last affected her sexually.

Gypsy or nay, there was no doubt that he was a splendid figure of a man.

She allowed her hand to linger against his chest, imagining how beautiful his body would be underneath his clothing. . . .

And to think she had seriously attempted to seduce a man like Girolamo Savonarola—a clown in comparison. And, even worse, the prior had rejected her in horror. In fact, she remembered with distaste, so great had been his horror that she had immediately thrown herself upon his mercy as a sinful mortal, unfit to be in the same room with a Chosen One like him. She had entreated him to forgive her and fooled him with her humiliating hysterics. Why not? She'd been fighting to obtain his protection . . . mayhap for her very life.

And the monk had finally relented, extracting a promise from her that she would allow him to find her a place to stay until she was ready to go on with her life. He also turned a blind eye to her plans concerning hiring a man to abduct Rodrigo da Valenti, obviously planning to plead ignorance should she be caught in her machinations.

For all that Lucrezia felt she'd done for him spiritually, he was being ungenerous with returning the favor. But she had unexpectedly snagged Fra Domenico, one of the pillars of San Marco, who hung on her every word . . . would have burned in hell for her, which he said he believed would happen after they began their clandestine trysts at the unlikliest times and in the unlikeliest places. The more sacred the place, the more titillating to Lucrezia, and the smitten Fra Domenico offered only token protests.

The more deeply he committed himself to her sexually, the less he seemed to worry about his immortal soul—and the more concerned he became with keeping her out of sight of the other brothers.

Lust did strange things to men, she mused. And women.

Rodrigo groaned softly, and moved his head. Lucrezia moistened his lips with a cloth dipped in water. Water tainted with a drug for sedation. She enjoyed sliding the slick cloth across his beautifully sculpted lips. A flash of desire hit her deep inside, and she dropped the cloth, so stunning was the sudden sensation.

When she'd recovered, she murmured, "All is well so far, *mio bello condottiere,* but should you misbehave . . . *ebbene,* I have a very special punishment in mind for you." Her smile was sudden, and beautifully evil. "A gift of death I stumbled upon in the *mercato* . . . smuggled in from the island of Murano." She removed the cloth from where it had fallen. "I wonder which unfortunate lost his life to provide me with such an exquisite gift?"

Fra Domenico entered as silently as a spirit and moved to stand beside her. He was a big man, with even features and an easy disposition. Until Lucrezia had stirred the ashes of his tamped passions and revealed a very passionate man physically.

He was wasting his life at San Marco, she'd decided. But that was his problem. . . .

She stood, and he asked softly, "Are you ready?"

She nodded. Such a pity there was no time to toy further with Rodrigo da Valenti—although she would have preferred him conscious for what she had in mind. "We need only blind-fold and gag him," she answered.

"Good. His stallion is harnessed to the cart and—"

Lucrezia turned on him in sudden fury. "Fool! The stallion will give us away before we leave the gates of the city! Valuable stallions don't pull carts!"

Fra Domenico looked taken aback. And offended. "I'm not stupid, Lucrezia, and 'tis still dark. We only need pass by the watchmen at the gate." He grinned then. "But mayhap you'll feel better if I tell you that with a little mud, a cropped mane, and a bulky blanket over his back, he's been transformed to ill-used and old. As for his high spirits . . ." He smiled slyly. "He was given a potion similar to what you gave his master—only he's still able to function. His sluggishness will appear to be due to his age. And you'll appreciate his strength once we're on the road south."

Lucrezia gave him her back and calmly proceeded to gag Rodrigo . . . until she felt Domenico's hand slide around her rib cage and caress her breast. "Not now!" she warned sharply, then placed the blindfold about Rodrigo's head. He moaned when she inadvertently came too close to his injury. Fra Domenico helped her sit him up.

"Make certain the corridor is empty," he told her. She lifted the cowl of her dark monk's habit over her head and moved to do his bidding; Fra Domenico hefted the unconscious Rodrigo to his shoulder with a soft grunt of exertion. Lucrezia turned to motion to him and saw him stagger beneath his burden.

"He didn't look so heavy," he said through his teeth.

"What did you expect from a *condottiere?*" she whispered as he eased through the door.

She couldn't make out his soft reply as he moved ahead of her down the passageway.

\* \* \*

Marco followed in the shadows on foot, for it was past curfew. He knew Rodrigo da Valenti was hidden beneath the straw of the small conveyance, somewhere among the wooden casks of what might have been honey or wine made at San Marco. His primary concern, however, was whether the *condottiere* was dead or alive.

He hoped, for the lady Giulietta's sake, that Valenti was alive. In fact, he'd been so unexpectedly concerned after he'd met and spoken with Maddalena on the road into Florence that he'd agreed to return to the city and help if he could.

And so, as the two-wheeled cart passed by his hiding place near San Marco, his cape tucked in his belt so as not to impede his movements, the Gypsy made a furtive dash from the shadows and dove behind it. Grabbing and clinging to the end of the cart frame, he nimbly hoisted himself over the rough board that acted as a low gate, and burrowed beneath the straw, carefully avoiding knocking himself unconscious by hitting his head against one of the casks.

Of course, he couldn't see a thing, but the casks were stable, evidently braced by blocks. He felt around him, and encountered a man's form in the confined area. He could tell by the warmth of the body, the rise and fall of the man's chest, that he was indeed alive. Further exploration revealed the facial features of Valenti, and a half-dry, sticky residue he encountered with his fingers that he feared was blood.

"Valenti?" he whispered in Rodrigo's ear. "Can you hear me? It's Marco." But there was no response he could discern.

One cart wheel jogged over an object in the street, jarring both men. Marco's hand thudded back against Rodrigo's chest. As a muttered sound of pain came from Valenti, Marco prayed the casks would remain secure, or they could both be pinned or injured. Or crushed.

He concentrated on his options: He could have killed the two monks who drove, the element of surprise on his side, but from the amount of time he judged to have passed, they were nearing the closest city gate . . . and guards. Which meant witnesses—mayhap capture and punishment. And certain death for a lowly *Zingaro* who'd dared to kill two so-called servants of God, no matter that they were involved in devil-spawned activities.

And then, too, because he'd calculated it to be only just after midnight, he knew that none of the city gates would open until dawn. Therefore, unless Carlo and Maddalena had a special pass to enter during curfew, precious hours would be wasted if he was trapped inside Florence awaiting them near San Marco.

He had to intercept them outside the city walls—the gate facing the direction of the principality of Monteverdi was the most logical . . . the Porta Romana. *Dio* . . . it was only halfway around the city!

Whatever he decided, he had to do it fast. They were nearing the gate.

Something incredibly dry filled his mouth, and he couldn't move his tongue. But at a particularly nasty jounce, the pain that splintered through his head made him forget his uncomfortable gag. It was pitch black around him, and he was covered with straw, flat on his back in a moving wagon or cart, from what his groggy mind could perceive.

He tried to remember how he'd arrived at this sorry state, and the image of Girolamo Savonarola flashed before his mind's eye . . . following him out into the passageway and. . . . Before he could think further, the conveyance bounced, increasing the stabbing agony in his head. There was sudden movement beside him, and someone's hand fell against his chest.

He remained perfectly still, thinking the other occupant

some kind of guard prepared to put him out of his misery i
he indicated he'd come to. Or, he thought with irony, anothe
body—perhaps this one dead—the hand of which had bee
thrown against his chest by the jouncing of the wagon.

"I have to leave, Valenti," said a voice in his ear.

The warm breath was definitely not that of a corpse, the
voice familiar. Rodrigo tried to speak, but to his frustratio
only a garbled sound came from his dry, scratchy throat. O
course. He was gagged.

"If you can hear me, 'tis Marco. I must intercept Carlo and
Maddalena. I'll lead them to you . . . on the road . . ."

Then Rodrigo felt the ropes at his wrists loosen and fall
away at the slice of a dagger; then his ankles were freed. Lastly,
the binding that held his gag in place was eased, although the
renewed hurt to his head at the change in pressure made him
feel faint.

"Don't do anything stupidly heroic, Valenti"—it definitely
was Marco—"unless they try to kill you outright. You're in
no condition, from what I can tell. We'll get to you . . ."

"Maaar-co," he whispered, but the straw was already
rustling as Marco slithered back from him. And then either he
was gone, or beyond Rodrigo's reach.

Well, at least he'd been freed. And he had the small dagger
tucked in the side of his boot . . . he hoped. If only he could
function more normally. Surely they'd also drugged him, for
his brain still felt sluggish, his perception fuzzy—more than
from the blow he'd evidently taken. And, as if in confirmation,
when he ran his tongue over his lips, he tasted a strange bitterness.

The cart came to a jerky halt—a gate, no doubt. There was
an exchange of dialogue, and for a moment Rodrigo was
tempted to try and sit up and reveal the nefarious plans of
these scheming brothers of San Marco. But he remembered
Marco's warning. If he remained where he was for a while,

until he'd recovered his wits and some of his strength, he might be able to crawl out of the wagon without the driver even knowing. He could hide then. . . .

The thought of hiding irked him in the extreme. For God's sake, he was a professional soldier! *Crawl* out of the cart and *hide?*

*Don't do anything stupidly heroic* . . . Marco's words warned again.

Crawling (or mayhap falling) from the back of a slow-moving cart was hardly heroic, he thought.

The cart lurched forward, sending pain shooting through his head. He wondered what kind of energetic mule they were using.

". . . large and frisky for such a task, brothers!" called a rough male voice. "You could lose your load. Better stick to your mules next time!" Laughter followed the remark, crackling through the chill, damp air.

"What do you give him? A snort of Trebbiano in his water pail?"

A male voice, edged with amusement, replied, " 'Tis a well-kept secret, my good man. Fra Luis here doesn't speak, but he can make a horse or mule do anything." And then the laughter faded as they left the city behind.

A monk with a sense of humor, Rodrigo thought. And a silent partner. What kind of adversaries would they be?

*Probably too much for you right now.*

The voice in his head sounded like the taciturn Marco again, and his pride suddenly began to smart in contention with his battered head, which prompted him to redouble his efforts to think his way out of his predicament.

After a while, the cart seemed suddenly to pick up speed . . . a frisky nag, indeed. "Whoah!" called the driver.

But rather than stopping, the cart lurched forward with such vigor that Rodrigo was actually thrown against one of the casks. The renewed hurt it caused in his cranium made him break out in a sweat, in spite of the cold.

". . . wearing off?" a muffled voice said. Fra Luis, who supposedly didn't speak? Rodrigo wondered.

The cart came to a dead stop, then leapt forward. With all the intensity he could muster, Rodrigo strained to concentrate on the dialogue rather than his acute discomfort, and the mists still shrouding his mind.

". . . don't know how long 'twill last," came the reply.

"Fool!" Fra Luis's voice was high-pitched with agitation this time . . . like that of a female. "You didn't give him enough! He'll end up killing us!"

And then a tendril of hope sprouted within Rodrigo's breast, for the uncooperative animal in the traces had to be Morello . . . his finely bred and dependable partner in war.

And who obviously was beginning to refuse to cooperate with two miscreants featherbrained enough to try to harness a highly trained stallion like a draft horse.

# Twenty-five

It was bad enough trying to explain to Paolo just why they were leaving the castle in such a hurry, and at that hour of the night. But when Giulietta insisted she was going along as well because her husband was in danger, pandemonium broke out.

Paolo wasn't the only one who obviously had real doubts about Giulietta hieing herself off to Florence in the middle of the night with three *Zingari*—never mind that one of them was a trusted servant of the Prince of Monteverdi.

Since both Dante and Caressa were in Pisa, and Nicco had accompanied them, the guards on duty were in agreement with their leader and disinclined to allow Giulietta—married or not—to leave Castello Monteverdi. In fact, all but one or two were eager to accompany Carlo in Giulietta's stead and rush to the aid of Rodrigo da Valenti, the man they knew and respected now.

With great drama, Maddalena threatened to lay a curse on them all if they wouldn't allow them to leave—Giulietta or no Giulietta. That didn't work, however, so in desperation Carlo grabbed the older Paolo and held a dagger to his throat while they exited the keep.

Giulietta was terribly upset at the prospect of the captain of the guard being harmed, but Maddalena had hissed in her ear, *"Cease* your mewlings, girl! If Rigo dies, 'twill be *your* fault—you and your thoughtless, selfish behavior . . . and now your equally foolish sensitivities! Carlo's no killer, but the guard doesn't have to know that." And she marched forward and toward the entrance of the keep, followed by Carlo and his hostage, a chastened Giulietta, and Aristo lurching along behind.

Maddalena was quickly off into the night like a spirit, leaving Carlo and the dwarf to bind and gag Paolo. They left him with two similarly trussed stableboys, then hastily saddled two horses and led them quietly to the edge of the forest. The three of them raced after the Gypsy woman, knowing Dante would be immediately summoned from Pisa, but unable to prevent it.

Maybe, Giulietta felt as the cold night wind whipped the edges of Aristo's borrowed cloak about her and stung her unprotected face, they could use her father's help, after all. She had none of Maddalena's reservations if the interceding of Dante and his men could increase the likelihood of Rodrigo's rescue.

Out of nowhere, the scathing words and haughty tones she had used against Rodrigo da Valenti over the months reverberated in her memory, flaying her with guilt and remorse. No wonder the proud Maddalena wanted nothing to do with those who ridiculed and condemned her people just because their ways were different.

And she, Giulietta, had been one of the worst offenders since she'd first encountered Rodrigo as a youth. *Dio al cielo!* she thought as a wave of guilt and a good dose of humility threatened to swamp her. It was a wonder that Maddalena was even allowing her to accompany them.

They rested briefly, halfway to Florence. Giulietta assumed that in addition to resting the horses, Carlo wanted to give the two women a respite from the steady pace, as well. Both she and Maddalena were impatient, but Carlo said, "We cannot enter the city until dawn anyway."

Giulietta's brief bemusement turned to anger. "My father could have provided us with a writ of entry!"

"Not from Pisa!" Maddalena snapped. "We'd still be awaiting his return."

"Hopefully, if Lucrezia is bent upon removing Rodrigo from the monastery, she must wait until dawn, as well," Carlo said.

Panic spurted through Giulietta. She glanced in the direction of the city, wishing they were there already.

But it was Maddalena who voiced all their misgivings. "The woman will stop at nothing to get what she wants—assuredly not so flimsy a thing as a piece of paper! She's evil and conniving, and I believe they're out of the city even as we speak."

Aristo pulled up just then, huffing and puffing, his features taut with pain. He sighed heavily as he pulled on the reins with his short arms—his feet didn't reach the stirrups, which had only made the ride worse, Giulietta surmised. She saw Maddalena's expression soften briefly as the woman eyed the winded dwarf. "Did you take your potion this eve?" the *Zingara* demanded.

Immediately, Giulietta dismounted and moved toward him, her own concern surfacing even as her fear for Rodrigo threatened to paralyze her. "Aristo," she said softly, "let me help you down."

He shook his large head. "Thank you, Mona Giulietta, but I cannot . . . move at this moment." He drew in a deep breath. "If I can just sit for a short time, I'll be better."

*"Maestro?"*

He looked at Maddalena. "Nay, woman," he said in some irritation. "In all the confusion I neglected to take my nighttime dose."

"I thought you carried it with you," Giulietta said, noting that he looked too miserable to care right now.

She reached toward his belt. "Is it in your pouch?" she asked. His belt had slid around his waist, and the attached pouch hung over his hip. Before he could answer, she fished inside it and pulled out a vial of liquid. "Is this it?"

At his desultory nod, Giulietta pulled out the stopper and held it up to him.

"Take *two* swallows this one time," Maddalena advised, "but no more."

Giulietta watched his Adam's apple bob in the moonlight, afraid that in his misery he would drink the entire vial.

"Why don't you return to Monteverdi, Aristo," she said gently as he corked the vial. Surely you'd be better off there, and you could tell my—"

"Don't send him home like a cur with his tail between his legs, *madonna*," Carlo said with unexpected terseness. "A man must do what he feels is necessary." He cut his gaze to her, and his expression seemed to say, Don't take that away from him.

Giulietta replaced the vial and watched as Aristo's breathing seemed to ease. Her heart went out to him. He'd had a miserable life under his first master. Then Caressa had entered his life. Giulietta remembered her mother telling her that Aristo had begun to change after meeting her . . . but first he'd been forced to betray her. After that, his remorse had given him the strength and courage to see the bishop for what he really was. And he'd begun to plan to sever the ties that bound them.

Dante had eventually placed his faith in him—and treated him like a man, not a freak. Aristo had defied Stefano Ruggerio and saved Dante's life some eighteen years ago, killing his former master in doing so.

It was obvious that the dwarf would have dropped dead off his horse before turning back toward Monteverdi. And Giulietta wouldn't be the one to order him to do so.

Carlo's voice broke into her thoughts. "We can only hope that they haven't left Florence yet. If they have, God help us unless we meet up with Marco before dawn."

"We'll think of *something*," Giulietta declared with more confidence than she felt. "I won't allow a barred city gate to keep me from getting to Rodrigo," she vowed with typical Alessandro tenacity.

They continued on toward Florence, with Carlo leading the way. As they neared the closest gate, Giulietta ignored her aching back and thighs from the long stretch of riding, the numbing wind, and the doubt and the fear that threatened her very sanity.

Never in her seventeen years had a loved one of hers been in imminent danger of death. . . .

"There . . . look!" Maddalena shouted to Carlo across the wind. She was pointing toward a small campfire beside the road leading southwest from the Porta Romana.

Carlo pulled ahead, one hand cautiously resting upon his sword hilt, and Giulietta silently said a brief but fervent prayer.

" 'Tis Marco," Maddalena growled just before Carlo motioned them forward.

A man moved toward them, the firelight behind him limning his form. It was Marco. Thank God! Giulietta thought, weak with relief.

Before Carlo even dismounted, Marco said, "They've managed to get him out of the city, hidden in a two-wheeled cart. There's no time to waste."

"How many are with him?" Carlo asked.

"Two monks."

"*One* monk," Maddalena corrected, staring out into the darkness with narrowed eyes. "The other is that *creature*. And Rigo is yet alive, isn't he? Injured but alive?"

"*Sì*. And we can take them if we plan carefully."

"But you have no horse," Giulietta pointed out.

He shook his head and swung away to stomp out the fire.

"I got out of the city by riding in the wagon beside Valenti," he said over his shoulder. "My horse is stabled near the monastery."

"Ride with Madonna Giulietta," Carlo said. "She's the lightest."

Marco moved toward Giulietta, his gaze meeting hers as if for her permission. She noted a look of deep respect in his dark eyes, before he said humbly, "I am dirty, *madonna,* and—"

Giulietta's mouth curved as she thought of how she must look—and smell—after a long and hard ride. She was tempted to hold out one foot in solemn humor to show off a shoe, but refrained, under the circumstances. She held out one hand to him and he vaulted up behind her.

She had no idea just how deep his respect ran . . . and that he was perfectly willing to give up his life for her because she had risked her own to care for his Maria.


Dawn began to break, the brightening Tuscan skies promising a clear but cold day. Rodrigo felt fully lucid now, the drug having finally worn off. His head still hurt like the devil—even more now, for the potion had also evidently taken some of the edge off his pain; he was also cold and stiff from lying scrunched between the casks on the hard wooden floor covered with only a layer of prickly straw. His cloak had been uncomfortably bunched beneath him, but once Marco had cut his bonds, he'd managed to free enough of it to wrap about him.

And the ride . . . *Dio!* but the ride had been the worst he'd ever taken in his life! Yet the fact that Morello continued to give his abductors an inordinate amount of trouble was a source of satisfaction and grim amusement to him. Served them right, damn their conniving souls to—

Suddenly, the cart leapt forward. Morello must have reared,

Rodrigo barely had time to think, for the vehicle then jerked to a stop and tipped backward, the stallion's shrill whinny piercing the early morning air. The top of Rodrigo's head stopped just short of ramming into the gate behind him as he swiftly braced himself against it with outstretched arms.

"Devil-beast!" shouted a female voice in obvious vexation, and it suddenly came to Rodrigo that "Fra Luis" was Abbess Lucrezia. "We're losing time," she cried angrily. "We'd have done better with a mule, you fool."

The stallion shrieked again, drowning out the monk's reply.

"Why don't you get out and lead him?" Lucrezia said. " 'Twas your idea to—"

"Hush, woman!"

Rodrigo pulled himself up until he could peer over the gate, hoping there was still enough straw covering him to conceal him from the two up front. He had to see the road and surroundings if he was to try and escape. He could only wait so long for Marco and Carlo, and for all he knew, his two abductors could attempt to dispatch him at any moment.

But not without a fight, he thought grimly. He reached down to pat the dagger reassuringly. By some small miracle, it was still in place. He dared to hope . . .

Until, with a jerk, the cart tipped again, wildly, and the gate broke open as a loosened cask crashed into it, spilling him onto the road. He barely had time to scramble sluggishly beneath the lower back end before the remaining barrels came tumbling out and bounced dully to the road about him.

He put two fingers in his mouth, gathered his breath, and whistled sharply. Morello jumped forward in instant reaction to the signal and went racing off down the road, the cart jouncing madly behind him.

Rodrigo turned to watch, and saw the two "monks" thrown from the runaway conveyance. If it weren't for the fact that they were both probably seriously injured—if not dead—he would have laughed aloud. But one figure lay sprawled in the road in what appeared to be an unnaturally twisted position. It remained unmoving. The other lay in a heap, still as death, as well.

They were his abductors—probably planned to murder him—but there was nothing humorous about death.

He whistled again, then a third time. Morello came to a screeching halt and wheeled about, the blanket flying. The cart was knocked to its side in the process, and the stallion dragged it back awkwardly toward Rodrigo.

He pushed himself to a sitting position, thinking to unharness the animal and ride him bareback to Florence. He glanced over his shoulder at the road behind him, listening for hoofbeats. He was still vulnerable to brigands who, along with unscrupulous mercenaries, infested the hilltops and castles along the old Roman road between Florence and Rome. It would be just his luck, he thought—saved by Morello, only to be slaughtered where he sat by thieves.

Honey oozed from two of the nearby casks strewn across the road, like liquid amber. Like Giulietta's eyes, came the unexpected thought. Giulietta. Again.

Always.

With an effort, he tried to push her from his mind. What was the use, anyway? He had to begin distancing himself from her, hardening his foolish heart, for even if Dante wouldn't hear of an annulment, Rodrigo knew he would never have her in the true sense. She would never accept him. He had to learn to expect much less from her than love. . . .

Morello moved restlessly, drawing Rodrigo's dark thoughts to the more immediate problem. The cart scraped along the rough roadbed a few feet with the movement; then the stallion reared in an obvious effort to rid himself of his awkward burden: an onyx silhouette against the gold-tinted firmament.

"Easy, my brave Morello," he soothed the horse, getting to

his knees. The world spun, but he forced himself to his feet, and stood swaying unsteadily until everything righted. His vision was slightly blurred, he discovered, but he determinedly moved toward Morello, one shaky step at a time.

The stallion whickered softly, then jerked up his head and blew out a spumy breath as Rodrigo approached, as if he sensed something was amiss with his master.

"Easy, boy . . . ," Rodrigo repeated, then grabbed hold of the bridle. He stroked the animal's downy nose, then buried his head in its foam-flecked neck as the world began to spin again and his head pounded like someone was using a hammer against his skull.

"You think to escape justice, *murderer?*" panted a voice from behind him. "Killer of innocents!"

He lifted his head, just as Morello neighed again and pawed the ground. He knew exactly who was speaking. But she was lying in the road up ahead. . . .

He moved slowly—he was incapable of anything more at that moment—and squinted at the road where the two bodies had landed. There was only one—still sprawled upon the ground.

A ghostly chill wafted over him like winter's breath, for death was near, he could feel it. He spun clumsily toward the figure behind him . . . and almost fainted from dizziness.

Her face swam in and out of his vision for a moment, but the image instantly burned itself into his brain forever . . . a specter straight from hell, with blood-clotted, auburn hair hanging limply from her exposed head . . . one eyelid split open and the eye bulging grotesquely. Blood ran down her pale and dirt-spattered face. Her nose was broken and sitting at an unnatural angle toward one cheek; blood and spittle trickled from her smashed mouth.

But it was the intensity of her hatred that made his blood run cold. Never had he seen such seething dislike as that smeared across her once fine features. The air fairly trembled with animosity.

" 'Twas an accident, Lucrezia . . . there were witnesses. Your hatred is ill-founded and—"

"I *will* take you to Rome, Valenti," she sneered through her damaged mouth, as if she hadn't heard a word he said. "To Gabriella di Corsini. Only first I'll kill you!" And she lifted one arm, a dagger clutched in her hand.

Rodrigo raised his left arm to meet hers, but her parody of a smile warned him there was more. . . .

Like a striking snake her left hand shot out from the folds of her dark robes, and Rodrigo caught the flash of crystal in the newly rising sun. As if suspended in time, the slender glass stiletto appeared poised in midair between them, the milk-white contents of its hollow blade sending mute horror surging through him.

Poison.

He made a desperate, drunken grab for it with his right hand, knocking the weapon toward his left side, where the stiletto grazed his ribs through his clothing before it shattered into a thousand shards and rained down upon the road.

It was a puny flesh wound, and the pain was nothing compared to the knowledge that lethal poison had penetrated his skin. Rage and disbelief flooded through him, and he went for her throat with all of his remaining strength . . .

And dimly heard the dull thunder of distant hooves.

He focused his narrowed gaze over her shoulder, his fingers still locked about her neck. She was jeering at him, but he couldn't make out her words for the roaring in his ears (or was it the pounding of horses hooves?), the lassitude invading his limbs. He began to sink toward the ground, pulling her with him. If he was going to die, she would burn in hell as well.

The last images he saw were of four riders racing toward

them . . . one a little man whose legs stuck out almost at right angles to the horse he rode, and beside him, the flash of the sun on red-gold tresses flying like a bright silk pennant in the wind.

But it was too late, he acknowledged with the last vestiges of reason before he succumbed to the toxin spreading through his system.

*Too late . . . too late . . . too late . . .*

As they came to a halt, Giulietta tumbled off her mare before Marco could move. She ran toward the fallen Rodrigo, her expression transfixed by terror. Dimly she noted Morello stood to one side, still harnessed to an overturned cart . . . a body lying farther along the road.

And a woman in monk's garb trying to crawl away from Rodrigo.

Lucrezia!

The others were close behind as Giulietta dropped to her knees beside her husband. "Rigo!" she said softly, feeling suddenly sluggish with fear. The blood on his face and in his hair was dried, but—

"Don't move!" Carlo warned Lucrezia, and she turned on him, revealing her disfigured face. But it was Marco who fairly emanated cold rage.

"Leave her to me," he gritted, and dragged her up by the neck of her robe.

Her good eye widened in recognition. *"You."*

*"Sì,* 'tis I. And you killed my Maria—refused to grant her entry to your sacrosanct cloister." He shook her with such ferocity that her limbs moved in spastic jerks.

"D-dirty Gypsy," she rasped. "You betrayed your own. You're the lowest of the low . . ."

Maddalena was working over Rodrigo, ignoring everyone

else. Giulietta was beside her and glanced up at Lucrezia's words to see the woman attempt to stick Marco with a dagger held in her right hand. But it was a clumsy move, and he knocked it from her fingers, then struck her in the jaw with his knuckled fist, sending her flying backward. She landed with a dull thud and lay absolutely still.

Without a backward glance, Marco walked to where the other monk lay and bent over him.

"What ails Rigo?" Giulietta asked Maddalena. "I see no other wounds but—"

"Look here," Carlo said, and squatted beside them to examine the pieces of broken glass reflecting the rising sun. He carefully picked up the glass hilt, which was still intact.

"He's been poisoned!" Maddalena cried softly. "Help me find the entry wound," she commanded Giulietta, and they quickly located the laceration on his left side.

The *Zingara* cut his shirt away with a small knife and bent over him. She began sucking on the wound and spitting the blood onto the road.

*Poison.* The word rampaged through Giulietta's mind as she watched, helpless, while Rodrigo's grandmother worked to save his life. She moved to take his head in her lap and stared down at his beloved face. His features wavered before her as tears filled her eyes, and she whispered a fervent prayer for God to spare him.

*If you hadn't run off to Santa Lucia, none of this would have happened,* screamed a voice inside her.

*I know you will have your way unless physically restrained . . .* Aristo's words struck her like well-sharpened arrows.

Her tears fell faster, spattered onto Rodrigo's face. "Help him, Maddalena," she pleaded through a throat constricted with emotion. "Save him, *per favore . . . ,*" she begged, unknowingly echoing her father's long-ago words to the Gypsy woman when Aristo had clung to life by a thread.

The dwarf was suddenly beside her. He awkwardly patted her shoulder, and for a moment, she buried her face in his chest—this beloved servant of her family, who had risked her father's displeasure for her on more than one occasion. His brief embrace felt comforting, and the faint, familiar scent of rose water reminded her of home . . . the haven of Monteverdi and the love of her mother and father.

She couldn't bear the thought of her helplessness while Rodrigo lay dying. "What can I do?" she whispered to Aristo. " 'Tis my fault, and if I lose him—" She couldn't finish.

" 'Tisn't your fault," he soothed her in his low, raspy voice. "The blame belongs to *all* of us."

"Is there a chance?" Carlo asked Maddalena, his expression grim.

She finally raised her face to his. "One never knows with poison. I removed all I could until I tasted no more. But it depends on how lethal it was and how much his body absorbed."

"I think we came just in time," he said, hunkering down and gazing at his brother's still features. " 'Tis a very fresh wound."

Giulietta caught the hope in his voice as Maddalena nodded. "We must get him to shelter . . . a bed, medicinals. And quickly."

Carlo nodded and stood, gingerly tucking the glass stiletto hilt in his belt. He motioned to Marco, and they moved toward Morello and the upset cart. Aristo stood stiffly and went to join them. While the dwarf held the stallion's head, the two other men righted the cart and brought it around to where Rodrigo lay. Quickly, Carlo unharnessed Morello and substituted Giulietta's mare.

Giulietta reluctantly stood and watched as the men carefully lifted her husband and laid him in the cart. She helped Maddalena cushion him with straw and cover him with his cape, then refused to leave him to ride one of the extra horses. "Someone can lead Carlo's horse to Florence," she said. "Or tie him to the back of the cart."

Marco and Aristo took care of the riderless horses. As they did so, Carlo met Maddalena's eyes, expectancy in his own.

Maddalena nodded at him, her expression thoughtful. "We'll take him to Florence rather than Monteverdi. It's closer," she said. Carlo vaulted to the front seat of the cart and coaxed the mare to swing around so that they were turned toward Florence. "And he has a house there," she added.

"What about Lucrezia . . . and the other monk?" Giulietta suddenly asked.

"They're both dead," Marco said. He sat astride Carlo's mount, holding Morello's reins. Aristo did the same for the horse Maddalena had ridden.

"And they can rot in the road for their treachery," the Gypsy woman added with a contemptuous toss of her head. The cart moved forward, with Carlo settling the mare into a brisk pace.

Giulietta carefully cradled Rodrigo's injured head in her lap, praying the poison that had entered his body wasn't enough to kill him.

# Twenty-six

They pushed the tired horses to the limit to reach Florence by late morning. Rodrigo was still alive, but pale and unmoving, his breathing shallow.

Carlo and Marco carried him into the town house while Maddalena dispatched Aristo to an apothecary. Giulietta hovered about trying to will Rodrigo to shake off his alarming lethargy. She fought panic in the face of his unhealthy pallor as Maddalena forced water down his throat, slapping his cheeks to keep him awake. At Giulietta's protest, the *Zingara* said to her, "He cannot sleep until I give him the elixir from the apothecary."

He choked on it at first; but with Carlo's help, Maddalena held him propped in a sitting position, and he drank some of the water. His long, black lashes fluttered, and he tried to speak.

Giulietta took it as a good sign, and wanted in the worst way to tend him. She was, however, intimidated by the regal Gypsy woman—something uncharacteristic for her. She set herself to straightening the bedchamber and standing sentinel but unseeing at the window, helpless and hating it.

Aristo returned, and he and Maddalena mixed an elixir of some kind and forced Rodrigo to drink it. Then more water, until he sputtered and turned his head in protest, the liquid dribbling down his chin.

Giulietta met his eyes once, briefly, but he didn't seem to

recognize her. "Why don't you go and prepare us a meal?" Maddalena asked her bluntly as evening fell. "The men need something to fill their bellies."

Giulietta met her arch gaze steadily, ready to object. She didn't want to leave the room.

"Or know you aught of such menial labor, *principessa?*"

Giulietta bristled. The title was pronounced with heavy sarcasm. "My lady mother is *principessa,* signora, not I. And I am not without a few culinary skills; but I won't leave my husband's side, no matter who commands it."

Maddalena brushed back a lock of dark hair from Rodrigo's brow. "You've done naught to help thus far," she said as she looked back at Giulietta, her deep blue eyes shaded with accusation. "Why this sudden unwillingness to leave the room?"

"You wouldn't *let* me help," Giulietta retorted angrily. "He's my husband, after all—"

"Which is exactly why he's lying here fighting for his life. If he had any common sense at all, he'd rue the day he ever met you."

Giulietta hesitated before she spoke, self-flagellation shimmying through her. "I'm sure he does now, signora, for he's already offered to agree to an annulment."

Now, why had she told this *Zingara* such a private thing? she wondered with one part of her mind. Perhaps it was because Maddalena obviously loved her grandson—was the only living immediate family he had, according to Dante. And, also, it was the only kind of atonement she could offer to this proud woman for having caused Rodrigo da Valenti such heartache . . . the admission that Rodrigo was not quite the romantic fool Maddalena had named him.

Maddalena's eyes narrowed for a moment; then she shrugged. "That is between the two of you. If he lives . . ."

Unexpectedly, her tone softened. "He sleeps now, and all we can do is watch and wait. He's in God's hands."

After she left the room, Giulietta approached the bed. There was a stool beside it, but she knelt, instead, and took one of his outstretched hands. She held it to her cheek, feeling his cool skin against the warmth of hers. Tears burned the back of her eyes, then spilled over onto his hand. "Stay with us, my love," she whispered. "I'll do anything if you'll stay with us." She put her lips to the back of his fingers and tasted the salt of her own tears. "Anything."

*He's in God's hands.*

She slowly raised her face as Maddalena's words came back to her. The *maesta,* a picture of the Madonna above the simple and narrow bed, caught her eye and shimmered through the blur of tears. . . .

Suddenly, the answer was there, like a divine revelation, and Giulietta realized what she had to do. It was the one thing she could do now if Maddalena spoke truly and Rodrigo's life was indeed hanging by a thread.

She was vaguely aware of a commotion downstairs, but didn't pay much heed as she concentrated on the right words for her prayer. A few moments later, however, she heard a familiar *click, click, click* on the tile floor. She raised her head and looked toward the door. A bedraggled Beau came into the room.

"Beau!" she whispered in consternation. His beautiful coat was filthy—wet in places and caked with mud. He favored one paw, as well, but his eyes were clear and alert. His tail swayed a few times as he limped up to Giulietta, and with one hand she scratched him under his chin, afraid to release Rodrigo's hand completely. "How did you get here?" she whispered.

But the answer was obvious. He'd come from Monteverdi in search of his master.

He pressed his cool nose to her cheek, then leapt upon the bed, curled up at the bottom, his eyes fastening on Rodrigo

as he rested his head on his paws. Giulietta's first impulse was
to shoo him away, for he was damp and dirty. But she couldn't
bring herself to do so after his courageous journey . . . and
he was at the very foot of the mattress, to the side of Rodrigo's
feet and out of the way, so what harm could it really do?

She gripped Rodrigo's hand with both of hers and touched
her brow to the back of it. She would make a bargain with
God. If he would spare Rodrigo, she would ask her father to
request an annulment from His Holiness, thus freeing Rodrigo
to find someone more worthy of his love.

She surely wasn't, she realized now. She had been judgmental, acting with prejudice and disdain . . . an embarrassment to the Alessandro name in more ways than one. In fact,
if she was absolutely honest with herself, much of her past
behavior had typified what many held against the nobility.

God in heaven, but she'd even called him a Gypsy bastard . . . flung his love in his face and told him he was after
her dowry and a place in the Alessandro family.

The one thing, she supposed, that could be counted to her
credit where any *Zingari* were concerned was her insistence
upon taking Maria into Santa Lucia. And she'd failed miser-
ably, for not only had she been forced to tend the stricken girl
in a lowly stable, but she'd also failed to save her.

Fresh tears gathered and sprinkled down her cheeks. "Please,
God," she whispered, clutching Rodrigo's hand as if it were a
lifeline, "I promise to ask my father to petition for an annulment. I'll set him free . . . just spare him. Please!" she sobbed
softly.

She lay there, her knees upon the hard floor, weeping over
Rodrigo's hand clutched in hers. Finally, she couldn't bear the
coolness of his skin. She straightened her stiff legs and back,
then carefully moved to lay beside the man she loved. Mayhap,
she thought, if she could impart any of her warmth to him, it
would help in some small way.

Studying his still but arresting features, she wondered once again how she could ever have thought him dark and unattractive, and came to the conclusion that that had been the only defense she'd had against the irresistible pull he'd had on her from that first night in the forest. She longed to plant a gentle kiss upon his molded lips, lips that smiled so easily, so beautifully—like a gift to any mere mortal within range of it. And the long-lashed lids that hid his splendid blue eyes from her . . . the straight, strong nose beneath demonishly winged brows. . . . But there was nothing demonesque about Rodrigo da Valenti. He was her dark angel, rather.

*If he lives, he won't be yours now.* The words tiptoed through her mind.

"But his life is more important than aught else," she whispered brokenly.

She gently rested one arm across his chest and anchored herself to his side, her lips inches away from his hair. She lay there, inhaling the scent of him as his hair tickled her nose, and willed him to overcome the poison that still threatened his life.

Over and over she silently, sincerely reaffirmed her love for him . . . and her promise to God.


Something cool touched her bare ankle, then the back of her neck, bringing Giulietta out of her sleep with a start. The two small oil lamps still burned, one on the table beside the bed, one set in a bracket on one wall, but the silence of the city around them and a glance at the partially shuttered window told her it was deep night.

Beau began to whine, and Giulietta looked at Rodrigo, barely aware that Beau had moved to the other side of the bed, his dirty front paws set against the edge of the mattress as he stood on his hind legs and tried to sniff his master's face.

Joy lit Giulietta's eyes, for Rodrigo's were open and his lips were moving. "Beau," he muttered in a voice husky with disuse, and tried to reach out his left hand. He only made it halfway across the narrow space, but the dog stretched his muzzle to meet it, his tail suddenly wagging furiously.

Giulietta pushed herself to a sitting position. "Rigo?" she inquired softly.

He turned his head with a grimace, leaving a streak of half-dried blood against the white pillow. His eyes brightened when they met hers, but he only said, "Water. Please . . . some water . . ."

Afraid to jounce the mattress, Giulietta restrained herself and moved cautiously to leave the bed and pour him a cup of water. Her footsteps must have alerted the others downstairs, for Maddalena appeared in the doorway, with Marco and Aristo behind her. Carlo had been dispatched to Pisa to intercept Dante and inform him of what had happened on the road to Rome, and assure him that Giulietta was well, even if Rodrigo was not.

Maddalena helped her lift his shoulders, and Giulietta raised the cup to his lips, her eyes caressing his beloved face as he obediently drank.

"Drink as much as you can, grandson," Maddalena told him. "Water not only dilutes any remaining poison, but cleanses the body of it, as well."

Giulietta handed Aristo the cup for more water, and as Rodrigo drank, she had the most powerful urge to press her lips to his sable hair. But she remembered her bargain . . . God had spared Rodrigo it seemed, and now she would keep her word.

"How do you feel?" Maddalena asked as they laid him back against a plumped-up pillow.

"A little fuzzy," he said with a lopsided grin that made Giulietta's heart turn over in her chest. "My head still aches like the devil, but otherwise I'm hale and hearty."

"Hummph," Maddalena grunted. "Hardly that. You're weak as a newborn."

Rodrigo caught Giulietta's eye and emitted an exaggerated sigh of resignation. Her hungry gaze clung to his before she realized what she was doing and looked away.

"Turn to your side, can you?" Maddalena asked him. "Your head needs cleansing and binding, now that you're out of danger."

Giulietta went over to Beau and bent to examine his paw. The farther away from Rodrigo she was, the better. It wasn't going to be easy, but she could avoid any further intimacy, no matter how innocent, to make it easier for them both.

"What happened to him?" Rodrigo asked as he lay on his side facing Giulietta and the dog.

"It appears he came to Florence on his own," Marco said, speaking for the first time as he looked on from the foot of the bed.

Rodrigo laughed softly, then grimaced as Maddalena stretched a strip of linen over his cut scalp. "He was never one to be left behind. Great Pyrenees are bold and courageous." Giulietta felt his eyes on her, but she deliberately remained absorbed in the examination of the pads of the dog's injured paw.

"Marco slew the abbess," Aristo told him, and Giulietta relaxed slightly as his attention turned to the dwarf.

"And the monk is dead also?"

Aristo nodded.

"You are very lucky," Marco said. From his belt he removed the glass dagger hilt Carlo had given him before the latter left for Monteverdi. "These, I understand, are manufactured on the island of Murano near Venice. The hollow blades carry the most potent of poisons."

" 'Tis just the type of weapon that *strega* would use," Aristo said. "No doubt she spent a goodly amount of gold for it at the *mercato*."

Rodrigo nodded and rested back against the pillow. "I'm surprised it didn't shatter when she was thrown from the cart."

"Aye. Or she could have impaled herself and saved us a lot of trouble," Maddalena said.

"You obviously deflected her blow?" Aristo asked Rodrigo. At his nod, the dwarf said, "Fortunately you caught only a fraction of the poison. Had she struck you full in the chest or belly, of a certainty you'd have died then and there."

Giulietta shivered at the thought, and her gaze automatically went to Rodrigo, then skittered away, color brushing her cheekbones. She stood and approached the bed. "I'm glad you're better," she told him in a low, unsteady voice, but her gaze didn't quite reach his eyes.

Rodrigo gave her a half-smile in acknowledgement, feeling a deep disappointment at her coolness. She obviously hadn't put their last argument aside. Nothing had really changed, it seemed.

He tried once more. "I see you dressed for the occasion, *cara*," he said softly. Gentle humor warmed his eyes, tinged his words, but she wouldn't meet his gaze.

He watched her blush deepen as Aristo said with an awkward chuckle, "We had no time to tarry . . . Maddalena appeared like magic at Monteverdi with Carlo in tow and stressed the need for quick action. Madonna Giulietta came from her bed and—" he eyed the shoes she still wore—"borrowed my shoes."

Under different circumstances, Giulietta would have found humor in the situation, but instead she was acutely conscious of all eyes directed to her feet—her entire person, she suspected. Maddalena would be silently disdaining, she already knew, the sullen Marco mayhap slightly amused, as was Aristo.

But it was Rodrigo for whom she wished to look beautiful. Or at least presentable.

Even Beau suddenly seemed to find her shoes of interest, for he began sniffing them with canine enthusiasm—as if they contained mouth-watering leftovers from a feast.

Swamped by uncharacteristic self-consciousness, Giulietta made a move with one hand to touch her hair, then stilled as pride intervened. "If you'll excuse me," she said, "I'll bring Rodrigo something to eat, for surely he—" she dared glance up at him—*"you* are hungry."

She turned and left the room with quick steps.

She realized her mistake before she even returned home the next day. The moment she saw her father coming toward them as they were traveling back to Monteverdi, she knew. There was no way he would ever agree to her requesting an annulment. She knew that now, even without speaking to him. *Idiota!* she thought in irritation. Her father had no doubt planned to marry them after Mario di Corsini's death. He obviously hadn't told her because he feared her reaction, and rightly so.

She decided it would have to be up to Rodrigo to obtain an annulment. Maybe it wouldn't be difficult to persuade him to approach her father, for it had been Rodrigo who'd brought up the subject in the first place.

Nonetheless, she felt physically ill at the very thought of having not only to lie to him, but then *persuade* him that she didn't love him, therefore relieving him of a wife who would constantly fling his birth in his face . . . and insult his honor.

The memory of his parting words that night returned with searing pain. How could she have given him the impression that she would do such a thing to him? *Continue* to do so during their life together?

*When have you done otherwise? Not since you've known him!*

As she walked slowly toward their bedchamber now, her steps slowed. The castle occupants were retiring after a dinner that included Carlo, Marco, and Maddalena. Rodrigo was much better—this was their first night home—but had pleaded being not quite himself yet. He'd left the board early, and she had deliberately remained behind, knowing and dreading what she had to do. . . .

Rodrigo stared out at the starlit night. He felt tired and listless, and his head still ached. More painful, however, was the ache in his heart. Giulietta had been cool toward him ever since he'd awakened the other night in his room in Florence.

There had been no joyful greeting, only, "I'm glad you're better." Those flat-sounding words weren't the words of a woman in love—not even the words of a woman who felt a lukewarm affection for a man. And her eyes hadn't met his.

He felt defeated—more than if he'd lost a tournament or even a battle—for there had always been a spark between them, unacknowledged on Giulietta's part, but definitely there. Now, it seemed, there was nothing.

He leaned his head against the thick, cold glass and closed his eyes tiredly. It seemed that he had managed to obtain everything but the one thing he'd wanted for most of his adult life . . . Giulietta. Nothing mattered now if he couldn't have her in the way he wanted her.

He wished . . . *Dio!* but it still hurt his head to think! And what was the use wishing, anyway? He remained standing before the window, his shoulders slumped with uncharacteristic defeat; then finally he straightened and swung away . . .

To see Giulietta watching him from just inside the door. Before she could clear her expression, Rodrigo thought he saw regret and despair etched on her features. But he couldn't be certain, and his vision still tended to play tricks on him. . . .

"We must talk," she said simply as she closed the door behind her. Beau came bounding up to her, and she bent to scratch him behind the ears, tempted to bury her face in his fur to escape Rodrigo's intense perusal. But she resisted the temptation.

He moved toward her, the natural briskness missing from his stride, she noticed. Then he checked, and motioned toward the two chairs before the hearth. The hearth . . . the chairs. . . . They'd made passionate love on one of those very chairs not long ago, before this very hearth, she remembered with a pang. A burst of hectic color splattered her cheeks.

She sat, and he, unexpectedly, did not. He stood at the hearth, one arm braced against the corner of the ornately carved mantel, watching her expectantly.

His color had not returned fully, although the bandage about his head was still a stark contrast to his skin. It reminded Giulietta painfully of his brush with death. She wanted to worry her lower lip, but steeled herself to reveal nothing about her inner agitation. The steady intensity of his eyes on her was unnerving in itself. He wasn't going to make this easy, she sensed.

"You left the board early," she said quietly (and thought how inane an observation it was). "How are you . . . feeling?" She glanced up at him.

"Better than this morn, thank you. But I tire much too easily." He paused. "Yet I suppose I should consider myself fortunate." His voice bore a hint of irony.

"Aristo said 'twill not last," she hastened to reassure him, smoothing the blue-green silk of her dress over one knee. She drew a deep breath in the wake of his silence and said, "You mentioned an annulment . . . I think my father would be more inclined to listen to you than me. He—"

"He wouldn't listen to me either, I'm certain," he interrupted her. "But the point is moot anyway, because I've changed my mind."

She looked up at him in bewilderment and felt an incongruous surge of hope, as well. Changed his mind?

His next words crushed that unexpected spark of hope, her bedside promise temporarily forgotten. "I need a wife as much as you need a husband, and our union appears to fit the mold now—an arranged marriage for political reasons, without any entangling emotions—which is fashionable among the gentility anyway." He gave her his profile, staring into the dancing flames. "Although, lest you misinterpret my words, I make no claim to gentility for myself. Rather, 'tis you I speak of."

She remained seated, staring at his fire-limned features, stunned. In spite of what he'd said, so obviously unmoved and matter-of-fact after what they'd shared, Giulietta dimly realized that he was forcing her to break her promise, and that *had* to be the uppermost consideration here . . . even though he couldn't know of it.

He looked over at her and said, "All those things you said about me the night before I left for Florence were true. For one so young, you are most astute, Giulietta. Therefore, I *would* be the greatest of fools if I let it all slip through my . . . greedy fingers. I feared contracting the plague as much as the next man, but my desire to wed you for all the wealth it entailed was uppermost in my mind when I took you to Father Antoine. And I saw no need to take the chance that you might persuade Dante to cancel the betrothal before the wedding because of your continued and vociferous objections."

The only thing that helped her keep her sanity in the wake of the brutal admission was the tattoo that kept beating through her brain, *the promise . . . the promise . . . the promise.* And the tiny voice that tried to tell her, *He doesn't really mean it. He couldn't . . . no!*

What did it matter anyway? she told herself sternly when she could marshal her wits. She had to set him free in the only way possible now. It was so simple. So painfully simple. *"Ebbene,* signore, you are free to find love elsewhere." Was that her voice? Had her stiff tongue and wooden lips uttered those callous words?

He said nothing for what seemed like forever. Then, huskily, "And you, as well, Giulietta. I would not stand in the way of that."

So steeped was she in her own misery that she didn't see the muscle spasm along his jaw, the fingers of his hands fist suddenly, and had no way of knowing that it was the most difficult thing he had ever had to say.


Marco left Monteverdi the next day, and Maddalena returned to where her people were spending the winter, promising to return in time for the spring wedding. Life settled back into its normal rhythm at Castello Monteverdi.

Winter slipped into early spring. Giulietta was miserable all the while, but made a brave effort to act as if nothing were amiss. Of course, her mother and father noticed, but for once said nothing, although Giulietta often caught Caressa's frowning gaze upon her.

She acted the perfect wife in public and before others in her family. But the natural sparkle in her amber eyes was dimmed, even when she smiled, which she tried to do frequently. And, of course, sleeping in the same bed but not touching Rodrigo was the hardest thing to endure. Giulietta would shut her eyes tightly and try not to remember the brief but blissful period of lovemaking that had begun at Father Antoine's cottage . . . and ended so abruptly when she had asked that incriminating question—and then taken exception to his honest answer . . . and the fact that he'd been right about her reaction.

Wedding preparations continued, and Giulietta tried to get caught up in them, for a diversion—although it was a poor diversion: preparations for a grand wedding which would only reinforce the fact that she would be his wife forever, and forever apart emotionally, sharing only his name.

As Lent—and therefore the day of the wedding—approached, Giulietta grew more and more somber, in spite of her intentions to appear otherwise. Surely God was punishing her, not only for all her past sins, but for her inability to keep her promise.

Early one morning, unable to sleep, Giulietta slipped from bed, dressed hurriedly, and went to the stables of Monteverdi where the cows were kept.

"Let me help you, Enrico," she said to the shocked stableboy, and pulled a milking stool up to one of the cows. Determinedly pushing up her sleeves, Giulietta made sure the animal's hind legs were secured and began, to Enrico's obvious astonishment, filling the pail.

She glanced up at the youth and laughed, her eyes suddenly asparkle. "You would be surprised, Enrico, at what I learned at Santa Lucia."

He returned her smile, still obviously trying to absorb the sight of Giulietta de' Alessandro milking a cow.

"This became my favorite task," she informed him, her eyes filling suddenly, "for I had a patient teacher . . . a wonderful teacher."

She never saw the tall, shadowed figure who appeared in the doorway, then silently moved away. . . .

# Twenty-seven

8 April, 1498

Giulietta kept her eyes downcast . . . and trained upon Rodrigo's clasped hands. She couldn't concentrate on what the Dominican friar in the pulpit was saying, for it was sheer torture to be so close to her husband and not able to reach out to him.

Even if Savonarola himself had been giving the sermon, Giulietta doubted that she would have been able to control her thoughts and yearnings with any more success. Many had thought he would dare take the pulpit himself this Palm Sunday, but after the cancellation of a "trial by ordeal" the day before between the Dominican and Franciscan orders, disappointment was rife, tempers were high.

And evidently Savonarola was smart enough to know when to remain within the sanctuary of San Marco.

The wedding was only three weeks away. Contrasting emotions twisted through Giulietta at the thought. Yet surely if she dared to break her promise to God, she would go straight to hell. And perhaps God would take Rodrigo from her anyway as further punishment.

But she hadn't been able to bring herself to broach the subject of annulment with her father. She didn't know which was worse . . . his agreement should she ask him, or the

prospect of eternal damnation for not asking as she'd prom
ised.

During moments of her deepest despair, Giulietta felt like
her vow to God had changed her into a vacillating, sniveling
coward.

Yet more and more often now, when she thought of her prob-
able punishment for breaking her promise, Giulietta thought
irreverently that it would be worth it. What woman in her right
mind would cast aside the affection of a man like Rodrigo da
Valenti? And she certainly wasn't as preoccupied with attaining
Heaven as those among whom she'd lived at Santa Lucia . . .
which was precisely the reason she'd hated it.

But they'd become virtual strangers. They talked—and they
did so mostly when in the company of other family members.
It was superficial and polite, and there was no mention of an
annulment.

In an effort to fight back her emotions, Giulietta raised her
head and looked toward the Dominican giving the sermon. To
her mortification, she felt heat stain her face, tears burn the
backs of her eyes. She suddenly had difficulty swallowing
around the clot of emotion in her throat. She closed her eyes
against her tears but kept her face lifted, silently entreating
God to help her. What better place than a cathedral? she
thought in growing desperation. She couldn't allow her tears
to betray her—not while standing between Rodrigo and her
father, with her mother near as well, and Nicco. . . .

Suddenly, Rodrigo's lips were at her ear, startling her. A
ripple of long-denied desire undulated through her at his warm
breath and whispered words: "Stay with your father, *cara.* I'll
be back . . ." And he slipped away into the sea of people
around them.

Giulietta looked over her shoulder, but he was gone. His
whispered endearment echoed around and around in her mind,
for it had held the promise of a rain shower to the tiny, ne-

;lected seed of her love that struggled like a wilted shoot to
emerge from the parched earth. It had also sounded like a
caress to her hungry heart. . . .

Before she directed her gaze forward again, however, a
dark-robed figure registered on the periphery of her vision.
The monk was huddled among a group of gaily dressed
Florentines, his cowl pulled forward and therefore shadowing
his bowed head. His presence was incongruous in the midst
of peacock-bright silks and brocades, but it was some eerie
and indefinable quality about the figure that had caught her
attention.

Without warning, he cast an awkward but furtive glance in
her direction, and Giulietta caught the flash of one eye. Inexplicably, a shadow passed across her very soul.

She faced forward and met Dante's eyes. One of his hands
closed over hers, imparting comfort, but not complete peace
of mind. . . .

"This wasn't a good idea," Rodrigo said to Carlo outside
the cathedral in the April sunlight. He shook his dark head.
"This idea of the prince to attend mass here . . . and today of
all days." A growing crowd was becoming hostile, menacing.
Many of the *Compagnacci* were among them, including Andrea Lenzi, Taddeo and Berto.

Lenzi was close by, eyeing the crowd around him. " 'Tis
going to be ugly," he predicted. "They're angry about yesterday—they wanted blood and got rainwater instead."

"One cannot help the weather," Rodrigo said with an ironic
twist of his lips. "The fires would have been doused by the
downpour."

"Too bad the rain didn't douse any tempers," Carlo replied
with a shake of his head. "I would get the women out of the
cathedral now, before aught happens."

Rodrigo nodded. There was no way the handful of them could control the swiftly growing crowd congregating in the *piazza* before the great Florence Cathedral. If anything, many of the youthful opponents of Savonarola were deliberately stoking the mob's anger.

Berto and Taddeo joined in, shouting imprecations at those inside the church . . . picking up sticks and stones.

This was no time to worry about going against the tide of opinion among the crowd—or defying the *Compagnacci* of which Rodrigo had pretended to be a part.

He began to move forward, shouldering his way toward the open front doors. Carlo followed on his heels. . . .


The crowd outside Santa Maria del Fiore was growing in size . . . and agitation. Giulietta could tell from the noise, the palpable tension pulsing in the air. She threw a quick look over one shoulder, but couldn't see Rodrigo. Why had he left? she thought. Where was he now?

A stone hurtled through one of the open church doors and landed with a clatter behind the congregation, startling some in the back rows. Then another, causing a woman to cry out in pain as it struck her. A hail of sticks and stones and oaths followed. The friar in the pulpit froze, his gaze going to the doors at the back of the church.

Suddenly, people appeared at several side doors that had been thrown open to the fresh spring air and sunshine. "Out!" Dante said in a low voice, and took both his wife and daughter by the elbow and steered them toward a side exit. Nicco followed protectively behind, trying to keep them all together.

But the predominant tide was surging toward the back doors, and Giulietta found herself being forcibly separated from her family. "Gietta!" Nicco called to her, but was jostled out of her reach.

When Giulietta realized it was useless to struggle, she ceased and found herself moving swiftly with the crowd toward the rear doors. Her eyes scanned the bobbing heads and panic-etched faces for Rodrigo. As she neared the doors, the noise from the crowd outside increased . . . and suddenly, she was out in the bright light of day. She stumbled twice and almost fell to her knees on the first set of stone steps, thinking surely she would be trampled.

How could she get out of the crowd? she wondered, but even as she thought it, the congregation began to disperse somewhat, giving her breathing room. Young noblemen shouted imprecations at the fleeing churchgoers, many of whom appeared headed toward San Marco. Sticks and stones flew through the air, as if to emphasize the verbal assault. . . .


Too late, Rodrigo thought in frustration as the congregation began to pour from the cathedral. He couldn't fight the swarm of panicked people—had already been separated from Carlo—and could only crane his neck to catch a glimpse of a young woman in yellow silk.

His heart jarred frenetically beneath his ribs; he tasted fear. To think he might lose her without ever having settled matters between them. . . . It was absurd, he acknowledged, petty obstacles in the face of possible injury or death. Life was too precious—too short to allow anything to interfere with happiness. . . .

Then he saw her, and watched helplessly as she was propelled across the narrow slab of marble traversing the front of the cathedral, just before the last four steps leading to the *piazza*. He fought like a madman to get to her, lost sight of her as she stumbled down the stairs, and redoubled his efforts to reach her. . . .


Giulietta saw a flash of scarlet on a tall form, a familiar face, and cried out, "Rigo! Here!"

Their eyes met. The crowd seemed to thin suddenly. A stick struck him in the head, bounced harmlessly to the stone *piazza.*

She threw herself toward him, feeling moisture trickle down her cheeks. "Rodrigo," she half sobbed with relief.

"Giulietta," he returned, his lips against the sweet fragrance of her hair. He squeezed her tightly, and she let out a soft gasp at the unexpected constriction of her ribs. "I saw a flash of yellow," he murmured breathlessly into her ear, giddy with relief.

She opened her eyes just long enough to see the dark figure come at them from over Rodrigo's shoulder. She instantly received the impression of grim purpose as opposed to strength, and instinctively knew the hooded monk wanted Rodrigo dead.

With a strength born of panic, Giulietta tried to shove him to one side. Her soft gasp of denial, however, and the spasm of rigidness that passed through her body, triggered his finely honed reflexes. Instead of allowing her to fling herself between him and the danger behind him, he pushed her away and spun around . . .

And felt the blood freeze in his veins.

The breeze had blown back the monk's hood, revealing a cropped auburn tonsure, and a face belonging in a nightmare.

Lucrezia, back from the dead.

He instinctively went for the woman's striking right hand, which held a wicked-looking dagger that gleamed in the benign spring sunlight as it descended toward him. But this time he wasn't weakened from injury.

"No half-measures this time, Lucrezia," he gritted softly into her mangled face. The force from his arm striking hers sent her dagger spinning through the air.

Without warning, another figure dressed in monk's garb came at him from seemingly out of nowhere, and yet another blade flashed in the sunlight. Giulietta's cry of warning made Rodrigo nimbly jump aside and swing to face this new threat, his sapphire cape flaring. But at the same time, Giulietta threw herself at the second monk's back. She shoved him with every bit of her strength at Lucrezia . . .

And watched with a dark satisfaction as he slammed into the abbess, his blade impaling her.

"Burn in hell for your treachery!" she whispered, and turned away from the gruesome sight.

They returned home, for no one wanted to stay the night in Florence after what had happened. Many of the congregation had fled to San Marco, the pursuing *Compagnacci* in their wake. The monks within the cloister, unbeknownst to Savonarola, had evidently gathered a small arsenal for just such an instance. "They panicked," Dante had told Giulietta later, "and loosened a pinnacle atop the cloister and sent it crashing down upon the heads of the mob in the square below. Some of the monks even took up lances against men who were attempting to set fire to the cloister walls."

"And what of Savonarola?" she'd asked, stunned at the turn of events, for after seeing that the assassin "monk" was in the hands of the authorities, Dante, Carlo and her father had gone to San Marco themselves.

"He took refuge in the library until a guard arrived from the *Signoria* with orders for his arrest. He was then escorted through the streets—through hooting and jeering people—and imprisoned in the tower of the Pallazzo della Signoria . . ."

Now, Giulietta stood alone in the room she shared with Rodrigo, and stared at the dusk-tinted horizon. The deep red of the setting sun reminded her of blood—Lucrezia's blood. . . .

A frisson of revulsion went through her, and she turned away from the bloodied sunset, her arms hugging her waist. Would she ever feel warm again? Or clean? No bath would ever cleanse her of the horrible memories.

"Lisa . . . ," she began, and looked up. Rodrigo was standing just inside the door. How long had he been standing there? she wondered, her heart jumping to her throat.

"I knocked," he said in quiet apology.

Attempting to shepherd the scattered flock of her thoughts, she nodded. "There's no need. 'Tis your room, as well."

He moved forward into the lamplight. His dark hair was still damp from his bath; his simple white shirt emphasized the teak tones of his skin. But his flame blue eyes were somber. He looked as if he wanted to speak seriously, and a knot of dread formed in her stomach. She wasn't sure of anything anymore . . . not even the correctness of her having attempted to bargain with a higher power.

Rodrigo had almost been taken from her again. What was the use of holding to a promise that was sheer torture if God meant to steal him away at the first opportunity? She'd almost lost him in a heartbeat in front of Santa Maria del Fiore today.

And then, too, how could he feel anything for her after four months of seeming indifference?

He stepped toward her, and Giulietta retreated back toward the window. "I wanted to thank you, Giulietta, for your willingness to put my life before your own. There are no words to express what it meant to me."

"I'm your wife. I couldn't have done anything less." *Nor could I have watched a Corsini kill you for a crime you never committed.*

He smiled a sad smile. "I disagree. Sacrificing one's life

for one's spouse is not part of any marriage contract that I know of."

She moved past him to sit on one of the two chairs facing the hearth, thinking to avoid his probing eyes. An idea came to her suddenly, but she didn't know if she had the emotional strength to carry it through. She drew in a deep, fortifying breath and said over her shoulder, "If you wish to express your thanks, then ask my father to petition for an annulment."

Silence reigned in the room for long moments. The hiss and pop of the small fire in the hearth, faint sounds from other parts of the keep, came to her, but Rodrigo said nothing at first.

She couldn't help but picture her life stretched endlessly before her without Rodrigo da Valenti at her side. For all the time she'd spent fighting him and the emotions he aroused within her, she still couldn't envision loving any other man.

*Love is not a consideration among the nobility.*

He came to stand before her, arms crossed, legs straddle-stanced, as if he were preparing for a disagreement. She dared to look up at him, and saw his face was set in bleak lines, his eyes narrowed slightly. "If 'tis what you want, Giulietta." He looked over her head for a brief moment, as if collecting himself before he added, "I thought I'd conquered any feelings of inferiority while strengthening my skills—and my confidence—in France. Learning how to ensure my future as an ordinary man with a little ambition . . ." He laughed softly, self-mockingly. "And then I returned to Monteverdi. And your disdain. But I swear to God, Giulietta, I never suspected what Dante had planned! God in Heaven, I'll not take the blame for *that!*"

She shook her head. "It has naught to do with that." Shame burned her face. "And I ask your forgiveness for any insult offered you, Rodrigo. If I could take them all back, I would . . . each and every one."

"Then why this wish for an annulment?"

She remained silent, sunken in misery.

Finally, he said quietly, "In an attempt to repay a favor that can never really be repaid—that of your attempting to shield me from an assassin's blade—I'll agree to whatever you ask . . . on one condition."

Joy and sorrow collided within her. "And that is?" she whispered, lifting her flushed face to his.

"Tell me exactly why you want our marriage annulled. A person doesn't attempt to throw himself between a spouse and death, then turn around and ask for an annulment. It makes no sense, and I think you owe me at least an explanation."

She shook her head.

He leaned forward and hooked one finger under her chin. As he lifted her face to meet his gaze, she was startled by the sudden anger that darkened his countenance. "What are you using *this* time as an excuse to put me off, Giulietta? You mayhap feel some affection for me, but I'll always be beneath you . . . different from your sainted ancestors. Isn't that it? I'll always be Ginevra's bastard son—the issue of a Gypsy and some philandering Tuscan, a blot on the pristine line of Alessandros?"

He swung away. In spite of her apology, he didn't want to hear the *real* truth from her lips. He knew Dante de' Alessandro had taught him differently, but the truth was that even his own daughter didn't believe it. It surely had to be easier for a prince to spout such lofty ideas—a man who had generations of blue-blooded princes running through his veins.

Giulietta stared at his proud figure before her. Every taunt, every insult she had ever used came back to her tenfold, bringing on a familiar flood of shame. "That has naught to do with it," she protested. "I couldn't find any fault with you—couldn't face my own part in what happened between us that first night. So, with my immense Alessandro pride at stake, I held at bay both you and the feelings you aroused in me, with taunts and insults . . . flimsy barriers to shield a coward."

"There is nothing cowardly about you," he said in a low voice. "But *why?* Why this pursuit of an annulment?" He turned back to her.

She went very still, and looked up into his beautiful blue eyes. "When you lay fighting the poison from Lucrezia's stiletto, I made a pact with God."

"Pact?" he said with a frown.

"*Sì.* I vowed that I would ask my father to petition for an annulment—set you free—if He would spare you . . . that I would free you to love elsewhere."

"Set me free?" He crouched before her, face-to-face. "If He would spare me?" The enormity of her promise took a moment to register. And when it did, he wanted to shout with relief, with happiness . . . to chide her for doing something so silly.

*And who are you to tell her her prayers are silly? To belittle so selfless a gesture, however misguided?*

Perhaps *this* was the ultimate wrong, he thought, for he'd actually threatened Dante in the face of the prince's refusal to go along with any plans to teach Giulietta a lesson by making her remain at Santa Lucia until spring. And surely she'd picked up enough piety in that cursed cloister to think up such an impossible and unnecessary agreement with God.

He watched tears form in her eyes and bit his lip to keep it from curving into a smile of relief. "Giulietta," he began, searching for the words that would soothe her, dissuade her from her belief. He took her unnaturally cold hands in his, pressed his lips to them. "I'm humbled by your sacrifice," he said gently, "but don't you think that before you make a bargain with God, you should consult the sacrificial lamb? Don't you think you should have at least talked to me?"

"You were between life and death . . . I could hardly have nudged you in the ribs and asked your permission! And now you're laughing at me . . ." Hurt rose in her eyes.

He shook his head. "No, never that, *cara* . . ."

"I'm an Alessandro, Rodrigo. I do not give my word lightly, nor do I go back on it. Especially to God after my weeks at Santa Lucia." A slight catch in her voice reminded him of a long-ago Giulietta, a delightful child who was still very much a part of the young woman before him. "Don't you see? I must ask my father to petition for an annulment . . . 'twas my part of the pact with God!" Her eyes were pleading and determined at the same time, and he immediately sobered.

It was a serious thing, he knew, a vow to God. But he couldn't allow this final obstacle to—

"Ahem."

Both of them looked toward the partially open door. "Forgive my intrusion, Gietta—Rigo, but I wanted to tell you myself that we have a visitor." Dante strode into the room, and Rodrigo stood. "However, I must admit to having heard your . . . confession."

Giulietta, mired in her misery, remained seated, her head bowed. She didn't see Dante's lashes dip in a wink at his son-by-marriage. "And as your father, Giulietta, I unequivocally decline your request for an annulment. I'll not break my bargain with Rodrigo, and I forbid you to break *your* sacred vows of matrimony with him, as well."

She stood then, and faced him. "But surely God will be displeased . . . I promised to set Rodrigo free—"

Dante's blond brows flattened over his eyes in a frown. "You've kept your part of the bargain, as I see it, but there was no guarantee I would grant your request. Furthermore, you had no right to speak for me in your bargaining, daughter.

Now, I suggest you wash your face and come to the great hall. Father Antoine has arrived early for the wedding, and I would give him a proper welcome."

"Father Antoine?" Rodrigo repeated, his eyes lighting. He looked at Giulietta, saw a fragile hope appear in her eyes in answer to his own. "Mayhap you can speak to him regarding some kind of suitable penance?"

"My thoughts exactly," Dante said. "Mayhap you can make your peace with God by donating to Santa Lucia out of your own personal funds . . . and promising to leave any bargaining with God to those who dedicate their lives to His service."

He turned to leave, and a third unexpected visitor came through the door, passing by the prince with an exuberance typical of his species. Dante rolled his eyes at the dog, threw one last look over his shoulder at Rodrigo and Giulietta, and disappeared.

To Rodrigo's consternation, the Great Pyrenees held Giulietta's damaged yellow slipper in his mouth.

"What's this?" she asked, wiping her cheeks with her fingers before she reached for the dog's offering.

Rodrigo blew out his breath, reluctant to reveal his secret. "Well, 'tisn't Aristo's, you can be sure."

She looked up at him as she caught the irony infusing his words. "But where was it all these months? And its mate?"

To her surprise, Rodrigo da Valenti blushed. "Until the *Zingari* left Monteverdi for the winter, both were hidden in Maddalena's wagon." He shrugged with what negligence he could obviously muster. "After that I . . . kept this one with me. Always." The last word dropped to a whisper.

Giulietta slowly stood, letting the slipper fall to the floor, thinking how sweet and romantic a man he really was. His long ago, unappreciated words came back to her once again: *There is nothing common about you, Mona Giulietta, nor was there anything in the least bit common about our meeting.*

But there was so much more to him that she couldn't even begin to name the myriad reasons she loved him so—had loved him ever since that first night when her heart would have driven her to the very towers of Monteverdi's keep to catch a glimpse of him had Aristo not intercepted her.

And how many times had she almost thrown this most precious of gifts away!

She stood on tiptoe and wrapped her arms around his neck, reveling in the feel of his own encircling her waist and pulling her close. "You were right," she murmured against his ear, "when you said you were different from the Alessandros."

He frowned slightly, suddenly finding it difficult to concentrate on her words with her lips nibbling at his ear and the sensitive hollow beneath it. "What . . . do you mean?" he asked tentatively, half-afraid of the answer.

She looked him full in the face, her love animating her amber-gold eyes. "The 'pristine' Alessandro line is peppered with rogues and scoundrels, Rodrigo da Valenti. But you're not one of them. Our children will strengthen the line through all the wonderful traits they will inherit from you."

He smiled, feeling suddenly reborn in her love and the obvious sincerity of her admiration. "I'm not so saintly as you think, *bellissima*," he said modestly. Then demons danced in his blue eyes. "Remember, I spent six years in France."

She lowered her lashes, then cast a glance at him through their silken screen. "Then I would have you teach me everything you learned there, *mio bello Zingaro*."

He threw back his head in soft laughter. "Everything, you say?"

She raised her face to his, and watched in fascination as his mouth slowly descended toward hers. *"Certamente!"*

Neither noticed as Beau picked up the discarded slipper and trotted toward the open chamber door with his prize. . . .

## Author's Note

Girolamo Savonarola's last sermon in the Florence Cathedral was given on Christmas day, 1497. In TENDER ROGUE I took the liberty of moving that sermon, and the events that cut it short, back a month for purposes of the story.

Also, after his imprisonment, Savonarola was tortured and, under the "exquisite agonies inflicted by the *strappado*," made all the confessions that were necessary. When the ropes were removed, however, he instantly retracted, thus requiring another round of torture. He and two of his most faithful disciples, Fra Domenico (not the Domenico in TR) and Fra Silvestro, were found guilty of heresy and schism and condemned to death. A scaffold surrounded by timber was erected in the Piazza della Signoria, and the three men were hanged in chains and burned.

Other Zebra Books by Linda Lang Bartell:

TENDER MARAUDER

TENDER WARRIOR

TENDER PIRATE

**PUT SOME PASSION INTO YOUR
LIFE . . . WITH THIS STEAMY SELECTION OF
ZEBRA *LOVEGRAMS!***

SEA FIRES                                   (3899, $4.50/$5.50)
by Christine Dorsey

Spirited, impetuous Miranda Chadwick arrives in the untamed New
World prepared for any peril. But when the notorious pirate Gentleman
Jack Blackstone kidnaps her in order to fulfill his secret plans, she can't
help but surrender — to the shameless desires and raging hunger that his
bronzed, lean body and demanding caresses ignite within her!

TEXAS MAGIC                                 (3898, $4.50/$5.50)
by Wanda Owen

After being ambushed by bandits and saved by a ranchhand, headstrong
Texas belle Bianca Moreno hires her gorgeous rescuer as a protective escort. But Rick Larkin does more than guard her body — he kisses away her
maidenly inhibitions, and teaches her the secrets of wild, reckless love!

SEDUCTIVE CARESS                            (3767, $4.50/$5.50)
by Carla Simpson

Determined to find her missing sister, brave beauty Jessamyn Forsythe
disguises herself as a simple working girl and follows her only clues to
Whitechapel's darkest alleys . . . and the disturbingly handsome Inspec-
tor Devlin Burke. Burke, on the trail of a killer, becomes intrigued with
the ebon-haired lass and discovers the secrets of her silken lips and the
hidden promise of her sweet flesh.

SILVER SURRENDER                            (3769, $4.50/$5.50)
by Vivian Vaughan

When Mexican beauty Aurelia Mazón saves a handsome stranger from
death, she finds herself on the run from the Federales with the most dangerous man she's ever met. And when Texas Ranger Carson Jarrett steals
her heart with his intimate kisses and seductive caresses, she yields to an
all-consuming passion from which she hopes to never escape!

ENDLESS SEDUCTION                           (3793, $4.50/$5.50)
by Rosalyn Alsobrook

Caught in the middle of a dangerous shoot-out, lovely Leona Stegall falls
unconscious and awakens to the gentle touch of a handsome doctor.
When her rescuer's caresses turn passionate, Leona surrenders to his fiery
embrace and savors a night of soaring ecstasy!

*Available wherever paperbacks are sold, or order direct from the
Publisher. Send cover price plus 50¢ per copy for mailing and
handling to Penguin USA, P.O. Box 999, c/o Dept. 17109,
Bergenfield, NJ 07621. Residents of New York and Tennessee
must include sales tax. DO NOT SEND CASH.*

# Taylor—made Romance From Zebra Books

**WHISPERED KISSES** (3830, $4.99/5.99)

Beautiful Texas heiress Laura Leigh Webster never imagined that her biggest worry on her African safari would be the handsome Jace Elliot, her tour guide. Laura's guardian, Lord Chadwick Hamilton, warns her of Jace's dangerous past; she simply cannot resist the lure of his strong arms and the passion of his *Whispered Kisses*.

**KISS OF THE NIGHT WIND** (3831, $4.99/$5.99)

Carrie Sue Strover thought she was leaving trouble behind her when she deserted her brother's outlaw gang to live her life as schoolmarm Carolyn Starns. On her journey, her stagecoach was attacked and she was rescued by handsome T.J. Rogue. T.J. plots to have Carrie lead him to her brother's cohorts who murdered his family. T.J., however, soon succumbs to the beautiful runaway's charms and loving caresses.

**FORTUNE'S FLAMES** (3825, $4.99/$5.99)

Impatient to begin her journey back home to New Orleans, beautiful Maren James was furious when Captain Hawk delayed the voyage by searching for stowaways. Impatience gave way to uncontrollable desire once the handsome captain searched *her* cabin. He was looking for illegal passengers; what he found was wild passion with a woman he knew was unlike all those he had known before!

**PASSIONS WILD AND FREE** (3828, $4.99/$5.99)

After seeing her family and home destroyed by the cruel and hateful Epson gang, Randee Hollis swore revenge. She knew she found the perfect man to help her—gunslinger Marsh Logan. Not only strong and brave, Marsh had the ebony hair and light blue eyes to make Randee forget her hate and seek the love and passion that only he could give her.

*Available wherever paperbacks are sold, or order direct from the Publisher. Send cover price plus 50¢ per copy for mailing and handling to Penguin USA, P.O. Box 999, c/o Dept. 17109, Bergenfield, NJ 07621. Residents of New York and Tennessee must include sales tax. DO NOT SEND CASH.*

## SURRENDER TO THE SPLENDOR OF THE ROMANCE OF F. ROSANNE BITTNER!

| | |
|---|---|
| CARESS | (3791, $5.99/$6.99) |
| COMANCHE SUNSET | (3568, $4.99/$5.99) |
| HEARTS SURRENDER | (2945, $4.50/$5.50) |
| LAWLESS LOVE | (3877, $4.50/$5.50) |
| PRAIRIE EMBRACE | (3160, $4.50/$5.50) |
| RAPTURE'S GOLD | (3879, $4.50/$5.50) |
| SHAMELESS | (4056, $5.99/$6.99) |

*Available wherever paperbacks are sold, or order direct from the Publisher. Send cover price plus 50¢ per copy for mailing and handling to Penguin USA, P.O. Box 999, c/o Dept. 17109, Bergenfield, NJ 07621. Residents of New York and Tennessee must include sales tax. DO NOT SEND CASH.*

**PASSIONATE NIGHTS FROM**

*PENELOPE NERI*

DESERT CAPTIVE                    (2447, $3.95/$4.95)
Kidnapped from her French Foreign Legion escort, indignant Alexandria had every reason to despise her nomad prince captor. But as they traveled to his isolated mountain kingdom, she found her hate melting into desire . . .

FOREVER AND BEYOND               (3115, $4.95/$5.95)
Haunted by dreams of an Indian warrior, Kelly found his touch more than intimate—it was oddly familiar. He seemed to be calling her back to another time, to a place where they would find love again . . .

FOREVER IN HIS ARMS              (3385, $4.95/$5.95)
Whispers of war between the North and South were riding the wind the summer Jenny Delaney fell in love with Tyler Mackenzie. Time was fast running out for secret trysts and lovers' dreams, and she would have to choose between the life she held so dear and the man whose passion made her burn as brightly as the evening star . . .

MIDNIGHT CAPTIVE                 (2593, $3.95/$4.95)
After a poor, ragged girlhood with her gypsy kinfolk, Krissoula knew that all she wanted from life was her share of riches. There was only one way for the penniless temptress to earn a cent: fake interest in a man, drug him, and pocket everything he had! Then the seductress met dashing Esteban and unquenchable passion seared her soul . . .

SEA JEWEL                        (3013, $4.50/$5.50)
Hot-tempered Alaric had long planned the humiliation of Freya, the daughter of the most hated foe. He'd make the wench from across the ocean his lowly bedchamber slave—but he never suspected she would become the mistress of his heart, his treasured sea jewel . . .

*Available wherever paperbacks are sold, or order direct from the Publisher. Send cover price plus 50¢ per copy for mailing and handling to Penguin USA, P.O. Box 999, c/o Dept. 17109, Bergenfield, NJ 07621. Residents of New York and Tennessee must include sales tax. DO NOT SEND CASH.*

# MAKE THE
# ROMANCE CONNECTION

# Z-TALK
## *Online*

Come talk to your favorite authors and get the inside scoop on everything that's going on in the world of romance publishing, from the only online service that's designed exclusively for the publishing industry.

With Z-Talk Online Information Service, the most innovative and exciting computer bulletin board around, you can:

- ♥ CHAT "LIVE" WITH AUTHORS, FELLOW ROMANCE READERS, AND OTHER MEMBERS OF THE ROMANCE PUBLISHING COMMUNITY.
- ♥ FIND OUT ABOUT UPCOMING TITLES BEFORE THEY'RE RELEASED.
- ♥ COPY THOUSANDS OF FILES AND GAMES TO YOUR OWN COMPUTER.
- ♥ READ REVIEWS OF ROMANCE TITLES.
- ♥ HAVE UNLIMITED USE OF ELECTRONIC MAIL.
- ♥ POST MESSAGES ON OUR DOZENS OF TOPIC BOARDS.

All it takes is a computer and a modem to get online with Z-Talk. Set your modem to 8/N/1, and dial 212-935-0270. If you need help, call the System Operator, at 212-407-1533. There's a two week free trial period. After that, annual membership is only $ 60.00.

## *See you online!*
*brought to you by Zebra Books*

KENSINGTON PUBLISHING CORP.